PRAISE FOR **The S**

"Readers young and old are sure to enjoy the fanciful humor and excitement that follow Jesse on his quest to find his grandmother. Priceless characters, clever wordplay, charming illustrations, and a story line so well-written it is a gift to read. An uplifting, highly entertaining book."
— Janet Auinger, ESL teacher, Berlitz School of Languages, Vienna, Austria

"*One moment of magic can transform your world.* This quote from *The Secrets of Windy Hill* says it all. This can't-put-it-down book is a perfect sequel to *Becoming Jesse*, filled with fun, suspense, and adventure. Even better, read it aloud!"
—Saverio Rebecchi, author, inventor, entrepreneur

"*The Secrets of Windy Hill* brings me into the imaginative atmosphere of another world. I couldn't wait to hear what the characters would say or do next. Jesse is an invention unto himself, with his innocent curiosity and wit and cleverness. Simply put, I've been encapturood by Jesse's story! May the good winds blow this book into the hands of thousands of children!"
— Patricia Cook, Elementary School Teacher

"A pitch-perfect story full of thrills and laughter and adventure. Brilliant! Or, as Jesse would say: Brillish! Yes, this is more Jesse magic."
— Paulette P. Smith, mother and grandmother

"It's excellent how we jump right back into action with Jesse. The story is so readable and immersive. I love the new characters, especially the animal look-alikes. It's a breath of fresh air to be back in this world, seeking adventure and holding on to all the Light and love of this story."
— Adela Bateman, parent and passionate reader

"I just loved the book. The story. The descriptions, the banter, the vocabulary. All are wonderful. I need more of Jesse. He is such an inspiration to adults and children alike. (Jesse and The Little Prince should meet!)"
— Mary S. Wright, Community Theater Founder and Director

"What a whimsical, entertaining, joyful story of Jesse, on a determined search to find his Grandma Jessica. It is enLIGHTening to witness the love and support given to Jesse, especially from his Uncle Conor, and the inspirational guidance from his deceased Nana, Dearie, from 'upstairs.' The adventures prove to be a page turner! Once again, a book to be read by oneself, or read to any age."

— Patsy Gallagher Snyder, Early Childhood Educator

"Jesse kept me on the edge of my seat! His adventures are irresistible. Best of all, Jesse still shines so much light on the world and wonders that are all around us!"

— Gay Wasik-Zegel, Elementary School Librarian and author of *Stop Means Stop!*

"I adore this book and the world created within! The unique characters and relationships, (mis)adventures, captivating plot twists, and emotional journeys are as rich and complex as they are heartwarming and delightful. Patsie McCandless artfully weaves in bespoke words, playful puzzles, historical nuggets, snippets of literature and fine art in such an effortless and engaging way. Kids won't even realize how much they're learning as the adventures unfold. Most importantly, they'll learn the lesson at the heart of the book: to keep your Light on, and let it shine brightly into the world!"

— Lauren Helmer, writer, editor, artist

"I couldn't wait to continue the journey with Jesse. The magic of childhood sparkles in Jesse, and his words — confuzzled, Diggity-boo, snollygoster — dance across the pages, leaving vivid pictures. Jesse approaches Elizabethtown with lots of adventures and Light Lessons — *and that Light shining through is so much needed in our world today.*"

— Kathy Dickenson, book lover

"I wish there were infinite pages of Jesse."

— K.R., nine-year-old boy

The Secrets of Windy Hill
Becoming Jesse ~ Book II

The Secrets of Windy Hill
Becoming Jesse ~ Book II

PATSIE MCCANDLESS

Copyright © 2022 by Patricia S. McCandless

All rights reserved. No part of this publication may be reproduced, stored, or transmitted in any form or by any means without written permission of the publisher or author, except in the case of brief quotations in critical articles and reviews.

The Secrets of Windy Hill is a work of fiction. Other than actual historical events, people, and places referred to, all names, characters, and incidents are from the author's imagination. Any resemblances to persons, living or dead, are coincidental, and no reference to any real person is intended.

Published by Light On Publications
For more information, visit www.PatsieMcCandless.com.

Edited by Lauren Helmer
Book design by Christy Day, Constellation Book Design
Cover and interior images by Patricia S. McCandless

ISBN (paperback): 978-1-7325066-3-3
ISBN (ebook): 978-1-7325066-4-0

Library of Congress Control Number: 2022914883

Library of Congress Cataloging-in-Publication Data
Name: McCandless, Patricia S., author.
Title: The Secrets of Windy Hill / Patsie McCandless.
Description: Paoli, PA : Light On Publications, 2022. | Series: Becoming Jesse, Book II
Summary: Jesse searches for his mysterious grandmother and learns life lessons while on his island quest.
Identifiers: ISBN 978-1-7325066-3-3(pbk.) | 978-1-7325066-4-0 (ebook)
Subjects: LCSH Grandmothers--Juvenile fiction. | Action and adventure – Juvenile fiction. | Mystery--Juvenile fiction. | Read aloud--Juvenile fiction. | JUVENILE FICTION / Boys & Men | JUVENILE FICTION / Mysteries & Detective Stories | JUVENILE FICTION / Historical / United States / 20th Century

Printed in the United States of America

*This is dedicated to children everywhere ~
those fireflies of Light
that flit into existence
and enchant our lives.*

CONTENTS

PROLOGUE . . . 1

PART ONE: CONFUZZLED . . . 3
- Chapter One: Zig-Zags . . . 5
- Chapter Two: Late . . . 10
- Chapter Three: Lights . . . 14
- Chapter Four: Accountings . . . 19
- Chapter Five: Astonishments . . . 24
- Chapter Six: Leaving . . . 28

PART TWO: TRAVELERS . . . 31
- Chapter Seven: Darks . . . 33
- Chapter Eight: All Aboard! . . . 38
- Chapter Nine: New Acquaintance . . . 41
- Chapter Ten: Memory-Fizzes . . . 44
- Chapter Eleven: Waiting for the Ferry . . . 48
- Chapter Twelve: Across The Bay . . . 53

PART THREE: WONDERLUSH . . . 57
- Chapter Thirteen: Harbor & Avenue . . . 59
- Chapter Fourteen: Windmill Road . . . 65
- Chapter Fifteen: Field of Dreams . . . 69
- Chapter Sixteen: The Barn . . . 74
- Chapter Seventeen: Ready or Not . . . 77
- Chapter Eighteen: Conor's Path . . . 80

PART FOUR: THRILL-DIGGING . . . 83
- Chapter Nineteen: Face to Face . . . 85
- Chapter Twenty: Scylla & Charybdis . . . 89
- Chapter Twenty-One: Explore . . . 93
- Chapter Twenty-Two: Up the Stairs . . . 96
- Chapter Twenty-Three: Phone Calls . . . 99
- Chapter Twenty-Four: Good Night, Windy Hill . . . 104

PART FIVE: QUIZZELS . . . 109

Chapter Twenty-Five: First Morning   111
Chapter Twenty-Six: Gemma   116
Chapter Twenty-Seven: End & Begin   123
Chapter Twenty-Eight: Star Wish   128
Chapter Twenty-Nine: Mailbox   131

PART SIX: B'JEEKERS!   135

Chapter Thirty: Amanda Wynne   137
Chapter Thirty-One: Breezes   140
Chapter Thirty-Two: The Secret   144
Chapter Thirty-Three: New Territory   147
Chapter Thirty-Four: Legacy   152
Chapter Thirty-Five: Treasures   155
Chapter Thirty-Six: Golden Afternoon   159
Chapter Thirty-Seven: Evening Blushes   162

PART SEVEN: WISKY-DOOLEY   167

Chapter Thirty-Eight: Farewell & Hello   169
Chapter Thirty-Nine: Ride   175
Chapter Forty: Linger Longer   179
Chapter Forty-One: You'll Never Guess   185
Chapter Forty-Two: The Basement   189
Chapter Forty-Three: The Farm   192
Chapter Forty-Four: Thinkers   195

PART EIGHT: DAISY-DASTER   199

Chapter Forty-Five: Lily's Offer   201
Chapter Forty-Six: Calamity   206
Chapter Forty-Seven: Today   211
Chapter Forty-Eight: Townsfolk   215
Chapter Forty-Nine: Bliss-T   220

PART NINE: DIGGITY-BOO!   225

Chapter Fifty: To Market   227
Chapter Fifty-One: Amici   232
Chapter Fifty-Two: Missing   236
Chapter Fifty-Three: Sly   241

PART TEN: SHIVERALS — 245

- Chapter Fifty-Four: Bad Tidings — 247
- Chapter Fifty-Five: A Little Magic — 251
- Chapter Fifty-Six: Brooding — 255
- Chapter Fifty-Seven: Compass — 260

PART ELEVEN: TRAPTURED — 263

- Chapter Fifty-Eight: Luggage — 265
- Chapter Fifty-Nine: Storm Coming — 269
- Chapter Sixty: Lily – Tina – Peggy — 273
- Chapter Sixty-One: Here — 277
- Chapter Sixty-Two: Between The Raindrops — 281
- Chapter Sixty-Three: I Can Tell You Everything — 285
- Chapter Sixty-Four: Treasure — 289

PART TWELVE: UNFURLING — 293

- Chapter Sixty-Five: Light On! — 295
- Chapter Sixty-Six: Celebration — 298
- Chapter Sixty-Seven: More Guests — 301
- Chapter Sixty-Eight: Lovey-Dovey — 303
- Chapter Sixty-Nine: The Set of the Sails — 307
- Chapter Seventy: Secrets Unfurling — 311

BOOKENDS

- Glossary of Imaginator People — 317
- Glossary of Imaginator Words — 323
- Discussion Questions — 333
- Acknowledgements — 336
- About The Author — 338

PROLOGUE

*Here is the stardust that dreamers know.
Wonder ... glittering. Secrets ... awakening.
It is your magic. Your Light.
Becoming.*

Salutations! I am Dearie, grandmother to Jesse O'Neil. Not so very long ago, I was an earthling. But I died last Christmas and am now in the Great Illuminations, which some call Heaven. From here, I will be your guide for Jesse's astonishing journey of misadventures, wonders, and secrets. But let's begin at his beginning.

Jesse was born at the stroke of midnight on New Year's Eve in 1947—an orphan. In the years that followed, he lived a wonderlush life filled with his everyday magic, his inner Light, shining out all over. Jesse shared every good wish with me and Conor—my bonny son—and all the dear families in our old brownstone apartments.

At age six, brillish Jesse began solving the secrets his mysterious mother left behind, and he discovered clues about his disappeared grandmother. No one knew a thing about her. But

Jesse dreamed, wished on the stars, and solved every puzzle!

Well, now I am gone. And Conor is leaving to begin his acting career with a theater in Boston. What will become of Jesse?

Ah. For Jesse, it is quite straightforward. Stouthearted, resolute, and often hilarious, he will simply undertake his journey accompanied by his uncle Conor. It is a journey that will take him far beyond the bustling world he knows in New York City to the remote, curious world of Windy Hill Farm on a small island in New England. Jesse is utterly determined to find Jessica, his long-lost grandmother.

But Jesse gets more than he bargained for, as he is catapulted from one bewildering surprise to another, discovering that there is much more to his quest than just his destination. For there are Light lessons to be found in every new person he meets ... every new secret he uncovers. And he is headed straight for a nest of secrets on Windy Hill Farm.

While he is on this adventure, Jesse must remember the ways of his inner Light. So I will be popping in from time to time to help Jesse keep that in mind ... and heart. Furthermore, I won't be alone, for also with me in the Great Illuminations, Jesse's father, James, and his mother, Jane, will be with our young adventurer, too.

I send my love and laughter and Light to my darling boys, Conor and Jesse. Of course, it is mostly Jesse's story—Jesse's quest. Like his star wishes, glittering in wonder, awakening in secrets. Becoming.

Light On!

PART ONE

CONFUZZLED

This puzzle piece.
How'd it get in my box?
It doesn't fit at all.

CHAPTER ONE

ZIG—ZAGS

"Yer goin' to jail, kid!"

A handcuff snapped around Jesse's wrist, and a pointed, pink nose zoomed in on him.

Jesse's mind zigged. *He looks like a possum.* Zagged. *A policeman?* Zig-zagged. *JAIL?*

He stood in Romano's Grocery, dumbfounded, clutching thirty dollars in his hand—which the Possum-Policeman abruptly snatched away, before clacking the other end of the handcuff to his own wrist.

"Nooo!" Jesse flailed. "My money!" Utterly bewildered, he was towed through a color wheel of fruits and vegetables, crying out to the young grocery clerk, "Gianni!"

Gianni stood paralyzed at the counter, his eyes wild with confusion. The Possum-Policeman hollered to him, "Phone the kid's family. Tell 'em he's at the Police Station."

Jesse's mind wheeled, *Police! I need Sergeant Hannity!* He spluttered, "Pl-pl-pl-ease, sir?! Just ask S-S-Seargant Hannity. Sergeant Hannity! He knows me."

The Possum spoke with a heavy New York accent. "You don' know Hannity. He made Detective. In anotha precinct." He tugged Jesse's handcuff. "I'm the Sergeant now."

Outside, Jesse was sweaty-hot. And hungry. He'd barely touched his lunch; he was so preoccupied with his travel plans. Now his stomach retaliated, grumbling, along with his thoughts: *I can't go to jail. I'm leaving New York City! Tonight!*

Desperately, he stammered, "S-sergeant, I-I'm only seven. Kids don't go to jail."

"That's up to Juvi."

"Ju-vee? What's ju-vee?"

The Possum-Policeman barked, "Juvenile Detention! It's jail! For kids—*juvenile delinquents*—like you!"

Jesse gaspered and his breath popped like water on a hot griddle.

The Possum-Policeman chewed his lip, thinking: *Hangnails! This kid's the pictcha of innocence. But that anonymous caller warned: he's clever, slippery. Don't be fooled.* He opened the patrol car door. "We gotta get to the Police Station. This is discombobulatin'."

Dis-com-bob-u-lating. Jesse frantically rolled the syllables over his tongue. They only tasted baffling. But inside the patrol car, he gagged on the stink of dead doughnuts and hot leather seats. Jesse's brain went black. He felt himself shaking. Tears salted his mouth. Dripped from his nose. Choking down a sob, he croaked at the Possum, "Why are you taking me to jail? And why did you take my money?"

The Possum almost shouted, "Look kid, we gotcha red-handed!"

Jesse's shoulders jerked.

"We saw ya! You and the Shock House kid! Their ringleada! He gave ya that envelope. An' next thing, we caught ya with the stolen thoity dollas! You're one of the Shock House gang!"

"Shock House? What?" Jesse faltered.

"The gamblin' den!"

"Ohhh, the Shark House." Jesse quivered, remembering that he was never to go near that place. From his pocket he pulled out a postcard. "This is what the Shark House kid gave me."

"Let's see that!" The Possum scanned the postcard-photograph:

"Elizabethtown Ferry." He turned it over and read: "C U" He looked at Jesse, "See You? Whatsit mean?"

Jesse rasped helplessly. "I don't know. But I do know that's my money. And I need it. I'm leaving tonight. For Elizabethtown." He put his chin up, adding clearly, "On my quest."

Regrettably, he heard the driver puff a laugh.

Sgt. Possum squirmed. "My hot bleeds for ya, kid."

Jesse's ears twitched. *Hot? Bleeds?* He imagined blood boiling, but Officer Possum thumped his chest, and instantly, Jesse realized: *OH! It's 'heart.' My heart bleeds for you.*

But the Possum was shaking his finger, saying, "Ya gotta stop ya thievin' ways, kid. Before it's too late."

Thieving ways? Jesse's brain jangled in a panic. Nothing was fitting together.

Inside the station, the Sergeant handcuffed Jesse to a tall wooden counter and stepped up to the Police Clerk sitting above.

Jesse's eyes followed and his thoughts gaspered, *Oh, my goggles! The Clerk! He looks like an owl!*

A shiveral prickled Jesse's shoulders. He remembered a Beatrix Potter tale of Old Mr. Brown, the owl, whose long, sharp talons traptured the rude, pesky Squirrel Nutkin.

Jesse watched the Possum whispering to the Owl. "I don't like pullin' in a kid," he wagged. "But we got an anonymous call 'bout all the stealin' up the avenue. This time, thoity bucks from the till at Romano's Grocery. When we turned up, this kid's standin' there, showin' off thoity dollas in his hand!"

The Owl's beak gnawed at a pen. "Brazen nerve!"

"Anyways, the anonymous caller said the kid was real clever, real slippery. From the gang at the Shock House. So, first thing, I clapped on the handcuffs."

"Pe-cu-u-liar," the Owl glanced down at Jesse and adjusted his wire-rimmed glasses. "He doesn't appear to be a Shark House urchin."

"Right, right. But the caller said don't be fooled by his innocent looks." He wheezed, "Well, see what's what. If ya need me, I'm takin' my dinna break in the back."

The Owl swiveled in his chair, uncapped the pen, and peered at Jesse long and hard.

Jesse's shining turquoise eyes looked back at him.

The Owl's eyes narrowed, and his feathery brows bristled. *Jiggery! This boy could melt a heart like butter on hot biscuits.* He looked away. *Best be on guard.*

"Sooo," he hooted, "this is the slippery culprit stealing from the businesses up the avenue." His eyes seemed to glow with a dark yellow light. "Now. You will answer my questions. No backtalk. No tribble-trap. No stories. Just the facts. Understand?"

The Owl's cantankerous temper was loud and clear. Jesse told himself: *Don't be rude. Don't be pesky. Don't be Squirrel Nutkin.*

At first it worked fine: name, birth, age, address.

Jesse answered, "Jesse Seamus O'Neil. January 1st, 1947. Seven. Brownstone apartment house between 5th and 6th Avenues ... near the Lady Bird Theater and the old Princess Theater."

But the Owl asked about his parents: "Occupation?"

"They are in the Great Illuminations."

The Owl stopped writing, "I thought I made it clear! No stories!"

Jesse winced. He took in a short breath, "They're ... dead ... sir."

"And WHOOO is your guardian?"

"Guardian?" Jesse quizzeled.

"WHOOO takes care of you?"

"Well, everyone, because Dearie died."

"WHOOO is Dearie?"

With every *WHOOO*, Jesse's heart thumped. He knew: *The Owl thinks I'm pesky.* He tightened his lips and concentrated on answering: "Dearie's my grandmother. Her occupation was she ran her *Lady Bird Theater.* But she's in the Great Illuminations too."

Officer Owl screeched, "No stories!" The hair over his ears puffed up, and Jesse swallowed a sharp dose of panic as the Owl exasperated, "Facts. No tribble-trap!" His head turned sideways, just like an owl. "Now," he quieted, "WHOOO is your guardian?"

"Well …" Jesse feverishly collected his thoughts. "Uhm … everyone. Everyone in Mac's apartment watches over me. Do you want all their names?"

"So you're an orphan with no living relative?"

"Well … yes … I am an orphan. But … I have my uncle, Conor O'Neil."

"Phone number?"

"Nobody has a phone. There's a phone booth in the lobby. But Conor isn't there now."

The Owl's head bobbed, "Enough!" He ripped the paper from the pad. "Enough! Enough!!" He called, "Ser-g-e-a-n-t!" The Possum appeared. "Take him to the Detectives. See what they can get out of him!"

Sergeant Possum released Jesse. But with legs wobbling, he zig-zagged dizzily into the Sergeant, who stiffly stood him up again. Stomach collywobbles growled through Jesse. He was hungry. He should be sitting down this very minute at the Maguire's supper table.

But the Sergeant prodded him toward a set of swinging double doors. Bleakly, Jesse realized, *This must be where the Detectives are waiting.* His lip trembled. *What will they get out of me?*

CHAPTER TWO

LATE

On the fourth floor of Mac's apartment building, Billy Maguire set the table for dinner. "Jesse's really late."

"Well," Grams Maguire hummed in her Irish tones. "He's likely still sayin' his g' byes. Like a snail to a herd o' turtles." She squawked her saucy laugh, tossed her straight white hair, and clicked out her false teeth.

Billy covered his eyes.

His mother, Teresa, ignored her. "We can't wait for Jesse. Grams and I have a church meeting." They sat, and she passed the cold platters. "Liam will be home late."

"And," Grams added, pushing her teeth into place, "your sister is babysitting Mac's Baby Grands."

"Yeah, Siobhan (Shi-VAUN) practically lives with Mac and Bridget's grandkids since their mama Rose died." Billy poked at the beans on his plate, adding, "Well, after supper, I'll go find Jesse."

They finished up quickly, and on the way out, Billy grabbed an apple, tossing it back and forth as he headed down the apartment stairs with his mom and Grams. On the second floor, they saw the apartment Misters gathering for Poker Night.

"Good evening Maguires," Mr. Schuyler greeted. "If you see Al Romano, please say we're waiting on him."

"Sure thing," Billy saluted and ran down to the street. At the corner, he turned to Romano's Grocery, where Jesse stocked the outdoor produce and sold his newspapers. Billy opened the door and was instantly stormed by a bellowing Gianni.

"I've been tryin' t' call ya! Nobody's answerin' the phone!" He blustered uncomfortably, on account he was seventeen and Billy was only eleven. "Jesse's in jail!"

"Whaaat?"

"In jail! Mr. Romano's been gone all day. Miss Peggy made a phone call and left early. Jesse was showing me his traveling money. A fortune! Thirty bucks! Then, outta nowhere a Policeman came in and put Jesse in handcuffs! Took him away. In a Police Car! There wasn't nothin' I could do!"

Billy spun around with his mind wheeling. But in the next instant, he spun back with an idea shining in his eyes. "You close up shop and go tell Mr. Schuyler!"

"Where 'r' you goin'?" Gianni spluttered.

"To find Jesse!"

Sergeant Possum ushered Jesse into the Detective Room. One rumpled-looking man sat there, elbows on the desk, head in hands. The Sergeant handcuffed Jesse to the chair.

"All yers, Detective Rocco. I gotta say, we caught him red-handed." Grimly, Jesse watched the Possum arrange the Owl's paper, the postcard, and the thirty dollars on Rocco's desk. He turned to Jesse saying, "Tell the truth, kid. Don't go down with yer house o' cods."

House of cods? Jesse wondered, *A fish house?*

Detective Rocco did not look up. The silence was long. And deep. Jesse looked out the tall window, as if he were gazing up at the stars from the bottom of a deep, dark well. But the steadfast moon glimmered back at him, and he thought of his dear darling grandmother, Dearie. He felt for her smooth white stone in his pocket, rubbing it softly, talking inside his heart, *Dearie …?* A cry quivered on his lip, his chin wrinkled, and he felt tears flooding his eyes. *No,* he told himself. *Stop. Breathe.*

All at once, he felt Dearie's darling voice:

Jesse, my love-adore, remember: Don't let reality tell your story! Close your eyes and watch this! See! Your Light! Feel your Light streaming. It's all yours, Jesse! Get into your Light stream!

Jesse wanted to hug her. But his arm. It was caught. He opened his eyes. *Oh! The room is filled with Light!* He heard Dearie's silvery laughter.

Let your Light shine, Jesse. Light on!

Straightaway, Jesse's brain lit up. *Oh! It's not house of cods! It's house of cards!* He sniff-snickered, *Thanks Dearie!*

But Detective Rocco was lowering his hands from his face. Jesse watched. Incredulous. *Really …?* A mask of dark shadows circled the Detective's inky eyes, like … *a raccoon! Great goggles!*

A tiny smile curled into Rocco's mouth, and he spoke softly, "So. I'm supposed to be *man-ning* the desks over supper break. But it looks like I'm '*kid-ding*' the desk."

Cautiously, Jesse smiled and he curioused, "Well … don't you get supper?"

The Detective reached for a black metal lunchbox and pulled out a stack of wax-papered sandwiches. "Let's see what *mi amore* packed for me."

He unwrapped a sandwich and Jesse felt his nose twitch. Ahhh! Savory ham on freshly made bread with sweet mayonnaise and tangy mustard. Jesse licked his lips and his hunger spoke right up: "Do you know? I can waggle my ears. I'll waggle, for one of those sandwiches."

"Ohh? Let's see."

Jesse's ears waggled like he was the Prince—maybe the King—of Waggling. The Detective leaned back, laughing out loud. "That's a first! Waggles!"

Best of all, he handed Jesse a sandwich. "You earned it! *Buon appetito.*"

Jesse wanted to cheer! When he opened the wax paper, it smelled so good, he thought his tongue would fall out. Then his teeth bit down ... *Mmm! Oh! There are pickles in here!* Out loud he hummed, "Mmm! *Delicioso!*"

That raised Detective Rocco's eyebrows. "My favorite word."

"Me, too, Detective Rocco!"

"Hm. Call me Rocky."

Jesse grinned, noting, "Rocky, your amor-ay must love-adore you."

"Love-adore?"

"Yes. She put all the things in your sandwich that make it a love feast."

Rocky picked up a framed photograph. His eyes gentled.

Jesse's heart quieted. "Like Mr. Romano. He loves Mrs. Romano. They're lovey-dovey."

Detective Rocky nodded. A calm silence drifted in, and Jesse tucked into the savory sandwich. Rocky pulled out a small bottle of milk and surprised Jesse when he offered him the first swig.

"Ahhh!" Jesse's white mustache grinned, "That. Is. Brillish!"

"Brillish?" Rocky chuckled at Jesse's words. But he said nothing. He stared at the phone. Glanced at the clock. Stared at the phone.

Jesse again bit into the delicious sandwich, his legs swinging out, as if he would vault out of the chair. But he was still handcuffed.

CHAPTER THREE

LIGHTS

Darting through traffic, Billy heard someone calling his name. *Is that Daddy?*

He saw the towering Liam Maguire, grinning through his thick red beard. "Daddy!" Billy flew into Liam's embrace. "Mom said you'd be late."

"Wind and tide got my tugboat home early."

"Daddy, Jesse's in jail!"

"Whaaat?" Liam's eyes snapped in disbelief. Blisterquick, he shouted, "Well! Let's go get him out!"

Down, down the avenue they flew, wheeling into the Police Station. But … no officers. They looked at each other.

A man at the visitor bench spoke up, "Suppah hour." He gestured to the apple in Billy's hand. "I could help youse … if …"

Billy looked at his apple … and handed it over. The man crunched a bite, swiped his chin, and pointed, "If you're lookin' for the kid, he's in there."

Detective Rocky cleared his desk. "Now, about all this stealin'…"

Jesse's throat contracted. Just the suggestion of him stealing made his heart sink.

"First. Did the Sergeant empty your pockets?"

"Well, no." Jesse brightened, and with his uncuffed hand, he awkwardly pulled out his treasured possessions. First, he held up a smooth white stone. "This is Dearie's stone, filled with the earth and with Dearie, and now it's getting filled with me." He smiled, then showed Rocky his orange pocketknife with the silver butterfly. "I found this digging in Mac's garden. And this … is my mother's thimble. Her kiss! Just for me. Remember? Peter Pan calls Wendy's thimble his 'kiss.'"

"Mmmm," Rocky softened. But abruptly, he switched tracks. "Okay! Details. Everything!"

"I'm confuzzled," Jesse flummoxed, "The Owl said, 'just the facts.'"

"The Owl?"

Jesse's cheeks burned red.

But Rocky guffawed. "Hah! The Owl! Right! Just the facts. But I want e-v-e-r-y-thing!"

"Really?" Jesse's eyes twinkled. "Okay! Well, I have my Circle of Lights, my guardians. First, there's my uncle Conor. He's the greatest. An actor. Just graduated college, so we're moving on. Leaving tonight. I *deranged* everything."

Rocky's smile curled back into his mouth. "And what did you *arrange*?"

"Well, I stock the outdoor produce for Mr. Romano's Grocery, and I found out that Ant'ny drives his truck for Mr. Romano from Connecticut to New York. He drops off the produce, then goes to the fish markets to take fish back to Connecticut. I never met Ant'ny, but tonight Conor's meeting him after his theater, to help him. So we can ride as far as Connecticut in Ant'ny's truck. It saves lots on our train tickets."

"Yeah. Where ya headed?"

"Conor's theater is in Boston. But first, we'll go to Elizabethtown, where my mother, Jane, grew up. I want to find her mother, my disappeared grandmother, my Lady Jessica. She's been my quest for over a year. Like Sergeant Hannity told me, I gathered all her clues and solved all her puzzles. And now, we're finally going." Jesse yawned, "Conor says, in the wee small hours of the morning."

Abruptly, the phone rang—and Rocky leapt for it. "Hannity! Where are you?" He shouted, "I'm waitin' here!"

Jesse sparked. *Oh, good! Hannity!* He listened to Rocky.

"Yeah, Juvi's coming. Once they book him, he'll never get out." Silence. "Name's Jesse O'Neil." Long silence. "Well then, get here fast!"

Jesse panicked. *Juvi? Jail for kids! I'll never get out!* Stunned, he rattled, *I – I'm ….* He couldn't finish his paralyzing thought.

Yet, in that petrifying moment, a bright rectangle of moonlight appeared on the floor. *Light!* Jesse knew. *My Light!* He felt Dearie again. *Shining.* Jesse sat up straight.

"Rocky … I was telling you … about my guardians! I have lots, and they all have kids. It's the greatest. Everyone in Mac's apartment building watches over me since my Dearie went to the *Great Illuminations* last Christmas."

Rocky looked at Jesse attentively. "And Dearie is?"

"My love-adore grandmother. She's, well, dead. But we visit a lot." Jesse soothingly fingered Dearie's stone on the desk. "Anyway, I have supper with every family in our apartments, every week. They're all love-adores."

"So? Why leave?"

Jesse's back stiffened. *Why am I leaving?* He knew why he was going. But … "Well. I love them," he stuttered. "And they love me. But … Well …"

Jesse looked away. He thought of the day Liam Maguire returned from being lost at sea. Jesse had surged with thrill-digging joy, but Liam did not take the slightest notice of Jesse. No one did. Liam was enveloped by his family. Jesse was left alone on the sidewalk. And he knew:

"I'm not ... well ... they're not ..."

"*Famiglia?* Not family?"

"No. Right." Jesse surprised himself. "I'm leaving, and going, for the same reason. I want my own family."

"*Famiglia!*" He smiled. "But who are these apartment love-adores of yours?"

Jesse sparkled again, and he told of all the families that lived in Mac and Bridget's apartments. It was a cheery, heartwarming account, finishing with the Maguire family.

"Liam Maguire, Teresa and Grams Maguire, and their kids, Siobhan and Billy. Well, I would say the Maguires are my favorites. Especially Billy."

A quiet *whoosh* rustled the air. The double doors swung open. Jesse swung his head.

"LIAM! BILLY! Glory BE!"

"JESSE!"

Detective Rocco was on his feet. "Stop! *Fermati!* You can't be in here!"

But the Maguires walked forward. Oh, how they hugged Jesse. Oh, how Jesse hung on. Sudden Lights bubbling up, sudden tears streaming down.

Detective Rocky watched them, knowing it would take more than hugs to set Jesse free. Nonetheless, this was a moment he couldn't take away from the boy.

But there was more! A sudden clamoring erupted outside the doors. Jesse knew those voices. The doors opened again and in tromped Jesse's Circle! The Misters! Bonheur, Gorecki, Schuyler! They swarmed around Jesse, all talking at once. Detective Rocco couldn't help grinning. He felt he knew them all.

Officer Owl flew into the room, "Gentlemen! This is not a church social!"

Sergeant Possum was right behind him. "Police poysonnel only! All visitors OUT!"

But a shot rang out!

It was the back door, banging open!

The room muted. In prowled a thin, imperious woman with fluffing, orange-red hair. Her flashing eyes inspected everyone and everything. Like a Fox.

Confuzzled, Jesse sighed, looking from her to the Raccoon, to the Possum, to the Owl. *Now what?*

The lady showed her badge. "I've been sent by Juvenile Services. I'll take the delinquent boy now."

CHAPTER FOUR

ACCOUNTINGS

The Juvenile Service lady. She stared, with her glinty Fox eyes trained on Jesse as if he were a wee rabbit she had cornered.

Jesse's heart sank to his belly button. *This is it. I'll never get out now.*

The room was heavy with silence as the Misters protectively circled Jesse. But another shot banged the back door open!

At once, Jesse's heart rocketed back up, as he saw Detective Hannity and Mr. Romano bolt into the room! Rushing to the desk, they deposited a long brown envelope and a stack of notebooks. Hannity whispered to Detective Rocky, and Rocky smiled.

Officer Owl and Sgt. Possum ogled as Rocky released Jesse's handcuff and declared, "It's official, Jesse O'Neil. You're free to go."

"Diggity-BOO!" Jesse soared! "FREE! I'm FREE!" He hugged all the Misters and Hannity.

The Juvenile Service lady put her long Fox nose in the air. "I came all this way? For nothing?" She stalked out, letting the door bang behind her.

Hannity pulled Billy aside, "We've got loose ends to tie up. You and Jesse wait outside."

Liam offered, "I'll take the boys."

But Jesse turned to Detective Rocky and hugged him, too. Chuckling, Rocky handed Jesse his thirty dollars and his postcard, with his orange jackknife, Dearie's stone, and Jane's thimble kiss. "*Buono, Jesse! Buono!*"

Jesse, Billy, and Liam strode back through the double doors, straight into a handsome young man, looking like a lost Hollywood star.

"CONOR!"

Jesse's uncle crouched, pulling Jesse to him.

"Oh, Conor!" Jesse was wrapped in Conor's arms, Conor's voice. "Jess. Oh Jesse."

Jesse felt tears flooding his eyes, but he grimmeled, repeating Dearie's old words: "Oh, Conor! I'm fine! So fine."

Conor grinned, "Yes you are, Jesse." He hugged him again. "Yes you are."

Back in the interrogation room, Hannity turned to the Misters. "Gentlemen, Detective Rocco and I have been running surveillance on a very slick young woman, a real snollygoster, robbing you blind and cooking your books."

Mr. Gorecki's deep voice asked, "Our mousey Miss Peggy?"

"More like a rat," Detective Rocky answered. "We discovered her operation in another precinct. Detective Hannity got himself assigned there to root her out." He added, "We don't have her real name. You know her as Peggy Banks."

Hannity continued, "We found her accounting books stuffed in her garbage can." He pointed to the notebooks. "And Mr. Romano made a positive identification."

Al Romano spoke up, "Yes. Miss Peggy is two ladies in one: Ours has short brown, curly hair, a funny nose, and wears little glasses. But the other Miss Peggy," he flustered, "is, uhm, ritzy-glitzy. Hard to tell, but both are Miss Peggy."

"Right," Detective Hannity cut in, "she's a sly act. She knew Jesse had withdrawn the thirty dollars cash for his trip, and she fingered him to the police."

Sergeant Possum realized, "This Peggy made the anonymous call?"

"Definitely. She didn't give a burnt fig if Jesse went to jail." Hannity shook his head, "Now, unfortunately, she got away. We have an all-points bulletin for her immediate arrest. And we'll go to the ends of the earth to catch her. But your money has not been recovered."

Amid the Misters' groans, Rocky smiled, "I'm just glad Jesse's free. He's *brillante!* 'Brillish'!"

The Owl and the Possum were back at the bench, staring down at Jesse. But their eyes were soft. Jesse smiled up at them, and the Owl hooted, "We are grrratified—*ahhhem*—that you have been released."

Possum agreed, "Yeah kid … yer … ya gotta good hot."

Jesse grinned, "Thanks. You've got a good heart, too."

The Possum pointed, "Good luck on yer quest." They both saluted Jesse.

Conor had to return to his theater, but the Circle of Misters enveloped Jesse, striding out of the Police Station together.

Liam merri-cheered, "Y' still got your shine, Jesse, me-boyo!"

He swept Jesse into a high, swirling hug, and Jesse saw the moon glimmering above.

Mr. Romano sang in his best Dean Martin voice, *"When the moon hits your eye like a big pizza pie—that's amore!"*

Jesse and Billy exuberated, *"Thaaat's AMORAY!"*

Liam and the boys led their singing parade, and Mr. Bonheur told one of his silly jokes: "Did you hear about the bones they found on the moon?" He answered himself: "The cow didn't make it after all."

Their laughter sang with *amore* all the way up the avenue.

Inside the apartments, they quietly climbed the stairs, and Mr. Gorecki's deep voice hushed, "Jesse, you are an adventure."

Each Mister embraced Jesse and wished him safe travels. But Billy's face silently conveyed: *Don't go, Jesse.*

Abruptly, rowdy shrieks blared from an open door, and out popped the three young Schuyler girls, squealing, "Jesse!" "Jesse's back!" "You're free!" Apartment doors banged open, and pajamaed youngsters ran to the railings, yelling:

"Jesse! Hey Jail Bird!"

"Were you behind bars, Jesse?"

"Did they give you bread and water?"

"Did ya get to keep the handcuffs?"

Liam raised his voice, "Okay kids. Jesse has to get going."

Young Andros Gorecki grumbled, "Come on-n-n! We wanna know all the whodunit stuff!"

Billy yelled in his Boss-of-the-Block voice, "I'll tell ya tomorrow."

The children moaned, but filed back into their apartments, with Mikey Romano singing the Roy Rogers theme song, *"Happy trails to you!"*

Mrs. Schuyler embraced Jesse. She had been his teacher at their Montessori school. He smiled up at her, "I'll always remember you, Mrs. Sky."

Billy puzzled, "Why are you callin' her Mrs. Sky? She's Mrs. K—for Katelijne."

"She used to be, but we were talking about imagination, and I said, 'The sky's the limit.'"

Mrs. Schuyler spoke, "And I said, 'The sky has no limits.'"

"Isn't that the greatest?" Jesse spurted. "So I gave her a new name: Missus Sky. It even sounds like her real name: Schuyler—Sky!"

Billy gave Jesse two thumbs up.

Little Elke Schuyler slipped under her mother's arm, "Jesse! I have a *Get Out of Jail Free* card for you, from our Monopoly game. For next time."

Next time? Jesse balked. *No!* But Elke was so sincere. "Well, thanks Elke. I'll keep it. Just in case." Then, strutting up the steps, he sang, *"Happy Trails to me!"*

But he saw Billy's eyes darken, looking like a flock of black birds had taken roost.

CHAPTER FIVE

ASTONISHMENTS

Jesse knew the dark things in Billy's eyes. He knew they would fly away—eventually. Jesse sent him his Lights, laughing on purpose, repeating the kids' questions: "*Were you behind bars? Did ya get to keep the handcuffs?* Diggity-boo! They think I was in a movie!" He laughed again—and Billy laughed with him.

By the time Teresa and Grams returned from church, Billy was full of himself. "We just got Jesse out of jail!"

"JAIL?" Grams wagged her Irish about. "Glory be to heaven and fifteen saints! You're joshin' us!"

But behind them, an old Irish voice reverberated, "No-o-o. No joshin'." It was Mac. "Siobhan and I jus' came from the Police Station."

Siobhan Maguire added, "Hannity told us that Jesse was in handcuffs all evening."

"Oh, good heavens!" Teresa hugged Jesse.

Grams peered, "Well, Jesse, you're all in one piece." Impishly, she clicked her false teeth out.

Jesse gaspered, "Oh Grams! Not that! Put them back!"

She clicked them back inside, and her mouth grimmeled, "Knock knock, Jesse."

He perked, "Who's there?"

"Freeze." Grams tittered.

"Freeze who?"

"Freeze a jolly good fellow! Freeze a jolly good fellow!" She shrieked her quirky laugh and everyone groaned. But Jesse hugged Grams. And she hugged him back, saying, "Now my jolly good fellow, let's not stand here like a penny waitin' fer change. I'll put the kettle on, and you can tell us your glar-ee-us tale."

It did seem like a glorious tale. From Jesse to Billy to Liam, they made short work of it, and they all sat sipping their astonishments, until Mac redirected, "Enough of that. Jesse, I've got somethin' for yer journey."

Siobhan furthered, "Oh. Me too."

Jesse's shoulders mounted in dismay. "Cracker Jacks! I'm supposed to travel light, with my mother's valise."

Teresa Maguire smiled. "I remember your mother, Jane, carrying that old leather traveling bag when she and James arrived here. Mr. and Mrs. James O'Neil!"

Jesse nodded, "Jane's bag is just right. I put in *Charlotte's Web*, so I know about the farm. And I've got my photos and Jane's letters that never got delivered to Lady Jessica because she doesn't have a mailbox. Plus, I packed Velvet—so Lady Jessica will know I really am hers."

Everyone qualmed at that till Mac held up Dearie's leather folder with the Triquetra design of three intertwining circles. "Bridget and I typed out *Dearie's Journal* of her travels when she was about your age."

"Ohhh! Mac! I can take Dearie with me!"

"Yup! Now, I have here one more story to add: of the famous Irish warrior-poet, Oisin (Oh-SHEEN) and his magical cat."

Gypsy-cat sat up at that, and the room begged Mac to read it. But it was time Jesse got to sleep. "The story will keep," Mac nodded.

Siobhan offered a spoonerism: "Another *dory* for another *stay*."

Jesse's ears waggled, translating with delight. "Another *story* for another *day!*"

She tickled the cat's ears, "Now, Gypsy, you're to live with us, you magical cat."

Jesse shiveraled … *All the things … I'll leave … behind.*

Teresa stood, "Jesse, your eyes are at half-mast. Let's fix the sofa and get you to bed."

Mac sat on the edge of the sofa with Jesse nestled under a sheet.

"One more thing, Jesse." He opened his hand. "This is my Travellin' Coin. A silver dollar, from the year 1900. Dearie's old friend, Elliot, gave it t' me, newly minted. Brought me the best of luck."

"You're confuzzling me. You and Dearie always said there is no luck."

"Right-cha are. This is a token of luck. Helps y' believe *All is Well*. Because no matter how much you plan, you never know what secrets your journey will present. Y' wanna stay in yer *Well-Being*. Just touch the coin and remember: *All is well.*"

"Thank you, Mac! A silver dollar! What great luck!!"

Mac hugged him. "Like *Oisin*, Jesse, follow your heart. It knows the way."

Jesse remembered those were Dearie's very words! He knew: *Dearie's here!*

With one last goodbye, Grams hugged Jesse. "Providence, Jesse! Yer journey is full of Providence!"

Jesse didn't understand, but Liam intervened. "You O'Neil boys will be fine."

The little black bird fluttered through Billy's eyes. "Well … Jesse?"

"I'll write you, Billy," Jesse promised, "I have another dream—to get a mailbox for Grandmother Jessica. I'll write you, about everything."

"Remember Jesse," Billy softened, "all the things you love in New York won't be in Elizabethtown."

CHAPTER SIX

LEAVING

"Jesse! Wake up! Come on, little man."
 Jesse was dreaming: *Stars. And Jane. And swirling lights.*
"Jess!"

He opened his eyes. "Conor!"

"Shhh!" Conor hushed. "It's late. Time to go. Ant'ny's waiting on us."

At the door, Siobhan appeared, like a dancer in a dream, offering Jesse a brown paper package. Jesse took it, whispering a spoonerism: "My *trappy hails* are waiting, Siobhan."

She sighed, "*Happy trails* to you!"

Jesse hugged her, but Conor pulled him away. "No scallylagging, Jess."

Holding the long, smooth, wooden railing, they darted down the apartment steps and out to the warm city street. Jesse was glad to be wearing his thin cottons and the sandals that Conor had cut out of his old brogans.

The truck rattled. Jesse waved at the smiling face in the truck window. "Ant'ny!" he called.

Ant'ny leaned out, "Call me Ant. My *amici*—my friends—call me Ant."

Jesse grinned, "Ah-mee-chee!"

But Conor was flinging their bags into the truck flatbed and lifting Jesse up and in.

"Golly-gee-whilakers! What a fish smell!"

"Sorry, Jess," Conor closed the tailgate. "Remember, free passage!" He bounded to the truck door, and hoisted himself in.

Jesse found burlap bags and made a cushion for his bottom. He leaned back against his valise with smiling thoughts: *Jane packed her dreams in this valise. Now it's got my dreams.*

The front door of the apartments opened, and Gypsy-cat pranced out with Siobhan and Billy, waving to Jesse. Billy's last words echoed through Jesse's heart: "I've known you since before you were born. You go find your disappeared grandmother. I'll wait for ya. I'll be here for ya, Jess."

The truck pulled away, and Jesse waved back. He knelt up, waving. He stood up, waving. But Siobhan and Billy only grew smaller. The truck bumped around a corner, and Jesse's bottom landed hard on the flatbed. Siobhan and Billy were gone. Jesse's heart bumped. It hurt. More than his bottom.

He took a shuddering breath. *Pivot,* he told himself. *Pivot.*

Swiveling, he looked into the rear window of the truck's cab. He could see Ant and Conor, and the headlights lighting up the road ahead. He lit up. *The road ahead! My quest!*

Jesse felt the truck wheeling through city streets, then moving upward, onto an Erector Set of a bridge. He looked at the sky. Opening up. No limits. Glittering. Streaming with stars. *It's my dream,* Jesse marveled at the sky diamonds. *My dream!*

But the truck rumbled down a narrow road, and the stars vanished in a strange, misting fog. Jesse shivered, remembering yesterday's jail fracas ... like jagged puzzle pieces that didn't fit together. His eyes grew heavy with sleep, and he drifted into the deep darks all around him.

PART TWO

TRAVELERS

My story circles the sun.

CHAPTER SEVEN

DARKS

I n the dark mist, the truck hit a pothole and Jesse's eyes flew open. *Uh-oh. I gotta GO!* He sat up and knocked on the window, "I gotta go peeps!"

"Peeps?" Ant guffawed but pulled to the roadside. "Okay, pick a tree."

Jesse jumped out. "A t-tree?" Jesse paused. "In the woods?"

Conor chortled, "Well, I don't see a toilet anywhere."

"Oh." Jesse remembered a day, playing kick-the-can in the courtyard, when Mikey Romano had to go peeps and used Mac's garden. But he spritzed everywhere, soaking his pants. Jesse would not repeat that.

Choosing a faraway tree, he pulled off his shorts and underwear, and hung them on a low branch. He had just started his business when he heard Conor's low voice.

"Jesse? Where are you?"

Jesse didn't answer. He was busy.

Conor yelled, "Jesse?"

A light went on.

Golly, Jesse startled, *a house! In the middle of nowhere!*

A door opened. Barking. A voice. "Go get 'em, boy!"

A hulking, hurtling silhouette ran straight for Jesse, barking to kingdom come.

Conor panicked, "Jesse!"

Bare-bottomed, Jesse yanked his clothes off the branch and ran—with the dark, barking dog galumphing after him. "Conor!" he cried out in a frenzy. "Where are you?"

"Jesse! This way! Come on!"

Ant started the truck, and Jesse stumbled toward the headlights. But he felt the misty night air tickling his bare bottom! Crazily, Jesse sniggled, *Discombobulating!* But he suddenly staggered. *Umph!* Fell. Onto damp moss. Oh, it tickled, too. Laughter gurgled out of him—in the same moment—the powerful dog vaulted! Landed! On top of Jesse!

Conor's heart howled, "Jesse!"

Ant bellowed, "Amici-i-i!"

But Jesse was rolling in laughter! The dog was licking him! His face, his arms, his hands. It tickled like nobody's business. Conor bounded through the trees, grabbing at Jesse's arms, dragging him away. But the animal excitedly licked Jesse's legs and almost got his bottom!

"Great Dane!" Conor exasperated. With the slobbering dog bobbing after them, he lugged Jesse away like a sack of giddy rabbits and hefted him over the side of the truck. But the dog still bounced and barked, even as Conor sidled into the cab. "That crazy dog wants Jesse!"

Ant stomped on the gas pedal, "That crazy dog wants my fish!"

Indeed, the animal still leapt after them, barking and snorting like a crazed bull. Jesse laughed out loud, as the looney dog chased the speeding truck. Until, bit by bit ... the dog slowed ... slacked ... stopped. Even the barking stopped.

Jesse called, "Goodbye, you big licker-tickler!" And the dog melted away into the thick fog.

Still giddy, Jesse awkwardly pulled on his clothes and lay back on his burlap bed. He heard Ant and Connor laughing, and his chest shook with a giggle-snicken. Another escaped his lips, until a long sigh, and a little snorkle, drifted him off to sleep.

When the truck stopped again, Jesse blinked into a heavy fog. Stiffly he stood and jumped out under a stingy streetlamp. He tapped the truck door, waving heartily. "Thanks Ant!"

"Bye, my little amici!"

"Bye, amici!" Jesse grinned.

Conor stood at the station door. "Jesse! This is it! Our train!"

Inside, a sleepy Ticket Master announced, "Tickets!" He looked at them and asked, "Window or aisle … ?"

Jesse stopped counting his money. Uneasily, he confuzzled, *I'll …?* He looked up and asked, "Window … or you'll do what?"

Conor laughed out loud. "*Aisle* seat, Jesse!" He answered the Ticket Master, "We'll take one of each."

With a droll smile, the man handed over the tickets and gestured, "Shore Line East. It's a far trot down the tracks."

Jesse picked up his valise. "This way!"

Slinging his arm around Jesse, Conor puffed, "I'll follow you anywhere, Jess."

"Well," Jesse opened the door, "maybe not into the woods!"

They both sniggled and walked together through the dripping, inky fog. Nothing much to see. But, "Conor … ? Do you feel that? The tracks? They're humming!" He smiled. It made him think of Dearie, how he and Dearie hummed together. But he looked down the tracks and gaspered, "Look! A Light! Shaking! Way down the tracks!" Jesse had a wild sensation. "Oh, my goggles! It's the *Banshee*!"

Conor's eyebrows danced, "Not a scary *Banshee*. Think of it as the Northern Lights. Remember, Jess? When you were only five, with Dearie?"

And all at once, here was Dearie!

On a frigid winter night, Conor and I woke you, Jesse, and took you up to the rooftop. The electricity was out all over the city. It was black as a coal bin, and we could see every star in the Universe! And the gossamer pink-yellow-blue-green swirling lights—the Aurora Borealis!

I first saw them as a little lass, watching them birl across the heavens over Scotland. They call them the Mirrie Dancers, swirling in the night sky. Mmm! Magic!

Now, through the dark, misting fog, such gossamer lights swirled toward Jesse. *The swirling lights,* he reflected. *Magic. In my star dream!*

Jesse was in a thrall of quivering lights. Streaming. He couldn't stop them! Surging. Closer. All at once, Jesse's vision lit up! On the inside! He jolted, "It's our train! Oh! It felt like ... magic!"

Conor smirked, "Come on, Mr. Imaginator! Let's get aboard."

Jesse pointed, "Conor, that's the Dining Car."

"Right. Not for us. Come on."

But Jesse stopped. A woman was staring out the window. She looked very stylish with pearls at her neck, blond hair whisking her shoulders, and not-to-be-missed red lipstick. Jesse had a strange sensation ... like she was looking right at him.

"Conor ... ?" But Conor was already down the line, heaving their bags on board, and Jesse skipped after him.

The O'Neil boys had this car all to themselves. Jesse sat in the velvety overstuffed seats, pushing the button, sliding his seat down-up-down, until, without warning, the car lurched.

"We're starting!" Jesse thrilled.

A Conductor strode in, calling, "Tickets!" He started to punch Conor's tickets but stopped at once. "You boys are goin' the wrong way! Didn't ya feel the jolt? We just uncoupled! This here train is goin' back to New York!"

"Great gargoyles!" Jesse cried. "We just came from there!"

CHAPTER EIGHT

ALL ABOARD!

"If y' hurry, y' can get to the Shore Line in time," the Conductor blustered. "But I mean *hurry!*"

Wild-eyed, Conor and Jesse leapt up, grabbed the bags, and ran! Jumping to the platform, they scrambled and Conor banged on the train door. The engine revved. Steam whooshed. He banged again.

Jesse jangled his stone and his silver dollar, *All is well. All is well.* And all at once, the door slid open! A Conductor shouted, "All aboard!"

The train stuttered forward just as they fell into their seats and Jesse yelped, "Great goldfish! That was close!"

He looked out the window, feeling suddenly dizzy. "Huhhh?" His stomach rolled. "We're moving backward!"

Conor smirfed, "It's just a sensation—called *widdershins*. The dizzy feeling will stop in a few seconds."

The train picked up speed, and as Conor said, the *widdershins* dropped away. They both settled in, feasting their eyes on the approaching dawn. Soft, glowing pinks lit up new clouds, sea birds slowly slid along the water's edge, and small craft gently rocked in a harbor.

Conor sighed and pulled out Siobhan's brown paper package. "Jesse, whaddaya think?"

Jesse's answer was to pull off the wrapping. On top was a postcard. Jesse cheered, "That's from Amanda Wynne!"

"And what does our favorite movie star have to say?"

"*Wishing you all the 'bliss-t' on your quest! Love, Amanda.*" Jesse beamed. "I love Amanda!"

"Me, too!" Conor agreed. "But what's this?"

"Golly! A drawing! Of me!" Jesse leafed through artful pages, overflowing with familiar faces. "Siobhan gave me her drawings! Look! Everyone in the apartments! And Amanda! And even Miss Peggy! Here's Gypsy! Oh, that cat! Ohhh, and Dearie! Look! Dearie!"

"What a gift," Conor enthused.

The keepsake entranced Jesse, but Conor's eyes slowly closed, and he fell sound asleep.

Jesse took out *Dearie's Journal: Oisin and the Cat*. He read the first story, transported to Ireland with Dearie. She was but a little girl, listening to Mac tell the tale of Finn McCouhl, the fabled Chieftain of Irish mythology, his beautiful wife, Sadbha (Sev) and their son, the warrior-poet, Oisin. Jesse felt a chill when the villainous Druid sorcerer, Fear Doirich, showed up. But he didn't count on the magical cat, Egypt!

"What a story!" Jesse whistled quietly. "But" he squirmed. "I have to go peeps again."

A sign over the door read: *Toilets – Dining Car*. Jesse wrote a note for Conor and yawed his way to the door. He could see through the door window that there was a connecting compartment between the train cars. But he knew nothing about the challenge of getting from one car to the next. He was about to find out.

Egh, the door's heavy! Jesse pulled with all his might and when it opened, he stepped around it. But without warning, the door thwumped shut—and Jesse was in a cyclone of Bang-Dang-Jack-Hammering racket! The air shrieked around him, streaking up from the side floor openings, where below, he could see the railroad tracks speeding by like blue blazes.

The floor was a bear-trap! A sliding metal floor plate! It slammed back and forth and side to side—gnashing at Jesse's toes!

Everything was clanking—rattling--jolting! It was as if he was inside his old can of coins and someone was shaking it—crashing and slamming him from every side! Jesse struggled to be calm. *All is … Oh, please! Let it all be well!* He summoned up his courage. *Jump! Jump over!* But the train jolted again, and the screeching metal snapped at his toes.

In all that wretched ruckus, he saw someone at the other door. It was the lady who had stared at him. *Help me!* Jesse mutely, frantically begged. *Help!*

The bear-trap-metal-plate grabbed at him again—but—*Glory BE!* The door opened! A hand and a shout reached out to Jesse, and the lady grabbed him, vaulting Jesse over the convulsing metal! She pulled him inside, and the door slam-banged shut.

In the stunning, blessed quiet, Jesse gulped her fragrance of lilies and saw her red lipstick smile at him. "Bathroom?" she asked, still smiling.

"Y-y-yes."

She pushed a button. A metal door slid open.

Amazed, Jesse entered a quiet, satin-smooth, metal bathroom: *Everything, metal! Good metal. But—I have to go back, through that metal monster!* He slowed down, took his time. When he finally slid the door open, the pretty lady was waiting for him.

"Better?"

Relieved and thankful, he answered, "Oh yes. Thank you."

The train door opened behind them, and through the appalling racket, Conor appeared, his face full of worry.

CHAPTER NINE

NEW ACQUAINTANCE

The lady extended her hand to Conor. "Lily Bankroft. Just assisting this young man."

Conor's smile showed his relief. "Thank you. You're very kind. I'm Conor O'Neil. This is my nephew, Jesse."

She instantly invited, "Won't you be my guests for breakfast? The waiter has promised a specialty." She didn't wait, but took Jesse's hand, leading them to her dining booth.

Jesse liked her deep, soothing voice as she said, "You have been through an ordeal, Jesse." She offered water. "Drink. It will calm you."

With the train jig-jogging, Jessie slurped the water—into his lap. *Ohhh, I am a Quatschkopf!*

Miss Lily graciously handed him a napkin, and he thankfully blotted it away. She passed him toast and marmalade, and he took it like it was melted gold on a platter.

This lovely, generous lady captivated the O'Neil boys. She was from New York, too, and they traded their city stories and their travel plans.

Jesse observed her drawing pad near the window. He pointed, "Miss Lily, your drawings?"

"Oh, these are copies I made." She held up a page.

Jesse focused, "A rabbit! Oh, wait. It's a duck!" Jesse giggled, "Gosh! It goes back and forth: rabbit—duck—rabbit—duck!"

"Those are optical illusions," Conor commented.

Lily smiled. "Yes!" She showed another.

Jesse stared, "I see two faces looking at each other. Wait. It turned into a fancy vase!" He giggled, "Oh, it keeps switching! It's a puzzle!"

"And here is another puzzle: the Eye of Providence."

"Providence?" Jesse wondered, *Grams Maguire said that.*

Miss Lily continued, "Yes. Providence is another name for God … or destiny. Do you see the eye surrounded by rays of light, enclosed in a triangle? It's used by the Freemasons, the secret society descended from the once, vastly rich Knights of the Templar. I believe it's a clue to their hidden treasure."

Conor's lips puckered, "You don't really believe that?"

Lily retorted, "Many of America's Founding Fathers were Freemasons. Why did they put the Eye of Providence on the Great Seal and the one-dollar bill? It's puzzling. And I love a puzzle."

"Me, too!" Jesse thrilled.

"My father drew this symbol often. Maybe he had a clue to the treasure."

Treasure. Jesse thought of Tim Braedon. He shuddered, remembering the criminal Tim Braedon kidnapping him, desperately trying to make him reveal the supposed treasure of Windy Hill Farm. *But Tim is in jail now.* Even so, Jesse's shoulders twitched with the jim-jams.

Miss Lily tucked the drawing pad into her large purse. When the waiter brought their breakfast, she gushed, "Ah, as you promised, very special bacon."

"Bacon?" Jesse saw a thick, curled *something* sizzling on the platter. "That's bacon?"

Winking at Miss Lily, the waiter smiled, "That, my man, is a pig's tail—just for you!"

Conor laughed, "Hold on to your tongue, Jesse! Let's try this."

The first bite was, Jesse crowed: "Dee–lishhh–eee–ohhh–sooo!"

Conor agreed. The little pig's tail was soon dispatched, and they tucked into the other plates of the wonderful breakfast.

Dishes were empty and Jesse's stomach was happy. But Miss Lily was fretting over her purse, "I spent a fortune on this, but the thread is unraveling."

Jesse wondered, *she keeps that bag so close, like there's a secret in there.* But he brightened, "I can cut that thread." He emptied his pockets on the table: his Dearie stone, silver dollar, Jane's thimble, and his knife.

She took the knife but couldn't cut it.

"I'll help." Jesse leaned over and saw a long, stuffed envelope in her purse.

Miss Lily quickly pulled it closed, "Never mind. It will keep."

Suddenly, the train was rattling, jittering, like crazed marbles on a tin plate. They were crossing a trestle bridge and the vibration jiggled everything—glasses of water and cups of coffee splish-splashed. Jesse laughed and his voice jittered, "Eh-eh-eh-eh!" That made him laugh even more.

Soon everything calmed, and he turned back to the table, collecting his pocket items. But he stopped. "My stone!" His happy, bright, jiggles of laughter—switched to panic. "It's gone!" His brain tightened with alarm.

The three of them looked everywhere: the booth, the floor, Jesse's pockets. Miss Lily said regretfully, "The train was shaking so, Jesse, it could have rolled anywhere."

Jesse's thoughts rolled about ... *How could I lose my Dearie stone? Golly-gee-whilakers! Why is all this bad stuff happening? I didn't plan this!*

CHAPTER TEN

MEMORY-FIZZES

D earie was in Jesse's thoughts.

Jesse, nothing is lost. Remember? It's somewhere. And remember what Mac said: "No matter how much you plan, you never know what your journey will present. Like Oisin, follow your heart-Light. It knows the way.

Jesse closed his eyes. "I have to believe. My stone will find its way back to me."

Conor agreed, "Right. Like your knife came back to you when Tim Braedon took it."

Miss Lily raised her eyebrow and put down her coffee cup. "Jesse, how will a city boy like you learn farming?"

"Well, in school, Mrs. Sky read *Charlotte's Web*, by E.B. White."

Conor added, "*Charlotte's Web* is the farm story of the little pig and the clever spider who saves his life. The author, E.B. White, and his wife, Katherine, came to dinner at our apartment. Their son, Joel, too. A great visit! E.B. told Jesse he didn't like his real name, Elwyn Brooks. He preferred Andy, and he really liked that Jesse called him Mr. Andy."

"I liked when Mr. Andy talked about his farm in Maine. He said he could watch the sea from his hilltop." Jesse's voice mellowed, "That's how I picture my grandmother's farm."

"Andy told you to always look for the presence of wonder." Conor and Jesse exchanged knowing smiles. Then Conor turned his attentions to Lily. "So, you're stopping in Union City?"

"Yes, I have an interview with a law firm there, Maxim & Tenet. They're opening an office in Port Haven that would be just my cup of tea."

Entering the city, Jesse read the signs and billboards:
Eclipse Coffee Syrup – You'll smack your lips if it's Eclipse!
Union Hotel – Spend a night, not a fortune!
Another billboard advertised the *Boston Museum of Art.*

"Look at the lights in that painting!" It was a tree leaning into a blue sea and sky.

"That's the 'Seacoast at Trouville'! In France," Conor proclaimed.

"True veel?" Jesse echoed. "You were there?"

"Yes! With Dearie and Galen—Pa—on the coast of France. That painting is by Monet!"

"Monay!" Jesse remembered Monet's paint-lights that made everything sparkle.

But Conor was hooting, "Oh! Union Station! Here we are!"

Lily smiled, "Our next adventure!"

Miss Lily Bankroft was showered with thank yous and goodbyes before the O'Neils headed for the bus station. Jesse cheerfully trip-trapped up the bus steps, following Conor to the high bench at the back. "Best view," Conor beamed.

Jesse marveled at the small, quaint towns as Conor shared his memory-fizzes of visits with Dearie. "This town is Brighton. We met Charles Dana Gibson here, at his sister's estate."

"Dana? Like your theater in Boston?"

"No, Dana like the famous illustrator of the 'Gibson Girls,' and the editor-owner of *LIFE* magazine. Gibson hired Pa to photograph, well, just about everything, everywhere."

The bus climbed a tall, green bridge and Conor excitedly pointed at the blue expanse of water, "Tanagasuq Bay! (Tan-ah-GAS-uk) Look at all the islands!" He named one after the other, blathering on. "Man! There's a whole fleet of Navy ships at anchor! They remind me of the ship we took to America, back in 1939: *The Continental Freight*."

"Oh, yes," Jesse nodded. "Dearie knew the family that owned that freighter."

Conor still enthused, "Oh, we sailed all over this bay. James rebuilt an old catboat, named *Bay Dancer*. Kept it at the little pier at Aunt Clare and Uncle Con's house. Hah! When we'd get hungry, we'd beach the catboat to feast on mussels."

Jesse touched his biceps, "You ate muscles?"

"Not those muscles!" Conor chuckled, "Mussels. Like clams, only in blue-black shells. We'd collect them off the beach, boil 'em in our bailing can, and enjoy our feast!"

Conor savored the taste of that memory, but Jesse confuzzled, "Conor? Why did we live in New York City if you like this place so much?"

"Oh, Port Haven was too small," he larked, "for our orchidaceous Dearie!"

"Or-kid-day-shus! Grams Maguire used to call Dearie orchidaceous!"

"It was Rachmaninoff's wife, Natalia, gave Dearie that name!"

"Rock-mon-ih-noff! The composer! Dearie loved playing his music!"

Conor nodded and they each shared a Rachmaninoff memory. Conor: with Dearie, Galen and James, visiting *Senar*, Rachmaninoff's summer home in Switzerland; Jesse: thrilling to Rachmaninoff's real-life escape from Russia in a horse-drawn sleigh.

"Golly!" Conor exclaimed as the bus stopped, "we're here!"

Jesse stepped down to a two-story brick building with a small gas station behind it. "Gee-whilakers! It's so little—like Lilliput!"

Conor inspected the posted Tanagasuq Bay Ferry Schedule. "C'mon Gulliver! If we hurry, we can make the next ferry!"

Jesse recalled the fantastic novel, *Gulliver's Travels*. He felt like the gigantic Gulliver on the tiny island of Lilliput. Everything felt so small compared to New York City.

They walked pell-mell down the cobblestoned Tunstall Street to Weaver Street. Conor halted, and Jesse looked up at a square church tower, like a wedding cake escalating to the sky, with a tall steeple and a shining gold weather vane. He imagined being the towering Gulliver, spinning the weather vane, licking the frosting off the cake. Jesse was hungry again.

Conor pointed, "That's Triquetra Church and its steeple is the landmark for the ferry." He guided Jesse to the corner, "Just down here." But, too late! A deep ferry horn throbbed through the air. "Oh dang!" Conor irked, "There she goes!"

CHAPTER ELEVEN
WAITING FOR THE FERRY

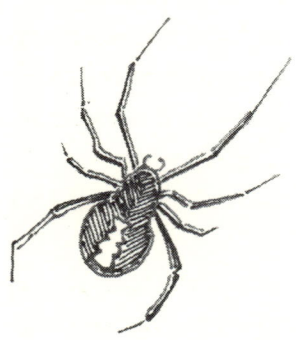

"We've got an hour till the next ferry," Conor exhaled. Jesse pointed to La Rosa's Cafe & Sundries, and Conor approved.

Inside, Jesse picked up *LIFE* magazine, showing Conor the cover picture of a distinctive stone house and barn. "This is how I picture the barn at grandmother's Windy Hill Farm."

Conor read the title: "'Stone-and-Shingle Homes ~ The Legacy of Charles Murray.' I remember that name from when I worked at T.J. O'Farrell's Lumberyard."

He shrugged and went to the counter to order sandwiches, while Jesse looked through the postcard rack.

When Jesse put his postcards and stamps on the sales counter, an old man at the cash register looked at him—and instantly gulped, his eyes bulging. Jesse smiled. But the man only stared back in a stupor. Conor stepped in front of Jesse, as the man whistered, "That's the Black Widow's child or I'm a frog in China."

Perturbed, Conor paid and steered a confused Jesse out the door. "Conor, what did he mean? Why was he staring?"

"Jess, he thought you were someone else."

Jesse was about to ask, *Who?* But they abruptly stopped in their tracks.

"O'Neil! Ballygomingo! Tis yorself!" A rollicking man boomed, "Dontcha know me? Tis yer old lumberyard boss! Morphy, meself!" A full brown beard and shaggy head of hair, all wiry and wild, poked out from under a floppy brown hat, atop his brown canvas work coat and big brown boots ... *He looks like a Bear!* thought Jesse.

"Murphy!" Conor shook his hand. "Regan Murphy! I can't believe it!"

"Regan?" Jesse curioused, not knowing such a name.

Murphy Bear's deep brown eyes eyes stared—stared stiffly—at Jesse. But his tongue was already in motion, and a rough paw reached for Jesse's fingers, "Pleased to make yer acquaintance. And what be yer moniker, laddie?"

"Jesse Seamus [SHAY-mus] O'Neil." Jesse grinned, thinking, *Murphy is like a big old Papa Bear!* But he wanted to know: "If you don't mind, what's Regan?"

"Regan means 'Little King'!" His eyebrows, all tangled and furry, frolicked over his eyes. "My granddaddy and my daddy worked the Dublin Ferry engines all the bally-ring-ding day. But not me! I'm a freight man—the Ferry Cargo King. Come, I'll show y' me freight buildin'."

Jesse followed like a little cloud on a breeze of familiar lilts, as Murphy kept up his Irish patter, saying, "We was deep sorry 'bout yer brother, James, killed in that construction accident. Yer Uncle Conor and Aunt Clare took it hard. God rest 'em. They didn't last long after that."

"No," Conor responded quietly. "It was hard. And last Christmas, Dearie died."

"So sorry," Murphy murmeled.

But Conor hugged Jesse about the shoulders, smiling. "Hey! We've got Jesse! Our little Mr. Imaginator!"

Jesse grinned and hugged Conor back, pointing to the side of the freight building, at a large, glassed-in map. "That's a marine chart," he said confidently.

"Aye," Murphy waved his thick fingers at it. "Tanagasuq Bay."

Jesse declared, "Tanagasuq Bay is a *ria*—a deep river valley that flows into the sea. And there's Elizabethtown, even though the name for the island is Nocanituq. (No-CAN-ih-tuk)"

"Diddly-ahten-dah!" Murphy exclaimed, "Y'r a right clever lad!"

Jesse focused on the chart, and Conor handed him a sandwich. "You have fun exploring, Jess. I'll be right over here with Murphy."

"Now, Conor," Murphy asked, "What're y' up to? And don't say six-feet-two!"

"I'm an actor," Conor smiled, "on my way to …"

Murphy interrupted, "An actor! Well, aren't you the cat's pajamas!" He made a *lah-di-dah* face, but Conor continued.

"Yup! I'm with the Dana Theater in Boston. But first, I'm taking Jesse to his grandmother in Elizabethtown. Jessica Roberts."

"NO!" Murphy gaspered, "NO! Not the Black Widah!"

Conor stuttered, "Wha-a-a-t …?"

"She'll eat him alive for breakfast an' spit out his bones fer lunch!"

Conor recalled that the old man at La Rosa's had muttered about a Black Widow. But he pshawed, "Murphy! You're an old gossip!"

"Yes, indeed! I know all the gossipy tittle-tattle! From a-way back."

Conor abruptly shut his mouth. Truth was, he knew nothing of Jesse's grandmother, this 'Black Widah' Murphy was raving about. Jesse's mother, Jane, had never talked about her mother or the farm. He wondered, *What does Murphy know? And why Black Widow?* Conor was suddenly all ears. And Murphy obliged.

"Ya has to know that the Black Widah is rightly named! All the people in her life died off: her grandmother, father, uncle, a husband nobody knows, all her farm help ... and then there's Jane. Y' say she's dead 'n' gone? It's dang dangerous to get near Jessica.

"The Black Widah—she's the only one left at Windy Hill. O' course, she learned her sorcery from Avery, her wicked-witch grandma who raised her. Avery lived in a summer mansion in Port Haven and wintered in Philadelphia. Had no use for Elizabethtown or Windy Hill Farm.

"But Jessica's Pa was a real likable fella. The islanders loved him. He was just a young colt when he married-up a London chorus girl, name of Susan. But when he brought her home, well, Susan wouldn't be livin' on no farm, nowhere! She abandoned their baby girl, Jessica, and skedaddled. Most say it was Avery. Paid her off, to get out and stay out.

"Well, little miss Jessica grew up. An' whaddaya know! The farm life wasn't good enough fer her neither. Ran away to the bright stage lights. Broke her Pa's heart, she did. He went to New York City to find her, but she sent him packin.' And the fates were agin' him. He was killed in a car accident on the way home.

"So then, well, the Depression hit. No more New York thee-ay-ters, so Jessica come back to the island—too late. Her Pa was dead and buried. God rest his soul.

"After the way she treated her Pa, no islander gave Jessica the time o' day. She were on her own, runnin' the farm.

"Desolate place. The wind sweepin' away any who dared walk down that long, dark lane to the Widah's door." He leaned close to Conor, "She's got some kinda black magic. She keeps everyone away, fer sure. Travelin' salesmen? She sends 'em packin,' screamin' like *Banshees*, down Windmill Road."

Conor blurted, "Enough!"

"Okay, okay. Well, with the Depression and the war years. No one paid her any mind. Besides she was so peculiar. Dressed in her Pa's clothes, she did! Looked like a tall, black crow."

Conor infuriated, "Black Crow! Black Spider! So, where did Jane come from?"

"Well, Jessica come back from New York expectin' the babe. Told people a married name: Roberts. But no husband ever showed up. Had baby Jane on her own. Islanders had nothin' to do with her; she had nothin' to do with them. Still won't. Goes over to Port Haven in her Pa's ole truck fer whatever she needs.

"Kept Jane hidden. Never sendin' her to school. Dressed her like a boy. Overalls, just like herself. Coat up to her chin, hat pulled down over that gorgeous head of hair. Once, on the ferry, the wind got hold of her hat, an' I saw that golden braid, circlin' her head like a halo!"

"Yeah," Conor murmured, "Angel Jane."

"Don't know about that. Apple doesn't fall far from the tree. Bad apples, every one. Avery, Susan, Jessica, Jane."

CHAPTER TWELVE

ACROSS THE BAY

"**B**ad apples?" Conor poked Murphy, "Did you ever meet Jane?" Murphy huffed, like a sulky Bear. "Not me! If the devil's knockin' at the door, I let God answer it!" He shifted his large feet, "Hup! Ferry's comin'! Gotta go."

"Wait Murph! Did you ever set foot on Jessica's farm?"

"Not me!"

"Murphy!" Conor exasperated, "Jane and James lived with us! In New York! Jane was beautiful—inside and out. She didn't get that way out of the blue!"

Murphy harrumphed, and Conor grabbed his arm. "I can tell you this: You're mad as snakes if you think you can stop Jesse from finding his grandmother."

Dismissively, Murphy shrugged and moseyed away.

Conor saw Jesse with his eyes alight, reading *Dearie's Journal*. *Jesse's Light!* He sighed. *Stick with that!*

At the ferry ticket booth, an old lady sat, absentmindedly collecting the coins. Jesse clicked his nickel into the metal dish and happily pushed through the turnstile. But when the lady saw Jesse, her eyebrows jumped to her straw hat. She stared. Stared like a frog on a fly. Jesse couldn't miss it. "Conor?" he flummoxed.

But Conor pushed him through and onto the ferry ... where the old deckhands stared at Jesse. Conor purposefully kept him moving, crowing, "I love this old boat, Jess! The *Governor Keane* Ferry!"

At the top, they went out on deck, where they aimed to watch all the sights. But they found: People. Staring. Jesse didn't know what all the staring was about. He decided not to care. There was so much to see.

Conor pointed, "There's Triquetra's steeple. Look north," he directed. "There's the Port Haven Yacht Club."

"That's where James and Jane first met," Jesse enthused. "Oh look, behind it! There's a sign! T.J. O'Farrell's! The lumberyard where you and James worked."

"Yup! And look beyond the fishing boats: Uncle Con and Aunt Clare's old house, where we stayed every summer."

"With the little pier sticking out?"

"Right! For James' catboat."

The ferry horn blew, and they steered out of the pilings like hands opening and fingers letting go, one by one.

Jesse gushed, "This is all beautiful!"

"Yes," Conor agreed. "It's as if every morning and every night, it takes a vow to be beautiful!"

Wanting to look everywhere at once, Jesse ran the deck—smack into Murphy.

"Watch out Jesse!" Murphy teased, pushing his Bear nose into Jesse's face. "If yer eyeballs fall out, they're liable to roll overboard!" He pulled Jesse to the side, showing off an old Torpedo Station and a timeworn fort at the harbor entrance: Fort Lafayette.

He told a first-rate story about the British Red Coats taking over Fort Lafayette. "Ya see, the American Revolutionary ships had to escape, so they waited till night. Tarred their sails black to camouflage 'em against the black sky. When the Brits realized they'd been hoodwinked, oh, how the cannons roared—like fireworks!"

He clapped Jesse's back, "Come lad, there's more to savor on this promenade."

The ferry moved into open waters, and at the harbor entrance, near Elizabethtown, Jesse noticed, "There's a house there. On a rock. In the middle of the water! And it looks like soup dumplings floating around it!"

"Yep," Murphy swaggered, his burly body galumphing along the deck. "Those smaller rocks are called 'Sheep Heads,' and that house built on a rock is called The Barnacle. True story," he said sensationally: "A monstrous tidal wave, in the Great Hurricane of '38 went clear over the house! But didn't she cling to those rocks, jus' like a barnacle! Oh, she lost her piers and water and 'lectricity, but she herself stayed put!"

They continued their promenade, and Murphy noted the big grey Navy ships tied up to the big round buoys, and the Naval War Institute beyond.

But Jesse noticed something else. The air. The water. Suddenly so still. Quiet. Jesse thought of the Monet painting. He felt he was standing inside a gem. Glittering with Light.

"Where did the wind go?"

Murphy looked at Jesse's radiant face. He felt the glittering. But he scratched his head and wagged sensibly, "Well, y' see, the prevailin' winds blow from the south, warm and steady. But when the bay gets calm, it oft means the north wind wants his turn. It'll storm up, get colder. There's a sayin': *Still skies and calm seas – North Winds soon blow as they please.* So, Jesse-me-boy, prepare for cold wind and grey skies!"

Jesse thought Murphy was telling a tale because the day still felt so warm.

"Come along now, laddie! I'll show y' what's in store for you on the island."

They moved to the foredeck to see the panorama of Elizabethtown. "Looky here," he pointed, "from the Barnacle-on-the-Rock to the Bay Traveler Hotel, there." He was telling a story about the Traveler Hotel that was floated down the bay to Elizabethtown, and the eighteen oxen needed to pull it up onto the land. But just then, they felt the ferry engines slow.

"Hup! Too late," Murphy conceded. "The *Ole Gov* has made it to Elizabethtown." He lamented, "Oh, there's ever so much more to show ya, Jesse."

"There is so much!" Jesse exclaimed. "I don't think I'll ever be done exploring! Conor! Adventures! My own adventures!"

"Oh, you'll have adventures!" Murphy glowered, "Adventures galore!" He moved to the stairway, glancing back at Conor with eyes full of warning.

PART THREE

WONDERLUSH

There is magic and mystery in your dreams.
A' times they guide. A' times they follow.
Always waiting...
for you.

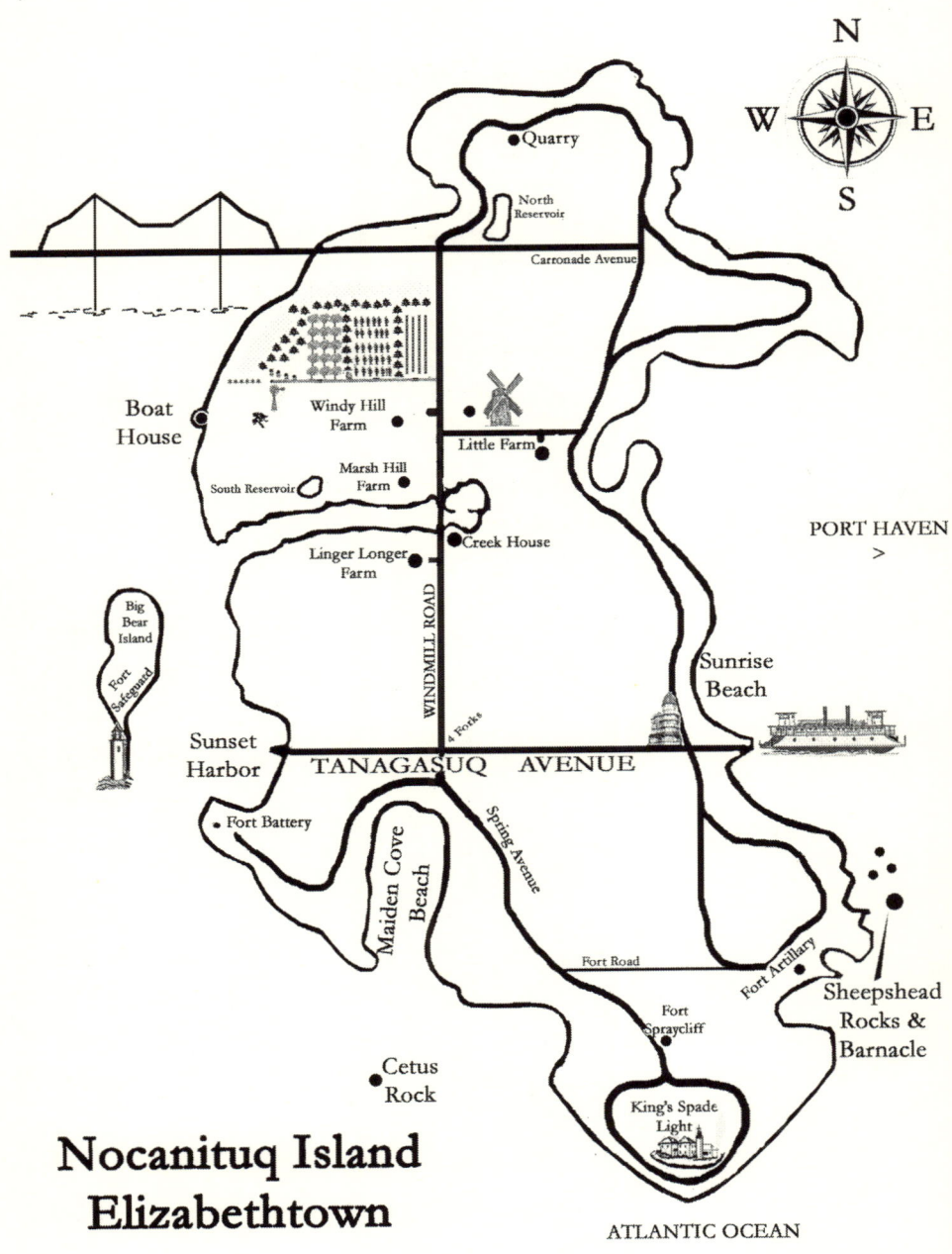

CHAPTER THIRTEEN
HARBOR & AVENUE

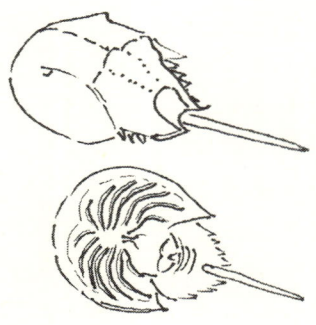

"We're here! Conor!" Jesse trumpeted, "Elizabethtown! Golly! Everything's so small. It really is like Gulliver's tiny town of Lilliput!"

He bustled off the ferry and ran across to the railings at the edge of the harbor, where he saw cement stairs leading right down into the water.

"Oh Conor! Can I go down?"

Conor laughed, "Okay!"

Jesse trip-trapped to the bottom of the cement stairs where the water gently lapped. He sat down, took off his shoes and dipped in his toes. "Oh! It's cold!" Conor joined him, and Jesse pointed, "Look! Little silver fish! Swimming like birds in a flock!" But unexpectedly, he shrieked. "What is THAT?"

Conor saw a dark shadow move across the sandy bottom.

"Good glory!" Jesse blurted, "It looks like an armored tank with a spear!"

Murphy's voice grizzled from the railing above them. "It's just a horseshoe crab. Ancient creature—been around since dinosaurs. Related to spiders."

Jesse knew about spiders from *Charlotte's Web.* Incredulous, he exclaimed, "That swimming tank is an *arachnid*?"

Conor reached into the water and grabbed it by the "spear."

"No, Conor!" Jesse yelled.

But the slick, dripping, brown shell was in Conor's hands. He turned it over and showed Jesse, "Eight legs! A spider!"

Jesse was newly fascinated, but Conor slid it back into the water as Murphy sounded off impatiently. "Come along now. There's more t' see, starting with Sunrise Beach, here," he pointed.

Jesse gushed, "Sunrise Beach!" He gamboled back up the steps to see umbrellas dotting a slow curve of gray sand. The beach was situated below a charm-bracelet of stately homes sitting high on a grassy hill.

"That's Harbor Hill." Murphy expounded, his big paw-feet padding across the street. He pointed, "An' this here's the old Bay Tower Hotel. Over there on that hill is the USO Hall and the Police Station. And at the bottom of the hill is our one and only pay-telephone booth."

Jesse's head was spinning. But Murphy's wagging tongue continued leading their feet up the street. "This here's Tanagasuq Avenue. Runs from Sunrise Ferry to Sunset Ferry." He looked up, "On the corner, there be A.P. Carey's Drugstore. A.P.'s got a right nice ice cream soda fountain in there. Now, goin' up Tanagasuq is Hopewell's Hardware, and up the street is our own branch of T.J. O'Farrell's Hardware and Lumber." He pointed across the street again, "Next up is Beef 'n' Bones."

Jesse surprised, "Beef 'n' Bones?"

"Yep, the Gado brothers. One's beefy-big, the other's bone-skinny. It's their meat market. Sell penny candy, too."

Jesse saw Beef and Bones inside the shop window. Staring.

More staring came from Viand's Grocery, next door: A little lady was standing inside at the plate-glass window. Murphy informed them, "That's Tilly Pickles. Well, Otillia Pickford. Always been called Tilly. When she was a young thing, she helped at Windy Hill Farm."

A little girl flounced out of Gardiner's Flower Shop and went nose to nose with Jesse, gushing, "You-u-u belong to the black spider lady!"

"Whaaat?" Jesse flabbergasted, his ears ringing with her nonsensical folderal.

"My Granny Grace worked at Windy Hill Farm when she was little and—"

Granny appeared. "That's enough, Nancy." But when she saw Jesse, her mouth fell open and her eyes stared wide.

Jesse heard Conor beckoning, "Jesse! Come on! A movie theater! Jess!"

Thrilled, Jesse trotted up the street. "Oh! *Bambi* is playing!" he said breathlessly. "Grandmother and I can go to the movies!"

With a toothsome grimace, Murphy cringed openly, and Conor shot him an elbow.

Jesse didn't notice. He was reading a sign at The Spa Soda Bar:

Don't stand there and be hungry—
come on in and get fed up.

The door opened and a jukebox blared the hit song, "Shake, Rattle and Roll." Jesse's smile turned to laughter as two young men danced down the steps, s-s-s-wivelin' their hips and knockin' their knees together. Jesse thought they looked ree-dic-you-lus! Dis-com-bob-u-lated!

Mac would say, *Have yer manners, Jesse. Don't be gawkin.'* But Jesse couldn't help himself. He gawked away—and giggled.

One of the dancers had a short cigarette at his lower lip and he called to Jesse, "Hey ankle biter! Think fast!" He flicked the cigarette butt at Jesse's feet.

Jumping aside, Jesse wondered, *Why would I bite his ankle?*

Someone yelled, "Hey, Cherry Lips! You really razz the berries! Come on! Shake that thing!"

Cherry Lips indulged, like a loony stork, elbows, hips, knees, a-knockin'! Wild! Cockamamie!

Jesse fell into paralytic laughter, almost drooling, and toppling against Conor's legs.

Conor commandeered, "Come on, Jess. These guys are crazy."

"Craaa-zy!" Cherry Lips chanted after them. "Later, man!"

Hiccuping with laughter, Jesse followed up the street. The Post Office and the Telephone Operators' building were near the corner. He remembered, *Grandmother Jessica doesn't have a mailbox or a phone.*

They crossed a narrow street as a foggy cold shivered up Tanagasuq Avenue. Jesse wanted his sweater. He put down his valise in front of a stone building with three big garage doors and a big horn on the rooftop.

Just as he opened his valise, that big horn *B-L-A-A-A-S-T-E-D!*

Jesse screeched! Rocketed up! Hung in the air! Plunged to the sidewalk! On all fours!

The horn kept blasting and Jesse kept screaming! Scuffling! Scrambling! Like a tiddlywink gone mad!

"Jesse! Jesse!" Conor danced around him, finally catching the sobbing tiddlywink and bustling him back to the corner. Jesse covered his ears, bawling and shaking uncontrollably.

Cars screamed up the street. Shrieked to a stop. Men jumped out, racing toward the blaring horn: the Fire Station.

Murphy was there, handing fire gear to the men jumping aboard the fire engines. Cherry Lips climbed up, and an older man elbowed him, pointing at Jesse. Staring.

Red lights flashed, sirens whined, and the fire trucks pulled out with a police car following behind. Finally, the horn blast stopped.

Murphy reappeared and from his scruffy paw, handed Conor a surprisingly clean white hanky. Conor dried Jesse's cheeks while Murphy blabbered. "It does give ya a fright, that fire horn. Speshly the first time y' hear it, speshly up close!" He snorted a big Bear laugh, "Tho' I never seen nobody fly up into the air like that! Come right up off yer feet, ya did! An' come down on all fours! What a sight! A real ballygomingo it was!" He laughed and clapped his hands.

Jesse laughed, "Ballygomingo!" He shook with the giddies. But his laughter subsided when he shivered from a rush of nipping cold. Up he popped, ran to his valise, and pulled out his sweater. Prompted by Jesse's move, Conor put on his own jacket. Dearie had knit that sweater for Jesse. She'd sat in the comfy chair by the parlor windows, clicking her knitting needles, weaving her wonderful energies into every stitch.

Jesse was wondering about his energies. *Bunky-dinks, Dearie*, he thought, pulling on her sweater, *what are all these terrible, zany, grotty, ree-dic-you-lus surprises? What's wrong?*

He heard her silver-y laughing words:

....

Ah Jesse, nothing is wrong. It's all new.

Just think of these surprises as thrill-digging adventures!

You are fine, Jesse. So fine! Travel on. Shine your heart-Light.

Believe! All is well. And so it is!

....

Conor saw Jesse with Dearie's knit cables up to his chin and felt Jesse was Jesse again. They held hands and strolled on—together.

Murphy was still blathering, and Jesse realized Elizabethtown had the same shops and businesses and churches as New York. Just smaller. Now, Murphy was bragging about Doc Nichols' office: "Me wife, Darlin,' is Doc's nurse! The best care anywhere!"

Jesse thought, *Oh, so there's a Mama Bear!* He smirfed to himself, but Murphy was jabbering and jawing on about the old Town

Library and the new Librarian: "Miss Bethesda Philhips, a right musty old maid."

They arrived at a crossroad, and Murphy puffed, "Four Forks. This here's the cemetery. Way back when, it was the Town Green, center of town. Used it to train the militia. Well," he hitched up his pants. "Here's where I leaves ya. You're goin' north, on Windmill Road, I'm turnin' south, on Spring Avenue." He saluted, "I'm off to me Darlin,' me own treasure of a wife!"

Boasting, Jesse pointed up Windmill Road. "My treasure is on Windy Hill."

Murphy leaned down on his knees. "And all the finest to ya, Jesse, lad."

Jesse wondered at his short, unconvincing laugh. It painted an empty smile across his Papa Bear chin, and he looked oddly … worried.

But Murphy straightened up, muttering to Conor, "Windy Hill's got more secrets than y' can shake a stick at. But first, y' hafta get past the Black Widah."

Conor glowered, and Murphy shifted, "And you, Conor, I wish y' good fortune in the Boston Beantown."

Turning about, he marched down Spring Avenue, whistling a tune. It took Conor a few notes, before he realized that Murphy's song was a funeral dirge, its dreadful notes dripping into the foggy air.

CHAPTER FOURTEEN

WINDMILL ROAD

They had walked a few blocks north when Jesse bent down. "Cracker Jacks! I found a penny! Dearie said it means someone is thinking of me." He looked up, "I think Dearie's here. I told her, when I go to Elizabethtown, I'd take her with me. I think she's here to help me *in-guess-tivate*." He chuckled, "I still gargoyle my words sometimes. I mean, *in-VES-ti-gate*."

"You keep your penny and Dearie close," Conor encouraged.

Jesse put it in his pocket, but he shivered in the cold wind. "Golly! I need more clothes—I'm so cold!"

"Cold?" Conor gusted, "Why Dearie would say it's simply tinteling!"

"I'm tinteling all over! Gosh, it's supposed to be summer! But I'm freezing!" He sat and rolled his socks up over his knees, singing Grams Maguire's knock-knock joke: *"Freeze a jolly good fellow!"* His canvas jacket didn't fit over his heavy sweater, but he flung it over his shoulders like a cape and buttoned it at his neck. He tied his cap onto his head with his long scarf, over his ears and under his chin. He was quite a sight.

Conor laughed heartily, "Jesse Seamus O'Neil! There are just so many inches of you, and right now every inch is ridiculous!"

A school bus passed them and some of the children pointed at Jesse, laughing.

Conor smirfed, "Hah! Little wonder!"

They saw the bus stop at the crest of Windy Hill, and some children got off, but they couldn't see where they went. Jesse and Conor trudged down the hill, and near the bottom, Jesse read a sign on a fence: *Linger Longer Farm – Horses Boarded – B. Philhips.*

"That's Miss Bethesda Philhips," Jesse noted. "*Linger Longer.* Hmm. I like it."

At the bottom of the hill, they reached an expansive marsh. A causeway road separated a ribbon of creek water on the left, and on the right, a wide blustery backwash with a little house at its edge. Bouncing with curiosities, Jesse bolted in that direction. "He-LLOOO!" he called into the foggy wind.

There were two trucks parked at the little house. One, a beat-up red pickup truck with a sign on the door: *Sure Lock Homes.* Jesse chuckled at that. The other truck was polished black, also with a sign: *Creek House – Seafood, Bait & Tackle – Peter Murphy, Owner, Proprietor.* A large wooden raft floated in the misty water, and a tall young man dressed in oilskin overalls and rubber boots was there pulling up crab cages.

Jesse ran down the plank and the man turned, shaking the cage at Jesse. Long crab claws scratched out, and Jesse jumped back.

The man laughed, "Green crabs and fiddlers! Best bait for blackfish." A pair of deep brown eyes glimmered at Jesse.

"I'm Jesse Seamus O'Neil. Are you Sherlock Holmes or Peter Murphy?"

He clucked a little laugh. "I'm Peter John Michael Murphy."

Jesse thrilled, "Those are all *Peter Pan* names!"

"Right! And believe it or not," he leaned toward Jesse like a conspirator, "my mother's name is Darling."

"This must be your *Neverland!*"

Peter's smile opened wide, quoting *Peter Pan*, "*Second star to the right'... !*"

"*And straight on till morning!*" Jesse grinned.

The fog rolled across the water in a glistening mist. Peter stopped talking and watched a long white bird stretching its wings like a graceful kite, its gossywim feathers sweeping over the water. Jesse was spellbound watching its thin neck and even thinner legs with bright yellow feet all topped off by magnificent wide wings sliding into the marsh grasses.

Jesse whistered, "What is that?"

"That is one of the enchantments of this creek marsh. A Snowy Egret, in the heron family. This is their summer home. They are a wonder, whispering through the air." His head turned to Jesse, "You get to see them, if you have eyes to look."

"I will. Thank you, Peter John Michael Murphy." He looked into Peter's deep brown eyes and added, "Today I met Regan Murphy."

Peter's face shadowed, "My Dad. But ..." he looked at Jesse knowingly, "he doesn't believe."

Jesse turned as Conor walked the plank, "Conor! This is Murphy's son, Peter! It's his Creek House!"

Conor had a memory-fizz: *Hmmm ... Murphy always bragged that his son, Peter, was a genius. Got into Harvard at sixteen. Went into big-time finance in Boston.*

Just then a man came out of the Creek House and joined them. *Oh,* Jesse thought, *this must be Sherlock Holmes!* But this man had a bushy ponytail sticking out of the back of his baseball cap. In one wink, Jesse thought, *Great goggles! He looks like Squirrel Nutkin! Golly! More animals followed me right here to Elizabethtown!* The Squirrel grinned, and Jesse saw that he was missing a front tooth. The man grinned anyway, and he looked even more like a Squirrel.

Peter introduced him, "This is Morton Mealy. Our local locksmith. He's here for bait."

Jesse smiled at the Squirrel, beaming, "We're here for Windy

Hill Farm!"

"Oh no!" Morton instantly blurted, "Y' don' wanna go up there! That old woman'll turn y' into a toad an' skin ya alive, I swear!"

Jesse's heart jolted. The raft seemed to spin in a dizzy *widdershin*.

But a heavy clam-rake stomped at Mealy's squirrelly toes. It was Peter. "No gossip here!" he commanded, "Go on inside; I'll bring the crabs."

Peter turned to Jesse, "*Those are my principles, and if you don't like them,*" he smiled, "*well, I have others.*" He smirfed at himself and said, "That's Groucho Marx." Peter leaned on his rake, adding, "People don't know what they don't know. And most gossip talks with the tongue of a shoe."

Jesse chortled, and Conor took the opportunity to introduce: "I'm Conor O'Neil, and this is my nephew, Jesse O'Neil. We're from New York City, going up to Windy Hill Farm. We'll be meeting Jesse's grandmother for the first time."

Peter nodded solemnly. "There's a first time for everything."

CHAPTER FIFTEEN
FIELD OF DREAMS

The cold wind gusted through the fog. Jesse shivered and Conor moved toward the plank, saying, "We'd best be going."

Peter cleared his throat, "Before you meet Jessica Roberts, there is something you should know." He leaned on his rake. "That farm. Well, Jessica worked and learned from her farm managers and her housekeeper. Oldsters. Steadfast and true. But, the Depression, well, it was hard. And it got harder, because, one by one, the oldsters died off. That left Jessica all on her own—with her little girl."

"Jane," Jesse volunteered. "Jane is my mother."

Peter nodded. "Beautiful, brilliant Jane." He exhaled. "But the Depression ... it brought the desperate beggars and tramps. Starving. Stealing. From Jessica's barn, her gardens, even got into her house. That was it. She had to protect ... well ... She got rid of them. She'll not abide any strangers. Ever." Peter looked at Jesse. "Just so you know."

Jesse had not a care, thinking, *We're not strangers. We're family.*

But Conor speculated, *We are strangers to her. What did she do to the strangers?* He thought uneasily of Murphy's words: *No one dares walk down her long, dark lane.* But he lectured himself, *Well, there's nothing for it now. We're almost there.*

He thanked Peter and led Jesse up the plank, where they heard Peter call, "Good luck to you. You're welcome to Neverland anytime."

Jesse beamed. "Thank you, Peter John Michael Murphy!" He skipped across the road.

Conor observed, "Jesse, do you know, this little causeway bridge was first built in the early 1700s? Back then, you had to pay to get through all the farmers' gates."

"Yes, you had to pay the Troll."

"No *Trolls*, Jesse," Conor smirked. "*Tolls*. You had to pay tolls."

Jesse ran past a brick Water Company building to walk atop an old rock wall. But it was in a sorry state, and he jumped down, yelping, "Oh! The ground is wet here!"

Conor saw Morton Mealy watching them, but he ignored him. Turning back to Jesse, he cautioned, "Don't step on any skunk cabbage! You'll reek to kingdom come."

Jesse yelled, "I can smell it! It stinks! I'm going up through the field!"

The fog-misted field grasses were sprinkled with wildflowers, and he took out his pocketknife, slicing away, filling his fist full of creamy-white Queen Anne's lace and blue chicory. "Conor," he called. "Flowers! For Lady Jessica!"

Conor waved, knowing that Jesse was in his element—finding his way. They were almost there! *All is well!* He kept walking up the very steep hill.

Jesse found a rough path leading to a stone wall. On the rise stood a tall, plain house. *Could this be Grandmother's?* He thrust his hand in his pocket, feeling for Dearie's stone. It wasn't there. But he touched Mac-Elliot's silver dollar, and suddenly, two dogs bounded toward him! One, a burly, black-and-tan thing and the other, a smaller, short-haired, reddish dog. Beyond them were two dark-haired, dark-eyed children, maybe a few years older than Jesse. The boy led a cow and calf, the girl had two goats. *Oh!* Jesse goggled, *They look like twins!* He hooted, remembering his Christmas star wishes, when Conor showed him the constellation Orion the hunter, his two dogs, and the Gemini Twins.

My dreams followed me here!

The dogs wagged their tails, barking happily. Jesse pet them, not caring about the slobbers they left on him. He looked up to the blowing, grey heavens as if a trail of stardust was tracing its way straight to him. But instead of stardust, thunder scudded through the clouds.

The boy and girl stopped. Stared. Well, Jesse was used to that by now.

The girl called, "Who are you?"

"Jesse Seamus O'Neil!"

Thunder cracked. Wind gusted. One of the goats bucked—right into the girl, knocking her over! Both goats galloped off, dragging the girl—on her bottom with her legs up in the air!

"Owa!" she cried, "Halt, Königin! Herzogin! Halt!"

Laughter exploded in Jesse's cheeks, even as he ran to help. *What a sight!* Sniggering with giggles, he caught the collar of one goat and gently touched the soft ears. Instantly, both goats stopped and nuzzled Jesse.

The girl leapt up, gasping, brushing at her pants. "How … did you gentle the goats?"

"I … just … I don't know," he flustered.

When the boy and the cows caught up, the girl spoke again, "What do you want?" She had a slight accent, making it sound like, "Vat do you vant?"

Jesse liked how she said 'v' instead of 'w,' and when she said 'the' it sounded like 'thee': *thee goats.* Like a little sing-song.

"Well," he answered, "I'm here with my Uncle Conor." He pointed to Windmill Road where Conor was making his way uphill. "We're here to find my grandmother!"

"Vat grandmutter?" the girl interrogated.

"My grandmother. Jessica. Here on Windy Hill Farm!"

The children looked at each other. The girl said, "Vee don't know any grand-boy."

He smiled and told them, "Jane is my mother."

Their eyes and mouths dropped open. They looked at each other. "Du meine Güte!" The girl whistered, "You are … Jane's?"

Jesse nodded, still smiling.

"Mein Gott!" She hesitated. "Jane? Is she here?"

"No. Jane and my father, James, are in the Great Illuminations." He saw their instant confusion. "They are dead."

"Mein Gott!"

"Yes. Well …" Jesse queried, "Could you show me where my Grandmother Jessica lives? I thought the farm back there was hers, but it looks empty."

The girl retorted, "That is the Marsh Hill Farm. The people are not here."

She gestured, "I am Margarethe, called Greta. This is my twin bruder, Mateus, called Matts. Vee take Guess and Who," she pet the cow and calf, "and the Queen and Duchess," she tapped the goats, "back to the barn. I say, you come."

Jesse looked at Matts, "What do you say?"

"Nothing," Greta answered. "He does not speak."

"Really? Why not?"

Greta looked perturbed, but she answered, "Matts only makes noise. Too many nincompoops make fun. So he does not try." They both turned away.

"Oh." Jesse followed them.

Greta called to the dogs, "Sadie! Red!" They kept barking at something but returned to lead the way along the rutted path.

Greta asked, "Vhy are you dressed like that?"

"Oh. I came up from New York City today."

"New York? This is how you dress in New York City?"

"Oh. No. It was blazing hot in the city, but it's freezing here. These clothes are all I could pull out of my valise."

The girl and boy nodded. "And the veeds?" Greta asked.

"Weeds?" Jesse echoed.

"In your hand. That vhite thing is Queen's Lace, but it is really a vild carrot."

"Wild carrot? These are flowers!" Jesse answered defensively. "They're beautiful, and free for the picking."

"Mmmm. Veeds." Greta said again.

Jesse smiled. He liked the way she talked.

They arrived at a beautiful wooden gate with a carved scallop shell on the latch. Again, the dogs barked at something, and Jesse wondered what it was. But all at once, he stood still. There was an enchantment in the air. Yet somehow it felt both dark and Light.

Muddled, Jesse was silent. The wind swirled with mist, almost obscuring the tall shadows of trees and muted traces of stone buildings. Jesse had not expected this. This deep uncertainty.

CHAPTER SIXTEEN

THE BARN

Jesse put his hand in his pocket, holding Mac's silver dollar. Elliot's silver dollar. Strangely, unbidden, the fogs lifted like a mysterious veil, and Jesse was looking at a barn. His mouth opened in a wide grin. "Like *LIFE* magazine! And Zuckerman's Barn in *Charlotte's Web!*"

Matts pulled the scallop-shell latch, the gate swung open, and Jesse followed the dogs, cows, goats, and twins on to Windy Hill Farm to the enchanted barn. At the lower level in back, Greta opened the wide barn door and Jesse followed the twins inside with a great breath of eager anticipation.

But instantly, he gagged! Stopped breathing! His lungs battled with an overwhelming stench. Matts pounded his back, forcing Jesse to suck in the foul air. "Ae-e-e-chh," he choked, pulling his hat and scarf over his nose.

Greta chuckled out loud, "This is the smell you vill learn to love!" Matts smiled wryly.

Jesse's eyes watered so, he could hardly see. Even so, he looked about for a pig. Or sheep? Geese? No. This was not *Charlotte's Web*. Jesse covered his nose. "Aegh, that smell!"

Ignoring him, Greta took charge. "Next, ve muck out. Clean out animal poop."

Matts opened three sturdy metal latches on a large door and swung it open, revealing a cement room about the size of an elevator, with high walls rising to the next floor.

"This is the vault," Greta tittered. "For the black gold," she tittered again. "The manure-poop from the animals down here and the chickens up there."

"Maneuver! That's the smell?" Jesse choked again and pulled his jacket off his neck.

Greta was laughing, "Not *maneuver! M-a-n-u-r-e*!"

"Sometimes I *gargoyle*, I mean *gargle*, my words." Jesse gagged.

Snickering at that, Greta and Matts pulled shovels from the wall and mucked out the stalls, taking the manure to the tarp in the vault. "Vhen the tarp is full, ve drag it outside to the pile. For the fertilizer."

With a hose, they washed the shovels over a low sink on the floor; then forked a pile of hay into the stalls and took the animals to their nice clean places. The animals were quite docile. Until … Queen-the-goat suddenly butted Guess-the-cow!

"Bally-go-go-jin-go!" Jesse bungled Murphy's exclamation as he backed away.

"It is Queen," Greta smirked, "showing her royal highness." Jesse thought the goat smirked, too. "Next the hens." Greta led them under the chicken platform, up the stone steps, and up another set of wooden stairs.

On the upper floor, they overlooked the stalls, with a door at each end: the left door was the color of a robin's egg. On the wall, hung a cross-stitch sampler with threads in the same blue, that read: *Gifts of God*.

"That cross-stitch is Jane. The blue door leads to the treasure rooms."

Jesse surprised, "Treasure? Really?"

The twins didn't answer. They turned to a line of chicken cages and cleaned again. Greta explained, "Ve use trap door here to shovel the chicken poop down into the vault below."

"Oh, a trap door!" Jesse marveled. "Clever."

Matts opened the cages and put in feed from a large grain cabinet on the wall, and Greta hosed fresh water into the little cage cups. Then she opened a flap and let in the chickens.

Willy-nilly, Jesse greeted the hens. "Salutations!"

"Salutations?" Greta flabbergasted. "No, these are chickens."

Jesse smiled, "I am saying 'Hello!' 'Salutations!' Like in the book *Charlotte's Web*."

She didn't answer. She commanded: "Back, Lady Macbeth! You also, Cleopatra! Back, Juliet!" She turned to Jesse, "The hens are named for Shakespeare ladies. Today they are prickly from the cold. Out in their fenced-in yard vith the Doodle-Doo."

"Doodle-Doo!" Jesse exclaimed, "The Rooster! You know *Peter Pan!*"

Greta looked askance. "Jessica named him Doodle-Doo."

Jesse moved close to pet the birds, and they cooed tenderly. Greta looked at Jesse, "How do you do this vith the animals?"

"I—just—pet them." Jesse stammered.

"That is helpful. But you vill have a lot to learn. If Jessica lets you stay."

Jesse's heart jolted. Again. *IF? IF Jessica lets me stay?*

CHAPTER SEVENTEEN

READY OR NOT

Uninvited doubt ballooned in Jesse's mind and his heart deflated. *Lady Jessica—my own grandmother—not let me stay?* This new, alien doubt took the Light-filled love in his heart and sent it swirling with dark, worrisome clouds into his brain. He stopped. *No! No IF! Pivot!* He closed his eyes and breathed. *Aech! That smell!* His watery eyes opened. He looked up at the row of high, square windows. He could see the fog drifting by. *Dearie … ?*

Keep shining, Jesse! Remember what Mr. Andy said: Look for the presence of wonder. It's waiting for you. Look! And Light on!

Jesse opened his eyes as wide as he could and gazed out the windows. Greta was looking at the clock high on the wall. She and Matts moved down the steps from the chickens, pulled off their rubber boots, pulled on their shoes, and went outdoors.

Following behind them, Jesse, sucked in the fresh foggy air like a sponge drinking water. But when he turned around … "Glory BE!"

Jesse was gazing at a wonder! A fully blossomed, fluttering, pink cherry tree. He felt Dearie in every petal … winking at him! "Dearie!"

"Not a Dearie," Greta murmured. "It is *Sakura*. Jessica says, *Wabi Sakura*. Japan-y for the 'vonder of one blooming cherry tree.'"

"Wa-bee-sa-kur-a." Jesse smiled. "A wonder!"

Greta added, "Jessica's Grandfather planted it vhen the barn was built."

Jesse hardly listened. He was in a wonderlush with Dearie. Slowly, his eyes moved up, above the cherry tree. Up, to the top of the barn roof … and more wonder! "Cracker Jacks! There's a little house up there! With porches on each side!"

"That is Jessica's Star Cupola. It is a vonder," Greta allowed.

"Wonder," Jesse almost laughed. "So much wonder here!"

"There is more," Greta carried on. "That is her carriage house. For old cars. Second story is office. Over there, that little stone mound is the first vell dug for the farm. There are many vells on the farm. Vindmills, also. For electricity." Greta turned around, "Jessica lives in that big house. Here are the gardens."

"Gardens?" Jesse puzzled. Plants were hanging in the air! Rows of poles stood with hooks at the top, for pails filled with young tomatoes, peppers, squashes. All airborne! Farther along was a glass house, and farther on were low stone foundations covered with glass doors.

Greta explained, "That is the greenhouse and the cold frames where Jessica starts the baby plants." To the right she pointed to rows of raised boxes. "More vegetables and herbs. Underneath, at the edges, are strawberries and marigolds."

"This is brillish," Jesse marveled. "Jessica is so clever. So *remorseful*." He laughed at himself, "I mean *resourceful*."

Greta and Matts paid him no mind. They moved toward a long building with porches at the first and second floors. "This last building has two parts: This end is vhere our father's old uncle and aunt lived; Joe and Mary Vareio. They helped Jessica vith the farm and baby Jane."

"That's my mother! Jane!"

"Yah!" Greta amazed. "So," she pointed to the far end of the long building, "that is Jessica's workshop, where she makes her furniture. Your grandmutter is there." Greta looked at Jesse sincerely. *"Ich drücke dir die Daumen.* In English it is: 'I press my thumbs for you.' It is like crossed fingers. Good luck."

"That's brillish! Thank you!" Jesse grinned.

"Yah. Ve must go. Home. To Little Farm. Goodbye."

Just like that. Goodbye. Jesse watched them disappear behind the garden.

Something rusheled at his feet. A grey striped cat was gazing into Jesse's eyes. Like the dogs before, it moved away from him and stopped, staring back at Jesse. Waiting for him.

Jesse's feet stuttered forward. "Ready or not, here I come."

CHAPTER EIGHTEEN
CONOR'S PATH

While Jesse discovered field and farm, Conor trudged up Windmill Road. At the top was a high stone wall that led to a long cobblestone driveway lined with tall purple-leafed maple trees, heavy with blowing mist. He couldn't miss the sign on the gate:

No Trespassing—Private Property

The wind whiplashed the branches above, and Murphy's warnings snapped through Conor's thoughts. *Black Widow. No strangers.*

Trying to calm himself, a memory-fizz took him back to their New York apartment, with Bridget and Mac, talking about Jessica.

Bridget shook her head, "And how would a beautiful girl like Jane ever come to have a dreadly mother? Never happen. Not in my book."

Mac added, "I'll bet you a doughnut hole, Jessica's a Lady of Light. Like Jane."

Conor inhaled, *That's what I want. I want Jessica to be a Lady of Light. Like Jane. Like Dearie. Just the right kind of grandmother. The kind Jesse deserves. A Lady of Light who will love-adore him. Watch over him ... like a little treasure.*

All at once, he heard Dearie:

....

Oh, yes Conor! That's it! That's how you want to feel.
Let it all unfold. Keep only the good energies.
No matter what.

....

Conor warily tossed the suitcases over the gate and climbed over, furtively moving behind a line of evergreens. He found a slim wooden gate and slowly lifted the latch, gulping, *Dang it! I am trespassing.* But he commanded himself, *Let it unfold!* In through the gate he went, hovering behind thick rhododendrons.

He stopped and marveled at the building construction: the high stone foundation; the row of small square windows; the long, steep, overhanging roof with stone drains on the ground below. *Simple. Simply stunning.*

A woman's voice was singing. He moved toward the voice and came to another part of the building with wide, sliding-door openings.

The voice sang clearly. A sweet old song from Irving Berlin: "Always" ...

I'll be loving you, Always! With a love that's true, Always!
When the things you've planned need a helping hand,
I will understand, Always!
Days may not be fair, Always! That's when I'll be there, Always!
Not for just an hour, not for just a day, not for just a year, but Always!

Conor was carried away by her soft, tender voice. *Oh, she is tender-hearted. Why did I ever listen to Murphy? Black Widah! Bosh!*

He peeked inside the doorway, and his breath caught in his throat.

PART FOUR

THRILL-DIGGING

Earthbound.
Yet I slip to the stars.

CHAPTER NINETEEN

FACE TO FACE

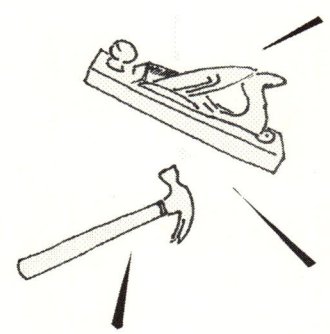

Conor watched Jessica. He stared.

Her shimmering, spun-gold hair was pulled up loosely, with errant tendrils sliding over her cheeks and one long braid falling down her back. She was still singing, and her tall, slender body swayed with her melody. Even in chambray and overalls, she was the picture of grace.

Conor silently acknowledged, *She's beautiful. And so young.* He chuckled: *Well, what did I expect? Some old hag? Jessica is Jane's mother, after all. Beautiful Jane and beautiful Jessica. Naturally, they resemble each other.* Somewhere in his thoughts was a flicker of another. But Conor didn't follow that musing right now. He focused on Jessica. And it struck him: *Jessica. Jesse. Look-alikes. Unmistakable.*

Jessica was sanding a chair in a large, tidy workshop. Conor realized, *She's a woodworker!*

Humming still, she smiled and took a little waltz step, holding up her pants legs like a long skirt. Humming. She twirled. Slowly. Turning. Slowly. Whirling. Bit by bit. Coming face-to-face ... with Conor.

She stopped. Her smile vanished into a crevice of ice. Her eyes frosted. She snatched a knife, and her voice matched the glimmering blade.

"Get off my farm!" She raised her arm and stepped forward.

Conor stood still. "I can't ..."

Jessica hurled the knife.

Conor ducked. "Holy smoke!"

She flung a screwdriver at him.

"Great Lakes!" Conor ducked again, but she had grabbed a long pitchfork, stabbing the tines at his chest.

"Get out!" She jabbed. "NOW!"

He put up his hands, feeling like an outlaw in the old West.

"Get OUT!" Jessica repeated violently, prodding him. But he lunged, yanking the pitchfork out of her hands.

Jessica gasped and backed up. She began flinging anything, everything. Wood. Blocks. Tools. She screamed, "Get OUT! GET OUT!"

"I—Listen! HEY!" Under the barrage, Conor dodged this way and that, using the pitchfork as a shield. But he saw a weighty planer and a claw-tooth hammer coming at him. He fended off the hammer, but the planer came whistling through the air, with head-on precision. *Thwunk!* Down he went. Crumpled into a pile behind the doorway.

Jessica backed away, falling heavily onto a bench, gasping for breath after breath. From the doorway, the grey-striped cat padded in and leapt into her lap. She clutched the cat, stuttering, "Oh Ellie-cat ... oh, my Ellie-cat! But the cat pulled away. Stared into her eyes. Unbelievably, she thought, it smiled at her.

Back at the doorway, there appeared a young boy. His face, his eyes, were smiling. Jessica did not move. The boy walked to her. He softly pet the cat, just once. Then his little hand went to Jessica's cheek, and he held it there, still smiling, with his deep, blue-green eyes shining at her like a mirror.

"It's you!" His voice was full of joy. "My own dear Grandmother. Lady Jessica!" He hugged her about the neck, cat and all.

The cat purred long and deep.

Jessica began to weep. To wonder.

Abruptly, the cat jumped down, to the pile that was Conor. Jesse turned his head and saw Conor … blood trickling from his head.

"Conor!" Jesse tore away from Jessica, falling at Conor's side, frantically pulling at Conor's jacket. His heart screamed! "Conor! Oh, please don't go, Conor!" Achingly, Jesse pleaded, "Conor! Please! Wake up!"

Conor moaned. His eyelids quivered. Opened. He saw Jesse. Heard his voice. "Oh Jesse!" He clutched Jesse to his heart. Lovingly, he stroked his hair, his back. "Ohhh, Jess … Jesse!" Slowly, he pulled himself up, resting against the wall, with Jesse in his arms, the cat licking his hands.

Unexpectedly, Jessica knelt in front of them.

Conor backed away from her, putting up his hands again, ready to fend off whatever she would throw. But instead, she offered him a cup of cool water. She washed his bloody head with a wet cloth, not saying anything. But he could plainly see that she had been crying.

Jesse sat with Conor, his eyes fluttering back and forth with encouragement and hope.

Jessica cleared her throat. "Conor …? You will have a modicum of bruising at your eye and perhaps, a small scar. Nevertheless, your *health shall live free, and sickness freely die.*"

"Thank you." But he instantly blithered at himself, *Ohhh, this is so bizarre! I'm thanking her! While she quotes Shakespeare at me!* He recalled Peter Murphy's warning. Jessica certainly knows how to get rid of a stranger. Yet, Conor felt contrite, wondering how many strangers Jessica must have had to dispatch over the years, alone on this farm.

Meanwhile, the cat was still licking him.

"Oh look, Conor!" Jesse cried, "Like *Oisin's* cat! Licking you!"

Jessica roused, "This is my Ellie-cat. But you know the story of Egypt! Oisin's cat!"

Jesse's head bobbed, as Jessica plowed into her next question. "And your mother, Jesse? Where is my Jane?"

For a moment, silence owned the room, before Jesse blurted, "Oh, Jane and James have gone to the Great Illuminations."

"Great Illuminations?" Jessica knew that phrase. *Papa used to say it when ... when ...* "Oh no!" she cried out, "NO! Jane! JANE!"

Jessica's eyes emptied. Darkened. She was falling. Plunging into a dark abyss. Her head dropped to her knees. Slowly, slowly, she keeled over.

No sound came out of her. It felt like time stood still. Then all at once, her body heaved violently, and she gave out a long, very long, keening cry. A strangled cry. A shattered cry. A cry that shivered and trembled through Jesse and Conor.

CHAPTER TWENTY

SCYLLA & CHARYBDIS

Jesse and Conor got Jessica to the house and into her bed, wrapped in a quilt stitched with yellow roses. Jesse sat on the floor beside her, while she slept under the spell of fathomless grief. He looked at her face, like the moon, shadowed with a light not her own.

Thunder rattled the fog-filled window, and Jesse felt his dreams rattle. *My dreams.* He sighed. *I didn't dream this part. I didn't. Did I?* His eyes closed.

....

Jesse. Your dreams have come true. Here you are. With Jessica.

   Let your dreams unfold. Trust them. Open your heart, and Light on.

....

Jesse knew Dearie was right. But still, he struggled with this unexpected turn of events. He saw Conor standing in the doorway, silently enticing him with a mug in one hand and a cracker tin in the other.

But Jesse didn't move.

Conor's mouth grimmeled. In the next instant, he popped his one good eyebrow, knocked his knees together and swiveled his hips, whistering, "Come on, ankle biter!"

In a whoosh of quiet laughter, Jesse got up and hugged Conor for a lingering moment, and they moved into the kitchen.

"I poked around here," Conor gestured outdoors. "The barn, the garden. Jessica's workshop is a wonder! And that cherry tree! Magnificent! It made me think of Dearie."

"Me, too." Jesse thought, *Wabi Sakura. Wonder.*

"I closed Jessica's workshop and got our bags. And your flowers."

Jesse remembered Greta and rusheled, "My weeds."

Conor brought mugs of steaming tea to the table, where he had put out the tin of crackers with a pot of goat cheese and a jar of jam.

Jesse sat and blew on his tea, peering at Conor. "Well," he breathed. "Grandmother Jessica didn't know Jane went to the Great Illuminations."

Conor wagged his head, "Murphy was right. Jessica knows nothing about us. Nothing."

"Nothing about us? Not even me?"

Conor touched his bruised eye, "I'm afraid not, Jess."

Knows nothing about me? Jesse imagined having to go back to New York City without a family to call his own. As if to snuff out the thought, he closed his eyes … into a darkness where he couldn't see. He couldn't feel his way through this dark uncertainty. His eyelids barely opened. He was looking at the floor. "Do you think … Conor … Do you think she'll want me?"

"Ohhh Jesse." Conor's heart crinkled. But his mind suddenly whirled like a tornado. "Aech, Jesse! We're stuck! Between Scylla and Charybdis."

"Silla and Ka-rib-dis!" Even in his distress, Jesse almost smiled, recalling how he loved Conor's storytelling of the ancient Greek tale of Homer's *Odysseus*: traptured between *"being devoured by the horrifying, six-headed demons of Scylla—or swallowed whole and drowned by the terrifying whirlpool of Charybdis!"*

But Conor was silently berating himself: *Eghh! What was I thinking? I can't possibly leave Jesse here. But I can't take him with me to Boston.* Conor felt the impossible sitting on his shoulders.

"Conor?" Jesse waited ... slowly pivoting back to his Light.

"What? What did you say, Jesse?"

"I think she likes me. I like her. She looks like the photos of Jane, doesn't she? Very pretty. When she's not crying. Maybe she just needs some tender *affliction.*"

Conor's mouth spurted, "I hope you mean *affection!*"

"Oh, affection. Right. She was real gentle taking care of you. I like the way she talks!" He took another sip of tea and rambled, "Her farm is great. Everything is so clever. She takes good care of everything. And there are two kids—Greta and Matts—who come to help her with the animals."

Jesse stopped and spread some cheese and jam on a cracker. "Conor," he said, gazing at him softly, "I think Jessica will be better when she wakes up."

Jesse, the eternal optimist, Conor thought to himself. *He wants to stay. Maybe, I could? No! Don't even think it! Not with Jessica out of working order. No! And besides, I really don't know a thing about her. I mean, will she want Jesse?*

"Conor ..."

"Jesse!" Conor blurted, "We don't even know if Jessica can keep you!" He saw Jesse flinch at that. "I'm sorry, Jess, but we don't know anything right now."

Jesse heard Greta's words: *IF... she lets you stay.* His shoulders twitched. *No. No. I have to pivot again.* Quietly he offered, "So ...? One step at a time? Like Dearie always said."

"Yes," Conor fumbled. "Uhm, well, how about we stay here for the night. We can't leave Jessica now ... not in the shape she's in. So ...

we'll check in on her in the morning. And go from there?"

Jesse brightened, "That sounds good."

"Meanwhile," Conor cleared the table, "I need to go into town and use the pay phone. Call the Dana Theater."

They cleaned up the dishes and moved outdoors where the dogs, Sadie and Red, capered around them. Conor turned and tousled Jesse's hair, lecturing, "Now don't you wander off, Mr. Imaginator. I'll expect to find you here, inside the house, when I get back." He hugged him. "This is no time to be finding mysteries. Stay put."

Jesse smiled at Conor, but he couldn't help thinking: *Stay. IF Jessica lets me stay.*

Conor gestured, "You'd best get back inside, and I'll be on my way."

Jesse smiled and sang, *"Happy trails to you!"*

Conor was off, down the driveway. Jesse stood a moment longer under the tall, darkly purple trees swaying with the cold, misty breezes. He looked up at them. They seemed to be standing, arm in arm, like they were watching him. Staring.

CHAPTER TWENTY-ONE

EXPLORE

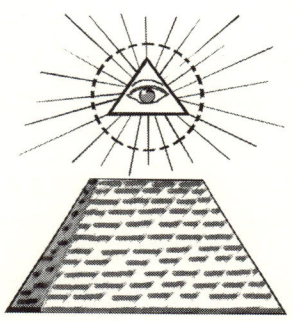

J esse checked on Lady Jessica: *still sleeping.*
Wandering back to the kitchen, he saw something twinkle at him and found glittering purple jewels piled inside a tall rock, inside a glass box.

"My goggles! Lady Jessica has her treasure right here on the kitchen shelf!" He sparked, *I wonder what else I can find!*

Near the kitchen entry, Jesse opened a door to an apartment, like a housekeeper's rooms. Then, adjacent to Jessica's bedroom was another bedroom. Jesse saw a copy of Jane's poem "Island," written in the shape of the island of Elizabethtown. Jesse marveled, thinking: *Jessica has a copy too! That poem was the beginning of all the secrets. My journey. To find Jessica. And I found her, right here on this island that Jane puzzled into her poem.*

"I think this was Jane's room," he whistered to himself as he poked about. "And what is this?" On the nightstand was a cylinder with tiles of alphabet letters all around. Jesse shook it. "Something is inside." But it was sealed. He turned it over and read: *The key will always be ~ you and me.*

"Who is you and me?" *Another secret,* he thought, setting it down.

Golly, exploring Jessica's house is an adventure. Indeed, every room was filled with gadgets and devices and riddles.

The office had a globe of Earth, with the sun and moon revolving around it! A binocular case was embossed with:

THE EYES – THEY SEE

Jesse thought that was silly, until he realized, "The letters for THE EYES! Golly, they're the same letters for THEY SEE! It's a clever anagram!"

On a shelf stood a small silver stand decorated with tiny rose flowers—but whatever was supposed to be in it was missing.

Jesse moved to the desk and picked up what he thought was a watch. On the cover was a blue-and-gold design. "Hmmm, the letter G, inside a wide V, under a pointy A—and on top is the Eye of Providence. Just like Miss Lily's drawing."

He had no idea what it meant. But surprisingly, his finger pushed the lid, and it swung away from the top. "It's a compass!" He wheeled in a circle, and the arrow held at a steady North. He turned it over. An inscription read:

When joy is your compass, you live your magic.

"Yes," Jesse inflated. He closed it and left it on the desk.

In the hallway was a broad, open staircase and beyond, an enormous living and dining room, skirted by a wide screened-in porch.

Everywhere he looked were more contraptions. A small log splitter on the hearth reminded Jesse of Mac's old contraption that could snap a small log into big sticks. On the grand piano was a stained-glass lamp that rotated, sending dancing colors onto the walls and ceiling; a small, old Victrola record player; and below it, a strange contraption with one straight antenna and one looped antenna. It was labeled: *Léon Theremin, 1928.*

There were stuffed bookshelves built into every wall, and on the side table, Jesse saw both *Peter Pan* and *Shakespeare*. Captivating artwork hung in gold frames, both oversized and postcard-sized and signed: *William Trost Richards*. Jesse liked his paintings, especially the full moon over the bay, with a moon glade sliding across the water.

Tall cupboards held beautiful blue-and-white chinaware and tiny, delicate statues: a rabbit, a bird hatching out of an eggshell, a monkey, a man with a bald head sitting on a mushroom. Jesse noted a card underneath them with a word: *netsuke*.

Circling back to the kitchen, he noticed rain spackling the windows and he remembered his flowers. *Hah,* he chortled, *my weeds!* He went to the pantry and reached for a vase, brushing a teapot decorated with yellow roses. *I guess Jessica likes yellow roses.*

Conveniently, a small sink there took care of watering, and he turned to take his flower-weeds to the kitchen table. But, to his surprise, he saw, "Another door! Cracker Jacks!"

He put the vase on the table and silently opened the door, into deep darkness.

CHAPTER TWENTY-TWO

UP THE STAIRS

In the dark, Jesse twiddled a wall switch, and a gloomy glow revealed: *Another stairway! A secret staircase?*

An exciting shiveral nudged Jesse's foot to the bottom step. His other foot rose all by itself, and he didn't resist. He was climbing up, up, through his own thrill-digging shadows, with his imagination on fire.

At the top landing were three doors—like three secrets. The left and center doors had no door handle. But the right door did. And it opened at his touch.

Jesse moved into a scrim of darkness, drumming with rain on the roof. He searched for a light switch, but his fingers found—"Eeewww! Ech! A dead bird! Aegh!" He flung it away.

Suddenly, his exploring didn't feel like an adventure. It felt ... skittley and spooky. Dreadly jim-jams shivered up his spine. He started to withdraw, but he lost his balance, and, falling back, his hand hit the light switch!

"G-r-e-a-t g-a-r-g-o-y-l-e-s!" His eyes exclaimed with his voice.

Jesse was aboard a magnificent yacht! He recalled the *Hispaniola*—the old sailing ship from one of his favorite books, *Treasure*

Island. Glowing wood and polished brass gleamed high and low. A bank of long windows marched across one wall with a long window seat and cupboards below that.

"This is glare-ee-us!" He chuckled, thinking of the way Grams Maguire liked to say "glorious" with her Irish brogue.

To the right, a beautiful carved wooden desk. On top rested another set of binoculars, and a brass telescope. The side of the telescope was engraved:

ASTRONOMER – MOON STARER

Jesse fingered the letters. "Another anagram?" He matched letter for letter. "It is! Somebody liked these word puzzles!"

Also on the desk was a box of stationery engraved with a scallop shell. On the floor was a thick Persian carpet with a scallop-shell design along the edges. Oddly, Jesse saw something perched in the middle of the carpet. He peered closer. It was … a feather duster! "Oh!" He giddied, "My dead bird!"

On the opposite wall were two round porthole windows where a dining table stood between high-backed benches. Next to that was a kitchen, a *galley*, with a sink encased in more polished wood, and an icebox below. Beside that was a cupboard. Jesse opened it and looked … down. "Oh! This is a little elevator! It must go down to the kitchen pantry!"

Wood railings above held crystal glassware and decanters, gold-rimmed dishes, and heavy silver mugs, all painted or embossed with the scallop-shell design.

Jesse opened a tall, shuttered door, and found two bedrooms with both regular and porthole windows, plus built-in bunks and storage. A bathroom, the *head*, was between the bunk rooms.

"I'd love to sleep in this snuggery!" Jesse gushed.

Returning to the main room, he saw a long table and again thought of *Treasure Island*. "This would be the table for rolling out sea charts."

Under another porthole window was a drop-leaf table with a treadle underneath. "That's a sewing machine, like Dearie's from her theater costume shop."

He moved to the tall doors on each side of the entry door and slid one open.

"Great goldfish! There's a toy store in here!"

Two miniature armies were lined up in formation on a tray: one army in red, the other in blue. Above and below were shelves and shelves of board games, puzzles, paper, paints, and art books! Jesse knelt down, pulling out a stand with a mirror and a light. "What is this contraption?" An embossed label answered: *Camera Lucida Projector*. "Oh, yes! Dearie had this for tracing pictures on the theater sets!"

He rocked forward, fingering a metal statue of Uncle Sam with his palm up and the words: *Support the War Effort – 1917*. Uncle Sam was waiting for a coin. Jesse took out the penny he had found and placed it there. Amazed, he watched the hand move down, and the coin slide into a slot! "A mechanical piggy bank!"

The rain was but a light patter now, and through the drizzles, Jesse saw lights flickering outside. He moved to the window seat at the slanted windows to see what he could see.

"Oh, great gargoyles!" He knelt closer to the windows. "Oh, no!"

CHAPTER TWENTY-THREE
PHONE CALLS

Walking down Windmill Road, Conor muddled, *So many questions. Jessica's still a secret puzzle.* His thoughts swayed with the rhythm of his feet ... *But Jessica doesn't know how good Jesse is at solving puzzles!*

Trekking past Peter Murphy's Creek House, Conor started up the hill as thunder rumbled through the scudding clouds and jostled the telephone lines.

"Telephone lines?" Conor's eyes followed the lines. He whooped, "Peter's got a phone!"

He walked back and knocked on the door. "Hellooo! Peter? It's Conor O'Neil."

The door opened and Peter welcomed, "Come on in!"

"Why!" Conor surprised, "your inside looks like an outside. You've shingled the walls!"

Peter beamed, "Welcome to my Nautical Knick-Knack Nook! Built like a boat, shingled like a barn!" He pointed, "My bait business there," he stepped back, "and my cabin over here. Mostly crates and cement block, but one day, it'll be my yacht."

"Nice life you're carving out for yourself."

Peter mugged and quoted Groucho Marx, "*Life is several billion cells that get to be you for a while!*"

Conor grinned, "I'll have to think about that one!" He glanced about. "Really. Very neat. Reminds me of Jessica's wood shop."

"She's a great woodworker. Big call for her furniture all over New England."

"Really?"

"Oh yes. She's made a name for herself."

"Really!" Conor repeated. "Well, she's the reason I'm here." He told Peter everything that had happened at Windy Hill Farm.

Peter nodded, "I did wonder about that black eye."

"Oh, it only hurts if I touch it."

"Then don't touch it," Peter chuckled.

Conor chuckled, too. "So, may I use your phone? I can pay you. It's long-distance. To Boston."

"Glad to help. I'll heat up some coffee."

Conor phoned the Dana Theater and, to his great relief, learned that they were waiting on other actors. He could take a few days more. Picking up the coffee mug, he saluted, "All is well!"

"That's what I like to hear!" Peter rejoined.

With rain drumming on the roof, the two young men talked away like long-lost friends.

Conor remarked at last, "It's been odd. Since we arrived, people have been staring—*just staring*—at Jesse."

"Yes," Peter smiled. "One thing you can be sure of: Tonight, just about every house in Elizabethtown is talking about the Black Widow and the boy who looks just like her."

That made sense to Conor. "Well, I left that boy alone. I'd best get back."

Peter offered, "It's dark and wet. I'll give you a lift." Grabbing a jacket, he opened the door, noticing the rain was but a light patter now. But looking up the hill, he shouted, "Oh, no!" He pushed inside and seized the phone. "Fire!" he yelled at the Operator. "Marsh Hill Farm!"

Within seconds, the Fire Station horn blasted into the night, and Peter jumped into his truck, yelling, "Conor! Get in!"

Back in Jessica's "yacht," Jesse could see inside the Marsh Hill house. Fire! Flaring at three boys—the tallest boy, pulling the others away. Then, three shadows, shooting across the field, framed briefly by the headlights of a truck that had pulled into the farm.

"That's Peter's truck! And there's Conor!"

The Fire Station horn blared. Sirens wailed. Jesse watched flashing red lights tearing down and up Windmill Road and into the driveway at Marsh Hill Farm. Instantly, they trained their bright spotlights onto the farmhouse.

In awe, Jesse watched the Firemen teams: peeling off fire hoses, sliddering them across the field like racer snakes, spouting water like a raging faucet. Ladders up. Axes chopping. Faster than he could believe, Jesse saw the flames extinguished! "Done and Done!" he exclaimed.

Firemen milled about and Jesse saw the squirrelly Morton Mealy—Sherlock Holmes. He was talking to a Policeman and kept pointing down to the Creek House and up to Windy Hill. He looked pesky.

All of a sudden, Jesse thought of Jessica. *Good glory, all this commotion!* But when he got to her room, Jessica was still asleep.

The back kitchen door opened, and Conor entered with Peter Murphy, followed by a Policeman.

"Jesse," Conor said seriously, "this is Chief of Police Patrulha. He has some questions for you."

"Am I going to jail?" Jesse ruffled. "I have a *Get Out of Jail Free* card."

Chief Patrulha tried not to laugh. "Listen young man, we know three children were in the farmhouse."

"Yes," Jesse agreed. "I saw them. The fire got too big, and they escaped!"

"My witness says you were one of the three children. That you met two others, running through Marsh Hill fields."

"Yes. This afternoon, I met Greta and Matts." He chortled, "Queen, the goat, butted Greta onto her bottom, and the two goats d-r-a-g-g-e-d her across the field! So, Matts and I ran after her."

"Let me finish," Chief Patrulha persisted. "My witness says the three of you disappeared but later returned and headed straight for the Marsh Hill farmhouse."

Jesse's eyebrows knit over his nose. "Well, I saw three someones in there." He took a breath, "But, nooo. It wasn't us. We took care of the animals, and Greta and Matts went home."

Jesse leaned forward, "Then I met Lady Jessica. That's what I call her. She's my grandmother. But she didn't know Jane was dead. Jane is her daughter, my mother." His voice turned sorrowful, "Lady Jessica's deep asleep. Not even your fire sirens woke her."

This was not going as Chief Patrulha had planned, especially when Jesse stood up and took his hand.

"Come upstairs. You'll see. Everything."

Up the stairs they went, into Jessica's "yacht."

"Oh! Meu Deus!" That's what Jesse heard Chief Patrulha say.

"Good glory and Great Lakes!" That's what Jesse heard Conor say.

Peter Murphy said nothing. But his eyes were bigger than the porthole windows.

At Marsh Hill Farm, the bright spotlights were still on, and they could see everything outside, clear as day. Jesse explained, "This is where I stood, and I saw the three boys running."

But Chief Patrulha stopped him. "I see. I believe you. My witness must be mistaken."

Peter muttered. "Morton Mealy. He could throw himself on the ground and miss."

"But I thought," Jesse wondered out loud, "Squirrel Nut ... I mean, Morton Mealy, was like Detective Sherlock Holmes."

"Mmm," Peter smiled wryly, "He'd like that."

Chief Patrulha was speaking, "Jesse O'Neil, you are one lucky boy to live here."

Jesse blurted back, "IF Jessica lets me stay."

CHAPTER TWENTY-FOUR
GOOD NIGHT, WINDY HILL

Jesse closed the door after Peter and Chief Patrulha. "Whew! I'm so glad I'm not going to jail again!"

"Right!" Conor puffed and turned to the icebox. "Let's find something to eat."

They pulled together a supper of leftover soup and thick slices of bread topped with the best butter they ever tasted. Jesse wanted to put up a tray for Jessica, but she was still sound asleep.

At the table, he eagerly shared his explorations, and they both marveled at Jessica's yacht design and Peter Murphy's hopes to construct a yacht room of his own.

Jesse was taking his bowl to the sink when Conor grinned. "So, I found a phone!" He waved his hands in the air as if he had discovered the North Pole.

"Oh, Jiminy Cricket! I forgot! What happened?"

"All good! Peter has a phone, and, well, I've got a few days more. So, we'll see. Listen, we've had quite a day! I'm beat! I say we clean up here, find our beds, and get some sleep."

Jesse yawned his agreement. "But first, I'm leaving something for Lady Jessica." He took his old stuffed bunny out of his valise and leaned it against his vase of flowers. "Jane's Velvet."

Conor hushed, "Yes, Velvet's home now."

Jesse pulled out the cigar box filled with his mother's undelivered letters. "I want Jessica to read Jane's letters. Whenever she's ready."

"Good idea, Jess. Maybe she'll heal all the sooner."

On tiptoe, they climbed the wide front steps to the gallery at the top. There they found four simple bedrooms with adjoining bathrooms and more floor-to-ceiling bookcases.

Jesse washed up and unpacked his valise, putting away his clothes and setting out the happy little framed photographs: one of James and Jane, and the other of Dearie and her husband, Galen, with their boys, James and Conor. Jane's embroidery threads were there, still wrapped tightly in the odd egg shape. He put that in the drawer of the nightstand. Then he took out his pocket items and added his thimble to the drawer.

His knife and silver dollar were laid on the tabletop, as he insisted to himself, "My stone. It's not lost." At the bottom of the valise was the Shark House postcard showing Elizabethtown. "C U" he shivered at the ominous note, fingering it. "This landed me in jail! I wonder who sent this?" His heart stirred with aimless worry, like a boat with no sails. Hearing Conor in the bathroom, he asked, "Will you lullaby me?"

Conor was surprised. He hadn't sung to Jesse in months, but gladly, he tucked Jesse under a quilt, and began the lullaby he had always sung to Jesse since the New Year's Eve Jesse was born: "*Silent Night, Holy Night ...*"

Conor turned out the light and Jesse gazed out the window. "It's so dark here. No city lights. Not even streetlights."

Smiling, Conor whistered, "It's in the dark that we get to see fireworks and fireflies ... the moon and stars ... and your Light, Jesse!"

Jesse smiled. He saw the clearing night sky playing peek-a-boo with the stars. Conor kissed him goodnight, and he fell into his dreamland: *Jane in bright stars and swirling gossamer Lights.*

∙⋖⋗∙

A gleam of moonlight awoke Jesse. It was shining on the silver dollar like a flashlight. He sat up and suddenly gaspered. Out the window the starry sky was dancing with streams of gossamer swirling lights! *My dream lights! Jane?*

Kafluffling into his clothes, he tiptoed down to Jessica's room. As he entered, he was only somewhat startled to hear Jessica gently call out, "Jane?"

Jesse looked out Jessica's window, watching the pink-yellow-blue-green sky lights—the Mirrie Dancers. How they rippled around the Star Cupola at the barn rooftop. And there was something else: the aroma of chocolate. Jesse smiled. *Jane!*

Jessica's soft voice called out again, "Jane?"

"Yes," Jesse answered her, "Jane is here!"

Time seemed to vanish.

Jesse and Jessica were in the barn. Conor, too. Jesse's eyes ogled, as Jessica pressed buttons on a pad hidden in the doorframe of the robin-egg-blue door.

The treasure door opened, and Jesse was sure he levitated into the room. He knew they were walking through floors of treasure rooms, and up, up the stairs, until all at once, they were in the Star Cupola … under an ocean of glittering stars.

Jesse's dream. Closer. Closer. He couldn't stop it. He didn't want to stop it.

Like a charmed spirit, Jessica opened the glass door and floated through, into the swirling, gossamer lights. Jesse and Conor followed, and in that moment, new Lights appeared. Hundreds of glittering Lights, pulsing like beating hearts. Jesse heard Dearie in his heart:

The Lights, Jesse! Here we are! All Lights.

Each of us, an enchanted jewel, a gem, glittering our facets.

Gorgeous, magnificent Lights! All connected.

We are all love-adores! Shining in endless love and joy.

And on earth—none, nothing more glittering than you!

Jesse breathed through his smile. *Dearie is here ... And Jane!* The smell of chocolate was unmistakable. *Jane's chocolate! Jane is here!* He knew. He remembered. His Lights: New Year's Eve with Billy on their apartment rooftop. He knew this special Light. The stars, effervescing into gorgeous gold and silver bubbles. And the smell of chocolate. *This is Jane!*

Oh! And James! He felt James standing with Jane, letting her shine. *Oh, so much Light! And so many love-adores! They are lighting us up!* He felt a gurgle of laughter, *Oh! I'm alight! Like the Rockefeller Christmas tree! And Conor is alight. And Jessica is alight.*

Lady Jessica! So beautiful! Lights bouncing in her hair, her cheeks, her eyes ... all around her. She looked like she was in a magic swirl of fairy dust. She was humming. Not out loud. Jesse could *feel* her humming within ... with the stars ... with Jane ... with wonder. He knew, *This is where I'm supposed to be.* His cheeks smiled wide, and he felt tears of wonder flooding his eyes.

Then Jessica murmeled, as if she had read his mind! "Ah! The stars! Jane! Glorious!" She reached out ... touching Jane. Inside the glowing, whirling Light ... the *Aurora Borealis,* like a sweeping butterfly net, capturing the Light, the stars.

Jesse heard her whister, "Exquisite! Jane!"

Slowly, slowly, slowly, the Lights rippled back into the night. Jesse and Conor and Jessica watched them fade and flutter away, until only the faraway stars were left in their eyes. Yet the Lights were inside them now, as they themselves had stood inside the gem of wonder.

Jesse looked at his radiant grandmother. A new word formed in his mouth: Gem. 'Gemma.' Shimmering. Becoming … 'Gemma.' Leaving Jessica behind.

Feeling all this, Jesse settled, *my grandmother—Lady Jessica—is 'Gemma.'*

Once again, time slipped them down the long, spiraling steps. Outside, they walked on a silver path. Like a snail trail in the night. But Jesse knew, it was really the path left by the stars. Jessica stopped. She looked to the sky. Her eyes gleaming with starlight … her face, a quickening of joy.

Inside, she fell into her bed, murmuring, "Jane. My Jane. Glorious!"

Jesse went to the kitchen and returned with Velvet. Crawling in beside her, he tenderly cozied Jane's old stuffed rabbit at his grandmother's cheek.

"Gemma," he hushed her new name.

He felt Conor kiss his forehead, and cover him with a quilt, before he sat in the stuffed chair in the corner and closed his eyes.

Only the bubbling stars and Mirrie Dancers knew the secrets awaiting the morning light.

PART FIVE

QUIZZELS

The day is not left to chance.
Change becomes.
Magic is.

CHAPTER TWENTY-FIVE
FIRST MORNING

The dawn sun opened Jesse's eyes. *Where am I?*

He rolled over. Conor was asleep under a quilt in a comfy chair. His grandmother slept on the bed beside him, with Velvet at her cheek. Jesse smiled, remembering last night's *Aurora Borealis*. He hushed her new name: "Gemma."

Footsteps sounded outside. *Greta and Matts are here!* Out into the golden morning, Jesse caught up with the twins.

"Did you see the fire last night?" he began.

"Vee saw the lights," Greta replied.

"Police Chief Patrulha thought WE started the fire!"

"Vhaaat? No!"

"I know! I told him I saw three boys inside the farmhouse."

"The Dorkings," Greta stated without a sliver of doubt. "Their names are Benedict, Angus, and Dominic. B-A-D." She looked at Jesse, "Did they catch them?"

"No."

"No. Dorkings. Like rat traps. Snap. But never caught."

Jesse was quiet. He heard Dearie:

'Rule of Tongue! No name calling!

It serves no one and only makes a tangle of hurt feelings.

You can heal a broken bone,

but the wound from words can ache forever.'

Quietly Jesse followed the cat into the barn. Zippity-pip, she skittered after a mouse!

"Diggity-boo!" Jesse hootled. "They're playing tag!"

Greta smugged, "Always the same game. Ellie-cat chases the mouse."

"Does Ellie-cat ever catch the mouse?" Jesse asked.

Greta's eyes looked cunning, "Not yet."

Jesse chorkled, and, thankfully, he didn't choke on the barn smell.

Matts handed him a pair of boots and went down to milk the cow, but Greta exclaimed, "The hens, they sound like hornets!"

Jesse ran up and found the birds wild in their cages. "Oh no! One of them fainted!"

"Yah. Ophelia faints in upset."

Jesse gently pet the bird, whistering, "Ophelia ..." The hen opened her eyes and cooed.

Greta stared at Jesse. "How ...?"

Jesse's shoulders quivered, "I just do it *instinkably*."

Matts and Greta snickled. She said, "Your hands are good. You help find the eggs."

Jesse's hands searched but came up empty.

"Delinquent hens!" Greta chastised and searched again. No eggs. "Ohhh!" She realized, It's vicked Dorkings!" She grabbed a pitchfork and stormed up to the hayloft.

Jesse followed. But he stopped at the trap door. The sun was shining on it just so. *The pull-ring ... it looks like ... the Eye of Providence!* He crouched down, but it disappeared. *What? I know I saw it!* He moved sideways, and the sun shone again, revealing the eye with a triangle and rays of light. *I can only see it in the light! My shadow makes it disappear!*

He touched the wood. *A secret! Is this trap door hiding the treasure?* He cackled. *In the manure room? Hah!* But he sobered. *Treasure!* He stepped up to the blue treasure-room door and flipped the door molding back, revealing ten buttons. The top button was labeled 'A'; the bottom button was a symbol: Ω. Jesse didn't know what it was.

Greta stomped back down the stairs, and Jesse tucked away his wonderings as she announced, "Dorkings slept here! And stole our eggs!"

"Last night! I saw them!" Jesse declared, "But, how did they get in here?"

"The Dorkings, they steal into any place. Like rats."

Jesse thought: *Templeton, the rat in* Charlotte's Web, *could get into anything.*

"Vell," Greta shrugged, letting the hens outside, "I milk Queen."

"Doesn't Duchess get milked?" Jesse curiosed.

"No. Goats need rest. She vill start again. Two months." Greta stopped. "Vant to milk Queen?"

Jesse's mouth grimmeled, "Sure."

He sat down. "I, uh … how do I find the, uh … the milk-makers?"

Greta shrugged, "Feel. You vill know."

His fingers arpeggio-ed along Queen's soft skin, unintentionally tickling her. Wildly, she toppled Jesse off the stool and butt him mightily. Onto his own butt! Jesse scoot-crawled away, with Queen and Duchess bleating, and laughter ringing through the barn.

Jesse was stunned. But the twin's giggles were infectious, and Jesse bubbled up a giggle-snicken, even as he rubbed his bottom.

"You are good sport!" Greta grinned. "Sit. I show you."

"I-I don't know about this." Jesse stuttered. But Matts nodded reassuringly. Greta's hands gently guided him, squeezing tenderly, firmly. Queen nuzzled Jesse as if in apology, and Jesse hootled, "This is thrill-digging! Milk-making!"

Jesse helped take the animals out to the field and gushered over everything, from the stone walls to the gate to the metal windmills on the hillcrest. Inside the pasture they reached a rolling green hill, and he stopped. Ahead was a stunted tree, framed by the beautiful, blue sea-and-sky. *It's "Trouville»! The Monet painting!* He felt the sparkling Light inside him. *Maybe I'm in a Monet painting! Maybe it's an* obstacle *illusion! No,* he laughed again, optical *illusion.*

Matts was pushing the long-handled pump, and Jesse watched the glistening water splashing into the trough. But he suddenly noticed that Greta was leaving.

"Oh, Matts," Jesse realized, "you have to get to school." Spontaneously, he clapped his flat hands twice, which is the hand sign for *school.*

Matts looked at him.

"I know you can hear me." Jesse offered, "This is a way for you to talk—in sign ... hand words." As he clapped, he repeated, *"school."*

Matts smiled and mimicked Jesse.

"Yes!" Jesse cheered, and they ran together to catch Greta.

At the fire-scorched Marsh Hill Farm, Jesse saw Peter Murphy's truck and dashed through the hole-in-the-wall. "Good morning, Peter!"

"Saint Patrick!" Peter jolted. "You startled the b'jeekers out of me!"

Jesse was startled, too. He was reminded of St. Patrick's Cathedral in New York City.

But Peter was talking. "I was so glad to see your grandmother's yacht room last night. I've dreamed of a room like that ever since I was knee-high to *Peter Pan* and the *Jolly Roger.*" Jesse beamed and Peter smiled. "For now, I'm meeting the caretaker and a carpenter to get this house back in shape."

A motorcycle roared up the driveway, and the rider pulled off his helmet.

"That is Charlie Lippley!" Greta crooned.

"Cherry Lips!" Jesse hooted.

Charlie looked at Jesse. "C-r-a-z-y man! We meet again!"

"I'm Jesse O'Neil from Windy Hill Farm."

Charlie stuck out his hand, "Charles Lippley. But I'm called Charlie, for short."

"That's funny," Jesse smirfed, "because Charles and Charlie have the same number of letters."

Charlie smirked, "Hmmm, Little Mr. Big Brain!" He grabbed a sack of tools from the truck. "Peter, have you got the key for the house?"

"No, but Ben'll be here any minute."

"Oh, man!" Charlie blurted. "I wanna get this done!"

Peter jiggered, "Keep your eyebrows on! Here's Ben now."

Another truck rolled in, and a man jumped out. Greta and Matts jumped back. "Ve must go!" She dragged Jesse away.

But Jesse called to Peter, "Glad to see you again! If you need anything, you're welcome—anytime!"

Greta sputtered at him. "You are mad! That is Mr. Dorking!" She pushed him, "You do not invite the devil to Jessica's farm!"

CHAPTER TWENTY-SIX

GEMMA

Greta scolded Jesse all the way to the barn, even as they put the full milk canisters and empty egg basket on the dolly. As they wheeled away, Jesse wagged, "Oka-a-ay!" But he didn't think anyone was the devil.

When Jesse opened the kitchen door, he heard Conor in the living room. Jessica was on the sofa, surrounded by Jane's letters and holding Velvet. Her clothes were rumpled, and her hair was falling out of a braid. But when she saw Jesse, a smile transformed her face, radiantly lighting her eyes. Jesse danced into her embrace.

"Ah love!" she raptured, holding Jesse. "'*Love is like a child that longs for everything it can come by.*'"

Conor saw that she meant every word of the Shakespeare she spoke, gazing at Jesse from head to toe.

"Oh, you are Jane, all anew!" she murmured, and pushed the letters aside, patting the cushion for him. "You have brought my darling Jane back to me! I will never forget the Lights of last night—filled with Jane!"

Jesse smiled, feeling their inner energies, their *brî*, bouncing between them. Conor whistered, "Jane's a FairLight, for sure."

Gemma sighed, "Yes. Jane's letters. Such love, in every word. Of her life in New York." Jessica quieted. "So very like my own life when I was a stage actress in the city. So strange, even as I lost my Daniel, she lost her James."

A sob snorkled in her throat. "Jane and James, Daniel and I. First and last love. Always." A cry escaped, "Oh, why have I lost all those I have loved? Papa, Uncle Trevor, Daniel, and now my Jane. My Jane."

Jesse's memory popped at the name, 'Daniel.' He remembered hearing it, way back when he was in the lightning storm with Billy. On his sixth birthday. He had heard that name: Daniel. Clear as a bell.

But Jessica was weeping, "Jane. All these years, how I wished for her."

"Why did Jane leave?" Jesse innocently quizzeled.

Jessica brushed away a wisp of hair. "I ... I should have known. Jane was a wanderer. Even at a young age, she would simply walk or bicycle away. Gone all the day. 'Exploring,' she would say."

Jesse smiled at that. But again, a sudden sob rushed through Jessica's throat. "Oh, I would look for her." She trembled. "From up in the Star Cupola. After she truly left, I could feel her on the breeze, in the sky." Her breath stuttered, "Last night, the Aurora Borealis, whirling through the stars. It was ... Jane."

Jesse hushed, "Yes, Jane was there. And Jane is here. Right now. Just like last night in the beautiful Lights." He moved closer to her, "But you can't have Jane when you're scrumpled up in only sadness. I found that out when Dearie went to the Great Illuminations."

That stopped Jessica in mid-weeps. She sat. Silent. Looking at Jesse.

Conor interjected, "Dearie, Jesse's Grandmother, explained it like that."

> *Yes! Our love-adores are in the Great Illuminations of pure love and joy.*
>
> *If you want to feel them, then that is the energy vibration you must become: love and joy.*

"It's like Peter Pan," Jesse explained. "If you want to fly with him, you need happy thoughts, and faith and trust. Oh, and pixie dust!"

Jessica wiped her tears and quoted *Peter Pan*, "*Oh, the cleverness of* YOU, Jesse!"

She looked at Jane's letters. "I have read only a portion of Jane's letters. But it is clear, Jane wrote only of love and joy and faith and trust. Not one word of reproach. Though I deserved it." Her voice whispered, "I severed all ties. I was obdurate. Yet, Jane did not renounce me."

She touched Jesse's cheek, "You have brought me Jane! Such love." She hugged Jesse close until he muffled, "Gemma, I'm smuffling!"

Jessica stopped. She quizzeled, "What is it you are calling me?"

Jesse explained, "Well, I used to call you Lady Jessica."

"My, my," his grandmother rustled, "Lady Jessica!"

"But last night," Jesse continued, "in the Lights, you looked like a gem. I saw Lights glittering inside you. And I thought of 'Gemma.' For you."

"A new name?" Gemma again gazed at Jesse. She considered, *New name ... new beginnings. Well!* A little giggle-snicken escaped. "I do believe I fancy my new name. Gemma." She showed off a fetching smile, and Jesse thought she looked more like a gem than ever.

"All righty then!" Conor copied an old Dearie phrase. "'Gemma' it is!" He reckoned the innocent impudence of Jesse was pretty magical. But more than that, he was amazed at Jessica's—Gemma's—recovery. Her venom and her grief had vanished. Conor was so relieved, for both his and Jesse's sakes.

Jesse saw the book, *Peter Pan*, on the table. He picked it up. "This is the same *Peter Pan* we have. Dearie used to say, 'We can hear Peter calling us into Neverland.'"

Gemma's face quieted, "I lived in those pages as a child. Even now I find a sweet comfort in the endless magic of Neverland. It is there, still."

Jesse and Conor smiled at that. But Gemma folded her hands and continued. "I shall save and savor Jane's remaining letters for a later time. At present, we have copious particulars to share. How shall we commence?"

"Come – enss …?" Jesse echoed.

"Begin. How shall we begin?"

"How about we start with breakfast?" Jesse beamed.

Gemma's larder spilled over in a morning feast that left Jesse exclaiming, "Golly-gee-whilakers! This is like a Christmas Day breakfast!"

"Yes indeed, Mr. Whilakers!" Gemma offered him a platter of pancakes. As she poured the warm maple syrup into the melting butter on his pancakes, Jesse watched it swirl together.

"Look! It's like the Aurora Borealis! On my plate!"

"Ah," Gemma smiled. "*Aurora* is from the Latin, meaning Dawn Goddess. *Boreas* is the Greek god of the north wind." She bent over his plate, "Yes, the colors of the dawn, blown by the wind. I do believe they are playing together on your pancakes!"

She sat down, smiling impishly as she slid her fork under an egg. "Well! I am so very hungry! I believe I could eat a horse—if I had one!"

"The way you talk, Gemma!" Jesse boggled, "It's like … reading a book!"

Conor wagged, "It is! And your Shakespeare fits right in."

Jesse wagged, too. "Jane told Conor how Shakespeare invented or wrote down almost 2,000 new words! It sounds like you know a lot of them!"

Wistfully, she smiled. "Jane loved Shakespeare, too. For me, it is odd that someone from the sixteenth century helps me explore the endless questions I often ask myself." She laughed, "I warn you, it is my habit to talk to myself. And I do believe I am getting expert advice!" With a shrug of her shoulders she added, "I suppose I am somewhat like a book."

Her eyes glimmered at Conor with a new, slightly sly expression. "Following our breakfast, I shall introduce you to one of my Chapters. Rather a grand surprise!"

Conor and Jesse looked at each other—and chewed on their curiosity with every lip-smackey bite.

At the back door, Gemma stopped to pull on a jaunty hat. Jesse liked it. "It looks like you have petals around your face, like a flower."

"My, Jesse! You are full of lovely compliments."

Jesse was first out the door and was surprised—by Peter and Cherry—Charlie.

"Hello!" Jesse welcomed, and straightaway turned to introduce them. But Gemma stood rigid and wary.

"Gemma," he gently pulled Peter forward, enunciating clearly, "This is Peter John Michael … Murphy."

Gemma's mouth wriggled. Opened. Smiled. "Truly? Peter John Michael?" She gestured to Charlie, "And is this Captain Hook?"

The balloon of tension popped in startled laughter and introductions. Charlie Lippley stepped forward, "It is a pleasure, ma'am. My great-grandfather built all of Windy Hill."

Gemma's mouth fell open. "Charles Murray? Truly?"

Jesse fizzed, "We saw that name on the cover of *LIFE* magazine!"

Charlie grinned, "The celebrated Charles Murray is my Great-Gramps! Well, he died last year, but my Great-Nanny Lyla still talks of this place."

Yes, Gemma thought, *everyone talks.*

Peter and Charlie explained their work at Marsh Hill Farm and that they needed a few tools that perhaps Gemma would lend.

Silence.

Gemma's eyes narrowed. But she looked down at Jesse, his eyes, smiling, glittering back at her. Slowly her feet moved, signaling them to follow to her workshop. Charlie efficiently chose a drill and several bits and a long slim saw. Peter assured her, "We'll take good care and have them back safe and sound."

Gemma's lips quivered ever so slightly, but she said nothing.

It was left to Jesse and Conor to bid goodbye. In silence, they headed to the pasture.

On the hilltop, Conor saw the stunted, leaning tree and reacted as Jesse had: "'Trouville'!" He twinkled, "We're in a painting! This place is beautiful!"

Gemma smiled, and they walked with her to a grassy road paved with old cobblestones. She flashed a devilish look at Conor. "You shall find a treasure at the end of this road!"

"A treasure?" Jesse echoed.

"Wha-a-at?" Conor amazed.

Both O'Neils impulsively broke into a run, bubbling all the way down to the rocky beach. Jesse felt like he was flying. *My treasure! Jane!* He looked at Conor, and felt, *James!*

At the beach, Jesse pointed north to a bridge spanning the bay. "It looks like another Erector Set bridge!"

Conor informed, "That's the Elizabethtown Bridge, to the

mainland." But he was looking at a stone building on the shore, topped by a pagoda-like roof; enormous doors stood over a long ramp with two metal tracks advancing straight into the water.

"A boathouse!" Conor shouted.

They saw Gemma enter through a side door, and they ran over the rocks and up the ramp, where Gemma was sliding open the doors from the inside.

Jesse felt a tiny shiveral in his shoulders.

There on a wooden frame sat a beautiful wooden boat, painted a deep hunter green. Conor walked around it, speechless. It was a catboat—*just like* ... He couldn't believe it! His hands stroked the gleaming, varnished wood, and brushed the rough, white canvas decking. He caught his breath, *Could this be ...? How could it be ...?*

Gemma's smile held the key to unlock Conor's puzzlement. "Look at the name, Conor."

Jesse stood, watching Conor. He put his hand in his pocket and felt the silver dollar. *What now?* A giggle-snicken gurgled in his throat. *Some kind of a surprise ... Another secret?*

Conor moved to the rear where the light was shining on the transom. There was the name: *Bay Dancer.* He inhaled a cry, all mixed up with thrill and delight and impossibility. "Bay Dancer!" he cried.

Gemma cleared her throat. "Yes, it is your brother's catboat, restored and ready for launching. Perhaps, it has waited for you."

Jesse smiled, knowing, *Dearie is here!*

....

Yes, Jesse! Surprise! Your timing is perfect! It's been waiting for you!

....

Conor cheered his tears away. "This is the biggest surprise ever! How ...?"

Gemma paused, "Let us put the catboat to sea, and I shall explain."

CHAPTER TWENTY-SEVEN
END & BEGIN

Conor lifted Jesse into the catboat. "You're going to love this, Jesse!" Jesse was in heaven, captivated with every new word, every new object. The lines and cleats, pintles and gudgeons, and every nautical step Conor and Gemma took. Before he even thought to say, "Cracker Jacks!" the catboat was down the ramp and floating in the water.

Conor helped Gemma aboard, then tied a dinghy to the bow, rowing them out to the mooring. Jesse smiled, hearing Gemma humming and singing a snippet of song: *"I'll be loving you Always..."* He felt himself humming as they rigged the sail, and he was thrilled when they let him haul on the main halyard.

"Heave!" Conor trumpeted. The canvas ran up the mast and Jesse felt the wind catch the sail. Conor released the mooring, and the *Bay Dancer* capered across the water! Gemma and Conor beamed, and Jesse whooped, "We're sailing!"

They sailed close to Big Bear Island, and Jesse recalled Murphy's marine chart of Tanagasuq Bay. But he focused on the island's old fortifications and the lighthouse on the tip of the rocky spit. *Oh, that's the lighthouse Jane painted for her Island poem! Oh, my goggles! And this is the catboat in her picture! My dreams! Coming true! It's real!*

Conor, couldn't wait to ask, "So, Gemma, how did you come to own this catboat?"

Gemma smiled wryly. "It is a tale of irony, *a little more than kin, and less than kind.*"

Conor noted, "Another Shakespeare quote!"

She exhaled, "I shall begin at the end. You see, when Jane married, I knew not where she was living. I never thought she would send letters. I never receive mail. Ever.

"After more than a year, I decided to finally ask after your family, at T.J. O'Farrell's. I found that your aunt and uncle lived in Port Haven. But they had died. Nevertheless, there was to be an estate sale." She paused, recalling, "A lovely woman with white hair and red cape was directing affairs."

Jesse turned with a start, "That was Dearie!"

Conor agreed. "My mother, Jesse's other grandmother. Dearie in her red cape! Unmistakable!"

Gemma was shocked. "I thought her to be an estate agent! She … she was your mother? Ohhh!" Gemma cooed in surprise.

"Did you talk to Dearie?" Jesse queried.

Gemma nodded, "Yes, I purchased a set of very fine tools."

"You have Uncle Con's tools?" Conor chuckled. "Well, I'll be!"

Jesse approved, "That is so fine!"

Gemma continued, "It seems this is a tale more ironic than I had supposed!"

Jesse chorkled, "You know what the opposite of irony is?" Laughing, he quickly answered, "Wrinkly!"

"Wrinkly!" Gemma laughed. "Well! In my wrinkles, I noticed this catboat! Your Dearie told me the owner—James O'Neil—had found it in a backyard up the bay in Brighton. That owner just wanted it off his property." Gemma's eyes sparked. "Also, I observed something that persuaded me to purchase this catboat." Her eyebrows arched,

"And, I must say further, I caused quite a stir on the ferry. I could hear the gossip: What is the Black Widow doing with a boat?"

Jesse bewildered, *Black Widow?*

But Conor yelped, thinking, *Sooooo, she knows her reputation!*

Yet Gemma looked dismayed. "Oh, if only I had the mettle to ask!" She slapped her knee, "For the sake of Heaven! I was speaking with your Dearie!"

Nonetheless, Jesse encouraged, "So, you restored the *Bay Dancer!*"

Conor interrupted, "Wait! What was it you observed?"

Gemma's mysterious smile returned, and Jesse got a little shiveral, thinking, *It's like secrets are popping out all over!*

Now Gemma was speaking. "Ahh, now we come to the beginning of the tale. In 1920, Papa had a sailing craft built. Ah, sailing! Such freedom! No didactic Grandmother Avery to rule my life!" She hummed. "Papa taught me to sail. I taught Jane. She loved it so. But the '38 Hurricane took our boat. Nothing left but the mooring."

Jesse curioused, "What did you name your boat?"

Gemma looked squarely at Conor, "We christened it *Scallop.*"

"Nooo!" Conor waggled in disbelief.

"Jesse," Gemma beckoned, "come sit by me." She showed him a carving on the inner transom-skirt.

Conor was bursting, "It's a scallop shell! I remember that scallop! Great Lakes, Gemma! This … this is your original catboat!"

Gemma blurted, "Yes! Yes!"

"Really?" Jesse flabbergasted, "This boat was yours? And Jane's? AND my father's?"

Grinning, Gemma nodded, and Jesse slapped the decking, "All this time! We've been weaving together! Dearie said so!"

....

So many weavings. They are the roots of our magic.
    We are the warp and woof, humming and weaving together.
    Spinning our very own fabric of life.

....

"Yes, our lives are entwined," Gemma breezed, "even when we cannot see it. Over the years, as I restored this boat, I came to understand that Jane loved James O'Neil—your father, your brother. Jane had chosen a wonderful man, who rebuilt this boat with his own hands. Jane was not mine anymore. She had married the love of her life. Just as I had.

"Thus, as I restored this boat, I hoped it would be a connection, intertwined with you O'Neils, back to Jane." Tears filled her eyes. "Though, now, Jane is gone."

"But here we are!" Conor grinned.

Even with her tears, Gemma's face showed off her fetching smile. "Yes! Dancing on the bay! Together!"

The morning sun warmed them as they zig-zagged, tacking toward King's Spade Light, at the southern tip of Elizabethtown, overlooking the Atlantic Ocean. They were skimming over the sparkling waters when Gemma shouted, "Look! A submarine! Coming into the bay!"

Jesse jumped up with eyes spinning! "Oh, my goggles! I see it! It's coming to the surface!"

But Conor did not join in his excitement. He was smirking.

Jesse focused. "The waves are crashing! But. Wait. The submarine. It isn't moving."

Gemma and Conor burst into chuckles.

Jesse tugged at Gemma's knees, "It's not a submarine, is it!"

"No," she confessed contritely, "I have hoodwinked you, Jesse. It is naught but the remains of the Cetus Lighthouse, from the '38 Hurricane."

"It really fooled me!" The catboat suddenly heeled, tilting dramatically. "Oh-OHHH!" Jesse tumbled into Conor.

"The swells are too deep," Gemma declared. "We must turn back."

"Ohhh! I wanted to sail to Boston!" Jesse grinned. "Then we could stay in your theater, Conor!"

"Theater?" Gemma's face startled, and suddenly, her voice fell like an ax between them. "Boston?" She turned to ice. Silent.

Conor looked guilty.

Jesse was bewildered.

CHAPTER TWENTY-EIGHT

STAR WISH

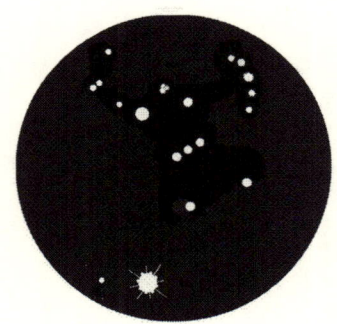

Fiercely, Gemma thrust the tiller to the gunwales and shoved the boom out over the water. Jesse felt the boat swivel and rock. Gemma stood up, grabbing the tiller like a sword, her tongue lashing out at them both. "I see your plan. You arrive at my farm. Turn my life upside down. Depart. In and out! Break the Black Widow's heart. No one will care."

She dropped to the seat, and Conor spoke, "Gemma ..." But she shot him a look that froze his tongue in place.

Jesse stood up. His hand on Gemma's knee. "That's not the plan, Gemma. The plan is ... well, it's my star wish," he blurted. "After Dearie went to the Great Illuminations, Conor helped me make my wish, on Orion's hunting dog, the Dog Star, Sirius. It's the brightest star. And my wish has been coming brighter every day."

He took a big breath.

"This ... I ... here's my wish: I want to live with you. I want to be your grandson forever and ever. Always. Conor can't stay. But I want to. Stay. With you. Can I, Gemma? I mean, may I? Oh, please?"

The fury in Gemma's eyes was swept away, and a tear dropped onto Jesse's fingertips.

"Ohhhh ... I ... foolish ... eghhh ... thinking the worst! I ... ohhh ... enough of that!" She pulled Jesse to her heart. "Yes! Yes! I *want* you to stay! More than anything in this world. *Yes!*"

Conor began to apologize, but Gemma waved him off.

"I am the product of an extraordinary father, also named Jesse, whom I dearly loved; and an extraordinarily demanding grandmother, Avery, whom I ... obeyed."

She continued, "I never knew my mother. She is a prodigious secret in my life."

Jesse repeated, "Pro-dih-jus." He quizzeled, "Does that mean big?"

Gemma smiled, "Quite big. You see, I knew only her name—Susan—and that she was a musical stage actress. Papa never spoke of her. Nevertheless, that does not excuse my behavior. I am horrified when I transform into Avery, as I did just now: accusatory, leaping to dreadful conclusions! I was far out of bounds. Conor, you have had no opportunity to speak of your plans. Furthermore, I never asked. Did I?"

Conor let out a deep breath at this transformation. "All righty then!" he smiled. "I have a request."

Gemma's eyebrows lifted.

"A mailbox. At your driveway." He raced on, "I'll get all the Post Office particulars."

Gemma sighed, thinking of Jane's undelivered letters. "A mailbox. Of course. You are quite right." She blurted. "Yes. It shall be done. Today."

Jesse beamed, "We can write postcards and letters! And get them, too!"

Gemma swayed with new energy. She reached into her rucksack and took out a worn paper tablet and a pencil. "Conor, would you take the helm? My mind is, all at once, percolating."

Conor happily sat beside Jesse with the tiller between them, watching Gemma. Jesse squintled, "Gemma looks like Jane. But doesn't she remind you of Amanda Wynne?"

Gemma's head came up, "Really! Amanda Wynne! The famous actress! That is a compliment for the ages!"

"So, you do go to the movies!" Jesse's eyebrows popped.

Gemma grinned, "Yes. In Port Haven. Always a treat!"

Jesse grinned back, "Great!" He saw the engraved scallop shell. Suddenly he remembered. *I know where I saw that symbol: Ω! Saint Patrick's Cathedral. On a Christmas banner. Just like the code pad: the A on top, that Ω on the bottom. Dearie called it "Alpha" and "Omega." But what does it mean?*

Gemma was deep in her drawings and notes. Jesse shook out his thoughts and rested his hand on the tiller. *Later. I'll talk to Gemma later.*

CHAPTER TWENTY-NINE

MAILBOX

Back at the farm, Gemma fixed a quick lunch and set everything in motion for the mailbox. She handed Conor the keys to her truck, saying, "Visit the Post Office for details of installing a mailbox, and O'Farrell's Hardware for a can of creosote to soak the wooden post below ground level."

Off he went, while Gemma and Jesse went to her workshop.

"Oh!" Jesse amazed looking at her drawings. "It's your house—only miniature!"

"Yes. It will be a basic box. The roof will be a bit challenging. Let us commence."

Jesse smiled and watched her make pencil marks on the wood.

"Measure twice. Cut once." She clamped the wood to the bench with the carpenter's vise and let Jesse turn the lever. "Around you go. Keep on until it is quite tight."

With the handsaw, she easily cut through. Jesse was impressed.

Next, she put a small nail in her mouth and took out a comb.

Jesse surprised, "You're going to comb your hair? Now?"

The nail and laughter came spitting out of her mouth. "Please observe," she grimmeled and placed the nail between the teeth of the comb. It clearly held steady. With a little tap, the nail went into the wood like a hot knife through butter.

"Now THAT is brillish!" Jesse was full of admiration.

Driving into town, Conor brewed an inspiration. *I am going to shine up Gemma's reputation!*

At the Post Office, he introduced himself, adding his and Jesse's background. Then he laid it on thick: "Gemma is wonderful, and her farm is beautiful and clever beyond belief. Oh, and she wants to reinstate her mail delivery."

Mr. Coleman remembered Jesse's letter. "Glad to hear the boy made it! New beginnings all around!" He handed Conor a paper. "These are details for the mailbox placement. We'll put Mrs. Roberts of Windy Hill Farm on our delivery route."

Next, Conor headed to T.J. O'Farrell's Hardware, reenacting the same script, genuinely bragging about Gemma. Then he drove to the ferry landing to turn around, and who was on the corner, but Murphy!

Murphy pretended to be shocked, "Jus' shocked I am to see yer alive, Conor! Tho' y've got a great bruise there! Y' can't say I di'n't warn ya!"

"It's nothing! Listen Murph," Oh, how he relished setting Murphy straight on all the Black Widow tales. "Jessica Roberts is THE most amazing woman! Jesse's in love! Renamed her 'Gemma.'" Conor snickered, "Revise your gossip, Murph!"

Murphy tutted, but they were both distracted by a squabble erupting in the ferry car lot. A young woman, in a wide-brimmed white hat, was flailing her arms like exclamation marks, from her car to the ferry, as she animatedly spoke to the Purser.

Murphy chuckled and quoted Will Rogers: "*There are two theories for arguing with a woman. Neither works!*"

Conor saw her, helplessly looking to the sky. He got a real good look at her.

"Amanda? Amanda Wynne?"

PART SIX

B'JEEKERS!

*The unforeseeable moment
may be the sweetest delight.*

CHAPTER THIRTY

AMANDA WYNNE

"Co-n-o-r O'Neil!" Amanda embraced him.

"Amanda! What are you doing here?"

Her Georgia accent drawled, "Oh, my darlin' Conor, I'd ask the same of you!"

Murphy's jaw dropped to the street, but he picked it up and jumped in. "Ma'am …? Yer car's banjaxed?"

"If *banjaxed* means 'I can't start my daddy's old car,' then yes."

Murphy was off. "I'll get Mr. Wheeler from his garage."

Amanda and Conor traded their news, and she was pleased—"as punch"—that Jesse found "his new grandmother!" But she almost exploded about Conor's Boston theater!

"Conor!" she buzzed. "Take a wild guess where I'm headed!" The brim of her hat went up and down, confusing the dickens out of him. "The Dana Theater! We'll be there together!"

"What? How …?"

"Ohhh, I was in New York, cryin' to Bobby Lewis, feelin' lost since Daddy and Mama died. Bobby told me, 'Amanda, go back to your roots. Get back on stage.' And, next thing, the brand-new Dana Theater called me!"

Murphy returned with a tall, spindly man. "This here's Charles Wheeler. He'll take a look-see."

Charles Wheeler took a long, silent look-see, and finally droned: "The cah needs serious ovah-haulin.' Batt'ry, oil, cah-b'rator, spahk plugs." He pointed, "Tires, too."

Amanda paused, stuttering, "Well … I … I …"

But Murphy declared, "Mr. Wheeler here can fix everything."

Wheeler motioned. "I'll need the khakis."

Conor baffled, "He needs a pair of pants?"

Amanda chuckled, "Not khakis—car keys!"

Murphy, still attentive, added, "Y'll hafta stay overnight, ma'am."

"Amanda, stay with us!" Conor cried. "At Gemma's farm!"

She smiled, but first turned to Murphy and Mr. Wheeler, gushing her appreciation.

Murphy, like a Bear in a tuxedo, ceremoniously took her proffered hand … and kissed it! To which, Conor briskly escorted Amanda to the truck. They left Murphy waving a besotted farewell.

Wildly wagging tails welcomed Amanda to Windy Hill. She laughed, "Whoop-de-do dogs! Such a greetin'!"

A shout came out of Gemma's workshop: "B'jeekers! It's Amanda!" Jesse hurtled into her arms, "Amanda!"

"Oh, Jesse!" She drawled. "My sweet-treat sugah-beet!"

The two laughed and hugged—till Amanda saw Gemma. "Oh! Forgive my manners. It is a bona fide delight to meet you, Gemma!"

Gemma was overwhelmed.

Conor cut in, "Gemma, I hope you don't mind. I've invited

Amanda to stay with us. Her car is being serviced overnight at Mr. Wheeler's Garage."

"Diggity-boo!" Jesse jumped. "Can she stay, Gemma?"

Gemma stood still. Speechless.

CHAPTER THIRTY-ONE

BREEZES

Jesse took his grandmother's hand, and Gemma, feeling a little less wobbly, let Shakespeare do the talking: *"I have invited many a guest, such as I Love ... and you, one more, most welcome ..."*

Jesse hugged Gemma.

Conor stuck to business. "Great! Now! I'll creosote the post and dig the hole."

"We're building a mailbox!" Jesse crowed. "Another dream!"

"Well, I want to pitch in!" Amanda offered. "Daddy always said, 'A little elbow grease helps any dream along!' I'll just change my clothes."

She took Gemma's arm walking into the house. They returned with Amanda looking like a honeysuckle rose in flannel and denim, her hair in a ponytail, bedecked with a ribbon.

Conor noticed, *Gosh, Amanda looks like Gemma. Hm, must be her hair, pulled back like Gemma's.*

Amanda broke in, "Now Conor, I'll take care of this creosote thing. You go dig that hole."

The tasks breezed along: slathering creosote, affixing small stones and cedar shingles to the box, and laying small tar shingles to the roof. Jesse screwed in the little red flag for mail pickup, and Gemma crowned the miniature house with its gabled roof.

"Oh! It is adorable!" Amanda exclaimed.

"Let us not get carried away," Gemma remarked sensibly.

Amanda slipped her arm around Gemma's waist, "Oh! Let's get carried away!"

"Let's carry it to Conor!" Jesse elated.

Conor had the post ready, and he screwed it all together, while Jesse whooped, "Cracker Jacks! We have a mailbox!"

"Yes!" Gemma delighted.

Jesse was suddenly aware that Greta and Matts had appeared, going home after their farm duties. They looked surprised to see someone new there. Jesse called, "Greta! Matts! Come meet my uncle Conor and Amanda Wynne!"

He introduced the twins, and they politely shook hands with Conor, but both beamed at Amanda, the famous movie star! Jesse didn't waste another minute, pointing to the mailbox. "Look! We built a mailbox! We can get letters now!"

The twins were grinning and gazing at Amanda, hardly noticing the new mailbox.

Gemma stepped in, saying, "The hour is late. Time to prepare dinner." Greta and Matts, still overcome with amazement, mumbled their goodbyes and walked across Windmill Road. But they kept looking backwards and giving little waves to the movie star.

Gemma took Amanda and Jesse to her *potager*: the kitchen garden and greenhouse. She left them to pick the vegetables, and they plucked away. Jesse pulled up a small clod of dirt with the lettuce leaves, and he remarked, "The plants are buried in the dirt, but the sunlight warms them up and they pop out of the ground! It's just like all the secrets I solved!"

Amanda drawled with a chuckle, "You're right, Jesse. Secrets can't possibly live in the dark with your love-adore Light shinin'! It's irresistible!"

Jesse began singing a song from Amanda's last movie, *Love's Breezin' In!* She joined in: *"No reason, just teasin'... so pleasin'... Love's br-e-e-e-zin'... in!"*

Swinging their overflowing basket, Amanda stopped to cut a bunch of blue wood hyacinths, and they capered into the kitchen. Jesse went to the pantry and chose a beautiful blue-and-white oriental vase for the flowers.

"Oh, no," Gemma stopped him. "Please, Jesse, not that vase. It is far too precious."

He fixed the flowers in another vase while dinner was prepared.

Amanda pointed, "My Mama would call those 'buxom' tomatoes!"

"What's buxom?" Jesse asked.

Conor's mouth wriggled and Amanda blushed like a tomato.

Gemma explained, "A buxom woman is one endowed with a large, full bosom."

"*Boo*-zum?" Jesse quizzeled.

Conor blurted, "Breasts. On a woman's ..." He made gestures around his chest.

"Oh, the ba-*zooms!*" Jesse picked up two tomatoes, holding them to his chest. "These *are* buxom!"

Conor hooted. Gemma and Amanda laughed so, they had to sit down.

Soon everyone was seated, and Amanda sighed, "Thank you for havin' me here, on this lovin' spoonful of a farm! If I may, I'd like to say my Mama's blessin'." She raised her glass:

*"Here's to those whom I love, and here's to those who love me.
Here's to those who love those whom I love,
and here's to those who love those who love me.
North, South, East, an' West—here's to you, I love the best!"*
"Blue Ribbon, you!" Jesse trilled as Gemma dabbed at her eyes.

While they ate, Gemma asked Amanda about her family.

"I have two older brothers. Much older … born in the 1920s. I was born in 1930."

"So," Jesse figured, "you're twenty-four years old. Just like Jane would be."

Gemma gaspered, but Amanda continued.

"Yes. Daddy said they saved the best for last! Mama and Daddy were such romantics! They met at the Philadelphia train station. She was in a terrible state, and Daddy tried to help her. What he did was fall head over heels in love with her!

"Mama had been a stage star. But she gave it up, with birthin' babies and keepin' house for Daddy. He was a lawyer, and both my brothers followed him into the law. Philip is in Philadelphia and Blair is in Boston.

"Mama loved that I followed in her footsteps." Amanda stopped. "Oh … I get weepy … thinkin' of Mama. I was with her when she died. But …" Amanda brightened, "just before Mama died, she started talkin' up a storm—and she told me a big secret!"

"Can you tell us the secret?" Jesse hoped.

Amanda looked sweetly at Jesse. "Well, I don't think it would hurt to tell, if you all want to listen."

"We're all ears!" Conor encouraged.

Gemma nodded, though, inexplicably, her shoulders shivered.

CHAPTER THIRTY-TWO

THE SECRET

Amanda's voice softened. "It was the middle of the night. Mama was callin' someone named Jesse."

Jesse's eyes lit up.

"I went in, and there was Mama, sittin' up in bed! I couldn't believe it! You see, she had been comatose. But there she sat. She asked who I was. And I … I answered, 'Jesse.'

"Well! Mama started beggin,' *'Oh, Jesse! Forgive me! Leavin' you an' our beautiful baby girl on your beautiful farm broke my heart! I tell you, Jesse, not a day has passed that I have not thought of you and our baby. My own babies don't know they have a sister. I don't dare tell 'em. Daddy would never get over somethin' like that.'*"

Amanda paused. "Mama was confessin.' To somethin' from ages ago. She said, *'Take my locket, Jesse! There's your hair on the one side and our baby girl's on the other. Take it. I know you didn't truly love me. I know your heart was set on … on … another. But let me show you how I loved you.'* Mama handed me the locket she'd worn every day, with photos of herself and Daddy. But hidden underneath each photo was a tress of golden hair.

"Then Mama grabbed my arm and said with such fierceness: *'Don't let Avery see it. Avery will take the locket—just as she took our baby and made me go away! Made me leave you and our baby! Promise me! Only give the locket to our baby. Promise! Oh, Jesse, forgive me. Forgive your Susan.'*

"All of a sudden, Mama stopped. She was filled with a beautiful light. Radiant. *'Oh!'* she spoke so tenderly. *'You have! You have forgiven me.'* ... And she died."

Gemma slumped ... and slipped off her chair. Collapsed on the floor.

"Oh! Heavens to Betsy!" Amanda jumped up, "What on earth?"

Conor knelt and held Gemma in his arms. "Amanda," he spoke strangely ... knowingly. "Amanda ... you'd better sit down. Gemma has had a shock. And you're next."

Mystified, Amanda sat.

"Amanda ... oh, I'm just going to say it." Conor whooshed: "Amanda ... *your* mother's first-born child, that baby you were just talking about ... It's Jessica." His voice loudened insistently, "Gemma ... is your sister, Amanda."

Silence. Long silence. Brittle silence.

It was Jesse who broke into it. "Oh, Amanda! It's your blessing! All the people we loved, who loved us: Dearie and Jane and James—and all of them—are helping us find each other. And they're really good at it!"

Amanda was glassy-eyed. Conor began, "Amanda—"

But she suddenly spoke. "I have a sister. I ... have ... Oh! I *told* Philip and Blair. They didn't believe me. A sister! They said it was only Mama's imagination. But the locket, the little tresses of hair. It's real. Jessica—Gemma—is real." Her lips curved, "We even look alike! I noticed the instant I saw her!" Her hands flew to her flabbergasted cheeks. "We are sisters!"

She stood up. "Conor, let me." Sitting on the floor, she gently enfolded her sister in her arms. "Gemma. You can wake up now, Gemma. We've found each other."

She looked up at Jesse with wonder in her eyes. "Jesse! I'm your Auntie, Jesse! Oh, Heavens to Betsy! I am your *Great* Auntie!"

Jesse burst, "B'jeekers! What a prodigious secret!"

Gemma's eyes opened. She touched Amanda's face. "I have a sister," she whispered hoarsely. "Her name is ... Amanda Wynne."

CHAPTER THIRTY-THREE
NEW TERRITORY

In the morning, Jesse awoke filled with astonishments. "Jigger-Jollies! I have my own family! I'm going to write everything to Billy and Mac!" He took out his postcards, and copied Gemma, tittering, "Now, how shall I commence?"

When he finished the postcards, he had another thought. He ripped off a piece of Siobhan's brown paper and drew the code pad for the treasure-room door: Alpha at the top, Omega at the bottom.

A

O O

O O

O O

O O

Ω

"There!" He put it in his pocket. "Now I'll remember to ask Gemma."

Jesse ran to the mailbox, with Sadie and Red scampering alongside. He popped in his postcards, and joyfully pulled up the red flag for mail pickup.

Across the street, he saw Greta and Matts standing at the top of a narrow lane, and figured, *Oh, down that road is their home. They call it Little Farm.* A woman walked up behind them, her head circled with a braid, wearing a long apron over a longer black skirt and a grey, buttoned vest over a white shirt. Crossing the street like a locomotive, she headed straight for Jesse and stood so close, he could see her wide, clear blue eyes, like cats-eye marbles, spinning into his own. Jesse felt his mind spinning.

"Jesse!" she declared with Greta's accent, but much thicker.

"Y-e-s ...?" He answered with a quiver.

Her face moved closer. Her fingers twiddled at her vest button. "Yah, you are Jane's son." Jesse shiveraled as she rasped, "But your eyes. Zey are Jessica's eyes." She pulled back. "Gut!"

With relief, Jesse echoed, "Goot."

Greta motioned, "This is our mutter, Margarethe."

"Mar-gar-ay-ta," Jesse repeated.

"Gut," Margarethe repeated. "Now, vee go." She led their little train up the cobblestone driveway. *B'Jeekers!* Jesse thought, wanting to tell his Amanda news. But he silently followed Margarethe.

Gemma, Amanda, and Conor were standing under the cherry tree in their workaday denims. Margarethe marched to Gemma, pulling a wrapped cheese from her pocket, "For you and guests." Fiddling with a vest button, she advanced on Conor. "You are ze onkle. Yah."

Gemma introduced, "Conor, meet Margarethe Vareio, mother to twins, Greta and Matts."

Margarethe shifted to Amanda, "And you ...?"

Amanda effused, "I am Gemma's sister, Amanda Wynne."

Margarethe's face became a palette of confusions. *Zis is Amanda Vynne? Movie star? Dressed like ziz? Vhat? Who is Gemma?* She shrugged and said out loud, "*Ich stehe auf dem Schlauch.*"

"What?" Jesse looked at Greta.

Greta giggled. "She is standing on the hose."

"Wh-a-a-a-t?"

"Like a garden hose ... the vater can't come out." Greta sighed, "It means she does not know vhat is happening."

"What a funny way to say it!"

"Yah. It's German." She turned. "Time for the barn."

Jesse signed 'barn' to Matts, and Margarethe stared at Jesse.

"Barn?" Amanda surprised, "I'll come along!"

Gemma and Conor chorused, "We'll come, too!"

Margarethe pivoted to Gemma, "I put ze cheese in ze icebox." Moving toward the house, she added, "Zen, I go. Goodbye."

Just like that, Jesse tittered.

Gemma realized, "Oh, I forgot my hat."

"I'll get it for you." Jesse ran to the house.

From the back entry, he saw Margarethe in the kitchen. The glass cabinet for the purple gemstone was open and she was fingering the gleaming facets. But when the back door slapped open, her hand snapped away. Jesse got a funny feeling. But he waved and grabbed Gemma's hat.

In the barn, Amanda and Conor cheered Jesse, watching him gentle the hens, collect eggs, and milk the goat, Queen. With all the hurrahs, he forgot to ask Gemma about the code pad and the Eye of Providence.

On the way to the pasture, Conor took Gemma's arm. "About

Jesse ... our little Imaginator! You know," he glossed, "we'll never have this day with Jesse again. Tomorrow, he'll be a little older. Today will be gone. And we can't get it back. I want him ... to bloom. Like your farm. Watched over, love-adored, like the treasure he is. I want him to have every moment of his childhood. His magic."

"Yes!" Gemma smiled lovingly. "I so wish Jesse to bloom!" She quoted her Shakespeare: "To *wear the rose of youth upon him*. I do wish to be up to the task."

A superb breakfast followed, and Gemma offered, "If you like, I shall tour you about Windy Hill."

Conor and Jesse smiled knowingly as she led them up the back stairway to the yacht room. Amanda twirled through the extraordinary room. "Ohhh, my! MY! This is nothin' less than spectacular!"

Jesse investigated the cupboard under the window seat. "Oh, look! Children's books! I have my own library!"

Amanda sat beside him, "Ah! *Winnie-the-Pooh*! Remember? Dearie took us to the Pooh Tour at the Fifth Avenue Library."

"Dearie knew the real Christopher Robin!"

"Yes, she did! We saw Galen's photograph of Christopher Robin standing inside the big tree. And Winnie, Piglet, Eeyore, and Kanga were there ... pretty shabby from all their lovin'."

"Those books have had their share of loving," Gemma remarked. "Grandfather, Papa, Me, Jane ..."

Jesse smiled, "And now me!"

Amanda twinkled at Jesse, then asked Gemma, "Why so many scallop shells?"

"The scallop! Papa's forefathers were Freemasons, honoring Divine Providence. The scallop is an old family design signifying the Protection of Providence."

Jesse mused, *This Providence thing! It's ... I don't know what it is!*

But Gemma changed direction, "Jesse, how old are you?"

Jesse chuckled, "Not *old*. I'm seven years *new*—because I've never been seven before!"

"How true!" Gemma smiled. "But when were you born?"

"Midnight, New Year's Eve! Church bells rang! And fireworks went off like crazy!"

Gemma grinned, "*... trailing clouds of glory do we come ... and Heaven lies about us in our infancy ...*"

Amanda clapped her hands and recited, "*... the growing boy, ... beholds the light, and whence it flows, he sees it in his joy ...*" She admitted, "I memorized Wordsworth's poem for my graduation recital! Now it reminds me of Jesse."

Gemma sighed, full of deeply humming happiness, resonating again with her new sister. She turned back to Jesse, "This yacht has been well navigated over the years. Would you like to take the helm?"

Jesse nearly knocked her over, "Oh, yes! Yes!"

She embraced him. "We shall move you into this bedroom bunk tonight!"

Next, Gemma returned them to the stair landing, to the doors with no knob. "The key is in my fingers," she swaggered, showing Jesse her empty hands. "One must know the magic."

CHAPTER THIRTY-FOUR

LEGACY

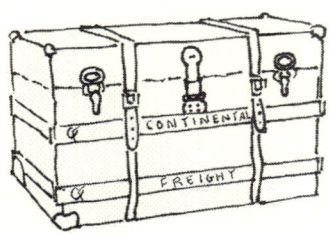

"Oh!" Jesse delighted, standing at the secret door, waiting for Gemma's magic.

She pushed on the edges of the door—and it popped open!

"Oh-hhh!" Jesse marveled.

"A spring lock!" Conor observed.

The door opened to the bedroom gallery where they had slept last night. The other side of the door was disguised as a bookcase.

Jesse amazed, "A secret door!"

Grinning, Gemma led on. "This next door opens to the attic stairs."

In the attic they found a large cistern, collecting rainwater for the house; boxes of art; and steamer trunks, revealing suits and dresses and riding attire.

"Such vintage clothing!" Amanda enthused.

"Yes. Jane was remaking these, before she left."

Jesse pointed at a painting in a heavy gold frame. "Who's that?"

"That is my grandmother, Avery. Painted by the famous John Singer Sargent."

Amanda grimmeled, "She looks like she could start an argument in an empty room!"

Gemma chuckled. "Quite."

"But look at her long necklace!" Amanda noted, "Every flower is set with diamonds! What happened to that small fortune?"

Conor interrupted, "Hey, look, Jesse! A poster by Charles Dana Gibson!"

"Ohhh," Amanda purred, "I love the Gibson girls!"

"Ah, yes," Gemma rallied. "During World War I, Papa worked with Gibson at the Naval Institute in Port Haven to create posters supporting the war effort."

Conor wagged, "And my Pa did photography for Gibson's *LIFE* magazine!"

"How coincidental!" Gemma surprised.

Jesse chittered to himself, *Except there are no coincidences.*

But Conor was gaping at a label on a steamer trunk. "I can't believe my eyes! This steamer trunk!" Conor yelped, "It was aboard the *Continental Freight!*"

"That's the ship you took to America!" Jesse recalled. "In 1939!"

Gemma baffled, "But that cannot be. My Uncle Trevor died in 1929. His shipyard in Philadelphia—*Continental Freight*—closed with the Depression."

Conor insisted, "In 1939, Dearie knew someone at *Continental Freight*."

She bewildered, "But how …?"

"Gemma," Conor began, "you told me your family had houses and a shipyard in Philadelphia. They didn't disappear." He grinned. "I'll bet you a doughnut hole, you have family property!"

"But I know nothing of that."

Conor tried again, "Gemma, you haven't had a post box all these years. There may be a dead letter file sitting in some lawyer's safe."

"Ohhhh …?" Gemma looked startled. "I never … it never occurred to me. I have lived so very frugally all these years, counting every penny." She see-sawed. "How could I have ignored such a legacy?"

Amanda chimed in, "Brother Philip's law firm is right in

Philadelphia! We'll put him on your properties like a bee to a honeycomb!"

Jesse hooted, "Another secret, Gemma! You own a shipyard!"

"I .... Oh! Everything is changing so quickly!" She looked at Jesse's dancing eyes. Not having felt this jubilation in years, she gushered into the moment, "I have a mystery to unravel!"

Jesse declared. "A secret treasure hunt!"

Gemma clapped her hands. "Yes! And a perfect segue to the treasure rooms! Off to the barn!"

CHAPTER THIRTY-FIVE
TREASURES

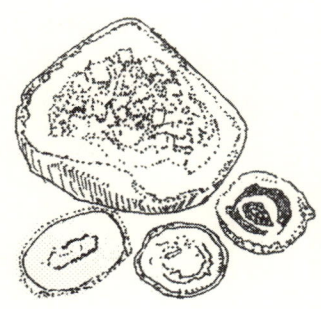

Jesse skittled outdoors, straight into the dogs, wagging at Peter and Charlie. He blurted, "We're going to the treasure rooms! Wanna come?"

"Whoa! Jesse!" Conor stopped him.

Charlie stepped back, "We just need another day with your tools."

Gemma had forgotten about the tools. Right now, she was euphoric. She looked at these two young men, thinking, *All these years of saying,'No.' Excluding. But Jesse says, 'Yes'—and look what has come!* Her elation ballooned. "First, allow me to introduce my sister, Amanda Wynne."

They stared at Amanda like a genie had popped out of a bottle. Their top lips didn't know what to do with their bottom lips. Amanda's hand floated before them.

Conor cut in, "Now, you shake hands and say, 'Hello'!"

They did so, with smiles all around, and Gemma gestured to the barn. "You may join us, if you wish."

Charlie enthused, "I'd be honored! All my life I've heard about your beautiful barn!"

As soon as they opened the barn door, Jesse asked Gemma about the manure room. "Greta called it a vault—for black gold."

"Ah Jesse," Gemma tittered, "you are a caution! *Black gold* is a euphemism for manure, since it is essential to fertilize the fields. And the manure room was referred to as a *vault* when it was originally an ice chamber, the ice being the old means of refrigeration."

Charlie added, "That ice was carved out from a quarry on the north end of Elizabethtown. Inside that cement vault, the ice blocks could last for months. I believe there's a wheel at the lower floor, to raise the ice to the top as it was used up."

"Why Charlie," Gemma startled, "how well you know such particulars!"

Charlie pshawed, "It's all my Great-Gramps."

Jesse wanted to ask about the Eye of Providence on the trapdoor, but Gemma moved on, unlocking the blue treasure door—this time with a key. She paused, "The collection is called *Dona Dei: Gifts of God*." And Jesse pointed at Jane's cross-stitch words: *Gifts of God*.

Inside were long tables with shelves of yellowed muslin covering mysterious lumps of ...*Who knows what?* Jesse wondered.

Folding back the muslin, Gemma explained, "This floor holds the fossil collection."

"These are jewels!" Amanda fingered the stones.

"Geodes," Gemma chuckled, "a type of gemstone. Those, like the kitchen amethyst inside the rock, are quite glittering. The flat, rounded specimens have been cut and polished. These deep blues are rare lapis lazuli."

"What are these swirling green ones?" Peter curioused, and Charlie noted, "They look like emerald tree rings."

"They are agate geodes," Gemma responded, "again, sliced and polished."

On the other tables they found: "Fossils of ferns in solid rock—and petrified wood!"

"A perfect nautilus shell!"
"Shell skeletons?"
"Gold!"
"No, that's pyrite—fool's gold."

Gemma interrupted, "We could go on in this manner all-the-day. Let us rise to the cupola."

Up the spiraling floors and stairways, they puffed for breath. But at the glass cupola, they gaspered for wonder. Out on the porch, Amanda spoke for all, "Ohhh! We are overlookin' the whole world! Such splendor!"

Then silence. And slow turning in a full circle.

No limits! Jesse reveled. *No limits!* Vast. Open. A dome of blue sky. Tails of fair-weather clouds. Invisible breezes. Sparkling grassy, leafy greens. Glittering marine blues.

Conor murmeled, "We're not in New York City anymore."

Jesse said not a word. He felt the breeze. He felt ... *Dearie? Oh, it's Jane!*

Listen, Jesse! Listen to the stillness in between.

The sound of silence. You. Standing in stunning, blessed wonder.

Gemma quietly broke the spell, and Jesse knew Jane had also spoken to Gemma, as she quoted her Shakespeare.

"*Oh wonder! How many goodly creations are there!*"

But she didn't expect Charlie to finish her quote: "*How beauteous mankind is! O brave new world, that has such people in it.*"

Gemma was amazed, and Conor whistled, "Man, oh, man, Charlie! Shakespeare *and* 'Shake, Rattle and Roll'! You're quite a combination!"

Peter snickered, "That's Charlie! *Blessed are the cracked, for they shall let in the light.*"

Jesse smiled, "Groucho Marx?" Peter smiled back.

By and by, Gemma led everyone back down to earth. Going out the robin-egg-blue treasure door, Jesse saw the wooden plaque above the doorframe: *Dona Dei*. But he hurried on, as Gemma was waiting outside to lock the doors. Jesse took her hand, "Gemma, your Star Cupola is gahslahzerous!"

Conor chuckled at Jesse using one of Dearie's favorite words, and Gemma tickled Jesse's chin, "My! That word sounds exceptional." But she jangled her keys, "Now where are Peter and Charlie?"

CHAPTER THIRTY-SIX
GOLDEN AFTERNOON

Conor stuck his head inside the barn, calling, "Peter? Charlie?" Nothing.

He stepped up to the blue door, and was about to go in, when Peter and Charlie came bumbling out.

Peter raptured, "That view will be with me forever."

Charlie thanked Gemma, "I'll try to describe this to my Great Nanny Lyla. She's almost blind now. This will make her day!"

Peter and Charlie headed back to Marsh Hill Farm, and Jesse piped up: "Gemma, could we take Amanda sailing?"

"Yes!"

The breeze was perfect, the sun was warm, and the views were splendid. They sailed around Big Bear Island and Gemma showed off the sights and the history: "The Indian name for Big Bear Island was *Quotenis*; the old fortifications are called Fort Safeguard—with the remains of the hospital buildings and soldiers' quarters; and there is Big Bear Lighthouse."

They sailed back into the harbor, past Sunset Marina, and Gemma pointed to the empty ferry boat slip, explaining, "Since they built the Elizabethtown Bridge in 1940, there was no need for the ferry to the continent."

Jesse looked west to the mainland. "You call it the 'continent'! I never saw that on all the maps I studied to get here."

Gemma's face shone with her beautiful smile. "Ah! Your wandering quest—to find me."

At that, Conor began singing: *"There was a boy, a beautiful, enchanted boy. They say he wandered very far, very far, over land and sea. Bright of eye, and never shy, and very wise was he."*

Amanda took up the second verse: *"Then one day, one magic day, he passed my way. And tho' we spoke of many things, fools and kings, this he said to me …"*

Jesse finished: *"The greatest thing you'll ever learn is just to love and be loved in return."*

The three smiled at each other, but Gemma had tears in her eyes. "I … have not heard that song."

Conor looked surprised, "You don't know Nat King Cole? He's one of the most popular singers out there!"

"I only know songs from the 1920s."

"Ohhh," Jesse remembered, "no radio."

Amanda clarified, "Well, that's Jesse's song. It's a long story that began with Dearie playin' the melody with Dvořák—"

"Truly?" Gemma surprised.

"Oh, yes," Conor concurred. "Dearie knew the most amazing people. Dvořák's tune was written as a song when Jane was pregnant with Jesse. And when Jesse was born, Nat King Cole made it a hit."

"It is *love*-ly."

The catboat danced back through Sunset Harbor, and Amanda chortled, "Oh, I am spoilt beyond-the-beyond! How am I to go back to my borin' old life!"

Gemma pulled in the mainsheet, "Amanda, I do not believe anything about you is boring!"

Jesse piped up again, "Well, I'm hungry beyond-the-beyond!"

Gemma noted, "Yes, the sun is over the yardarm. High time for a high tea!"

Up the hill from the beach, Jesse pointed, "A fox!"

Gemma quieted. "Ah, magical, mischievous Kitsune is back."

"Magic?" Jesse quizzeled.

Gemma explained. "The Japanese legend says that every 100 years, the clever Kitsune fox gains a magical tail—up to nine tails. Then it can shape-shift into anything—a tree, the moon, even human form.

"There are two Kitsune: the good and wise *zenko* foxes, and the dangerous *yako*, often disguised as a beautiful woman."

"Dangerous," Jesse repeated. "Does the fox go after the goats?"

Drolly, Gemma looked at Jesse, "Queen and Duchess …?"

"Oh." Jesse smirked. "No. The goats would butt the dickens out of a fox! But the chickens?"

"Yes, the chicken pen must be kept safely locked from such a knave. Remember that, Jesse."

CHAPTER THIRTY-SEVEN
EVENING BLUSHES

Conor and Jesse set up the porch furniture, then joined Gemma and Amanda in the kitchen, preparing a smorgasbord of leftovers.

Gemma hummed that *Always* song and reminisced as she stirred up dessert. "Jane delighted in strawberries and cream! Mmmm. She loved to d-r-i-z-z-l-e the berries with m-e-l-t-e-d chocolate. Nonpareils!"

"Yummm!" Amanda hummed, taking the shortcakes from the oven.

"When Jane visits with me," Jesse added, "I smell chocolate!"

Gemma startled, "Why, I, too, have had that experience! It is an extraordinary sensation!" Gemma went on, "Chocolate! Nonpareils are still my favorite."

Jesse noted, "Chocolate is a kangaroo word!"

"Oh?" Gemma quizzled.

Conor explained. "A kangaroo mother carries her baby—*joey*—in her pouch. Kangaroo *words* carry a baby word, with the same meaning."

Amanda sparked. "Chocolate carries the *joey* word, 'cocoa'!"

Gemma's mind flickered. "Where do you find these ideas?"
Conor, Jesse, and Amanda laughed, "Dearie!"

Out on the porch, Jesse sat at the table and scarfed down everything offered. Quite content, he patted his stomach. But he sat bolt upright when Gemma appeared with the dessert.

"Oh my, oh MY-oh!" Amanda exclaimed, "This is a bonbon of strawberry shortcake!"

Jesse salivated at the hills of whipped cream, the slumping strawberries, the juices soaking into the warm biscuit. Keenly, he sunk his fork into the concoction and didn't stop till every crumb was devoured. Then he scraped the plate. Finally, he picked up the plate and licked it clean, sighing, *"Delicioso!"*

Gemma, Amanda and Conor astonished, "Jesse!"

He looked up. "Oh." He put the bare plate down, instantly aware of his pitiful manners. "Uh … I'm sorry."

Amanda chuckled, "The secret potion got hold of you!"

Secret. Jesse's eyes flicked, and he took out his paper drawing of the code pad. "Gemma, could you explain this secret?"

She looked at it. Sipped her tea. Answered curiously, "I could …"

"Would you …?"

Conor's eyebrow lifted, "Sounds like a puzzle."

"It is a puzzle," Gemma allowed.

Jesse's eyes lit up, "I love to solve puzzles!"

Her lips grimmeled. "So you have said." She went to her office, returned, and handed Jesse a book: *The Alphabet Around the World.* "Here are three clues:

1. Find two alphabets: one ancient and one medieval.
2. Use the alphabet letters and the numbers evenly.
3. Translate the code words into an ancient language."

"Great Lakes!" Jesse opened the old book, "This is a puzzle!"

But the puzzle was postponed by barking dogs and a loud car horn. It was Regan Murphy! Driving Amanda's car! Accompanied by a pretty little lady, dimpling self-consciously.

"Special Delivery!" Murphy blustered.

"Oh, I thank you, from the bottom of my heart!" Amanda spouted, though she kept her hands to herself.

"This is m' wife, Darlin," Murphy gestured.

"I had no idear!" Darlin chirped in her New England islander accent, "It's so bee-u-tee-ful here!"

Murphy introduced: "This is young Jesse ... and there's Conor O'Neil ... and o' course, Amanda Wynne and the Black ... er ... Mrs. ... uh ... Mrs. Roberts."

Conor filled in, "We call her Gemma."

Murphy turned an embarrassing red. Conor could almost feel the man trying to get both feet out of his mouth.

Amanda moved next to Gemma, smiling, "Gemma is my sister!"

"No!" Darling exclaimed. "Reeelly?" They were dumbstruck, at the news and the remarkable resemblance.

Conor tittered to himself, *Now the island has some big gossip!*

"Do come inside," Gemma offered, surprising herself. "The tea kettle is hot, and we have fresh strawberry shortcake."

"Delicioso!" Jesse crowed.

Gemma led them back through the white garden of daisies, peonies, and baby's breath nodding at her. Murphy and Darling were enchanted. Even in her denim work clothes, Gemma was a vision of grace.

They all sat in delightful conversation, and Darling gestured, "You have a good peek of the watah from here!"

Jesse translated that to 'water,' and he smiled blurting, "Darling—is that your real name?"

"It is," she whimsied. "My mother wanted to name all her babies from *Peter Pan*. She got Wendy, my oldah sistah. But then, all she got was me! She almost called me Nana, but luckily decided against calling me a dog! Instead, she gave me the last name: Darling!"

Jesse grinned, "And you gave all the boy names to Peter! Peter, John, Michael!"

"Yes!" Darling added quietly, "When we knew he was to be our one-and-only baby, he got all the names at once." Darling's cheeks blushed in roses, as a rosy light glowed on them all.

Conor gestured to the west, and they gazed at the sunset clouds, spreading like shimmering red satin.

Jesse liked the way Murphy suddenly stood up, like a Papa Bear, saying, "Well! Ballygomingo! The day is done. Departin' time."

Conor offered to drive them home. As they strolled to the car, Murphy remarked to Gemma, "I am impressed to the hilt, ma'am, at the beauty here."

Darling cut in, "Yes! You must be as busy as a moth in a mitten!"

But Murphy was not finished, "Yes, ma'am, it is a tribute to you, takin' care all these years."

Gemma looked innocently at Murphy and Darling, "I suppose then, this is the death knell for the Black Widow …?"

Darling gasped. Murphy stopped. Came to a complete stop. He let out a huge belly laugh, bending over, leaning on his knees, laughing. "Ballygomingo!" He gurgled. "Oh! Ma'am! I daresay, the Black Widah will be heard of nevermore!"

From the car, Murphy rolled his window down and pointed to the sky, quoting an old seafarer's expression. *"Red sky at night, sailors' delight!"* He grinned, "Bodes well for a beautiful day on the morrow."

Tomorrow, Jesse flustered. *Amanda and Conor leave tomorrow.* He tried to take a breath, but his lungs were squishing his heart.

PART SEVEN

WISKY-DOOLEY

*In a rush,
my heart spoke
before my tongue.*

CHAPTER THIRTY-EIGHT
FAREWELL & HELLO

Silently, Conor gazed at Jesse, standing on the ladder of his bunk-bed, watching the dawn gather in Marsh Creek.

"If I close my eyes," Jesse murmeled, "I hear the gulls over Liam's tug in New York and at the creek here—at the same time."

Conor's breath skipped. "I … I'll do that, too, Jess—listen for the gulls in Boston and picture them here with you."

Jesse was all at once crying, shaking, bawling into Conor's shoulder. Conor held him. Just held Jesse. Loving Jesse.

Tumbling thoughts cascaded with Jesse's tears. *Oh Conor! Don't leave! Don't go! Please! Don't leave me!*

He all at once heard Billy Maguire's voice: *Don't go … Don't go …* Jesse couldn't make sense of it. He knew: *This is all part of the plan … our plan.* But he didn't feel the adventure, the thrill-bumps. He felt … alone. A deep sob gurgled through him. Conor hugged him closer.

Jesse closed his eyes and held on tighter. His hand touched Conor's cheek. It was wet with his own tears. He felt Conor take a deep breath and Jesse breathed, too. Deeply. Keenly thinking: *I have to … I have to pivot.* He rubbed his eyes and cheeks. "I don't … want to cry."

Conor swiped his face and cleared his throat, "No, but, Jesse, sometimes we feel this … this upset … on the inside … and we just have to let it out. And that's fine." He grimmeled, "So fine, as Dearie would say."

A titchy little snorkel gurgled in Jesse's throat and bubbled up into his nose. He chuckled, "I sound like the goats snorting!" At that, he overheard the twins below. He rubbed his face again and sniffed. "Greta and Matts are here."

"I'll tag along," Conor offered. "The kids won't mind."

Jesse smiled weakly, "You never know with Greta."

Amanda and Gemma were in her bedroom. From the hallway, Conor and Jesse heard Gemma's tears.

"Oh, loneliness is settling in my bones. *O, me alone! Like to a lonely dragon …*"

"Lonely," Amanda gentled, "is a kangaroo word—with the word *one* inside. But you're not *one* anymore! You've got Jesse!"

Conor took Jesse's hand and they headed to the barn.

Greta gawked at Jesse. "Your face … vat is wrong?"

"I …" Jesse fumbled. "Conor's leaving."

Greta was perplexed. She looked at Matts. They each reached to Jesse, brushing his arm, his shoulder, clearly wanting to help him. He was so touched, his eyes flooded again. Double-quick, Greta raised her chin, saying to Conor, "If you are here, you must vork! You vill help?"

"If that's agreeable."

Greta shrugged with a little smile, "Do not be a menace."

"Do you mean to say," Conor mocked, "I cannot be wicked?" All at once he rubbed his hands together and cackled like a cartoon villain, "Mwa-ha-ha-ha! Curses! Foiled again!"

All three hooted at his act, and Greta pointed at Conor, "Yah! Ve make the villain collect the eggs!"

Then, when Conor grumbled about the barn smell, she mockingly reprimanded him with, "Complaining is the squeaky vheel!"

He chuckled and grandly bowed to her, and Jesse wagged his head, as she continued to bestow her abrupt advice through every task. But walking back from the pasture, out of the blue, she surprised them all: "So, Conor, you and Amanda Vynne vill marry?"

Jesse and Matts gaspered and Conor sputtered, "Uh … no!"

Greta responded, "Gut," and smiled at no one in particular.

At the kitchen door, Amanda called, "Greta! Matts! Join us for breakfast."

Jesse turned to Matts, signing *breakfast*—his fingers together at his mouth, then moving under his extended arm, with his fingers pointing up.

The three of them went in, signing breakfast over and over.

Washing their hands, Jesse bubbled, "I love the animals. Maybe, I'll be a vegetarian!"

Amanda chuckled, "And eat only vegetables?"

Gemma informed, "Vegetarianism was called the Pythagorean Diet, practiced by the ancient Greek philosopher, Pythagoras. It was changed, one hundred years ago, to the Vegetarian Diet by the Vegetarian Society in Ramshead, England. Be that as it may, the word you want, for the care of animals, is *veterinarian*."

"Vet-er-a-NAR-ee-an," Jesse echoed.

Greta pulled out a chair. "So, Amanda and Conor leave today." She and Matts made the snaking sign for *journey* that Jesse had shown them. "But Jesse stays." Gemma beamed, "Most assuredly, yes."

"Gut. Next to Dorkings, Jesse is the angel."

After breakfast, Conor and Amanda readied to leave, and everyone went outdoors. Hurtling up the driveway came Margarethe, thrusting a gift basket into Amanda's arms. "For your journey to ze Boston city." Then, twiddling a button, she declared, "Now, I go to Germany."

"What?" Jesse blurted. "She's going to Germany?"

Gemma brushed his hair back, "She uses the ham radio to talk to her friend in Germany."

"Oh!" Jesse wanted to watch Margarethe use a ham as a radio, but, surprisingly, Charlie Lippley's motorcycle arrived.

Amanda grinned, "Gemma, I do believe you have company!"

Charlie had a camera, and he took photographs of everyone.

Conor watched him keenly. "He reminds me of Pa," he murmured to Jesse. "Always had a camera. That camera even looks like Pa's." Charlie aimed at Conor, and he mugged with Jesse in a big hug.

But the dogs began barking. A small, stylish white sedan pulled in the driveway. Charlie whistled, "A Nash Metropolitan! Slick!"

It parked under the cherry tree. The door opened. And out stepped Miss Lily Bankroft!

A vision! Lily looked enchanting, as pink cherry blossoms twirled about her shoulders and carpeted her feet. She stepped toward them like the Empress of Japan.

Charlie clicked his camera, noting her red satin blouse and her matching red lipstick. Everyone ogled Lily. But Margarethe screwed her button and glared. She did not "go to Germany" on the ham radio.

Jesse hugged Miss Lily. "I remember your perfume! Lilies! So nice!"

Everyone noted Lily's deep, beguiling voice. "Jesse, I brought you something!" She hung her ever-present handbag on her other arm and held out her hand. "I found it in my handbag!"

Jesse gaspered. "My stone! Oh! Glory BE! My stone! It's back! Oh, thank you!"

Conor joined them, "Welcome, Lily!"

"I am sorry to crash your celebration!"

Conor amended, "It's actually a farewell. Amanda and I are driving to Boston."

Amanda took over, introducing Charlie and the Vareio family.

Lily gawked at Amanda, who trumpeted at the last: "… and this is Jesse's Grandmother and my sister! Gemma Roberts!"

"You're sisters?" She looked at Jesse and Conor, "You didn't tell me!"

"We didn't know!" They beamed, and Jesse asked, "Miss Lily, how did you find us?"

"I just came from Port Haven, where I am now officially working at Maxim & Tenet Law Offices. I thought I'd try to stop in and see you, so I took the ferry across, and the Purser gave me directions here."

"So you got your dream job!" Jesse beamed.

"Yes! And I have my car. Now, I just need an apartment."

Gemma's brain wheeled like a whirligig. *I recounted to Amanda how lonely it will be without them. I wonder. Why not …?*

Looking at Lily's red-lipstick smile, Gemma had a momentary pause, and Shakespeare invaded her thoughts: *And some that smile have in their hearts, I fear, millions of mischiefs.*

But she scolded herself, *Preposterous!*

Wisky-dooley, Gemma offered, "Lily, you are welcome to stay here at Windy Hill."

Margarethe's mouth opened and her eyes darkened. She swiveled her button but said nothing.

Jesse popped, "Oh Miss Lily, you'll love it here!"

Lily was flabbergasted. "I … don't know what to say. This is most … generous … most unexpected!"

"Say yes," Conor opened his hands.

"Well … yes!"

Conor tapped Charlie's shoulder. "Let's get her luggage." Pulling her bags from the car, Charlie followed Conor into the house, and they moved Lily into the old housekeeper's rooms by the kitchen door.

Conor and Amanda ignored Margarthe's suspicious mood. They turned instead to a poignant farewell. Embracing Gemma, Amanda overflowed, "Now dear sister, you can't be lonely anymore!"

Jesse waited at the car. Amanda and Conor held Jesse, blinking away goodbye teardrops. Gemma watched them, overwhelmed by her surging emotions. Gemma had fallen in love again. Gazing at these three love-adores, she was filled with joy and love, mingled with leavings of sorrow. Her heart followed Jesse as he chased the car down the driveway.

At the gate by the road, Jesse stood with Red and Sadie and Ellie-cat, holding his stone and waving, watching the car roll away. Down the hill, and up again. Gone.

The three Vareios were heading back to Little Farm, but they stopped at the gate with Jesse. He heard Margarethe mutter, "*Pech gehabt!*"

Jesse looked to Greta, "What did she say?"

"You have tar."

"Tar?"

"It means you have bad luck."

Margarethe's clear blue, marble eyes spun into Jesse's. Twisting her button, she rasped, "It is ze devil wears red."

CHAPTER THIRTY-NINE

RIDE

Miss Lily was in her rooms unpacking, which allowed Charlie a word with Gemma.

"I'm waiting for Peter. He's bringing your tools back," he explained. "But I wanted to say, my Great Nanny Lyla told me Windy Hill was Great-Gramps' all-time favorite project. It's the model for our house at Carlyle Place. And she is tickled to have another Jesse back at Windy Hill."

Gemma was all appreciation. But she saw Jesse returning. "Oh, Charlie, could I enlist your help?" She led Jesse and Charlie into the carriage house.

Jesse curioused, "What's under the canvas?"

Gemma pulled the tarps away, revealing a Benz Motor Wagon and a 1928 Ford Model-A sedan.

"Wowzer! Man!" Charlie exclaimed. "That's the first Benz! 1886! And this is an old Ford—the 'A-Bone'!" He blabber-gabbed with details as Gemma pulled back another tarp, inviting Jesse: "Bicycles, Jesse! Your choice!"

Charlie gushed, "Wow! These bikes are crankin'!"

Jesse gawked. *It's Christmas in June!* A dusty red bike caught his eye, and he pulled it out. "This is it, Gemma! Just right!"

"And it is in exceptional condition."

Charlie found an air pump and filled the tires. "Man! This rubber is indestructible. Let's check the chain. Always want a *well-oiled bicycle*."

Jesse guffiggled, "Or a *well-boiled icicle!*"

Gemma clapped, "Why, that is a spoonerism! Bravo, Jesse!"

Charlie finished up. "Okay, Jesse, your chariot awaits!"

"I know how to ride," he beamed, climbing on. "In New York, I rode Andros Gorecki's bike." Jesse rode round and round the cherry tree with the dogs following. Then he headed down the driveway.

"Jesse!" Gemma called. "Come back!"

The cobblestones here were too bumpy. Jesse couldn't turn. He yelled, "I'll turn around on Windmill Road."

The dogs stopped when Jesse reached the smooth road. They seemed as surprised as Jesse when the tires slid away in the sand, and zippity-pip, the bike rolled down hill!

"Cracker Jacks!" Jesse felt the wheels spinning! He pushed the pedals backward, trying to brake, but they only spun around.

"No brakes!"

The bike hurtled down-down-downhill—with no way to stop. *Help!*

But he heard cheering on the inside.

....

Jesse! Hold on! EnJOY the ride!
 Hold on! And Light On! No matter what!

....

Jesse knew it was Jane—and James! He grimmel-grinned and he held on!

He saw Peter, at his truck, shouting, "Jesse! Stop! Brake!"

"No brakes!" Jesse bellowed, screeching past the creek.

Oh! Jesse spotted a swath of roadside grass. *That'll slow me down. I'll fall onto the grass!* But suddenly—right in front of Jesse—a lady stood up! Jesse's mind zipped, *B'Jeekers! Where'd she come from?* But too late—he rocketed into her! She flew! Jesse soared! The bike catapulted!

Sprawled in the grass, Jesse heard Peter running. He heard Charlie's motorcycle. He saw Gemma. *Gemma? Leaping off the back of Charlie's motorcycle?*

"Jesse!" She vaulted to him. "Jesse!"

Jesse wailed, "Oh, Gemma! I ran her down!"

Gemma pulled Jesse into her arms.

Peter calmed, "Charlie's the Fire Station Medic. Let him check Jesse."

As Charlie checked him over, Jesse could see the lady he had run down: her full skirt fanning around her, cinnamon hair waving about her delicate face, her garden hat laying guillotined in the grass.

He saw Peter beside her, looking like the Prince kneeling beside Sleeping Beauty. Charlie soon crouched beside them, "Oh, good gravy! Jesse brained the new librarian!"

Peter gaspered, "This? Is Bethesda? Philhips?" He was thinking of the prim little lady in the old-fashioned hat, gloves, and suit, walking to and from the library. His dad, Regan, said she was a "musty old thing." Confounded, he whistered, "But … but … she's b-beautiful!"

Jesse crawled to her. Gemma was right behind, grabbing the watering can and giving Bethesda a few drops.

Jesse pleaded, "Oh! Please wake up!"

Gemma gave her a few more drops of water and Bethesda Philhips fluttered her eyes. She drew in a deep breath. Coughed. Sat up. In Peter's arms. She looked around. Absurdly, her first words were, "My … hat …?"

She stopped. Pointed at Jesse. He drew back. But she twittered in a delightful accent, "I never! Quite unbelievable!" She shook her head, "I flew! Ho! I flew into the pansies!" She hooted, "Yes! Well! Preferable to the roses!"

Jesse marveled. Dearie would say her accent was the Queen's English—very British.

A truck pulled in the driveway with a horse trailer behind. It was heading for the paddock but stopped post-haste.

"Bethesda!" A handsome man, dressed in riding attire, raced to Bethesda.

"Oh, Father! I am quite all right. Just a rather exciting mishap!" Another laugh slipped out of her cheeks.

He helped her up, steering her away from Jesse and company. But she stopped him. "I am fine, Father. Please don't make a bother."

She turned, again pointing at Jesse. "You, young man! Have got some answering to do!"

CHAPTER FORTY

LINGER LONGER

Bethesda Philhips bright-eyed Jesse, "Do you have a name?"

Jesse's eyes lit up to match hers. "I'm Jesse O'Neil, and this is my grandmother, Gemma, from Windy Hill Farm." He was shaking her hand, "I'm so glad you are all right, Miss Bethesda! I really didn't mean to brain you!"

She laughed lightly. "A bit naughty, that!" But she smiled, shaking hands with Gemma. "We are neighbors!" She pulled her father forward. "This is my father, Bertrand Philhips."

Gemma stepped back self-consciously. But he stepped closer, with a slight bow and an English accent, "It is a pleasure."

Bethesda turned to Charlie and Peter, but she suddenly stuttered like a parrot, "Th … thank … y … you."

Peter handed her the errant hat, and stuttered back, "Our … our pl … pleasure, ma'am."

Charlie winked, "Charlie Lippley and Peter Murphy, at your service. Glad we could help."

Bertrand Philhips pulled on his daughter's elbow, "Bethesda, if you are up to it, I need your touch with the new horse."

Peter and Charlie, Gemma and Jesse politely exited toward the roadside.

Jesse observed, "Mr. Philhips is very *extinguished*."

Charlie chuckled, "That's *distinguished*, Jesse."

"Oh. Distinguished," he corrected, and turned to watch Mr. Philhips back out the high-spirited horse. Abruptly, the animal reared! Broke away! Bolted out the driveway! Straight toward Jesse!

Jesse stood. Still. Calm. Breathing.

The horse slowed, gentled, nuzzled Jesse. Then it nuzzled Peter! And Gemma!

Bertrand Philhips looked them up and down, "You know horses!"

"No," Jesse and Peter said simultaneously.

"Yes," Gemma admitted, "but not for ages." She pet the horse's neck.

"You—all three—have the touch. Like Bethesda." Bertrand gestured toward the paddock, "Would you? He's quite skittish."

Jesse took one rein, and Peter took the other, both grinning like two sunny-side-up eggs.

Following along, Gemma vied with her wits, wanting to say … something … engaging. She saw the rose bushes and murmured. "I love yellow roses. But Windy Hill has none remaining."

Now Bethesda spoke smooth as velvet, "We are happy to share our yellow roses. Meanwhile, the horses need exercise."

Bertrand quickly followed up, "Yes, if ever you would like to ride …"

Gemma knew she was the one stuttering now, "Yes. That is … well … it has been years."

"Oh," Bethesda adjusted her hat, "the horses know."

Gemma stopped fretting and sighed giddily. *Never in a thousand years would I ever think to be communing with a horse and conversing with new people.* She joshed inwardly. *Or riding a motorcycle!* She looked at Jesse. *It is all Jesse!*

She exhaled, "We shall see." She touched Jesse's shoulder, "Lily is alone at Windy Hill. We had best get back."

At the roadside, Peter collected Jesse's bike. Unfortunately, the culvert was slippery, and he stepped in a patch of skunk cabbage.

"Oh," Gemma objected. "I am terribly sorry, Peter!"

Jesse held his nose, "Stink-a-roooney!"

Ignoring it, Peter set the bike at the roadside and offered, "A cool drink of water?"

Gemma replied gratefully, "Water. Yes."

Charlie laughed, "And you have GOT to change those shoes! Whew!"

Outside the Creek House, Peter left his shoes on the stoop. Inside he opened his arms, "My Nautical Knick-Knack Nook!"

Jesse rolled that on his tongue like a burping frog: "'Nautical Knick-Knack Nook'!" In high spirits, he laughed, "It's a *nosey little cook* in a *cozy little nook*!"

Gemma quirkled, "Another spoonerism from Jesse!"

Jesse kept fizzing, "This is Peter's yacht! Look! He's got a galley! And a sailor's hammock for a bed!"

Peter boasted for Charlie, "The plumbing, electricity, telephone— that's all Charlie's doing. He's the best."

Charlie larked, "Peter knows enough to learn from the mistakes of others."

"Only because," Peter graveled, "*You can never live long enough to make 'em all yourself.*" He hmphed. "Groucho Marx."

Gemma smiled and realized that both she and Jesse were thoroughly enjoying this Creek House visit. Lily was postponed for now, as she crackled, "Peter and Charlie, the two of you are a comedy!" She thought further, *Peter is quite clever, and Charlie Lippley has many talents.* Out loud she observed, "Peter, you need proper wood and tools." For the second time today, she surprised herself. "You are welcome to my workshop."

The water in Peter's glass sloshed up in exclamation. "Well! Thank you!"

But abruptly, Gemma was staring at a framed picture. "That … is … Jane's."

Jesse stepped close. "It's Jane's 'Island' poem!" He turned to Peter. "Why … how … did you get it?"

Peter's face went red. "Jane … Jane was my best friend."

"What?" Gemma and Jesse surprised.

"I met Jane … on the first day of second grade at the Keane school. She was so … different. All the girls were in dresses, but Jane was in overalls. I liked her right away. She spent the morning in class asking question after question. Anyway, at noon, I went home for lunch, and she followed me. Said she'd play with me after school." Peter's deep brown eyes stared into his memory banks. "Some of my greatest adventures were with Jane."

The confusion in Gemma's face softened. "Ah. Then Jane was not alone in her wanderings."

Jesse blurted a laugh. "That's the greatest! Maybe WE can have adventures!"

Charlie chuckled, "I think you just did! That bike ride?"

Peter smiled. "Well, let's get you home."

As they came out of the Creek House, a white heron slid across the water. They watched the white wings, flinging elegant feathers into the blue yonder as it descended into the long, lush grasses.

"Did you see that?" Jesse enthralled. "It was …"

"An enchantment," Gemma nodded.

Jesse perked, "That's what Peter said the first time I saw the Snowy Egret heron! It's an enchantment! If you have the eyes to look!"

"Jane called it *Gifts of God*." Peter pointed at Jesse, "And you! You have a memory like a bluefish!"

"Is that good?" Jesse asked.

"It's excellent! Jane used to say, 'Bluefish remember. You can count on them, always returning right here to Tanagasuq Bay.'"

Jesse skipped to the truck to help Charlie put his red bike on the flatbed. Before he and Gemma got in the cab, they overheard Charlie teasing Peter.

"So, Pete, you sure got your head full of that redhead over yonder!" They both chorkled.

Jesse looked up at Gemma, sniggling, "Lovey-dovey!"

Red-faced again, Peter drove them home to Windy Hill.

When Lily saw Peter's truck, she joined them, appreciating Charlie's demonstration to Jesse: "These are the handbrakes you use to stop the bike."

Jesse gave them a try. "Oh! Okay! I do have brakes!"

They went to Gemma's workshop with the borrowed tools. This time, Peter's eyes and tongue openly ogled, "I'd give a lobster's tail for a workshop like this!"

Charlie chuckled, "I think you'd have to give over the whole lobster!"

Lily laughed lightly, "I'd take that!"

Jesse fingered the leather tassel on Gemma's tool pouch. *I remember ... these tools belonged to Uncle Con.*

But Lily picked up the pouch, smiling at Peter and Charlie, "My, this leather is as handsome as you boys!"

They tittered, but turned, flipping through Gemma's wood selections.

Lily silently slipped outside.

Peter picked up a large scrap of cherrywood. "Perfect for my galley sink!"

Charlie ran his hand over it, "A great door."
Gemma generously offered, "Take it with you."
Peter was agog. "I … didn't mean …"
Gemma smiled brightly. "I did."

After they left, Lily, Jesse, and Gemma went inside. But at the kitchen table, Gemma stopped in alarm. Distressed, she pointed to the table, "Do you know how this came to be here?"

CHAPTER FORTY-ONE
YOU'LL NEVER GUESS

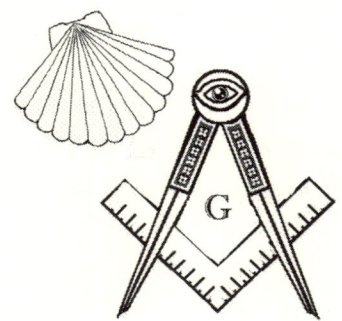

On the kitchen table was a handkerchief, embroidered with yellow roses.

"I think," Jesse patted it, "there's something inside it."

White as the hanky, Gemma unfolded it.

"Ohhh," Jesse marveled, "one perfect, pure white scallop shell!"

Gemma caught her breath. "Lily, was someone here while we were out?"

"No …"

Jesse wondered, *The Dorkings? But why would they leave a hanky?*

"Come." In her office, Gemma pulled out a wooden box. "Open this, Jesse."

He flipped a scallop latch and raised the lid to behold a set of three white scallop shells, placed on handkerchiefs embroidered with yellow roses.

Gemma explained, "The first shell appeared when Papa was five years old. The second, when I was born; the third, when Jane was born. And now this fourth shell …"

"For me?" Jesse wondered, "Is it because I'm here?"

Gemma pulled him close, "It would seem so."

"A mystery!" Jesse smiled.

"Yes," Lily acknowledged. "And here is another mystery." She picked up the compass and tapped the blue-and-gold design.

Jesse pointed, "What is that design?"

From her desk, Gemma pulled out two geometry tools: a compass and a square.

Jesse compared the tools to the blue-and-gold design. "Ohhh, I see! These aren't alphabet letters. The A is the compass tool, with a little pencil attached to it. And the wide V is the square. But, what does it mean?"

"The answer is in the 'G.'" Gemma explained, "The Freemasons, of which Papa and Grandfather were members, believe that God is the Divine Architect of everything in the Universe. The compass and square are the tools of every architect."

With the compass, she drew a perfect circle, and with the square, a perfect right angle. "In the circle and the angles of the square, we find the perfection of everything in the Universe, God's magnificent creations."

"But," Lily noted, "Freemasons are a secret society. We don't know the real meanings."

Jesse acknowledged, "Miss Lily believes the Freemasons hid a great treasure somewhere."

Lily made light of it, "One never knows."

Gemma read the compass inscription:

When joy is your compass, you live your magic.

She looked at Lily. "If there were a secret treasure on this farm, I would have discovered the magic ages ago."

The afternoon twirled away, touring Lily through Windy Hill. She was intrigued with every clever detail. They ended at the beach, and Jesse asked, "Can we take Miss Lily for a sail?"

"Oh, no!" Lily put up her hands, "I get seasick. But I will keep the home fires burning if you want to take a spin."

"Oh," Gemma retorted, "I would not think of abandoning you on your first night here. Come. It is nigh time for dinner."

After dinner, Lily made a tea tray and set it between the comfy chairs in the living room. Jesse sat alone on the long sofa, observing only two cups on the tray.

He capered away and returned with a small mug. Gemma and Lily stopped talking as he poured tea for all, blabber-gabbing:

"This has been a great day! Even though Conor and Amanda left, you came, Miss Lily. And I got my stone back! And Greta and Matts and Margarethe and Charlie and Peter were here. Oh! And I had a rollercoaster bike ride!" He joked, repeating Bethesda's words with her accent: "A bit naughty, that!" He held up his hands, "And somebody sent a scallop-shell mystery."

"Jesse," Gemma stopped him. "It is time to prepare for bed. You may read before lights out."

"Oh!" Jesse gulped and put the mug on the tray. "Goodnight, Gemma!" He hugged her and kissed her cheek. "Goodnight, Miss Lily!" He giggled, "Don't let the *beg buds* bite!"

"Goodnight, Mr. Spoonerism!" Gemma beamed.

Jesse headed to his yacht room with his alphabet book. "Golly! There are so many alphabets!" He paged through the beautiful Arabic, ancient Phoenician, intriguing Hebrew, and stunning Egyptian alphabets.

He was searching for the Omega—Ω—from the code pad. And there it was! At the end of the Greek alphabet: *Omega*.

"And here's the 'A' at the beginning! *Alpha*!"

Jesse was thrilled. "Greek is one of the alphabets! I solved the first part!"

He pulled out a postcard to write to Billy all about his new-old bike and his rollercoaster ride with no brakes! He ended with, "Amanda and Conor left. You'll never guess! Miss Lily Bankroft—the lady from the train—she's living with us!"

CHAPTER FORTY-TWO

THE BASEMENT

In the morning, Jesse had already finished the chores and was eating a bountiful breakfast when Miss Lily appeared.

"Gangbusters! You've been up for hours." She laughed lightly, "Obviously, the dawn and I are not on speaking terms."

Gemma chuckled, "Farm life is not for everyone."

"No. And, I'm afraid I don't do a farm breakfast either. I'm a coffee and toast girl."

Jesse soon realized Miss Lily's routine: coffee, toast, lipstick—and out the door.

Jesse, on the other hand, learned the farm routines hour by hour. He remembered Wilbur in *Charlotte's Web* spending his routine hours scratching itchy places and standing perfectly still. Whereas Gemma was always busy with the house, the buildings, the farm, and her workshop.

This morning she took Jesse to the basement with her gentle, but insistent, "Come."

They began in the larder room, where stood a large generator for electricity, next to which was an even larger freezer chest, and against the walls were rows of tall metal shelves.

"I am utterly grateful that my old farm manager, Joe Vareio talked me into purchasing these shelves and the extra stove, as well as the freezer chest. We bought them for a song, from a restaurant that closed during the Depression."

Jesse quizzeled, "Does a song mean it didn't cost very much?"

Gemma nodded and Jesse looked at the floor-to-ceiling metal shelves, filled with baskets of root vegetables and rows of canning jars. "Everything's so neat."

Down a short hallway, Jesse saw another of Jane's cross-stitch samplers:

Look not sorrowfully into the past. It comes not back again.
Wisely improve the present. It is thine.

"*Thine* … that must mean *yours*." Jesse shrugged, "That's like Dearie says: 'Live today. Yesterday is gone.'"

"You loved your Dearie," Gemma gentled.

"Oh, yes."

She touched his cheek. "Come."

They entered the laundry room where the old tub-washing-machine was agitating in a rhythmic chorkle all its own. Unconsciously, Jesse waggled his ears to its catchy tempo.

Gemma startled, "Haunts alive! Your ears! They're … waggling!"

"Dearie taught me! And she learned it from James Barrie."

Gemma flummoxed, "*Peter Pan* James Barrie?"

"Yes! Dearie knew all sorts of Imaginators."

Gemma had a funny look on her face, but she took his hand. "Next, our radio room."

On the table, Jesse saw the transceiver, microphone, and logbook. He felt like he was in a secret code room. A coded picture hung on the wall: letters made from hundreds of black dots. He chortled when he read it:

The Morse Code – Here Come Dots.

"Another anagram!" Jesse hootled. "Somebody likes to play with words!"

"Papa and Grandfather Harrison would challenge each other with puzzles. Grandfather installed this ham radio."

"You mean it's really called a *ham* radio?" Jesse smirfed.

"Yes. It truly is. Papa used it to keep abreast of the global contributions to science, engineering, industry—and weather. He updated the system and taught me how to use it. One day, I shall teach you. I communicate with freight drivers and ships regarding my lumber and furniture shipments—also with meteorologists for reports of stormy weather."

Jesse giggled, "You're a HAMster!"

Gemma looked appalled, "Are you calling me a rodent?"

"Oh, I … I …"

CHAPTER FORTY-THREE
THE FARM

"I am teasing you, Jesse!" Gemma laughed.

"Oh!" he laughed, and she boshed, "Hamster indeed!"

Ellie-cat followed them into the barn loft, and Gemma climbed the step-like bales to the very top. "We do this before the heat of the day."

"What?" She tumbled a bale, knocking him down. "Gemma!"

"Come," she grinned, "help me roll them down."

But Jesse ran up—and rolled down himself! Bumpity-down! Then he popped up to the top and gave Gemma a little push!

"Whoa!" Down she bumpity-rolled! With Jesse rolling after! Both covered in hay!

Zippity-pip, two streaks of grey flashed across the floor. Jesse saw Ellie-cat madly chasing a scurrying mouse.

"Crazy! They're still playing tag!" Jesse had a sudden, unaccountable feeling that his father James was there. He curioused, *James?*

At the same time, the mouse stopped. Sat up. Looked at Ellie-cat. And scooted under the hay.

Jesse whooped, "Game over!" He felt James, grinning, laughing with him.

Gemma cheered, "They live to play another day!"

The two of them giggled and poked each other with hay straws, until Gemma rolled over and got up to fork hay down to the animal stalls.

"Come."

They went down to a large garage, housing several tractors of different sizes. She pulled on her hat, opened the wide outside door, and climbed up on a tractor. "Come!"

Jesse climbed aboard, strapped in, and they chugged out of the barn, along a tree-lined lane flanked by moss-covered rock walls. Jesse pointed, "Look! Your fox!"

"Kitsune," Gemma declared. "He looks like a prince of the forest. But under that glowing fur coat, is the cold heart of a thief. He is an ostentatious, deceptive knave. Remember that."

Jesse didn't know all her words, but he figured the fox was not to be trusted. Indeed, Kitsune abruptly disappeared. "Oh! He's gone!"

But Jesse noticed squirrels. "Look at that! A squirrel dug up a nut—like it knows the secret hiding place! Look! It shoved it in its mouth! Nuts!"

"Hickory nuts. The Algonquin Indians called them, *chinquapin*."

"*Chink-a-pin*. That's catchy." He settled on the seat, "There's so much to see," he looked at Gemma, "and learn."

The tractor passed a group of beehive boxes, an orchard, and entered a huge field of grassy-looking plants. "Corn," said Gemma, pointing. Back and forth they went, dragging the spring-claw cultivator behind them, weeding row after row.

"So tidy!" Jesse hummed.

"Yes. Next week, the potato field."

On the way back, they stopped at the orchard, and she took down a ladder and buckets. "Open the gate, will you Jesse?"

But Jesse sat up higher, pointing, "Someone is sneaking. At the beehives."

Gemma barely looked. "The bees will make short work of any intrusion."

Jesse hopped down from the tractor. At the gate he found a tall rock, imprinted with a verse:

Fruit of this tree – Falling free – Proves Isaac's old discovery.

"Who's Isaac?"

Gemma only replied, "That is one of Papa's Riddle Rocks. You solve it as we work." She pulled open the tall stepladder and climbed up, humming a song. Jesse heard her sing, *"I'll be loving you … Always …"* But she stopped. Holding a branch, she declared, "These apples need pruning."

"You're going to put prunes …? In the apples?"

She burst a laugh, "Ohhhh! Jesse!" She showed him a branch filled with small apples. "Every one of these apples sprouted from an apple blossom. You can see that too many apples have bloomed. Hence, I cut off the extra apples, down to one apple, often referred to as 'King's Fruit.'"

Jesse pondered aloud, *"Blossom. Bloom."* He suddenly laughed, "They're kangaroo words!"

Gemma's eyebrows lifted, "Why so they are!" She clipped off a string of apples that fell to the ground. "Nevertheless, Mr. Kangaroo, your task is to retrieve the fallen apples. Place the substandard fruit in the black bucket, the worthy apples in the red bucket."

"For apple pie!"

"Not with these. The substandards produce chicken mash and compost; the worthy apples make pectin to thicken my jams—also cider vinegar, though only for housekeeping purposes."

Abruptly, a cry rang through the woods, "Owww! Aeghhh! Owww!"

CHAPTER FORTY-FOUR

THINKERS

A swarm of bees chased three screaming boys through the trees, heading for Windmill Road. Just in time, the school bus pulled up and they safely clambered aboard.

Gemma swaggered with a little smile, "You see, the bees took care of the intruders."

"You were right," Jesse smirfed back. Watching the bus pull away, he added, "You taught Jane at home … will you teach me?"

Gemma looked thoughtful. "We shall see."

Jesse sighed, "Anyway, those boys are the Dorkings." He repeated from Greta, "Benedict, Angus, and Dominic. B-A-D."

Quietly Gemma responded, "Judgment is not helpful. The Dorkings have their own troubles."

"Oh … uhm … yes. Right." Jesse flustered, remembering, "Dearie told me: *I don't need to blow out someone's candle to make mine glow brighter.*" Jesse felt in his pocket for Dearie's stone tinkling against Mac-Elliot's silver dollar. "And I have to remember Dearie's Rule of Tongue. *Let the words on my tongue taste delicious.*"

Gemma was taken aback. "You—and your Dearie—are quite … intriguing." She inspected Jesse's work. "Ah, this is fine, Jesse. You have reduced my job by half. We shall finish the whole orchard."

He picked up another apple. "Gemma? On Riddle Rock. Is Isaac—Isaac Newton?"

"Yes."

"Then I know! *Isaac's old discovery!* It's GRAVITY!"

"Bravo, Jesse!"

Farther along the apple trees, Jesse found a circle of stones. "There are words on the stones!" Walking roundabout, Jesse read:

You can count the seeds in one apple.

But who can count the apples in one seed?

He chortled, "Can't answer that! It's not a riddle, it's a 'Thinker'! Oh, Gemma," he called up to her, "Try this Thinker: *Why is 'abbreviated' such a long word?*"

She chuckled. "Ha! Superb! Try this! *Why is it that sheep do not shrink when it rains?*"

Grinning, Jesse offered another: "*Why isn't there mouse-flavored cat food?*" He chiggled, "Your turn!"

Gemma was silent for a few seconds, then blurted: "*How can even the most careful person overlook his nose?*"

Jesse applauded and marveled, "Gemma, everything here is so—so wondrous!"

"Papa always said, 'Wonder is the beginning of wisdom.' Perhaps invention and inspiration are in that place: of wonder."

"Dearie told me that, too! Always look for the wonder!"

Gemma dimpled. "I *wonder* if it is time for our noon repast."

They ate lunch out on the porch, cleaned up, and headed to Gemma's workshop.

"Golly, no scallylagging around here!" Jesse teased.

Gemma set Jesse to sanding the rungs for the chairs.

"Gemma, I have a spoonerism! *Be fruity* is *free beauty*!"

She was working the lathe. "Since you are so clever, here is a song puzzle:

> *Mayr-zee doats and do-zee doats*
>
> *An little lamb-zee di-vee –*
>
> *A kiddle-ee-di-vee, too – Wouldn't you?"*

Jesse didn't know what he was singing, but it was a fun. Before he knew it, Greta and Matts arrived. "All ready?"

Greta speed-walked ahead ... like Queen the goat!

"Golly, Greta," Jesse pulled on his boots, "you need some merri-cheers."

"I do not know merri-cheers. I know only Dorking bullies."

Jesse pivoted, "Well, I don't want the Dorkings to ruin our day." Greta's eyes rolled like a bagel. But as Jesse gentled the animals, she felt gentled, too.

After chores, Jesse invited Greta and Matts to his yacht to read *Dearie's Journal*. They settled into the cozy quarters, and Jesse introduced: "This is how Dearie became an Irish gypsy."

When Jesse finished reading, Greta said, "Yah. Read more."

"Okay. This is how Dearie got her name."

When Jesse stopped, Greta sat up, "This is gut book."

They heard a car, and Jesse tootled, "Miss Lily is back!"

Greta jumped, "Ve must go. Goodbye"

Matts signed *Thank you* and *Goodbye*. And they were gone.

Lily entered the kitchen with a bouquet of lilacs and a small pastry box. "Hello, Jesse! I've had a marvelous day! How about you?"

"Yes!" he laughed, "The farm is … marvelous!"

"Oh, I know just the vase for these lilacs!" She took the blue-and-white vase.

"Gemma says this vase is too precious." He put it back on the shelf and Lily blithely took another vase.

At dinner, Lily raved about her job, the people, and the little shops in Elizabethtown. "Everyone is so friendly!"

Gemma smiled tepidly. But afterward, Lily delighted Gemma with tea, pastries, and lilacs. Jesse saw only two cups and two lemon squares. He understood: He was not invited.

PART EIGHT

DAISY-DASTER

*Calamity arrived
at the door we left open.*

CHAPTER FORTY-FIVE
LILY'S OFFER

With a goodnight kiss, Gemma embraced Jesse. He understood. Gemma did not do "tucking in" like Dearie did. Jesse was on his own. He turned away, but Lily took his hand.

"Jesse, tomorrow afternoon I'd like to help you bring the animals back to the barn. Tell Greta and Matts they have the afternoon off."

"Oh, that will be great!"

Humming, Jesse headed to the back staircase, but in the pantry, he stopped. His eyes frowned. *Where's Gemma's blue-and-white vase? I know I put it here!* He stopped. *Maybe Gemma put it someplace else.*

He eagerly dashed up to the yacht room. There he found Velvet, waiting on the desk. "Thank you, Gemma!" He propped up his dear old bunny to show her his code-pad drawing with *Alpha* at top, *Omega* at bottom, and eight buttons between.

"Hmmm, I've got the ancient alphabet: the Greek *Alpha – Omega*. Now I need a medieval alphabet that divides evenly for the buttons."

Distracted, he pushed his chair out, and noticed the book cupboard door was ajar. His imagination sparked at all the choices of Jane's books. He felt Jane. Smiling.

> *Jesse, you know the real magic of books! I have watched you ride with Sir Galahad on his quest for the Holy Grail and hide with Jim Hawkins in the apple barrel aboard the Hispaniola. And Peter Pan was at your bedroom window looking for his shadow! Imagination! It lasts and lasts! It's in everything you want to be. And become.*
> *Read on, Jesse!*

Jesse grinned like a Cheshire cat and pulled out a book:

Magic Potions and Spells ~ Bewitch, Enchant & Hex Anyone

He eagerly opened the cover. "Oh! The pages are empty!" He flipped through and found on the last page:

Oh, the magic webs we weave, when first we practice to believe!
– Danielle Jane Roberts

He thought about this day. *It is magical here! I have so much to write to Conor. It needs a letter!*

He pulled out the scallop stationary and happily wrote:

Dear Conor,

I love this farm! I love Gemma!

He went on and on, writing of the laundry, the ham radio, the hay bales, Ellie-cat and the mouse, riding the tractor, the orchard and Riddle Rocks, the fox and the bees and the boys …

Velvet slumped onto his paper, and Jesse stopped. "Yes, I'm tuckered, too, Velvet. Let's go to bed." He turned out the light, snuggled with Velvet, and felt himself carried away into his deep, blue, velvet sleep.

Jesse heard Greta and Matts and opened his eyes. *Morning!*

Diggity-boo! He was up, washed, dressed, and out!

At the barn, Greta questioned him straightaway. *"Dearie's Journal!* Vhat next?"

"Oh no!" Jesse insisted, "You have to wait! *My zips are lipped!*" He smiled at the spoonerism from his days with Dearie. But Greta and Matts didn't understand, and Jesse explained, "It's a fun way to say, *'my lips are zipped.'*"

They still didn't get it.

"My lips are sealed tight as the manure door!"

They all giggled at that, and Jesse remembered, "Oh! You have the afternoon off today. Lily and I will take the animals to the barn."

"Miss Lily?" Greta frowned, "She does not like animals. They do not like her."

Jesse ruffled. "Golly, you act like she's going to put a spell on them!"

Greta didn't argue, but she demanded, "You vill read *Dearie's Journal*?"

"Well, come by after the barn chores."

In the afternoon, Jesse was in his yacht room, studying the alphabet book. He had come upon the Latin, or Roman, alphabet and the changes to it over the centuries.

Originally, 23 letters. But three letters were added: J, V, W in medieval times.

"*Medieval times!*" Jesse hooted. "This must be it!"

He read on, "The medieval Latin alphabet matches our English alphabet today, with 26 letters."

"But," Jesse puzzled, "26 doesn't fit equally with the number pad."

Lily's car rolled in, and Jesse looked out the window. She waved, calling, "Jesse, I'll be ready in a jiff!"

Together they walked to the pasture. She was talking a blue streak, all about the treasure and the code to the treasure room, the Freemasons in the family, and the valuable things in the house and barn. And big money. Jesse didn't pay much attention. He noticed that Ellie-cat was leaping at Miss Lily's fingers, and Lily picked up the purring cat. At the pasture she enthused in her deep voice, "Oh, this view is a knockout!"

But, instantly, Queen the goat put her head down, running at Lily full tilt!

"Gangbusters!" Lily cried, frozen to the spot.

Jesse stepped in front of her, and the obstreperous goat turned away. But Lily urged, "You take those nasty goats, I'll take the gentle cows." She pulled the cows' leads, with Ellie-cat snuggled on her shoulder, licking her hand, while Jesse explained the mucking out.

"Oh no," Lily groused. "I'm not much of a farm girl. How about you take the goats inside and do the mucking out. I'll tend to the cows and chickens."

"Okay, I can do that." Jesse cheerfully went inside and began the mucking. But he heard Lily cry—

"OH! Jesse! Help!"

Jesse ran outdoors. "Great gargoyles!!" There was the fox, Kitsune, skulking into the *open* chicken pen! The hens were flitting in raving conniptions with the fox bouncing-pouncing after them! Jesse was horrified as the fox snapped up Juliet and scrambled out!

Chasing after the fox, Jesse yelled back to Lily, "Close the chicken gate!"

Ophelia had fainted, and the rest of the hens fluttered like lunatics. Before Miss Lily could close the gate, they scuttled out, squawking and screeching.

Lily was rubbing her hands together, then wildly shooing the animals. She pushed and pushed the backside of Guess, and the cow moved away. But suddenly Ellie-cat leapt on the cow, sniffing, and clawing up her backside. Guess wheeled about, eyes on fire, and bolted into the woods—with Ellie-cat riding like a steer wrestler in a rodeo, and Who the calf loyally galloping behind.

In desperation, Jesse gave up on the fox and tried to catch the cows. But they were crazier than ever—bawling and bellowing! The upset was contagious. The bleating goats wildly banged the barn door, the chickens flapped in frenzied delirium, and the dogs barked like demented troubadours.

Jesse was utterly discombobulated. "What the dickens?"

Amidst the pandemonium, Greta and Matts appeared.

"Oh mein Got!" Greta pushed Matts, "Go help!" She turned, "I get Gemma!"

CHAPTER FORTY-SIX

CALAMITY

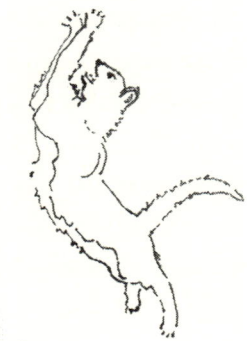

In a red rant, Gemma took over.

Lily looked as traumatized as the animals, and Gemma sent her back to the house. Then she wheeled on Jesse. "You! Muck out the barn stalls to spotless perfection!"

To Greta, "You collect the hens!"

To Matts, "You put Who in the barn. I shall fetch Guess."

With sweat rolling down his cheeks, Jesse grabbed a shovel and steadfastly mucked out. His mind raved. *Great gargoyles! Miss Lily was scared out of her wits! And, what the dickens? Ellie-cat is crazy! Queen, too! And the cows! And who opened the chicken pen? The Dorkings? Somebody did.* But Jesse didn't have an answer. *How could this happen?*

After much effort, all the animals were back in their remarkably clean stalls. Except Ellie-cat. She was left chasing her tail and rolling in the grass. Gemma stood, breathless, towering above the children, her eyes boring into Jesse.

"You have put our livelihood at stake, Jesse. The milk will be spoilt for tomorrow, and we have lost Juliet to the fox." Her voice rose with intolerance, "After this fiasco, Jesse, any mischief with the animals, and you shall be on duty, mucking out until doomsday."

"But ... I'm not doing any ... mischief," Jesse moogled.

Gemma was grievously unconvinced. "I have never seen the animals thus!" Her head shivered, "Jesse, you are a Calamity John! You have induced the animals to extreme excitement. And you were negligent in keeping the chicken pen closed."

Jesse was horrified. He had no idea how this calamity happened. Outrage boiled in his mouth, but before he could say a word, Matts wagged his head, *No,* and Greta stepped forward. "The cow and calf run avay, the goats butt everything in sight, the chickens are crazed."

"Great gargoyles!" Jesse confounded, "I didn't do that!"

Greta nodded in agreement, "It is not Jesse. His hands, his voice—they gentle the animals. Always."

"Be that as it may ..." Gemma rattled off something Jesse did not understand: "*Res ipsa loquitor! It speaks for itself!* Jesse was the one in charge." Gemma inhaled sharply. "Jesse, please leave off your 'thrill-digging' adventures, as you call them. Think calm thoughts. Please. For all our sakes."

"Yes," Jesse tried to calm and he murmeled, "I can do that."

He followed Greta and Matts outdoors, but, needless to say, there was no reading of *Dearie's Journal.*

Lily set the table in the kitchen with fresh flowers. But dinner was late. When they finally sat down, she was lavish with apologies. "I am so sorry to have caused such upset."

"There is no need to apologize," Gemma clipped. "Jesse knows his duty."

He nodded. "I won't *lo-kwee-tor* again."

In spite of herself, Gemma's lips melted into smile. "The Latin phrase is: *Res ipsa loquitor.* Literally: *The thing speaks for itself.* In this case, all the evidence points to your delinquency with the animals."

Jesse remembered the Possum Policeman back in New York City. *He said I was a joo-ven-ile dee-link-went. Maybe that's Latin, too.* Out loud he said, "I don't want to be a delinquent."

"No." Gemma agreed and took a breath. "Hence, there is something you should know, Jesse. This farm—everything in it—this is my ... *our* ... world." She looked to the window. "When I was little, this place was my sanctuary. Papa, Joe, Mary, Hannah—oh, all the magical people who worked here—taught me the lessons of life. Seasons of blossoms and harvest. Seasons of hibernation. But always, the work."

Her face turned back to Jesse. "Living on a farm is a guardianship. It is hard. There is work. Every day." She nodded slowly. "When Papa was alive, there was money to provide for everything. But the Great Depression ... well, there is no money. The animals are our livelihood. If we lost the animals, this farm would wither." She shifted uneasily in her chair. "I have borne witness to farms that have withered. Sold-off for mere pennies." Her eyes closed, and when she opened them, she said, "Please remember, Jesse, you are a guardian. Without the animals, we have no farm. We have nothing."

Again, Gemma gazed out the window and sighed a line from Shakespeare, "*So weary with disasters ... I would set my life on any chance to mend.*" She looked into Jesse's eyes, "I doubt this disaster will happen ever again." With a long sigh she lifted her glass to Jesse and smiled, "To refreshing beginnings!"

In a gush of relief, Jesse raised his glass.

Gemma watched Jesse and thought of Conor's words: *Today will be gone. And we can't get it back. I want him ... to bloom.* She thought of her Shakespeare utterances: *He wears the rose of youth.* She thought, *Yes, he does.*

Her glass was still raised as she offered, "Perhaps we shall go for a sail tomorrow afternoon."

"Oh, Gemma!" Jesse perked contritely. "That would be great!"

After they cleaned the supper dishes, Jesse excused himself to go up to his yacht room. He propped himself on the window seat, paging through the alphabet book. But he was not in the mood for puzzling. He still had a nagging feeling of frustration at being accused of not being able to handle all the animals. He felt he didn't deserve the blame for it. His heart rustled with the prickly feeling of unfairness, and his mind seesawed back and forth with blame—trust—whose fault—being dependable—responsible. A big puff of his breath cleared the air, and he knew: *Gemma's right. I was in charge. And I don't want to be a Calamity John.* He sighed. *Now, I have to stop thinking about it. Put my Light On. Lighten up. Yeah, that's it! Lighten up.*

He opened *Dearie's Journal*. *Oh this is just right!* Jesse smiled. Dearie was visiting a monastery in Ireland, and she met an extraordinary man from India, dressed in a gorgeous silk tunic and pantaloons with a turban on his head and lustrous slippers on his feet.

Jesse was captivated, but sleepy. With Velvet, he nestled into his bunk and drifted into his wispy-slips.

A noise jolted Jesse awake. He listened. Noises. *On the roof? In the attic? Someone is prowling! The Dorkings?*

He sat up. Footsteps. Above. Jesse sat still. Something—someone—is in the attic.

He smelled a faint fragrance. Lilies.

Is it Miss Lily? No, she's downstairs. I gotta tell Gemma.

He got out of bed, but in the dark, he accidentally pushed over the chair, and it clattered on the floor. He picked it up and made his way to the doorway. But he stopped. Another noise—a click. *The spring-door!*

Jesse mincey-toed down the stairs.

Miss Lily was in the kitchen. "Jesse? What's wrong?"

"I need to find Gemma."

"She's in the basement."

He clambered downstairs. Gemma was counting canned goods and checking a list.

"Jesse?"

"Oh Gemma! It's not my imagination! I heard noises—footsteps—in the attic! Someone was up there!"

Gemma's head tilted. She smiled. "Jesse, it's the seagulls. They land on the roof and strut back and forth. It does sound like walking across the roof, but it is not human."

"Oh."

"My, my, Jesse," Gemma derided, "You are a Calamity John! Such tribulations!"

"I'm sorry, Gemma. I—oh, it's just one daisy-daster after another."

Gemma chuckled, "Today was a daisy of a disaster! But there is no need for sorry." She sighed, "As I said earlier, not everything is a thrilling adventure. Best go to your bed now." Her mouth grimmeled, and she added: "John …"

A giggle-snicken puffed through Jesse's cheeks, "I don't want that! Goodnight Gemma."

She hugged him, "Yesterday is gone. Tomorrow is a new day."

Back in his yacht, Jesse turned on the light and took out his last two postcards for Billy and Conor. He was out of stamps. "I'll buy stamps tomorrow."

He wrote of the mess that he and Lily conjured. Shaking his head, he sighed, "Calamity John!" Writing the addresses, he thought, *Gemma says tomorrow is a new day. I sure hope so!*

He went to the bathroom for a glass of water. The mirror looked at him. *Calamity,* it declared. *Calamity John!*

He leaned in. *Am I?*

CHAPTER FORTY-SEVEN

TODAY

Greta had nothing good to say about Lily and the fiasco.
But Jesse only replied, "Yesterday is gone." He found another egg and smiled, "Today is today. I'll read an extra Chapter of *Dearie's Journal*."

"Gut. Today is last day of school. We celebrate."

"I'll ask Gemma if you can come sailing with us," Jesse cheered and signed *sailing* for Matts. "And I'll bring *Dearie!*"

"Yah!" Greta grinned.

After breakfast, Gemma stood up, "Come. We shall prepare for the Port Haven Market."

In the basement, Jesse heard voices and followed his ears to the radio room. Margarethe was talking into the microphone. He didn't understand what she was saying, but she sounded ... normal ... like she was really talking.

"Cracker Jacks! She really can talk to Germany!"

"Yes," Gemma said, "Ham radios can connect you across town

or across the world." She handed him two baskets and they went to the larder, filling them with jars of honey, jams, apple butter, and pickled vegetables.

Jesse remembered, "It's the last day of school. Can Greta and Matts come sailing, too?"

She nodded, "That is a lovely idea, Jesse."

She remained in the basement, while Jesse climbed to the kitchen.

Miss Lily was drinking her coffee, gazing at the sparkling amethyst geode. Jesse heard her buzz, "This must be worth a small fortune."

Jesse thought of Margarethe's fingers—twisting her buttons, touching the geode. But he thought, *Don't be suspicious!* He told Lily, "Gemma says it is a gemstone, but not valuable."

"Hmm. Added to the ones I saw in the barn, it's a treasure."

"Oh," Jesse chortled. "You think everything is a treasure!"

The toaster snapped and Jesse jumped, "Your *post topped!*" He giggled, "I mean, your *toast popped*. Hey it's a spoonerism, and it just popped out of me!"

Lily smiled, buttered her toast, munched, and sipped her coffee. Out of the blue, she remarked, "I know Gemma keeps a key to the treasure rooms," she looked at Jesse, "but, I'll bet you know the code for the rooms!"

"Not yet!" He grinned. "Oh, by the way, we're sailing this afternoon. Supper will be late."

"Splashing good!" She smiled, pasted on her lipstick, and was out the door.

Jesse helped Gemma prepare for market, setting out crates, baskets, and a folding table.

She explained, "Margarethe will add her breads and cheeses, milk, cream, and butter. This is how we sell our produce."

Confounded, Jesse gulped, "Like *this*?"

"What …?" she flubbed.

"It's not very, well, presentable. Mrs. Romano always *presented* everything. Like a gift. I helped her gussy it up!"

"Gussy up?"

"Yes." He pointed, "The vegetables need a butcher paper wrap … ribbons on the jars … napkins in baskets … a tablecloth … oh, and an umbrella."

"Really …?"

"Yes. Customers like it."

Gemma was intrigued. Jesse brought Gemma to the yacht art cupboard. "We can make labels for the jars! All we have to do is copy your scallop stationary with the Camera Lucida!"

She quickly understood, and they copied and glued, beribboned and gussied up with delight. Further, they collected all kinds of items from the linen closet and attic. Gemma was astounded at the transformation. "Presentation! Everything looks quite inviting!"

"Splendish!" Jesse smiled. "Oh, and Gemma? I know the first clues to the Treasure Door."

"Do you?" She smiled.

"Yes, I have the *Alpha – Omega* from the Greek alphabet, and the 26 letters from the medieval Roman alphabet. But I don't know how they fit." He added, "YET!"

"A useful word is 'yet.'" That was all. No hints.

"Oh, and after lunch, I want to ride my bike into town to buy more stamps and postcards."

Gemma sounded surprised and concerned. "I am not one to venture into town. Are you accustomed to doing errands?"

Jesse responded, "Yes. I did errands every day in New York City."

"Alone?"

"Yes." He paused, "And I know my way around here. Murphy showed me."

"Really. Well. I see I have another child wanderer on my hands."

Jesse hummed, "Dearie would call it *whirly-wandering*. You know, like a delight."

Gemma still hesitated nervously, but she smiled and single-mindedly switched tracks. "Well then! I have a bike satchel for you."

Jesse loaded up his new-old satchel and pushed his bike to Gemma's workshop.

"I'm going now, Gemma. Do you need anything?"

She smiled, "Not a thing but you, Jesse."

Wheeling down Windmill Road, Jesse's heart sang … with the elegant white herons gliding into the marsh … waving to Peter … passing Linger Longer Farm. He continued, up and over the hill, and in no time, he was in town, on Tanagasuq Avenue, with more than stamps and postcards in mind.

CHAPTER FORTY-EIGHT

TOWNSFOLK

At Four Forks, Morton Mealy startled Jesse, pointing at him from the window of his truck. "I'm watchin' you, kid! Got my eye on ya!" He laughed, showing off his one front tooth, looking more like the pesky Squirrel Nutkin than ever.

Jesse shiveraled. But his smooth stone jingled with his silver dollar in his pocket, and he rode on.

Once in town, Jesse noticed that people were not staring at him. They waved and even called him by name. At the Post Office, Mr. Coleman cheerfully sold him stamps and postcards. Jesse buoyantly headed down to the flower shop, where Granny Grace Gardiner and her gabby granddaughter, Nancy, lightheartedly sold him one perfect, long-stemmed yellow rose. Elated, he crossed the street to a welcoming Beef & Bones and bought a little brown bag of chocolate nonpareils.

It didn't matter who or where, the townsfolk talk was pretty much the same:

So, Jesse, you've settled in just fine.
I hear Windy Hill had a famous guest! Amanda Wynne!
My! She is sister to the Black ... to Miss Jessica!
And there's a new guest staying with you. A Miss Lily.
Good company for your grandmother. And how is your grandmother?

Jesse answered with a grin every time, "We call her Gemma. I love her! I love Windy Hill!"

As he pushed his bike past Viand's Market, Tilly "Pickles" Pickford rushed out the door, grabbing Jesse's bike by the back fender.

"Young man!" she gasped. "I will not be put off. It is high time we met!" She held the fender. "You are Jesse O'Neil. You are son to the woman whom I helped bring into this world."

Jesse was surprised at that, but Tilly continued her blabber-gab.

"I know your eyes, Jesse. From your mother and your grandmother. It's love shining out. And I want to tell you how happy I am that you have come. I have always wished the best for Miss Jessica. But she has been as lost as last year's Easter egg. It is gratifying to know that you are here to find her."

She rattled on. "I hear only the best about you. You are Miss Jessica's second chance. And I believe in second chances. Now, my name is Tilly Pickford. You tell Miss Jessica 'hello' from me. Tell her I am praying for her. Tell her I always have."

"I will, Miss Tilly."

"Don't forget!"

"Yes, I will tell her."

He swung on board his bike, riding up Tanagasuq avenue, back to Windmill Road. His thoughts were a-jumble.

Well, one thing's for sure, it takes a lot longer to do anything in a small town than in the big city. Everyone talks! And everyone knows everything. Golly. Everything.

But they seem nice. Friendly. Kind. It reminds me of Mac's apartments.

He headed to the creek and his bike picked up speed as he whizzed downhill. His silver dollar jingled with his stone, and his thoughts followed, round and round with the wheels—one idea spinning freely to the next. All of a sudden, he shouted, "Oh my gosh and golly! That's it! The alphabet letters! The numbers! That's it!"

Jesse vigorously pedaled up Windmill Road and into the cobblestone driveway. He jumped off his bike, parked it in the carriage house—then dashed up to his desk.

"So, 26 letters! But! I take away 1 for the 'A'—that's for Alpha. And another 1 for the 'Z'—that's for Omega. That gets me to 24 letters! And that divides evenly by the 8 buttons left! Great goggles! Three letters for each button!"

$$
\begin{array}{cc}
\multicolumn{2}{c}{A} \\
\multicolumn{2}{c}{1} \\
B\,C\,D & E\,F\,G \\
2 & 3 \\
H\,I\,J & K\,L\,M \\
4 & 5 \\
N\,O\,P & Q\,R\,S \\
6 & 7 \\
T\,U\,V & W\,X\,Y \\
8 & 9 \\
\multicolumn{2}{c}{\Omega} \\
\multicolumn{2}{c}{0} \\
\end{array}
$$

"This is so thrill-digging! I can spell out a code word with the numerals! Wait till I tell Gemma!"

He stopped. "Oh! I forgot! Gemma's presents!"

In the pantry, Jesse fit the rose into a tall, skinny vase and rattled the nonpareils into a glass dish. Both went on a tray, and he marched to Gemma's workshop, with the dogs parading alongside him. "Oh, you dogs!" Jesse grinned at them, "Let's surprise Gemma together!" He stepped in to present his gifts.

"What is this?" Gemma amazed, "For me?"

The dogs yipped and Jesse nodded. And, oh! Gemma's hug!

"I'm smuffling!" She left Jesse gasping for breath. "You need practice hugging!"

"Ohhh?"

"A little too tight!"

She chuckled at that and led him back to the house, where they each had one or two (or three) nonpareils. Jesse told her of his trip to town and all the people who remembered her and prayed for her, especially Tilly Pickford. "Everyone was so nice, Gemma."

"Tilly Pickford." Gemma smiled.

But Jesse rambled on. "And they know me! Golly-gee-whilakers, they know everything!"

Gemma's shoulders fell, *Hmm, they know everything.*

In the quiet, Jesse stepped closer to her. "Gemma, I hope this isn't calamity. But, sometimes, Miss Lily talks—about a treasure here on Windy Hill. And all the valuable things here. She talks a lot about money. Big money."

"Oh, Jesse, what are you imagining? Lily is an independent young woman, making a respectable living. No, there is no treasure on Windy Hill, yet Lily may enjoy thinking so."

Jesse nodded, "Okay."

The twins arrived, and, like a carefree breeze, Gemma welcomed them. "While you tend to the animals, I shall prepare a rucksack of goodies for our celebratory sail!"

Jesse opened the back door, "And I shall tuck *Dearie* into your rucksack!"

The animals were very cooperative, and the sailing party met outside the barn, just as Lily drove in.

"We are off for a sail." Gemma addressed her, pulling on her hat. "I have prepared a cold dinner, but it will be late."

Lily smiled, "I'll have it ready when you return."

Gemma's smile gleamed, "Delightful!"

"Take your time!" Lily beamed, looking quite pleased with herself.

CHAPTER FORTY-NINE

BLISS-T

Their late afternoon excursion was the very best. Jesse called it, "The bliss-t!"

Greta and Matts helped with the sails and lines, and Gemma gave them turns at the tiller. Jesse was singing, *Mayr-zee doats, and do-zee doats* ... On and on.

Greta quizzeled, "Do you know vhat you sing?"

"No."

She nodded. "Think of female horses. And vhat they eat."

Jesse sang the tune, "Feee-male horses eat their oats."

"No!" Matts and Greta guffawed. She asked, "Vhat is a female horse?"

"Um ... a mare."

Greta clicked her tongue, "Mares eat ...?"

"Mares eat oats?"

"Yah!" Greta clapped. "And deer and lambs and baby goats?"

Jesse sang haltingly, *"Mares eat oats ... and does eat oats ... and little lambs eat ... ivy?"*

"Yah!"

"A kid will eat ivy, too—wouldn't you!"

"Yah! Sing!"

Greta's singing sounded terrible. Jesse had never met anyone who couldn't sing. He looked at Matts, who was silently smiling in his peculiar way. Jesse looked at Gemma, who shrugged, "Greta sings in the key of her own invention."

Singing the silly puzzle song, they zig-zagged back and forth, tacking through the west bay. Jesse had fun playing the submarine trick, and it amazed Greta and Matts. But that was the cue to swivel about and head home. With the quiet breeze at their backs, Gemma pulled out her treats, and Jesse pulled out *Dearie's Journal*.

Her journal Chapter came to life when a tiny kitten found little Dearie near a crystal river, and the curious boy—Elliot—discovered them both.

Greta gestured, "More!"

Jesse indulged them, reading of Old Barrett and his smooth white stone. Jesse passed his stone to each of them, and Greta held it tightly, while he read of the horrific storm.

Gemma amazed, "That was exceptional, Jesse. Would you read another Chapter?"

Jesse read on but stopped while they moored the boat. With everything ship-shape, Gemma prompted, "We must know what becomes of little Dearie and her cat! Let us finish the Chapter here in the boat."

They lolled with the rippling waves as Jesse read of Dearie's stormy night and the unexpected morning.

With the setting sun, they slowly trekked up the hill. But abruptly, Jesse pointed at the barn. "Look! The treasure rooms! There's a light on!"

"Yah!" Greta blustered, "Look!"

Gemma looked, but the light had gone out. "Perhaps it was the sunset reflection."

Jesse objected, "I don't think so. Someone is up there!" The twins nodded in agreement.

Gemma's eyebrows lifted with the corners of her mouth, "Now John …"

"But Gemma!"

"John …?"

Jesse stopped. He knew better. *Don't pick a quarrel*—he smirked—*even when it's ripe. That's what Dearie would say.*

Greta and Matts said their quick goodbye, and Gemma and Jesse entered the kitchen. Lily set aside her sketch pad and gestured to supper awaiting them.

Gemma was so grateful, "Thank you, Lily. You are an angel."

Lily smiled, "I simply dished up what you prepared."

They tucked in, enjoying the dinner comestibles and the conversation. "Oh, I almost forgot!" Lily noted, "I saw three boys prowling at the gardens and behind the barn."

Jesse thought: *Dorkings. The light in the treasure rooms.* But he remembered Gemma's admonition not to judge. Gemma nodded, and, like Jesse, said nothing.

Instead, he looked at Lily's drawings. "After dinner, I'll share my drawings that Siobhan did for me!"

But after dinner, Jesse heard the piano. He knew the music. Dearie used to play it on the Victrola in the evening parlor. Now Gemma was playing it on the piano: Rachmaninoff's *Rhapsody on a Theme from Paganini*.

Jesse stood next to Gemma. "Dearie said Rachmaninoff wrote this by turning Paganini's violin melody upside down. So, I said it should be called *Theme from Ininagap*. That's 'Paganini' ... well, backwards!"

She smiled faintly and continued playing. It was that soft part that squeezed Jesse's heart. He closed his eyes and was delighted to see his Lights flickering with each lovely note, showering him with a deep sense of love.

Just then Lily entered, clattering the tea tray. The music ended.

"Oh, don't stop, Gemma!" Jesse appealed. "That's my favorite part!"

Gemma closed the piano. "Rachmaninoff will keep. He always does."

Jesse's mouth went down in the corners. It seemed Gemma stopped playing because of Miss Lily. *Even though I asked her to keep playing my favorite part.* But he felt whiney, thinking that. He turned from the piano and cheered, "Dearie knew Rachmaninoff! When she was young. She met him in Russia. And Conor visited him in Switzerland."

"Really," Gemma's head tilted. "Papa knew him, too. When I was young, he introduced me. In Philadelphia. I recall Rachmaninoff's hands. So large, they completely enveloped my own."

She moved to the comfy chair and Lily plopped into the other chair.

Jesse noticed that there were still only two cups on the tea tray. Even so, he held up Siobhan's drawings, and both Gemma and Lily gave him their attention.

He shared each of the faces from his New York apartments. Gemma was particularly interested in Dearie.

"I have seen her ... that face ... somewhere."

"Yes," Jesse reminded her, "when you bought James' catboat."

"Hmmm ... that must be it."

The last picture was of Miss Peggy.

Lily startled.

Gemma looked at Lily. Gazed back at Siobhan's drawing. "Why Lily, Miss Peggy looks like you. Her nose and hair are different, but there is a strong resemblance."

"Really?" Jesse looked at the drawing.

Lily's mouth twitched, "Well ... truth to tell, Miss Peggy is ... a cousin. But Miss Peggy is a Peg-Puff—that is, a young woman who acts like an old one. We rarely saw one another in New York." She looked at Jesse, "But how funny that you knew her!"

Back in his yacht, Jesse wrote postcards to Conor and Billy—of riding his bike to town and solving more of the secret code for the treasure room, sailing with Greta and Matts—oh, yes, and the light he saw in the treasure rooms.

Treasure, he wrote, *That's all Miss Lily talks about! Oh, and you'll never guess! Miss Lily Bankroft is Miss Peggy's cousin!*

PART NINE

DIGGITY-BOO!

*Whatever you may undertake,
 let it bring forth bliss.*

CHAPTER FIFTY

TO MARKET

It was extra early in the morning when Jesse traipsed down the back steps with his code paper in hand. A morning fog coated everything, glimmering through a sieve of sunlight as Jesse left his shoeprints in the wet grass. He was inside the barn before Greta and Matts and he stood, staring at Jane's cross-stitch: *Gifts of God*.

"That's the code, I just know it. But what's the ancient language? Gemma called Grandfather Harrison's collection 'Dona' … something."

Jesse had seen it with his own eyes, heard it with his own ears, but he had not yet puzzled it out. Instead, he chuckled, remembering the song *Dona Nobis Pacem*.

Ha! I thought it was 'Donut No Cheese Pasta'! Ohhh! He chorkled. *Nooo! It really means 'Give Us Peace.'*

Dona, his thoughts repeated, *Dona. It means 'Give.' Gifts! Gifts of God.*

"I remember now!" He gaspered, "It's on the plaque inside! *Dona Dei!*"

Jesse excitedly wrote out *Dona Dei*. He put a matching code numeral under each letter: 2-6-6-1, then 2-3-4. He flipped open the molding, heedlessly dropping his code paper. Feverishly, he pressed 2661 234—CLICK! The treasure-room door opened!

Behind Jesse, the barn door opened, too. But it was not Greta and Matts. "Miss Lily!"

She didn't enter. She smirked, "I know. It's far too early for me. But Gemma said she's loaded the truck and gone to Little Farm to load up Margarethe's things. You and the twins need to hightail it with the barn duties." Her head tipped up to the treasure door, "Jesse! You solved the code!"

"I did!" he hopped. "I can't wait to tell Gemma!"

Now Lily stepped into the barn. "I can't wait for you to share it with me!"

"Oh no!" Jesse closed the door. "You have to solve it yourself!"

The barn door opened again and Greta hootled, "Market today! Let's go!"

Jesse stepped down to milk Queen. Behind him, Miss Lily picked up his code paper and slipped it into her pocket. Turning, she cheered, "Have a hunky-dory time at the market!"

Milking Queen, Jesse crowed, "Hunky-dory! You excellent goat!" His brain synapsed, *Hunky-dory, I've heard that before. Like 'gangbusters'… Oh, I remember … it was Miss Peggy! Miss Lily's cousin! I'm remembering everything today!*

The three children clambered aboard Gemma's truck, nestled into the cargo bed, and they rolled downhill, into the fog … misting over the creek and into the rooftops of Elizabethtown.

Excited to be on the ferry again, Jesse pointed, "Let's go up top! It's thrill-digging!"

Greta intoned, "Ve do not dig thrills. Ve sit in truck."

Jesse climbed out and knocked on Gemma's window, "Let's go up," he pointed.

Margarethe leaned forward, twisting her button. "Nein. Ve stay. On guard."

Jesse shrugged, and waved Greta and Matts to follow. And they did!

In the lifting haze, the bay views were mystical. Jesse eagerly walked the decks, pointing out all the sights, and telling Murphy's tales.

Matts signed *sailing*, and Greta grinned, "It is like sailing!"

When they pulled into Port Haven, Greta gushed, "Ve do it again on the ride home!"

They drove off the ferry and uphill, crossing Bellaire Avenue at the top and pulling into the huge, grassy Freeman's Field. They were early and took a place right up front. The children helped set up, and Jesse used clothespins to secure a sign on the umbrella: *Windy Hill Farm*. Everything glowed in the morning sun that burned off the fog. Margarethe, Matts, and Greta were surprised and pleased by the presentation. "Yah! Gut!"

The field filled up quickly, creating rows of vendors, followed by early-bird customers that swarmed about Gemma and Margarethe with *oohing, ahhhing,* and buying! The beribboned jars, vegetables, and breads flew off their table. Greta, Matts, and Jesse oversaw the dairy items in the large, ice-filled copper bin, and Jesse felt a 'giddy' in his throat every time they lifted the beribboned copper lid. Success was fun!

The day was June-perfect, with a breeze that cooled and a sun that warmed. Later, as the customers slowed, Jesse and the twins joined the children playing tag on the old baseball diamond at the far end of the field. Jesse had a clothespin in his pocket, and he got a new idea.

I'll carve a little peg from this clothespin, and we can play a game of Indian Bases, just like we played in the courtyard back in New York City.

He sat down on the grass and sliced off the ends of the clothespin. *Oh, one of these sticks can be the prop for the peg!* As he twiddled the little peg from the top of the clothespin, he chuckled, "It looks like a little hickory nut. A chinquapin! I won't call it Indian Bases anymore, I'll call it Chinquapin!"

In no time at all, the other children joined in his game of Chinquapin, flipping the little peg off the prop and into the air, and whacking it with a stick. The hitter ran the bases, while the other players caught the Chinquapin peg in the air or tagged the base with it.

Greta was last to step to the plate. First try, she smacked the peg right on the nose! It popped up—and she smacked it again—whizzing it past Jessie's ear—and into the outfield!

Everyone was crazed, racing after the little peg, jumping up and down, yelling up a storm. "Chinq-ua-pin! Chinq-ua-pin!" Throwing it from one to the other, they exclaimed, "Chinq-ua-pin!"—as Greta jet-streamed around the bases.

Jesse couldn't believe how fast she ran. "Cr-a-a-a-zy man!" he hooted.

Someone threw the peg to him—and he had to toss it to Matts, waiting at home plate. A race! Greta or the peg! Which would reach home-base first?

A shout rang out, "Run! Greta, run! Run!"

Jesse looked. *Cracker Jacks! It's Gemma!* She was shouting like a carnival barker!

The peg fell to the ground and Greta safely crossed home base! Gemma applauded, shouting, "Hurrah! Brava, Greta!"

Jessie and Matts jumped around Greta in her triumph—and Gemma, quite breathless, joined them, exclaiming, "I have not witnessed such excitement in a chinquapin's age!"

CHAPTER FIFTY-ONE

AMICI

Gemma radiated happy triumph. "We customarily have our lunch here, but we have sold all our wares! I suggest a picnic lunch at home in our Star Cupola!"

Packing up the empty baskets and bins was a sweet reminder of their success. Jesse heard Gemma tell Margarethe, "You and I have so often relied on our own resolve."

"Yah," Margarethe agreed, twisting her button. "Grit."

Gemma closed the basket lid. "I feel such delight to have Greta and Matts and Jesse bring the fresh and fun. It does not feel like grit."

Amici! Jesse thought and he grinned, as smiles and laughter filled the truck all the way to the ferry.

On board, they all visited with Murphy, strolling the decks and taking in sights, which Gemma and Margarethe had not enjoyed, Jesse snickered, "In a chinquapin's age!"

Jesse ran upstairs to wash up, grab *Dearie's Journal*, and dash ahead to the treasure room. There on the floor was his code paper.

"Oh good!" he picked it up, tapped the code, and proudly pulled the treasure-room door wide open—as wide as his grin.

Greta opened the barn door behind him, and gaped at Jesse, "How did you open the door?"

Gemma was right behind, puffing her surprise, "Jesse! You …! Why you are the cleverest boy! You deserve to enter first—with all *Pomp and Circumstance!*" She sang the notes to Elgar's famous music, and Jesse triumphantly marched in!

The cupola was as glorious as ever. Margarethe opened the glass doors and windows, and the breeze cooled as Gemma unpacked the picnic basket with a flourish. She had yellow-rose napkins tied up with yellow ribbons around Margarethe's chicken-salad-stuffed rolls. Jesse grinned at her *presentation*, and they all smiled when she passed a little jar of pickles, also tied with a yellow ribbon. More yellow adorned the thermos and jar of chocolate nonpareils.

All in good time, they put up their feet and leaned back, as Jesse opened the journal for a Dearie story. Margarethe inquired, "Vat is zis?"

Greta explained a bit to her mother, and as Jesse read aloud, they all entered the Irish countryside of 1897 and Dearie's adventures. "Dearie is seven and the Irish gypsy Travellers are visiting a monastery in Ireland."

Margarethe looked at Jesse, "Zis Dearie—she is your grandmutter?"

Greta answered, "Yah, Little-girl-Dearie is Jesse's grandmutter." She rolled onto her stomach. "Begin?"

Everyone giggled at the story of Dearie's cat and his unfortunate escapade into the catnip garden. Oh, the comical conniptions!

Jesse flashed back to Ellie-cat: *licking Lily's hands, crazily clawing the cow, chasing her own tail, and rolling in the grass. Catnip? But where would she get catnip?* No answer.

Nonetheless, he read to the end and was met with pleas for still more.

"Again!" Margarethe grinned.

"Golly!" He marveled, "You really like Dearie!"

"Yah! Again," Greta wagged, and Matts signed for *more*.

Jesse enjoyed reading about Dearie and Mac and the intriguing visitors they met in the monastery. But Gemma stood. "This is decidedly engaging, but regrettably, we must tidy up and prepare for the afternoon tasks."

"Yah!" Greta stretched, "Time to get the animals."

Gemma and Margarethe went down the spiraling staircase, while the children closed the windows and doors. When Jesse got down to the first-floor treasure room, he twirled around victoriously.

"Come," Greta ordered, ignoring his little celebration. "The animals vait."

But Jesse noticed something. The corner of the muslin was turned up. He only had time to lay it flat, as Greta pulled him out of the room.

"The animals get *mürisch*."

"Murish?"

"Grumpy." She looked sideways at Jesse, "But later—one Chapter more?"

Matts faced Jesse, signing, *book*. He grinned and Jesse grinned back.

In Jesse's yacht, he read more of Dearie and they felt the magic flowing from Old Barrett's talk of glittering eyes, looking for the vivid colors of nature. And the remarkable Indian man explaining the spirit—the Light—always inside each of us, especially when you look for it.

Too soon, the western sun peeked through the windows and Greta, soughed, "Vell. Ve go now. Goodbye." At the door, they turned, "Thank you."

Jesse sat smiling, staring after them, thinking, *amici*.

But the sun distracted him as it flickered on the wall of the galley. His eyes went up to the dishes and glasses and silver mugs. *Someday we'll eat in here at my galley table. We'll send all the food up in that dumbwaiter!*

But it's time to go pick vegetables with Gemma. At the door he stopped. His head turned back. He stepped back. His eyebrows accordioned, looking at the galley.

"That's not right." He moved closer, counting the dishes. "There are only six. There are supposed to be eight." He moved sideways, "Same with the glasses. And the silver mugs. They're missing!"

Jesse did not go to the garden.

CHAPTER FIFTY-TWO

MISSING

Jesse went to Gemma's office. The leather-cased binoculars: missing. He went to the living room. The painting of the moon glade: missing. He slid open the dining room cupboard. The little statues of the bald man and the rabbit: missing. The blue-and-white china—two large plates and bowls, two little plates and bowls, cups, and saucers: missing. *And don't forget Gemma's blue-and-white vase!*

Jesse felt calamity bursting in his chest. *Gemma did not put all these things in a different place! Some pilfer-looter took them! The Dorkings? They could have taken them when we were out sailing? Or today during the market? But how'd they get in?* He heard Greta's voice, *The Dorkings—they steal into any place. Like rats.*

"The treasure rooms!" He ran out to the barn, frantically tapping in the code. He folded the muslin back, smelling Lily's perfume, and noticed that everything was arranged differently. His eyes scanned up and down, across the table.

Oh no! The lapis blue geode—rarest—most valuable: missing!

Jesse's head was spinning. *Tell Gemma! Yes. But be calm. No Calamity John.*

Gemma was still in the garden. He calmly walked under the

cherry tree, but just as he was about to cross the driveway, Miss Lily drove in. She bounced out of her car, calling, "Hello, Jesse!" and walked with him to Gemma. "I have had another marvelous day. How was your market day?"

Jesse didn't get a chance to reply, as Gemma recounted the details of this wonderful day. Jesse stood silent, wondering, *Dorkings. But wait a minute! Why would the Dorkings take dishes? And if they did, why take only two of everything? There are three of those boys.*

He looked at Lily. *Could Miss Lily be taking things?* He thought of her perfume aroma in the treasure room. But he suddenly felt like a Calamity John. *Don't be ridiculous!*

He decided. *I'll keep my mouth shut. I'll write to Conor. See what he thinks.* To his surprise, he saw the mailman stop at their mailbox, and he ran down the driveway. He was utterly delighted, "Two letters! Oh! And a postcard."

The postcard was a picture of New York City. Jesse turned it over. *C U soon.* He remembered the day he left New York City. The Shark House kid gave him that other postcard.

"Who is sending this?" But Jesse shrugged, eager to read Conor's letter.

Dear Jesse,

Your dreams came true! You and Gemma were born for each other! I'm sure you are learning more and more of farm life each day, and you will have wonderful tales to tell!

And my dreams have come true. Rob Dana, the theater owner, is wonderful! His daughter is his right-hand man—so to speak—and she is wonderful, too. It's great to have Amanda here. It's like Dearie's theater. All good. So good.

> *It's great that we can write letters to each other. And I'm happy to know Miss Lily is there for you and Gemma. Just so you know, if ever you and Gemma need help, you can count on Peter Murphy. Well, all for now ...*
>
> *Love, Conor*

Amanda's was next:

> *Dear Jesse,*
> *Well, I declare! You have found the most beautiful island and the most beautiful farm with the most beautiful grandmother—my sister, Gemma! This Dana Theater is wonderful, but if I had my druthers, I'd love to live there with you. I think of darlin' you every day! You are a treasure! I'm happy to know that Lily is there for both you and Gemma.*
> *Take care, you love-adore!*
> *Your Great Aunt (!) Amanda*

Wrapped in loving words, Jesse floated up the driveway as the dogs began barking at a truck turning in. "Oh, it's Peter! And Charlie!"

Gemma and Lily smiled when they saw them. Charlie hopped out and opened a satchel, holding up the black-and-white photographs he had taken. Gemma invited them to her workshop, where he placed them, one by one, on her work bench.

"Oh, my! These are wonderful photographs!" Gemma bubbled. "Everyone is so jolly!"

Jesse squeezed in between Lily and Gemma and saw photos of Amanda and Conor. He held up his letters, "Amanda and Conor!"

But Lily spoke over him, "Oh this one is a treasure! I'm in a snowfall of cherry blossoms! May I have this?"

Charlie grinned, "Take them all! I developed them myself, so I still have the negatives."

Smiling, Gemma stacked them up, "We shall enjoy perusing these after dinner. I believe I shall create a new scrapbook when I have the time."

Peter smirked, "Groucho says, *Time flies like an arrow. Fruit flies like a banana.*"

Gemma quirkled. Then she tittered, "Oh! Fruit flies. Insects. That is amusing."

"Yup, that's our Peter!" Charlie slapped him on the back, "a porcupine needling us with his Groucho jokes!"

Ignoring him, Peter held up a long, rolled paper.

"Ah, your blueprints." Gemma reached for them, "Let us see what you have created."

Jesse wanted to see Peter's plans, but Lily took his hand, "It's left to us to bring in the harvest." At the *potager*, she picked up the basket. "I wanted to tell you, Jesse. I've been fitting up my rooms, with a little artwork. And I took some things from your yacht—dishes and glasses and such. I do like my late-night snacks."

Jesse felt his shoulders fall in complete relief. *Thank-golly-goodness I didn't say anything!* He blurted to Lily, "Well, someday I'd like to eat in my yacht. But till then, it's okay."

He showed Lily his letters, saying, "Conor and Amanda are love-adores!"

"Yes! A treasure!"

Jesse decided to overlook her treasure craze, and answered sincerely, "I know this place is full of treasure!"

Gemma left the men in her workshop and joined Lily and Jesse in the kitchen, "Oh, I see you are underway with the vegetables." She smiled, "Thank you, Lily. Your halo is shining!"

Jesse thought that was a neat way to say that Lily was an angel.

Quickly, a cold chicken dinner was on the table, and Jesse shared his Conor and Amanda letters. Gemma was heart-touched with the glowing references to her, as was Lily.

But a knock at the door interrupted, and Peter's head appeared. "Sorry to barge in," he began. "Gemma, we were looking for your leather tool pouch, but we can't find it."

Oh no! Jesse churned, *something else missing! Oh, my goggles! Is it Peter and Charlie taking the things? The lapis geode is missing—and they were in the treasure room—alone!*

Lily's velvet voice warmed, "Jesse, I remember you had that case the day I arrived."

"But I ..." he stumbled, still stuck on the possibility that it could be Peter and Charlie.

Gemma stood up. "I must have put it aside in my rush to prepare our presentation for the market. I shall find it tomorrow. Thank you for informing me."

"Thank you," Peter smiled, "As Groucho says, *We've had a perfectly wonderful evening. But this wasn't it.*" He chuckled, waving his hand. "I hope you find the tool pouch."

Charlie poked in, "We'll be back to show you our progress. Have a good night."

Lily fingered her knife and her red lipstick curled, "Good night, boys."

CHAPTER FIFTY-THREE

SLY

Lily prepared the after-dinner tea tray and Jesse bid them goodnight. He was keen to write to Conor and Amanda and Billy.

He told each of them pretty much the same things: *solving the treasure-room code; the market in Port Haven (He told Billy to thank Mrs. Romano for her ideas about presentations.); playing Chinquapin; reading* Dearie's Journal; *the missing things and Miss Lily's explanation that she had taken them to decorate her rooms ... and the mysterious postcard.*

He finished with: *Well, everything else is hunky-dory, as Miss Lily and Miss Peggy like to say. Love, Jesse*

Jesse fell into bed, turned out the light, and yawned heartily. But just as he was drifting off into his wispy-slips, he heard a deep hoot, followed by a sharp yelp. Startled, he sat up.

"Golly! It's so dark here!" He peered through the window and found a slip of the moon hanging over the Star Cupola, with a bright star cradled in its crescent. As Jesse gazed at the beautiful sky picture, another hoot sounded, and the silhouette of an owl opened its wings and launched off the barn roof into the deep dark air. Jesse chuckled, remembering Officer Owl back in New York and all the other animals that seemed to ripple through his imagination.

With that, another yelp rang out. And there, at the cherry tree, was another animal: a lone fox, gazing upward. They stared at each other. Jesse saw a sly, clever look glinting in its eyes. "Kitsune," he whistered, and the fox scuttled off. Jesse scuttled back to bed.

Downstairs, Lily and Gemma were cozied up, sipping tea and chatting, still sharing their wonderful day.

"Speaking of wonderful," Lily raised her eyebrows, "Jesse has solved the code for the treasure-room door! I watched him open it this morning."

"Yes, he is quite the clever one. He seems to know and understand things far beyond his age. And his ability to solve puzzles reminds me so of my own Papa."

"Hmmm. Well … Gemma," Lily began a new topic cautiously. "Something has happened that I must share with you. Jesse doesn't know that I saw him, but I truly think you should know. The oriental blue-and-white vase? Jesse wanted to put it in his yacht room, and he … well … it is broken. He was so upset he threw it all away. I don't want him in trouble, but I didn't feel right keeping it from you."

Gemma gaspered, pausing a moment before she spoke. "I am disquieted. Not for the vase. It is simply an object—yes, a precious one to be sure. But I am disturbed that Jesse would not speak to me."

"Oh, please don't talk to him about this. At least not now. Jesse is just a little boy. Alone here with two women he doesn't know. He needs to feel safe and secure. To trust us. He needs to feel he can rely on us. I know you lost your daughter, Jane. Let's not lose Jesse."

Gemma's eyes were leaking at the edges. She pulled out a handkerchief and dabbed away the wetness, smiling weakly at Lily. "Thank you. You are an angel."

The morning barn duties were filled with Greta's bubbling recollections of their market-day successes. "The ferry ride was great! Your present-tations! And I love the Chinquapin!"

Jesse suggested, "How 'bout we play Chinquapin again this afternoon?"

"Yah!"

"Maybe Gemma will play!"

They set up the game between the barn and the carriage house—and Gemma was thrilled to join them. She came out of her workshop with a perfect-sized batting stick.

"A Chinquapin bat: properly sized to properly strike the Chinquapin!"

Hitting and yelling, running and shouting, catching and hooting—were all accompanied by the excited dogs, barking and racing about! The game went on and on. When Gemma raced safely back to home base, she twittered, "I have not exerted myself in this manner in …"

"… a Chinquapin's age!" Jesse snickled.

Gemma bent over, resting her hands on her knees, "I believe I have utterly stretched every muscle in my body—including my vocal cords." She stood up and surprised them, "Shall we pause for an ice-cream treat? We can go into town. To A.P. Carey's drugstore."

Agog, Jesse followed her indoors as she went to her pottery jar for her change. "Are you sure you want to go into town, Gemma? I mean …"

"I shall mirror your example, Jesse. If you can do it, I can, too!" She put her forehead to his, "Gangbusters!"

This didn't even sound like Gemma. But she smiled, bounding to the old truck and taking the driver's seat. The three youngsters bounced into the back of the truck, heading for the corner drugstore in town.

As Gemma parked the truck in front of the block of storefronts, Jesse saw Miss Lily's car. "Look! Miss Lily's in the telephone booth down the street."

Gemma's face beamed, "Ah! Perchance she would like to join us. Jesse, would you please offer our invitation?"

Now that sounded like Gemma.

Jesse saw Morton Mealy in his truck. He decided to take a shortcut, past the pesky squirrel, by scrambling up the dirt path to the top of the hill, above the telephone booth. He was about to slide down and knock on the glass booth, when he heard Lily's voice turn shrill:

"Stop calling me Tina Braedon! You know how I hate my name!"

Silence.

"No! Tim! Don't come here! You'll muck it up! Like you did at the Shark House."

Silence.

"No, brother dear," she said in that velvet voice of hers, "I've got everything in place. I'm in now. They think I am an angel. I know every inch of this place. And I know how to make Jesse tell me where the treasure is."

Silence.

"Not if I get the treasure first!" She hung up.

PART TEN

SHIVERALS

The sea change
blew tranquility
into turbulent shivers.

CHAPTER FIFTY-FOUR

BAD TIDINGS

Jesse froze. Heart pounding. Breath stopping. He gawked at Miss Lily. Still standing in the phone booth. Jesse could see her checking her lipstick in a little mirror.

Oh please! Don't look up! Don't look up!

He bolted backward, crab-crawling to the dirt path, slinking down to the row of shops … his mind in wild alarm. *Tim Braedon is Lily's brother? Her name is really Tina? Tina and Tim! Brother and sister! Oh, my goggles! Nothing Lily said is true! Wait! Isn't Tim Braedon in jail?*

He stopped. *Tell Gemma.* He stopped again. *No. I can't.* He felt Gemma's pooh-poohs: *'Calamity John!'* Jesse took a deep breath. T-H-I-N-K, *he told himself, remembering Dearie.*

....

Jesse, if you are facing something gruff and rough, you can always stop and do your
    T-H-I-N-K. Remember?
    T: Take a deep breath.
    H: Hold yourself high.
    I: Imagine how you really want to feel ... right ...
    N: Now. And finally ...
    K: Know: All is well.
    Do you feel it, Jesse? The stillness. The calm. Look for it.

....

Jesse had to take a deep, deep breath before he felt his calm, before he truly felt, *All Is Well.* He quietly asked himself, *Do I go to the police?* But he answered himself: *Don't be a calamity. I don't know anything. Nothing has happened.* He breathed again, *Ohhh? What about all the missing things?* He wagged his head. *No. I don't know. What if Gemma did put them away?*

He turned around—right into Miss Lily. His autopilot invited: "Ice cream?"

"Oh Jesse, you are the best! Just what I need!" She took his hand. Jesse felt a jolt go up his arm. Into his heart. But she held on, and they walked into the drugstore together.

Licking his ice cream, Jesse was quiet. He thought, *Greta and Matts were suspicious of Lily from the beginning.* He tilted close and whispered to them, "I have to talk to you."

They nodded, and Jesse swiveled on the stool, facing Gemma, "Can we walk home, Gemma? Greta and Matts know the roads through Harbor Hill, and I want to learn that way."

"That is a brilliant idea, Jesse," Gemma rusheled. "Lily and I shall enjoy our ice cream and meet you at home."

The three children were no sooner out the door when Lily licked her ice cream and leaned toward Gemma. "I feel like I am the bearer of bad tidings. Jesse is such a dear, but I think you should know, he is collecting things. This morning I saw him, putting the Uncle Sam penny bank, and that coded cylinder, some shells and geodes inside the dumbwaiter."

Gemma stopped licking her ice cream. "Oh, dear," she paused. "Jesse? Thieving?" She swiped the napkin across her lips. "My possessions are not ostensibly important. But I must speak to such purloining."

Lily quickly interrupted. "There's more. You see, I was on the phone with my cousin, Peggy, in New York City. Jesse was arrested for stealing."

"Arrested? Jesse?"

"Yes, stealing cash from the produce business where he worked. It happened just before he left to come here."

Gemma's eyebrows puckered. "This is a horse of a different color." She was silent, her eyes shifting back and forth. She looked at Lily. "It is incongruous. Jesse? Pilfering?"

"I have a thought," Lily tilted her chin. "Conceivably, Jesse's thieving is a way to feel he has something of his own. After all, he's been uprooted from his old life. Maybe if you give him something personal. Like the things he carries in his pocket. Something like that compass you keep on your desk. You know, something from you. Keep up his faith with you. Then later you can talk to him about … pilf– … purloi– … stealing."

Gratefully, Gemma looked at her, "What a wise idea. Oh, thank you, Lily. I know I say it often enough, but you truly are such an angel."

The three children were no sooner out the door when Jesse gasped his story to Greta and Matts—beginning with his kidnap by Tim Braedon back in New York City last Christmas. It was a long story. He ended with Lily's phone call and the two C U postcards he had received. "They must be from Tim! He's coming here!"

Greta stopped, *"Ich glaube, mein Schwein pfeift!"*

"What?"

"I think my pig is whistling!" She wagged, "It means—this is unbelievable! You must tell Gemma." Matts nodded in agreement.

"No!" Jesse exasperated. "She's traptured. To her, I'm a Calamity John and Lily's an angel."

Greta understood. "Yah, like Dearie's story of Fear Doirich and Sadbha." She nodded, "Gemma is traptured by Lily."

"Tricky. Lily is so tricky!" Jesse's head wagged. "She makes up a story for everything! She's just like Tim Braedon!" He gasped, "Oh, no! That means she took everything, and she must be selling everything! And this stupid treasure! There is no treasure!"

"Yah, but Lily thinks there is. And her brudder, too—this Tim Break-In—he vill come. You need grown-up help. Police."

Jesse was thoughtful. "In New York City I knew the Police—Hannity and Detective Rocco." He smiled, *and the Possum and Owl!* "But here ... well, I know Officer Patrulha."

They reached Windmill Road and looked down to the creek. "Peter!" Jesse shouted. "Conor said, if I need help, I can count on Peter!"

The twins brightened, and Greta said, "Yah! Peter! Tell Peter everything. He can call police."

Jesse shiveraled, thinking of Tim Braedon. "If Tim is out of jail, he'll be here. Soon. I just know it."

CHAPTER FIFTY-FIVE

A LITTLE MAGIC

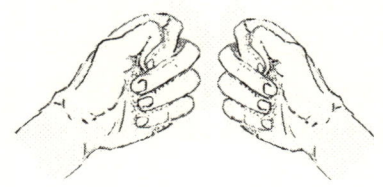

At the Creek House, Peter was standing on the large wooden raft floating on the breezy water. Running towards him, Jesse blurted, "Peter, we have to talk to you!"

Behind him, Greta exclaimed, "Help!"

Peter stopped them, quietly pointing to the marsh grasses. "A fox. Clever, patient."

"Kitsune," Jesse murmeled. "A knave and a thief!"

"You're likely right, there," Peter swayed with the raft, "He's smelling out the nests of the white herons, for sure."

The children watched the fox raise his nose to the late afternoon sun. He yelped! Clear and sharp. Then he tunneled through the long grasses, and popped out into the field, heading back to Windy Hill. Jesse thought, *Just like Lily-Tina. She'll be back at Windy Hill.*

But Peter jiggered a laugh, corralling the children up the plank, and quoting his favorite, Groucho Marx: "*Now, you can leave in a huff, or you can leave in a minute and a huff!*"

Jesse was not amused. Peter didn't want to hear their story. Peter's way. No gossip.

Deflated, Jesse held his tongue, while his hopes flowed away like water under the creek bridge. He took out Dearie's stone and Greta reached to touch it. "Yah," she murmeled. "Yah."

Peter stood at his Creek House door. "Jesse, your uncle Conor said to call him if you need help." He opened the door. "Call him."

The three children looked at each other, and wide-eyed, they stepped inside Peter's "Nautical Knick-Knack Nook." He pulled a pad of paper off the wall. "Here's Conor's number."

"How do you have Conor's telephone number?"

"Conor called me and left a telephone number if you needed to reach him." Peter handed Jesse the phone receiver.

Speaking to the operator slowly and deliberately, Jesse heard the phone ringing on the other end. When Conor answered, he held the phone so that Greta and Matts could hear.

"Jesse?" Conor questioned, "Is everything all right?"

"Oh Conor! I'm so glad to hear you!"

Jesse closed his eyes and felt a warmth flood over his heart. His sparkles blinked behind his eyelids, and he felt his Circle of Lights. He had no idea how big his Circle truly was, but at the moment, it didn't matter. He felt safe. And protected. And loved.

"Yes, Jesse," Conor reassured, "I love hearing you, too. But why are you calling?"

Jesse told him of all the things gone missing. But when he repeated Miss Lily's telephone call with Tim Braedon, Conor was dumfounded. Nevertheless, he didn't want to frighten Jesse. He spoke lightly.

"I think you're on to something, Jesse. I'm going to call Hannity in New York and see what's up. In the meantime, you sit tight. Act like nothing is going on. Don't tell Gemma anything more. It sounds like Miss Lily has her all wrapped up. You just sit tight. And if you need anything, you go straight to Peter. He can sort things out for you."

"Okay. Sit tight," Jesse repeated to Greta and Matts. "I will, Conor. Oh, I'm so glad I talked to you, Conor." He smiled, adding, "All is well!"

He felt Conor smile, "And so it is!"

Greta took Matts hand and held it tight, "Conor is goot," she said sincerely. "He vill call Police." She touched Jesse's arm. Matts squeezed her arm, and she added, "Ve sit tight, too."

"All good," Peter smiled. "Now you can leave *in a huff!*" This time they chuckled.

Outside, Greta turned to Jesse. "Good luck. *Ich drücke dir die Daumen.*"

Jesse smiled and they all pressed their thumbs.

The dogs barked their welcome-home greeting when Gemma's truck pulled in. Jesse was setting the table for dinner, wondering how to act like nothing was going on. When she walked in, he impulsively hugged her, blurting, "Gemma, that was a great ice-cream treat!"

But unexpectedly, he pulled away. "Uhhh …" His stomach rolled, lurching up into his throat. His mouth opened in a large O—and a cannon shot of a BURP erupted—"*B-U-RRR-P!*"

Jesse was astonished. "Oh …! Oh golly! I … excuse me!"

But Gemma was laughing. Jesse looked at her face. She was exploding in laughter! Her body, collapsing in laughter! He blurted a great laugh himself—as big as the BURP! The two of them sparked each other like firecrackers, pointing at each other, laughing their heads off, doubled up, holding their bellies. Jesse gasped, shaking uncontrollably. He slapped the table, and for no reason at all, it made him laugh harder. Gemma fell into a chair, and he heard a long, "A-h-h-h-h-h …" He looked up at her—and their giddies erupted again.

Jesse thought of Old Barrett's saying:

One moment of magic can transform your world.

He never thought a BURP counted as magic, but it certainly changed his little world. He loved the ridiculous, euphoric laughter.

This was the scene that greeted Lily. She looked from one to the other. But there was no explaining such hysteria. She walked to her rooms, and the sound of her heels clicking across the floor made them go mad with more laughter. Gemma helplessly dangled in her chair, and Jesse draped himself over the side of his chair.

Gradually, their hooting-howling slipped down the rungs of laughter ... and dissolved. Jesse went to Gemma and stood at her knees. "Cracker Jacks! That was a giggle-snicken to the stars and back!" He kissed her forehead. "I love you Gemma ... right up to the stars! I'm gonna rub in my kiss so you can keep it with you." He gently pushed his fingers around her forehead ... as he had done for Liam Maguire—oh, it seemed like ages ago.

Gemma pulled Jesse close. Her eyes were already wet from so much giddiness, but a tear trickled out. And feeling somewhat confused, she couldn't help herself, whispering, "I love you, Jesse. To the stars ... and back here to Windy Hill."

CHAPTER FIFTY-SIX

BROODING

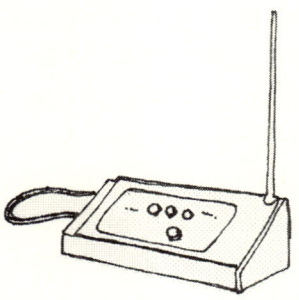

After dinner, Jesse interrupted Gemma's tea. "Gemma what is this *Theremin* machine? With the one loop antenna and the one straight antenna?"

Gemma smiled at Jesse's curiosity. "It is a musical instrument." She pulled it out, placed it on the piano, and plugged it in. "The antennas feel the vibrations in my hands. The one is for notes that go up and down with my hand movement. The other antenna is the volume."

Slowly, an eerie, unreal sound came forth ... mysterious ... ghostly.

"Oh, my goggles! I feel shiverals all over!"

Lily had her hand at her throat. "That is frightening!"

Gemma chuckled. "Yes, it is quite unearthly! But I do not wish to frighten you."

She unplugged it, saying, "Lily, I want to tell you how very fond I am of you. I enjoy your company so, and you are a model of young womanhood. So accomplished. So clever."

So wicked, thought Jesse, feeling wicked for thinking so. He shiveraled. *No. I have to remember my Rule of Tongue: Make sure the words on my tongue taste delicious.* He sighed, kissing Gemma goodnight and light-footing it up to his yacht.

Lying on the bed with *Dearie's Journal*, Jesse moogled. *I've got a case of the feisty-dregs.* He thought of Greta's word for it—*mürisch. Yeah, I'm grumpy. Elizabethtown is not New York City. Gemma is not Dearie. And ... I am missing Conor ... and Amanda, too.* He prickled and smirfed, *Great Aunt Amanda! Amanda would drawl at me: 'Jesse, yew can just get glad in the same pants yew got mad in!'*

He giggled and commanded himself, "Pivot!" But he sighed, "Pivot to ... what?" Jesse hugged *Dearie's Journal* to his chest. All at once, surprisingly, he heard ... Jane!

Oh, Jesse! You are a love-adore!

You know you love Gemma and Ellie-cat and Sadie and Red. You love this farm, the gardens, the fields, the Star Cupola! You love Greta and Matts. Peter, Murphy, and Darling. Charlie, too. You love going to town: past the Creek and Linger Longer Farm, Bethesda and Bertrand Philhips. The town shops and the people.

Suddenly, Jesse knew that James was here, too.

Listen, Jesse! You know! You love sailing and every day outdoors. Oh, you love the barn! The animals. You even love the manure pile. (Jesse smiled.) *Well maybe, 'like.'* (He chuckled.) *Maybe you're just used to it.* (Laughter twinkled through Jesse's heart, and he heard Jane finish.)

Oh, Jesse, be the love-adore you are!

Ellie-cat hopped up and strode across his bed. Jesse—and Ellie—didn't know they were about to be entertained!

First, Jesse noticed the tops of Ellie's ears, reflected in the mirror on the wall: two little grey triangles moving across the bottom of the mirror. Ellie saw them, too. She stopped. Stared. Moved to the left. Oh! The triangles moved with her. She sat up. Startled. Her head was looking back at her. As she stared at herself, her paw slowly reached up behind her head, curiously patting her ear. Her eyes kaleidoscoped, wide and spinning.

Jesse wanted to laugh. But he didn't move. This was enchanting. Ellie-cat was discovering her ears! Over and over, she moved this way and that, watching her triangles move with her, and sitting up, to eagerly—strangely—pet her own ears, pawing at them like they belonged to some other animal.

Jesse couldn't contain himself another second, and laughter burst from his cheeks. He lay on his bed, giggling, watching Ellie-cat examine her soft, furry little appendages.

"Ellie! You are a love-adore!" He rolled on his side, "I guess we're both love-adores! And that feels lots better than Calamity John."

He tickled Ellie's ears and moved to his nightly rituals: kissing Jane's thimble and laying out his knife and stone. It was so good to have his stone back. He grimmeled, *It wasn't lost!* But a dark shiver passed through his shoulders. *Miss Lily. She had it all the time.*

Still, he shook himself and tapped Velvet on the nose. He picked her up, as his head hit the pillow. Like Ellie-cat, she was softer than ever, though the velvet bunny had lost most of her stuffing and the threads on her face had faded. Jesse held her close to his cheek and closed his eyes, feeling Ellie-cat curl at his feet.

The sun rose like a ball of fire, and Jesse felt the heat in the morning mist. Oddly, Lily was out early, just as Greta and Matts arrived.

Jesse felt relieved. Lily would be away all day.

"Vhat is news?" Greta asked, as they opened the high-mounted barn windows.

"Nothing really," Jesse's shoulders twitched. "Gemma told Lily she adores her." His chin shuddered. "I went to bed."

Greta assured him. "Ve sit tight. With you, Jesse."

Walking back from the pasture, Matts touched Greta's hand and she remembered, "Oh, today we go with Mutter to Port Haven. In the afternoon, you get the animals alone."

Jesse wiped the sweat trickling down his cheek, "Don't worry, I can do it." He thought, *And no daisy-daster.*

Maybe it was the heat rising. Maybe it was the gentle cows and the feisty goats. Maybe it was remembering the laughter with Gemma. But, when Jesse returned for breakfast with Gemma, he did not sit tight. He told. He blabbed. The story of Tim Braedon.

"Tim Braedon," Gemma mused, "That is a name I seem to know."

"Yes. You knew Tim Braedon's father. Tim told me his father worked here during the Depression and he knew you and Jane—when she was little."

"Ah. Yes." Gemma's shoulders shivered slightly. "Yes. That is it."

Jesse continued with his story of the younger Tim Braedon in New York City, stealing, pawn-broking, and kidnapping. Gemma was horrified when she heard 'kidnap.'

"Why are you telling me this, Jesse?"

"Because Miss Lily is Tim Braedon's sister! I heard her on the telephone. Her real name is Tina. She's stealing things. And Tim is out of jail, coming here. For the treasure."

Gemma boshed, "This is preposterous. The fact that she is his sister does not make her a thief." She sniffed. "You are giving rise to something dangerous. I do not perceive Lily as a dangerous person, and certainly not a thief. Your imagination is getting the better of you. Lily is at work all day. She has no time to undertake a search for treasure. Let us talk no more of it."

Jesse moaned inwardly. *Conor was right. I should've kept quiet. What if she tells Lily?*

Gemma stood up. "Come."

Jesse followed her to the pantry, where she opened the dumbwaiter. He peered inside, his nose smelling Lily's perfume, his eyes puzzling. "Why is the Uncle Sam Bank in here?" He pulled out the tray, and picked up the cylinder, covered in alphabet tiles, from Jane's room. There were shells and pyrite and small geodes on the tray, too. "Why are these here?"

"Jesse," Gemma's lips thinned, "remember: *res ipsa loquitor ... it speaks for itself.* You placed these things here."

"No ... Nooo *loquitor!* I didn't. I would never take these things. I ..." His thoughts stampeded like an army on horseback, and he almost shouted, "Oh no! Miss Lily did this! Can't you smell her perfume? She is so tricky! She's blaming me!"

Gemma was bewildered. *Lily? Jesse? Who is telling the truth?*

"Come." She led him to her office, turning on the small wooden fan and sitting at her desk. She reached for the compass with the blue-and-gold Freemason design. "This is a directional compass and a moral compass. Both. To find one's way. It is a symbol of integrity, honesty, and honor. And it is a continual gift. From one generation to the next." A faint smile crossed her lips, and she said, "I now gift this compass to the next in line—you, Jesse."

She gently dropped it in his hand, quoting Shakespeare: *"To thine own self be true."* She sighed, "Find your way, Jesse. Find your True North."

Jesse was speechless. He was aware of wings fluttering in his heart. Yet he felt a decided *thump* in his throat.

CHAPTER FIFTY-SEVEN

COMPASS

Jesse let the compass fall into his pocket, and hugging Gemma, he quoted Jane:

"Oh, the magic webs we weave, when first we practice to believe."

Gemma embraced him, and they each wondered about the other ... the love and trust they wished to feel. *All is well,* Jesse breathed hopefully. *All is well.*

In the barn, Jesse pushed the hay bales down and spent the morning weeding the garden; Gemma opened the cold frames and planted the greenery from the pots. After lunch, she went to her workshop, and Jesse decided to re-explore Windy Hill—with the aid of his new-old compass. All over the house, he discovered that the rooms were perfectly square to north, south, east and west. He saw the architect's square on the compass lid. *Everything fair and square*, he smiled.

But his smile did not last long. He also discovered that more things were missing: another small, framed art piece, two silver chargers, and the crystal salt-and-pepper shakers. "Golly, Miss Lily is robbing Gemma blind! Oh, and what about the treasure rooms?"

He dashed outdoors. Instantly, he felt the humidity. So thick he could almost taste the heat in the air. Opening the barn door he felt the dense smell of cows, goats, and chickens ... hay, grain, and manure. In the treasure room, the 'missings' were easy to see: every shelf from every table on the first floor was missing items. Miss Lily had not even bothered to rearrange them or cover them with the muslin. He could see that the pyrite, the green geodes, and beautiful clear amber were gone, but he wasn't sure of anything else.

His thoughts ran wild, *I need to drag Gemma over here. Make her see!* But he knew—she did not want to see or hear. *Miss Lily is an angel. And that's that.*

Leaving the barn, he decided to explore the second floor of the stone carriage house. Gemma once said it was an old office nobody had used in years and years. He climbed the stone stairs, noticing, "Ohhh! It's so nice and cool in here!"

At the top, he peered inside. "Definitely an office." Long rolled papers filled a standing metal box labeled: *Blueprints*. Jesse sat at a high, slanted drawing desk with stacks of old tablets on a shelf. Hopping down, he noticed another room around the corner wall.

It was a parlor. A dusty blanket and pillow were left rumpled on an old sofa. He murmeled, "Someone slept here." Looking closer, he added, "Hmmm, a long time ago." Beside the sofa was a small chest. In the top drawer: a half dozen loose cigarettes, so old the paper was yellow-brown and brittle, a matchbook, sticky-looking wrappers of chewing gum and beef jerky. pencils and erasers. In the bottom drawer were old socks and yellowed t-shirts, a collared shirt, and a moth-eaten sweater. He reckoned, *Someone left in a hurry. Left this stuff behind.*

Jesse had a memory-whiff. Mildew. *Oh,* he shivered, *Tim Braedon. Aech!*

He plopped down on the sofa, and the cushion tilted upward. A pencil poked out. Putting his hand down the crevice, he felt a tablet of paper. It was filled with pencil drawings. "Gosh, these are optical illusions." His brain skipped a beat. *Like Miss Lily's drawings. And here's ... the Eye of Providence!* He stared at the drawings. His eyes focused on the signature: *T. Braedon.*

Jesse's mind bounced. *Tim Braedon? No ... not Tim. It's Tim's father! Tim told me his father had been here. Yes. His drawings are just like Miss Lily's, especially the Eye of Providence: the triangle and rays of light, just like the invisible Eye on the trap door to the manure room.*

In Detective mode, Jesse was putting the puzzle together: *Tim and Tina Braedon. Brother and sister. Searching for treasure. Just like their father.*

Now Tim Braedon is coming here! Jesse held his head with both hands. A light snapped in his mind. *Tina—Miss Lily—wants the treasure. All to herself. If Tim is coming, she must be going after it. Soon.*

PART ELEVEN
TRAPTURED

*It was dark
inside that laugh.*

CHAPTER FIFTY-EIGHT

LUGGAGE

A car pulled into the driveway, and Jesse looked out the window of the carriage house. *Miss Lily. But why is she parking at the barn?*

Jesse saw her going back and forth to the trunk, moving items, clearing space. She had on her red blouse. He thought of Margarethe, twisting her button and warning: "It is ze devil wears red." *Margarethe knew the whole time.*

Jesse watched Lily pull something out of her purse and go into the barn. When she came out, she deposited something back into her purse, and left it in the car. Swiping at her brow, she tossed her hair back and sauntered to the house, a curious smile stuck in her red lipstick.

What is she doing? Jesse decided to find out.

In the dreadly heat, he silently opened the door of her little white car and skinnied through. He accordioned to the floor and reached for Miss Lily's purse. *Now, what's so secret?*

Pulling the purse open, he saw a bottle of pills in the pocket at the top. In the bottom was the long brown envelope he remembered from the train ride. He opened it and found a stack of stuffed envelopes, each with a business card at the top. He read: *Schuyler—Bonheur—Romano—Gorecki. The apartment Misters ... back in New York City?*

Under each card, a running total of dollar amounts went down the side. The first was dated from January. *That's when Miss Peggy started working at the Misters' businesses.*

There was one other envelope, set up in the same way, but it read: *Antiques and Collectibles ~ Union City.* Below was written: *Windy Hill.* With a long list of items. Jesse recognized the missing items. Even the tool pouch was listed.

Opening an envelope, Jesse gaspered. "Diggity-Boo! It's filled with bills! BIG MONEY!" He opened each envelope. "Oh, my glory! Whopping money!"

Jesse was sweating. It was hot-Hot-HOT! But he sat, dripping astonishments.

He reached for the other luggage bag. Pressing the latch-button, the top popped up, and Jesse's bottom popped off the floor!

Ewww! What IS that? A hairy dead animal? Great gargoyles!! But he calmed. *Ohhh. It's a wig. Curly brown hair.* He thought of Miss Peggy. He looked deeper inside. *A pair of eye-glasses, like Miss Peggy's. A funny little piece of rubber—like a nose guard. A navy-blue dress with the plain white collar like Miss Peggy's. A small, plain purse like Miss Peggy's.*

Oh—my—golly—gargoyles! His eyes waggled. *There is no Miss Peggy! There is only Miss Lily. Miss Peggy-Lily-Tina-whatever-her-name-is! She ... oh, my gosh ... she really is an optical illusion! And a tattle-lips liar!*

And Jesse was certain: *This money belongs to the New York City Misters. And Gemma! C-r-a-c-k-e-r Jacks!*

His lips drew tight. He shut the luggage lid and put the envelope in the purse. Sliding out of the car, he took the purse in one hand and the luggage bag in the other, and sliddered down the hill behind the barn. His brain was ticking like a stopwatch.

I have to hide this from Tina and Tim. Keep it safe. Conor said, sit tight. But I need help. I'll go tell Peter. Oh, but first I have to get the animals. No, first I have to hide these. I know! In the chicken-grain cabinet!

Entering the lower barn, the heat and smell almost knocked him over. Nonetheless, he ran up and slid the bags into the cabinet. Closing it, he looked at the clock high on the wall. "I've gotta hurry."

It was hotter than ever when Jesse came out of the barn. Grasshoppers were springing out of the fields like popcorn, and birds were darting after them like arrows. The dogs were nowhere to be seen. But Jesse figured they were too hot to tag along with him.

Out in the pasture, Jesse saw Monet's leaning tree, shading the lolling cow and calf and the two languid goats.

But Jesse was surprised by a burly little bundle, waddling around the trunk of the tree. It clawed its way upward and sat in the crook of the branches. Jesse gaspered, seeing the black mask around its bright black eyes.

"A raccoon!" Jesse thought, *Detective Rocco—Rocky Raccoon! I could really use his help. I've gotta go get help!* But the cows mooed. The goats bleated. Calling him to his farm duties.

The animals ambled slowly through the muggy air, and Jesse felt another Rocky: Rachmaninoff. The *Rhapsody on a Theme from Paganini.* It seemed to pulse its gentle adagio through each hoof, softly hitting the earth. Rachmaninoff's calming music ruffled through Jesse's mind like the ruffling grasses in the fields.

Getting the animals into the barn, Jesse again felt the urge to get help, so lickety-split, he mucked out, put the stinky-hot manure in the vault, washed the shovel and put down clean hay. He ran up to clean the chicken cages, dumping the poop into the trap door. Lastly, he poured water and grain into the hen cages, let the chickens in, and closed up the barn.

Outside, he stopped. The fox! Kitsune was standing at the stone wall. It's eyes glittering, its nose sniffing. It yelped, and Jesse jumped, thinking, *It's yako! The dangerous Kitsune. Disguised as a beautiful woman. It's Miss Lily-Peggy-Tina!*

Jesse ran. Down through the fields toward Peter's Creek House. He saw Morton Mealy's beat-up truck, rattling up Windmill Road. Sherlock Holmes—Squirrel Nutkin—did not wave. But someone in the passenger seat waved. Jesse didn't see who it was. Likewise, Jesse didn't see Mealy stop at the top of the hill. He didn't see the passenger get out, salute goodbye to Mealy, and disappear into the woods behind Windy Hill Farm.

CHAPTER FIFTY-NINE

STORM COMING

Jesse saw Charlie working on the motor of a skiff moored at the creek. Peter was across the street, on his creek raft, preparing for bad weather. Jesse ran down the plank to help, quietly handing him the rakes and traps and buckets. Peter stored every jot-and-tittle in a huge cupboard built onto the back of the Creek House.

Charlie arrived and they went inside. Jesse followed, silently. Once inside, Peter poured water, saying, "Sometimes Groucho Marx is serious. He once said, *I, not events, have the power to make me happy or unhappy today. I can choose which it shall be.*"

They sat on his galley benches, and Peter looked at Jesse, "Don't let events decide for you, Jesse."

Jesse thought that sounded a lot like Dearie. "My other Grandmother, Dearie, told me that: *Don't let reality tell your story.*" He tried to speak calmly, "My story is, I really need your help. Now. I can't call Conor. There's no time for him to get here."

Between gulps of water, Jesse wheezed out his story, adding the finer details: "Tim Braedon. Somehow, he's not in prison. And Miss Lily is his sister, Tina. And they are after a treasure. But that's not the worst."

And he told him all about the BIG MONEY, and the wig, "And I'm pretty sure Miss Lily is really Miss Peggy—from New York City!"

Peter and Charlie were mum. Peter drank down all his water and stood up. He peered out the window. "Storm's comin'." He turned. "Jesse, you need to get home." He looked in Jesse's eyes, glowing like turquoise embers. "You know, Jesse … if Jane wanted to figure out something, she'd be perfectly calm and still. She'd picture how she wanted it to be. And … things worked out." Peter smiled supportively. "Whatever happens, Jesse O'Neil, be calm and still. Sit tight."

"That's what Conor said. But … can't you call the Police? Or something?"

Charlie cautioned, "There's a lot goin' on you don't know about."

"Like what?"

Peter shifted uneasily. He looked at Charlie. "Well … like, her stolen car. The Police here are already on to Miss Lily. All her deceptions. She's a con artist."

"*Deception. Con.*" Jesse puzzled. "*Con* is a joey word for the kangaroo word, *deception.*"

Charlie chuckled, "Man, oh, man, Jesse! That brain of yours!" He tapped Jesse's head, but said seriously, "Listen, I shared a photo of Lily with the Police. They know she's a con artist. She's wanted by the Police in New York, New Jersey, and now here."

"As a matter of fact," Peter added, "the law firm she says she works for … Maxim & Tenet? Well Mr. Tenet happens to live right here in Elizabethtown. And he's never heard of Miss 'Snollygoster' Lily."

"Really? But where does she go every day?"

"Jesse …" Peter breathed out a long puff, "let me … let it sort itself out. Sit tight."

Charlie nodded in agreement, "Jesse, you just stay away from Lily." His cherry lips curled into a little smile, "And keep hummin' your Jesse charm. Keep shinin' your Light."

Jesse smiled faintly. "It's not so easy."

Peter quietly pushed Jesse toward the door. "Things are happening fast. Charlie and I will take care of whatever needs to come next. Right now, I don't want you out on the marsh in this comin' storm. Get back to Gemma."

Charlie smiled encouragingly, "You git on home quick, y'hear!"

Through the dark, eerie clouds rising over Marsh Hill, Jesse pushed himself through the hot breezes. He was thinking, *Sit tight—Shine my Light—Sit tight—Shine my Light.* The rhythm of his feet tread through the long grasses, and he felt again the melody of Rachmaninoff's *Paganini Rhapsody*. Gemma's piano notes moved up from his feet. Into his chest. His heart. His breath. He remembered Dearie's story of Rachmaninoff's escape from Russia.

Sergei and Natalia Rachmaninoff—and their girls—were horrified to find that Russian revolutionaries had taken over their home, Ivanovka. The entire house. The revolutionaries allowed the family one little room together. They were traptured! That is when the Light went on for Rachmaninoff. He knew. He knew his Lights. They would escape. Just before Christmas. Take flight. By the light of the stars. And, do you know, Jesse?

That is just what they did! Shining free!

Jesse breathed. He breathed Rachmaninoff's rhapsody in every footfall. He felt himself shining. His Light. Shining. Calm. Still. Like the music. Still. Like Jane. He smiled. He seemed to float up the hill. Floating. Fluttering, as each tender note showered him with a deep sense of love. And Light.

When he got home, the light of the sun had disappeared behind the dark, stormy, clouds rising like chimneys. As he moved to the back door, he stumbled over something. "Whaaat?" He saw Sadie and Red. Big lumps lying on the ground. He chortled, "What are you two doing down there?"

The dogs didn't move. Jesse knelt beside their limp, still bodies. He felt his Light tremble. "Oh no! What's happened?" He didn't know, but he couldn't leave the dogs outside with this storm coming. He rolled the dogs onto their blankets and dragged them into the kitchen, calling, "Gemma! GEMMA!"

No answer.

CHAPTER SIXTY
LILY – TINA – PEGGY

"Gemma?" Jesse called. He saw Ellie-cat's water and food dishes, oddly untouched. But no Ellie-cat. He moved to the living room, full of flickering lights and eerie music. There was Miss Lily, moving her hands at the *Theremin* and watching the little stained-glass lamp rotating its colors around the room. Gemma was not there.

Something was very wrong. Jesse felt his Light tremble again. "Where's Gemma?" he called to Lily.

"Ohhh." She purred, turning down the volume, "Gemma ran off with some handsome man who came to the door. Something about a horse. Convenient, isn't it?" She turned. "It's just me. And you."

Jesse quiver-quavered. "But the dogs. Sadie, Red. I ... think ... they're dying! I brought them into the kitchen. It's going to rain and—"

"You really are a Calamity John!" Lily derided him. "The dogs are fine."

Lily sounded funny. Her deep voice was gone. She sounded like ... like Miss Peggy!

Jesse gulped. *Sit tight—Shine my Light.* He turned back to the kitchen. "I ... I've gotta help the dogs."

"Let them be," Lily commanded, her eyes glittering like the fox. "Trust me," she sniffed, "they're fine. For now."

"I don't trust you!" Jesse suddenly challenged. "You're all lies and tribble-trap!"

"So right!" She cackled outrageously. "Hah! How easy it was to twist you around my little finger. All of you. You didn't stand a chance!" Her laugh guttered, "I'll never forget how I helped you with the animals! A little catnip goes a long way! And how lucky to have the fox pay a visit. I wonder how that chicken pen was left open!" She laughed. It was a laugh Jesse had never heard before. Dark, bitter, nasty.

"Everything went my way! The attic noises? The light in the treasure rooms? Gemma's explanations were perfect! I couldn't have asked for a better sidekick! Gemma! Spouting her stupid Shakespeare! Ha! Little did Gemma know she was eating right out of my hands!"

She flicked her hands, laughing, and the music loudened and moaned. "And you even left your code paper for me! It was a cinch to open the treasure-room door!" She sighed with satisfaction, "I had all the time in the world, to take whatever my heart desired. What with your bike ride, your sailing outing, and the market day? Thank you so very much!"

Lily looked triumphant. "I think I'll take this little lamp along, too. And maybe a few more paintings." She crossed the room, lifting one of the small, framed seascapes. "They fetch a pretty penny!" She put it on the dining room table and turned, smirking, "Ha! You and Gemma! Right around my little finger!"

Jesse blurted, "I know who you are! Tina Braedon!"

"Don't call me that!" She yelped at Jesse and wrenched the *Theremin* plug out of the socket. Her tone took a fiendish turn. "For now, the animals are just asleep. But if you want to keep them all ALIVE, you will help me."

Jesse felt the jim-jams slither up his spine. "All the animals? Did you poison them?"

She laughed. That horrible laugh.

Jesse burst, "What have you done?"

"Well now, Jesse," her sour-creamy voice taunted, "you help me, and I'll help you and your precious animals. Then I'll be out of your life. Tonight."

"No!" Jesse cried. "You fix the animals now!"

"You're wasting precious time, Jesse." She haughtily folded her arms. "The animals' lives depend entirely on you."

"Me?" He thought of Gemma's words about the animals, the farm, their livelihood. He couldn't let Gemma lose this farm. He stood very still, a small sob puckering in his throat.

"Oh, for city pigs! I don't have time for this!" Lily jumped at him, raising her voice, "Jesse! If you want to save this farm, you help me!" She grabbed his arm, "Now!"

"Owww! Let go!" Jesse looked at Lily's dark-red fingernail polish … her fingers looked like claws … and they did not let go. Jesse gasped. "What do you want?"

"You know what I want. You're so good at solving puzzles. You know a lot more than you let on. It's time for our treasure hunt."

"But," Jesse thrashed, "there is no treasure!"

"Don't try that on me. YOU said it before! *You know where the treasure is.*"

"Nooooo! The treasure … it's … I … I meant Gemma."

Lily held Jesse's arms like a vise, "And Gemma will lose everything if you don't help me get my hands on that treasure. Time is running out!"

"I … All right, all right. I'll tell you."

"No! You'll show me!"

Jesse moaned. Trying to think, he felt a spark of Light. "I … it's … in the barn."

"The barn is a big place …"

"The … the hen room," Jesse spurted reflexively.

Lily smiled crookedly and dragged Jesse into the kitchen, past the lifeless Sadie and Red, and out the door. Jesse shivered in the hot wind, swirling like wild, swooping crows.

All at once, Ellie-cat was there. Walking beside Jesse. Like his guardian.

Lily trudged Jesse to her car, jerking open the door and thrusting him onto the front seat. "Don't move!" She opened the glove compartment and pulled out a flashlight. But instantly, she halted. "My bags! They're gone!" Standing up, she bang-danged her head on the doorframe and Jesse heard a curse gutter in her throat. She groaned, "Tim. Tim's here!"

Jesse felt his stomach flop. *Tim. Tina.* Rain began to splat in huge drops. Over and over, they seemed to say: *Tim. Tina. Here.*

CHAPTER SIXTY-ONE

HERE

Jesse's mind was spinning, spinning like a whirlpool. *Tim. Tina. Tim. Tina. Eaaagh! Scylla and Charybdis!* His heart thumped. But Lily grabbed his arm and fiercely hauled him out of the car, prodding him with the flashlight. The rain was falling in buckets and Jesse saw Ellie-cat in the rain-spotted light beam, like a wet little mop, hopping a few steps, leading the way to the barn.

Jesse felt *Dearie's Journal* words. He had read it to Greta and Matts and Gemma. *The cat led them through the storm … waiting like a patient shepherd.*

Dearie! Jesse breathed. But Lily flung open the barn door and rammed him inside. Trying to kick the cat out of the way, the door slipped out of her hands—and clicked shut. Jesse was sprawled and dripping on the stone floor, plunged into a deep, dense, smothering darkness. Alone. In that timeless moment, his heart choked, and he felt something sharp gushing up inside him. It was a sob—a burning cry—that quaked … graveled … in his chest, his throat. He wanted to let it out. To scream, to shriek into this horrible darkness. But no sound came out. It was as if he was inside a nightmare—traptured.

Something touched his cheek—he jerked back! But the something licked his face. "Ellie-cat!" he whistered, pulling her wet little body close.

Instantly, the barn door opened, and Lily leapt inside, slamming the door behind her. Jane's cross-stitch shivered against the wall, and Lily pointed the flashlight at it.

Gifts of God. Jane. Jesse breathed. He stood up and closed his eyes. A sudden spark ignited in the dark behind his eyelids. Jesse's Light brightened. Brightened again. *Dearie's here!* He smelled a whiff of chocolate. *And Jane! Oh!* He wanted to jump for joy!

The rain juddered across the roof, but Jesse heard something skittering, up in the dark hayloft. Ellie-cat jumped down from his arms. Yet she did not move. She sat, staring. Jesse felt … James! *James is here, too!* Jesse's brain was all at once wide awake.

Instantly, he distracted Lily, exclaiming, "Someone's up in the hayloft!"

Lily directed the flashlight upwards into the darkness. Two small, glowing red eyes boldly stared back at her. She screeched! Rocketed up! Jesse darted past her to the door!

But Lily seized him, shrieking, "Oh, no! No, you don't!"

The chickens spooked, and their hysterical squawks sent Lily into another hopping, squealing panic. Wildly she jabbed Jesse up the stairs, pushing him to the railing, furiously commanding: "Look at the animals, Jesse! Only you can save them!"

He saw the cows and goats lying on their sides. Like the dogs. Like they were dying. He tried to breathe. The chickens scratched and screeched, and Jesse thought, *Ophelia probably fainted*. But he quickly realized, *Lily didn't poison the hens!* With relief, he instinctively sipped a deep breath, but *Aegh!* The manure smell was intense. Jesse wanted to smell Jane's chocolate. But Lily's perfume mixed with the manure in a sickening odor, muddled with another stink. Jesse knew that stench. *Skunk cabbage! Somebody stepped in skunk cabbage. Tim?*

Lily gagged, too. Waving the flashlight, she charged Jesse, "Turn on the light!"

Ellie-cat twirly-purred Jesse's legs, with a soft, wet comfort. His thoughts burbled, *All is well. All is well.* And even in this dark storm, his Light burbled back: *And so it is. And so it is.*

He answered Lily, "I don't know where the light switch is. I haven't been here at night."

"Liar!" She pushed him against the wall, and again, Jane's *Gifts of God* trembled—in the precise moment that a powerful lightning bolt flashed! The windows blazed like glaring headlights. Not a half-second later, a barrage of thunder crashed in a gigantic boulder of pandemonium—exploding on top of them! Quaking the rafters, shivering the windows, shuddering the walls ... quivering the very air! Jesse was shaking so, he wobbled to the floor.

Lily screeched again, "Find me the light switch!" She clobbered Jesse's arm with the flashlight, and he stammered. "I-I don't know where! Honest!"

Pushing her sopping hair back from her face, she menaced in her deep voice, "Time's up Jesse. If Tim is here, you know what he'll do." Jesse didn't know what Tim would do. In the dark that followed the lightning, he felt the whip of Lily's squall, yelping at him: "Gemma's farm depends on YOU, Jesse! The treasure! NOW!"

"All right. All right!" Jesse's bottom scooted closer to the wall, under Jane's *Gifts of God* cross-stitch. He felt safe again, protected. His hand went to his pocket, and he jangled his stone with his silver dollar. He stood up. Straight. He had just a moment to breathe. To T-H-I-N-K.

Slowly, deliberately, Jesse lifted his arm and pointed.

Lily flashed the light down the row of cages. But it was too dark. The light didn't reach past them. She hesitated "What? What's down there?"

"A trap door," Jesse answered. "It's a trap door to the vault. There's a ring in the floor to pull it up. The ring is the Eye of Providence. When you shine the light on the door, you'll see the *Eye* and the *triangle with the sunrays*. The treasure is hidden in there."

"Thank you, Jesse. Thank you very much."

It was not Lily's voice.

It was Tim.

A flashlight lit up from the far end of the cages and a face floated in the dark: Tim was a ghastly mask of shadows, wafting on the stench of skunk cabbage.

"I told you I'd be here. Didn't I, Jesse?" He laughed, "C U!"

All at once, Lily's voice transformed to her deep, burnt velvet. "Hunky-dory, Tim! You made it! Wouldn't Daddy be just pleased as punch knowing both his kids found the treasure he could never have!"

"One of us is getting the treasure, that's for sure," Tim chided. "Me!"

He aimed his flashlight at the trap door. "Well! Whaddya know! It is the Eye of Providence!" He bent down and pulled on the ring. But instantly, Lily raced past the cages.

The trap door swung upwards. Tim yelped, "Oh no y' don't!" He tried to push her away. But her momentum carried her to the trap door opening. Pushing, grabbing! The two of them tumbled in! And plunged down!

Lightning flashed, thunder cracked, and screams burst—in horrifying shrieks. Jesse felt his way to the trap door and peered over the edge. Lily and Tim were down at the bottom. Tangled together. The flashlights silhouetted their snarled bodies—disgustingly sticking to the manure pile. They were screeching to kingdom come. Tina and Tim Braedon. Stuck in the cow dung, the goat droppings, the chicken poop.

CHAPTER SIXTY-TWO
BETWEEN THE RAINDROPS

Lowering the trap door, Jesse stood up in the dark. Though he was shivering, he could still feel Dearie and Jane and James. Ellie-cat circled his feet and he picked her up, nuzzling her wet fur and her cold, wet nose. She licked his cheek, but jumped from his embrace, meowing her way through the dark, still guiding Jesse. He felt his way along the hen cages, and moved to the steps, heading for the door. But the door opened. Someone stepped into the barn.

The light flicked on. There stood Margarethe. Like a statue. Very still. Listening. Muffled screams rose from the manure room. A slow, tiny smile curved into Margarethe's lips. Then, all at once, her eyes focused, and she gasped, "Jesse! Come!"

Jesse leapt down the steps into her embrace, and she pulled him close. He felt his face buried in her buttons, but he clung to her, shaking.

"Jesse," she asked determinedly, "vhere is Gemma?"

"Gemma! Lily said she went down to the Philhips' horse farm …"

"Aaahhh …" she breathed in relief. "Ah!"

Ellie-cat was purring like a locomotive and scratching at the door. Margarethe nodded and took Jesse's hand. "Yah. Now ve go."

Out the door, into the pouring rain, Margarethe and Jesse ran toward the house. But all at once, sirens and red flashing lights came speeding up the driveway. Though getting wetter by the second, and still trembling, Jesse stopped and stared. There were cars galore!

"Glory BE!"

Margarethe pulled him to the dry shelter of the back overhang and Jesse watched in disbelief as police cars pulled in. Right up to the barn. He saw Police Chief Patrulha jump out with two other men. Two more police cars pulled in, and all the Police ran inside.

Through chattering teeth, Jesse wondered out loud, "H-how do they know T-Tim and T-Tina are in the b-barn?"

Margarethe answered. "I see moving lights. I call. Ham radio."

Jesse turned and looked up at her. "Y-You?"

The other vehicles had stopped. Conor and Amanda jumped from her car. Gemma leapt out of her truck. Running through the headlights of rain. Picking up Jesse. Engulfing him in their embrace.

Cascades of comfort shuddered through Jesse. He shook and shivered with thankful tears mixing with raindrops on his cheeks.

Margarethe opened the kitchen door and drew them inside, where Conor fell into a kitchen chair with Jesse wrapped about his neck. Gemma, weep-sobbing and bewildered, tumbled onto the next chair. Amanda stood between them. "Now, now ..." she pet Jesse's hair and Gemma's back, soothing them through her own tears, "Oh my darlin's, hush now, my darlin's."

Doc Nichols and Darling bustled into the kitchen. Brushing off the rain on their shoulders, they moved toward the little family. But Margarethe waved them off, directing the Doctor toward the dogs, still unconscious on their blankets.

Confused, Nichols and Darling looked at each other like two fish out of water.

Margarethe spoke, "You are not veterinarians, but you vill do." She disappeared down the hallway.

Doc and Darling shrugged. Opening his black case, he took out his stethoscope and they both knelt beside the limp animals.

Peter and Charlie came in. Dripping, they dangled at the kitchen doorjambs as Murphy appeared, too. He paced back and forth, his boots wetting the floor, and his tongue spraying the air, "Ballygomingo! Everything's happenin' faster than a lightnin' bolt down a rainspout!"

Margarethe returned with a warm quilt. Gemma took it and tenderly wrapped it around Jesse. He was still trembling and crying quietly in Conor's arms. Unsure of what on earth had transpired, Gemma and Amanda leaned into them, but both were blinking away their own unstoppable tears.

With a twist of her button, Margarethe turned away and commandeered the kitchen. "Everyone! Sit!"

Murphy continued to pace the floor, but Margarethe's eyes drilled into his until he reluctantly took a seat. She turned to the tasks at hand, boiling water for coffee and tea and buttering stacks of toast.

Doc Nichols murmured to Darling, "It appears the dogs have gone under from a sleeping potion. But I need to know what sleeping potion and how much."

Darling went to the table. "Jesse," she said, touching his shoulder, "I know this is upsettin', but can y' tell me anything about what medicine the dogs took?"

Alarmed, Jesse replied in a thick cry, "S-Sadie and Red didn't T-TAKE anything! Miss Lily poisoned them! She … she poisoned the b-barn animals, too!"

Gemma tried to cover her groan and Jesse looked at her

sorrowfully, adding, "B-But maybe not the ch-chickens." He looked back to Darling. "Lily said they would be f-fine. They'd sleep it off. B-But then, she s-said if we waited too long, they would d-die."

Quietly, Darling asked, "Do you know what Miss Lily gave them? Do you know where it is?"

Nodding his head, Jesse answered, "Y-Yes. I saw a b-bottle of pills in Miss Lily's b-bag. I hid it in the g-grain cabinet." He hesitated. "There's B-BIG MONEY in her purse—"

He didn't get to finish. Charlie banged his chair back and ran out the back door to the barn.

CHAPTER SIXTY-THREE
I CAN TELL YOU EVERYTHING

Inside the barn, Lily and Tim stood in the low sink, handcuffed, while a Sergeant hosed off the manure and the stench of skunk cabbage. Lily's deep voice sobbed to Chief Patrulha.

"Thank God you got here!" She wept, "Tim threatened to kill Jesse! Just like he poisoned the animals! Unless Jesse told him where the treasure is hidden!" Shaking, she bawled, "He threw me into that-that manure room!" She sniffed pitifully. "I-I don't know h-how Jesse got free. Or h-how this-this monster fell in on top of me!"

Tim sneered at her, "You are a big, fat liar. Just keep making it up. You always do."

Charlie entered, vaulting up the wooden steps to the railing, where he could see the animals sprawled below. He motioned to Chief Patrulha, who walked up the stone steps, and up to the chicken cages. The two Detectives followed, and Charlie opened the grain cabinet for them. Patrulha made a clicking sound and his head went up and down, as he pulled out the bags. He handed the luggage case to one Detective, the purse to the other.

Lily gaspered. She stopped crying and turned viciously on Tim, her voice shrieking, "YOU! Always MUCK it up!"

Charlie reached into the purse, explaining, "Doc Nichols needs this pill bottle." He ran back to the house.

※

Doc Nichols looked at the bottle. "It's a form of clonazepam—an anticonvulsant and antianxiety medication. It's sometimes prescribed as a sleep aid. The problem is, if an animal is given too much, its blood pressure goes way down, and it can suffer a complete collapse."

Gemma groaned again. But she saw Jesse's doleful face and knew her moans were making things worse. Quietly, she swiped at her tears and put her hand on his, smiling weakly.

Jesse stared at her. She looked like … she looked like Jane. And Jesse smelled chocolate. He smiled. He had stopped shivering, and he could feel his breath calming. He felt warm and, once again, protected … and loved. Quilt and all, he moved off Conor's lap and put his arms around Gemma. "All is well, Gemma." He smiled into her shoulder and whispered in her ear, "Jane is here." He felt Gemma's embrace tighten around him.

The Doctor was speaking again. "Mrs. Roberts? There is an antidote to clonazepam. It's called flumazenil. But it requires a complicated intravenous application. So, first things first. Let's count the pills left in the bottle, and you give me the count of all the animals that have gone under. We'll see if this is serious enough to warrant the antidote."

Gemma tried to speak, but nothing came out. She cleared her throat, but only a squeak of sound was heard.

Jesse spoke up, "A cow, a calf, two goats and the two dogs."

Doc Nichols counted out the remaining pills. He smiled. "The animals will be fine. They do need to sleep off the effects, but they were given a very small dose. It's not serious." He packed up his black bag, saying, "We'll just check on the barn animals before we leave you in peace."

Doc and Darling exited, but the door opened again. Chief Patrulha entered with the two Detectives behind him. Jesse bounced between the chairs. "Hannity! Rocky!" He barreled into them, hugging them both at once.

"*Buono,* Jesse, *buono!*" Rocco smiled. "You know, hiding the bags was smart. But tricking those two into the manure room! That was brillish!"

Hannity added, "Y' can be on our Detective Team anytime."

Chief Patrulha was astonished that these two New York Detectives were so ... friendly... with a little kid. But the Chief needed testimony from the little kid. "Let's get on with it," he motioned them into the dining room. Conor and Amanda, Gemma, and Jesse followed them. They all sat down at the long table and Margarethe brought a tray of steaming mugs of coffee and tea and a plate piled with warm, buttered toast. The Chief grabbed a mug and appealed to Jesse, "I need a timeline on everything that happened here tonight. Can you help me?"

Jesse leaned in, "Yes! I can tell you e-v-e-r-y-thing."

In between sips of tea and bites of toast, he proceeded to tell e-v-e-r-y detail. Patrulha was taking notes, and he had to keep flipping the pages, trying to keep up with Jesse's litany of facts.

Conor shook his head at Jesse's account, while Amanda several times put her hands to her cheeks, and Gemma several times caught her breath. But Hannity and Rocco just grinned.

"Jesse," Rocky beamed, toasting Jesse with his mug, "Billy shared your postcards with Mr. Romano in New York City, and he brought them to us. You gave us our first lead. Then Conor's phone call to us—with your info on Tim and Tina Braedon—that cinched it."

Jesse looked thoughtful. "I keep wondering, though. Why wasn't Tim Braedon in jail?"

Hannity shifted in his chair. "Good question. The Shark House got him out on parole. But believe-you-me, he's goin' right back in! For attempted robbery and breaking his parole."

Jesse nodded, "Sergeant Hannity, do you remember that big snowstorm last year, after New Year's Day? When I began my quest to find my disappeared grandmother?" Jesse smiled at Gemma. "Hannity told me to collect clues. Like every snowflake in the blizzard." He snickled, "Well, I think I collected another snowstorm of clues!"

"Yes, you did, Jesse," Hannity chuckled. "And thanks to you, the money will get back to the Romanos, Schuylers, Goreckis, and Bonheurs. And you'll be happy to know, we followed Miss Lily's trail, and found the antiques dealer she was selling to, up in Union City."

"Right," Rocco furthered, "We have been working with him, giving him marked bills to trace Lily. And best of all, he has set aside all the items Lily stole from here."

"Ohhh …" Gemma moaned. She was beside herself with remorse, and rivers of tears rolled down her cheeks.

CHAPTER SIXTY-FOUR

TREASURE

Amanda held Gemma's hand and Jesse smiled at her, "Gemma …? Everything is fine, Gemma. So fine."

Chief Patrulha cleared his throat and stood up, "Well. We have plenty of evidence and testimony. I think we're done here. Thank you, Jesse."

Jesse hugged Gemma close, and they all walked back to the kitchen. Hannity and Rocky were set to go, and Jesse moved to hug each of them with his thank-yous and goodbyes.

He saw Chief Patrulha touch Margarethe's shoulder, "Thank you, Margarethe. Your call on the ham radio was crucial. Your timing was perfect."

"Perfect," Jesse echoed, hugging Margarethe. He looked up to her face, to those pale, pale, clear-blue eyes. "Thank you, Margarethe, for taking care of me. And everybody."

"Yah." The corners of her mouth lifted just enough to count as a smile, and Jesse recalled Dearie saying, *Yes, lifting the corners of your mouth lifts the corners of your heart.*

When Jesse turned around, Peter and Charlie were grinning at him. He let out a rush of air and moved between them.

"And thank you. For … whatever you did. Sorting it out."

"Don't thank me," Peter scuffed his hands together. "Those New York Detectives had this all in hand—alerted the Elizabethtown Police last week. Seems you sent some postcards?"

Charlie grimmeled, "But we had to keep everything hush-hush. Ya never know who knows what in this little town."

Murphy waggled, "That's the honest truth. Gossip buzzes through this town like a herd o' mosquitos!"

Peter and Charlie pulled back, their faces ballooning with ironic smiles. But they did not comment. Even Jesse understood: Murphy's Papa Bear tongue was a great buzzer of gossip.

Doc Nichols and Darling poked into the kitchen. "Don't worry," Doc reassured, "the barn animals and the dogs will sleep this off." He looked at Jesse, "You'd best get to bed and sleep this off, too." And to Gemma, "You, too, Missus. The Doctor orders bed rest. Now."

Jesse shook the Doctor's hand, saying, "Thank you." And Gemma stepped forward to shake his hand, too, adding her own appreciations. "I thank you, exceedingly."

Bending down, Darling kissed Jesse's cheek, saying, "You are one smaht boy!"

Jesse looked back at her with buoyant surprise, wondering what 'smaht' meant. But Murphy grinned to Jesse, "Diddly-ahten-dah! You are a smarty-pants!"

Darling took Murphy's arm. "Regan, we're taking Margarethe home. Everything is settled here."

"Ballygomingo!" Murphy swallowed his tea. "The sun'll set in the east afore anything's settled after this!"

As Margarethe moved to the door, Gemma took both her hands. They stood. Just holding hands, until Margarethe smiled and said, "*Aus die maus*. Zee mouse is out of here. It is over. Yah. I go now. Goodbye." And she was out the door.

Grabbing an umbrella, Jesse walked Margarethe to the car. Gemma joined him and they waved goodbye.

Jesse hugged Gemma again. "Do you smell it? Chocolate?"

Gemma gaspered, "Yes …! Jane! Jane is—" But her voice broke.

"Here," Jesse finished. "Jane is here!"

Gemma put her arm about Jesse, and they waved to all their company, as the cars circled over the cobblestones around the cherry tree, their headlights shining, shining in the soft rain.

Leading the way back to the kitchen, Gemma sighed, "I must take a lie-down." She took Amanda's arm, and they went to her bedroom.

Conor put his hands on Jesse's shoulders, "You're gonna fall asleep on your feet! Let's get you up to bed."

"First, I want to check on the dogs." He knelt beside them, petting their soft ears, hushing, "Sadie. Red. You have a good night sleep now. You'll wake up just fine in the morning." He patted their heads, stroked their backs, and whistered, "So fine."

He went in to kiss Gemma goodnight. She was falling into her deep wispy-slips, but with Jesse's embrace, she murmeled gently, "Oh, Jesse … I love you so, Jesse." His heart fluttered and he smiled, touching her cheek as he had done the first time he saw her.

Amanda was sitting in the comfy chair next to the bed and she pulled him onto her lap.

"Jesse," she hushed in her Georgia drawl. "Dearie's here. Stirrin' up old memories. She's remindin' me of the first time I ever set eyes on you. You. Baby Jesse. Lyin' in that dresser drawer in Dearie's Costume Shop. Your eyes twinklin' their turquoise at me! You. Just a bundle o' Light an' Love." She touched his cheek, "It's who you are, Jesse O'Neil. You can't help it. You're the reason we-all are here. Your Light just shines us all together."

Jesse's head rested on her shoulder, and he closed his eyes.

She whistered, "Oh my darlin,' Jesse. All is well."

His eyelids rose to half-mast and his head lifted ever so slightly. Gemma was under her quilt of yellow roses. Conor stood tall in the doorway. Jesse felt Dearie and Jane and James. He quirkled a thought: He had his treasure. He knew Amanda was right. *All is well. Really well.*

PART TWELVE

UNFURLING

*Let your story unfurl
like a sail in the wind
bearing you grace-fully onward.*

CHAPTER SIXTY-FIVE
LIGHT ON!

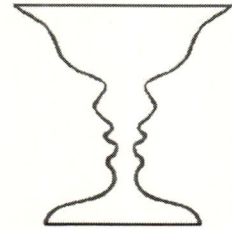

The morning sun was already warming the breezes, glimmering on the rain-washed leaves outside of Jesse's porthole windows. Inside, it dappled and danced on the walls of his bunkroom, prodding him to roll over. But he was still in the web of his wispy-slips, and he pushed his face into the pillow. But insistently, a sunbeam settled across one eye, and both eyes flipped open.

"What time is it?" He looked to the window. "Did I miss Greta and Matts?"

He washed and dressed in double-time and headed downstairs. At the kitchen he smiled, seeing the dogs, Sadie and Red, frisking out in the yard. But he heard Conor and Amanda talking with Gemma in the living room. He was about to rush in when Gemma burst into tears.

"Hopeless! Oh, I am hopeless! I did not protect Jesse. I am meant to be watching over my …" she smothered her tears, "my precious … ohhh … my Jesse!" Her voice turned severe, "But I failed utterly! He endeavored to tell me of Lily's wiles. But did I listen? No. I blundered! Just as I blundered with Jane. I did not listen. Oh, when will I learn?"

She put her fingers to her temples. "I believed Lily. The stories she concocted about Jesse. She convinced me to be wary of him. For all heaven's sake, she told me Jesse was arrested for thievery in New York City."

Conor nodded, "That, well, that was true. He was. And it was all Lily's doing. She was playing the part of Miss Peggy then, and she engineered the whole fiasco that put Jesse in jail."

"Ohh!" Gemma groaned. "I invited the devil. I left Jesse to face her cunning schemes. Alone."

Amanda poked in, "Oh now, simmah down, Gemma. You are goin' way overboard!" She smiled, "You just gotta shake the sugar tree. It's right here, Gemma. Shake it! And let the Light of love and grace fall all around you!"

Conor joined Amanda, "Listen to your sister, Gemma," he chortled as he sat forward. "I have proof positive of how much Jesse loves you and loves living here with you on this farm, because he wrote it all down in letters and postcards."

Right there, Jesse entered the conversation. He went to Gemma and hugged her about the neck. She hung on, and on, until Jesse softly pulled away.

"Gemma," he spoke soberly, "we were both fooled by Miss Lily. Like an optical illusion."

Conor amazed, "Right! She made us think she was the beautiful vase!"

"When all the time," Amanda revolted, "Lily was hidin' her black-hearted face!"

Jesse's head went up and down. "I think she was really the Kitsune fox! The dangerous *yako!*" He rambled, pulling together the words from Peter and Charlie, and even Lily. "Miss Lily-Peggy-Tina is a professional. A professional con artist. And she's wanted by the Police all over. She knew exactly how to wrap us around her finger. She's a *gollysnotter*—I mean a *snollygoster*. We didn't stand a chance!"

Gemma snickled surprisingly. "Oh Jesse, your manner of expression! You sound like an Agatha Christie Detective!"

"Maybe," Conor interrupted, "that's a good way to look at it, Gemma. It's a story. Your story."

"Hmmm," Gemma wandered. "I once knew a superb storyteller. He could weave a tale from the merest cloud of an idea. And he always made it come right in the end."

"Yes." Conor grinned, thinking of Mac. "And in the end, you came out fine. All is well." He gave her a dose of her Shakespeare: *"Unbidden guests are often welcomest when they are gone."*

"Heavens to Betsy! That's the truth!" Amanda agreed.

Jesse crackled, but he hung on to Conor's other words. "I felt *All Is Well* last night. It felt like the Star Cupola on our first night here. When we saw the Aurora Borealis. And the stars. And Jane and James and Dearie." He whistered softly, "I felt my Light on. I knew they were with me last night in the barn."

Abruptly, Jesse jiggered, "And all the people came to help! Margarethe was wonderly! Doc Nichols and Darling took real good care of the animals. Chief Patrulha and his Policemen were ready for everything. And Detective Hannity and Detective Rocco came all the way from New York City!" He swished, "Conor and Amanda drove down from Boston! Peter and Charlie, and Murphy, too! They all came to help. We have a Circle of Lights! Right here!"

Jesse stopped. Unexpectedly, he saw someone he did not know. Right outside the window.

CHAPTER SIXTY-SIX

CELEBRATION

Jesse went to the window, and there were Margarethe, Greta, and Matts, returning from the pasture and barn. He ran out, steering between the leaps of Sadie and Red, and the hugs and cheers from Greta, Matts, and even Margarethe. But there was a man there—with dark hair and dark eyes that perfectly matched Greta and Matts.

Greta gestured, "This is Mateus, our Pais—father ... in Portuguese. He is off work today from the ferryboat engine room."

"Mah-tay-us! I'm so glad to meet you!" Jesse welcomed and invited, "Come inside! Amanda and Conor are here, and Gemma is feeling lots better."

Mateus put up his hands, "Oh-no-no. We will not intrude."

But Margarethe interrupted "Yah!" She put her hand on Jesse's shoulder, "I vant to know—signs." She pointed to Matts.

They bundled into the kitchen and found Gemma and Amanda and Conor humming along, preparing breakfast. Gemma gladdened, "Ah, your timing is impeccable. Let us serve you a breakfast filled with gratitude!" She quoted her Shakespeare: *"I can no other answer make but thanks. And thanks, and ever thanks."*

Jesse sparked, *Gemma's back!*

After introductions, the children were sent down to the larder for extras, and at the bottom of the stairs, Jesse stopped the twins. "How did Margarethe know to come to Windy Hill Farm last night?"

Greta and Matts squirmed, until Greta blurted, "Margarethe! Mutter! She guessed something vas vrong. Ve try to sit tight, but you do not sit tight vith Mutter."

Jesse laughed, admitting, "I blabber-gabbed, too!"

They filled the basket with jams and honey and headed back upstairs, to a table bulging with delectables.

"Golly," Jesse hootled. "This is a celebration breakfast!" He signed *celebrate* to Matts, his fingers making the 'C' and his wrists tapping and spiraling up.

Briskly twisting her button, Margarethe shouted, "Yah!" She pulled on Mateus, "You see? Jesse, again! Sign!"

Jesse and Matts and Greta signed *celebrate* together, and Mateus smiled while Margarethe jubilated, "Yah! Jesse, you teach us." She pointed to her family.

Gemma interrupted, "One moment." She went to her office, returning with a book. She held it in both hands and showed off the title: *Sign Language – American School for the Deaf.*

Margarethe grabbed the book. "Ve learn!" she exclaimed. "Togezer! And now, Matts can speak!"

Jesse was just as excited, adding, "That's the same book Siobhan used when she taught me!" He looked at Matts, who eagerly watched his mother flip through the pages, and Mateus put his arms around his children, saying, "Yes, we will talk in sign! Together!"

After clearing up their fab-u-lush breakfast, Margarethe put down her dish towel and declared in her fashion, "Ve go now. Goodbye." At the door she turned, "Danke!" She held up the book, "Tausend Dank."

Gemma heartened, "A thousand welcomes to you."

They all went outside, waving them down the driveway. But a truck was driving up the driveway, and Jesse recognized it right away.

"It's Bethesda Philhips! And her father, too!"

Jesse watched Gemma's cheeks go red as she murmeled, "Oh, Bertrand."

CHAPTER SIXTY-SEVEN
MORE GUESTS

Bethesda got out of the truck first, donning her big garden hat. She was wearing her full skirt, and she had that captivating look, highlighted by her fresh, luminous, rosy cheeks.

Amanda purred to Conor, "And who do we have here?"

Bethesda waved and leaned into the truck bed, lifting out a potted rose bush. Her father opened his door and stepped out, looking dapper in old-fashioned linen pants and vest.

Conor murmeled to Amanda, "And who do we have here?"

Bertrand took the rose bush from Bethesda but set it down. He strode to Gemma, smiling and making that little bow of his. "Gemma, I hope you will forgive our intrusion. But, since we could not contact you, we decided to stop by, on the chance you would be in. I—we—want to thank you for your help with *Tempest* yesterday. That horse would have gone wild in the thunder and lightning if it were not for your calm serenity."

Jesse took note that Gemma was blushing again. She said formally, "You are quite welcome. And you are very welcome here." She introduced everyone, and Bethesda extended her hand to Amanda, "We had heard that Amanda Wynne was your sister, but we never expected you would be visiting now."

Bertrand shook hands saying, "We are only dropping off a yellow rose bush for you, Gemma. Our thanks to you."

"How kind," Gemma beamed. "I believe I shall plant it here by the kitchen door."

Instantly, Bertrand moved to place the rose bush at the back door.

Another truck rambled up the driveway, and Jesse hopped, "It's Peter and Charlie!"

Charlie was out first, saluting everyone in general, and saying to Gemma in particular, "Just checking you're all okay, after your ordeal last night."

"Ordeal?" Bertrand asked.

Charlie chuckled, "You may be the only people on the island who don't know! The phone lines have been jammed! Everyone's talking about last night's capture of two criminals. Right here on Windy Hill Farm."

Bertrand and Bethesda were shocked. But Jesse was busy noticing that Peter was silently sneaking looks at Bethesda. Jesse stepped forward, "Let's go drink tea. Out on the porch."

Gemma beamed, and Jesse directed, "The porch is over here. Just follow me."

The conversation began with lots of blah-blah-blahs, describing the many moving parts and people of the past night. But Jesse was not interested. Even when Charlie hootled about how clever Jesse was to trap the criminals in the manure room.

Bethesda gaspered, "It sounds like a frightening mystery book. Perhaps it is something you would sooner forget?"

Jesse smiled at her, "Yes. Yesterday is gone." He paused, "I want to know about you. Where did you come from? And why did you come to Elizabethtown?"

CHAPTER SIXTY-EIGHT

LOVEY-DOVEY

Gemma was disquieted yet pleased by Jesse's questions. He could get away with being so blunt.

"We are from the beautiful Isle of Wight in England," Bethesda smiled, "East Cowes."

"What did you do there?" Jesse curioused.

"For generations, we kept horses," Bertrand answered. "Our surname, Philhips, actually means 'lover of horses.' The odd thing is that I am not really a horse person. My wife, Pim, was the expert."

He was suddenly mum, and Bethesda continued, "We lost my mother, Pim, trying to get her ill sister out of London during the Blitz in 1940. And we lost my brother, Bowie, in Belgium, at the very end of the war in 1945."

Conor inhaled sharply. "Yes, we lost my Pa in that Battle of the Bulge."

"My dad, too." Charlie barely nodded.

"So many. So close to coming home." Bertrand tried to speak, but he stopped. When he resumed, he talked of family in Elizabethtown. "My brother, Berwyn Philhips, came to Elizabethtown years ago, in 1920, after the Great War. We came to live with him in 1946, after

World War II. But Berwyn passed on last year. Bethesda and I are the only Philhips left."

Bethesda rounded up, "Mother was also the librarian in East Cowes, on the Isle of Wight. I followed her into her books and completed my schooling here, in Boston. Now I am the Elizabethtown librarian." She asked Jesse, "Are you one who enjoys books?"

"I have my own library!" Jesse crowed. "You should see!" He swiveled to Gemma, "May I take Bethesda up to see my yacht room?"

"Certainly, if she is willing."

"Oh, I am intrigued," Bethesda beamed.

Jesse looked at Peter, "You and Charlie should come, too. Peter, you'll get lots of ideas for your 'Nautical Knick-Knack Nook.'"

Amanda and Conor looked at Jesse. They looked at each other, and grinned with the same thought: *What do we have here?*

For Charlie and Bethesda, this was a first visit to the yacht room. Peter showed them about, and they blatantly ogled. Then Jesse and Bethesda sat on the floor and opened his book cupboard. She gasped, "Why, this IS a library!"

Peter smiled and remarked, "*Outside of a dog, a book is man's best friend. Inside a dog, it's too dark to read.* Groucho Marx," he admitted contritely.

Bethesda chuckled. "Oh, Groucho Marx! One of my favorite comedians!" But her attentions returned to the cupboard, and she pulled out a book—"Rudyard Kipling's *Jungle Book!* Of all the stars and planets!" She opened to the title page, "1894! This is a first edition! And it's signed!" She read:

"*A favorite, for a favorite ~ Rudyard Kipling.*"

Bethesda fell back, lying on the carpet with the book clutched to her heart.

"Oh, no!" Peter knelt next to her, "Are y-you o-okay?"

Jesse looked at them and snorted a little giggle-snicken. "Um," he stood up. "Charlie, I just remembered, there are blueprints and drawings in the carriage house office." He took his hand, "Let's go get them." His head rolled toward Peter and Bethesda, "We'll be right back."

Out the back door, Charlie stopped Jesse, "If I didn't know better, I'd say you're playing cupid!"

"Is cupid a lovey-dovey?" Jesse asked, walking toward the carriage house.

"Yeah, I guess you'd say that." Charlie explained, "Cupid is the mythological baby with wings who shoots his love arrow, making people fall in love."

"That is a lovey-dovey," Jesse grinned. "But I think Peter and Bethesda already got shot with the love arrow." He looked back at the porch, whistering, "And I think Gemma and Bertrand got the arrow, too." Another giggle-snicken erupted, and Jesse beamed, "I love the lovey-doveys!"

Too soon for Jesse's liking, the guests were all gathered outside, saying their thank-yous and goodbyes and shaking hands all around. Bethesda invited, "You are all welcome to our Linger Longer Farm. The horses will be waiting for you," she smiled, "along with father and me, of course."

Bertrand touched Gemma's arm, and looking into her eyes, he bowed slightly and said, "Until next time."

Jesse looked around the circle. He was feeling—loving—his Circle of Lights. This farm, all these people. He heard Dearie's silvery laugh:

....

Oh, Jesse! The Light! It just glitters. It's what Light does. It can't be helped. You know it in the glintaling stars and sun and moon ... the sparkling water and air ... glistening leaves and flowers ... radiant birds and beasts—even Queen the goat! Mmm-hmm! Everything Lights up! But nothing—and none—more glittering than all of you!

....

Jesse looked around his circle. *We are all Light! And we're all connected!* He looked at Conor and Amanda and Gemma. *Lovey-dovey,* he chuckled quietly. *This is my lovey-dovey family.*

CHAPTER SIXTY-NINE
THE SET OF THE SAILS

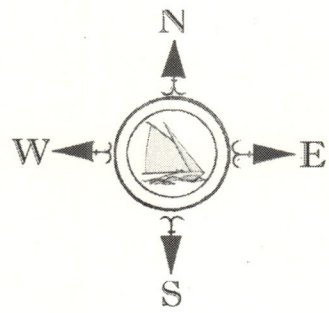

Jesse was standing among the daisies watching Conor tease Gemma, holding both her hands and joshing, "Mayhap, Gemma? It is a good thing that you don't have a telephone. Look at all the company that shows up!" He laughed and kissed both her hands, "Very … (kiss) … attentive … (kiss) … company!"

"Yes," Gemma nodded, taking her hands back and blushing to the wild, blue yonder. "Nevertheless, after last night's unspeakable episode, I am determined to find a way to afford a telephone again."

"A telephone!" Amanda enthused, "That would be grand!"

Jesse stepped forward with a small crown of daisies in his hands. "For you, Gemma!" Gemma laughed and bent down to receive her circlet of flowers, while Jesse happily intoned, "Gemma! The Queen of the Family!"

"Oh!" Gemma surprised. She was the picture of grace, especially as she quoted her Shakespeare: *"My crown is in my heart, not on my head: … it is called content, a crown it is, that seldom kings enjoy."* She pulled Jesse into her arms, burbling, "Yes! I am quite content!"

As Jesse kissed her cheek, he felt the breeze. It was rushing through the tall purple maples along the driveway and swirling around

Amanda's full skirt, lifting it like a sail. "Let's go sailing!" he hooted and took Gemma's hand.

"Oh yes!" Amanda approved, taking Jesse's other hand.

Conor whooped, "Count me in!"

Rowing out to the catboat, Jesse was thoughtful, "You know, maybe we should change the name of this boat to *Scallop Bay Dancer*. Then it tells the whole story."

"That is a brilliant idea, Jesse," Gemma approved, straightening her hat. "That will be a winter project in the boathouse."

Jesse liked thinking about winter with Gemma on Windy Hill.

The catboat danced back and forth across Sunset Harbor, and Gemma remarked, "An old poem says, *It is the set of the sails, and not the gales, that determine which way we go.*"

Amanda spoke up, "Let's set our sails for that lighthouse at King's Spade."

"To King's Spade Light!" Conor crowed, and Gemma steered them out of the harbor.

Jesse was becoming familiar with all the sights they passed. At Big Bear Island Lighthouse they moved through the channel near Elizabethtown's Fort Battery, and under the rolling fields of a large farm. As they moved southward, they sailed past the old Revolutionary War Battery, where the mouth of the bay opened wide before them.

Remembering the submarine trick, Jesse touched Gemma's knee, with a questioning glint in his eye. She nodded with a smirk.

Abruptly, Jesse shouted, "Look! Golly! There's a submarine coming in the bay!"

"Oh!" Amanda exclaimed right on cue. "Oh, my stars! Will you look at that! What a surprise! A submarine! Oh my! Is it comin' up or goin' down?"

There was no response. She heard a definite snicker. Amanda looked at Gemma and Conor. They had big grins on their faces. She looked back at the "submarine."

"Wait a sweet minute! Oh! That's not a submarine, now, is it! Why! It's some old rock foundation!" She huffed dramatically. "Well! I never!" She grinned. "Jesse, I shall remember this! You wait! I have a few tricks up my sleeve!"

Jesse giggled. "It was worth it, Amanda!" he winked at her.

"OH!" she exclaimed in mocking outrage, "Daddy told me never to trust a man who winks!" Amanda laughed. "That seals it, Jesse!"

Their laughter sparkled across the water as they neared the curling waves washing over the rocks at King's Spade Light. This was farther than they had ever sailed, and Jesse could clearly see into Maiden Cove Beach. "I have lots of exploring to do! All over the island!"

Gemma nodded, "You are like my Papa and Jane! Another explorer in the family!"

"I see the King's Spade grey stone light tower," Conor remarked. "But what are those white buildings?"

Gemma answered, "The lightkeeper's family lives there. I believe the other buildings are military installations known as Spraycliff Observatory."

Jesse memory-fizzed. "I remember Roald Dahl told me there was a radar station here!"

"I imagine that is true," Gemma said. "Spraycliff has military secrets, even today."

"It looks like an isolated place to live," Amanda noted. "The storms. Like last night. And the waves. They must be fierce."

"Those waves are our signal to turn back," Gemma said, pushing the tiller all the way to the starboard side. Jesse let the mainsheet slide through his hands and the sail wafted out almost perpendicular to the boat. Running with the wind, they headed home, skimming over the water, breezing up like a kite pulling on its tether.

Jesse turned around and announced, "I'm thirsty!"

Gemma was amused at Jesse's straightforwardness and was enjoying her own high spirits. "You have come to the right place! This boat is equipped with provisions!" She reached to the after deck, pulling out her rucksack. "Jesse, come. Take the helm."

"Oh-Ka-a-ay!" Jesse thrilled.

She put her hand over his, pointing with the other one, "Simply direct the bow of the catboat straight on, toward the Big Bear Lighthouse." Smiling to beat the band, Gemma offered the canteen of water to Jesse. "You may have the honor of the first drink."

She rustled through the canvas bag again and came up with a tin container. Flipping the latches on it, she presented: "Saltine Crackers!"

Next, she took out cans of sardines and deviled ham.

"Saltine crackers and sardines! Oh, just what I'm hankering for!" Jesse smiled, wiping the water droplets from his mouth.

Conor opened the sardines while Gemma used a can opener on the deviled ham. She searched through her bag again.

"Oh, I forgot a spreading knife," she muttered.

"You can use my knife!' Jesse offered.

"You have a knife?" Gemma was surprised.

"I carry it in my pocket." He smiled, "Always."

Amanda smiled, too. "I remember how you found your little orange knife, diggin' in Mac's garden. I love that darlin' butterfly!"

Gemma's eyes squintled. She gaspered deeply. "Did you say, Mac …? Butterfly …?"

But Jesse was explaining, "I was digging in Mac's garden in the courtyard, and I dug this up! The little blade is broken, but it makes a swell screwdriver!" He pulled out the blade to show Gemma. "I've had my knife for over a year! I use it all the time, more than I can count!" He handed it over to his grandmother.

Gemma was still. A large tear softly spilled from her eye and dropped upon the butterfly.

CHAPTER SEVENTY
SECRETS UNFURLING

Jesse's orange butterfly knife lay in Gemma's open hand like it might flutter away. Gently, she touched the silver emblem of the butterfly. It seemed she had stopped breathing. A lump rose in her throat. She closed her eyes and another tear spurted out.

"Gemma?" Jesse began. But she reached into her pocket and pulled out … Jesse's knife!

Jesse amazed, "Cracker Jacks, Gemma! What a magic trick! How did you get my knife into your pocket?"

Gemma looked like she didn't know whether to laugh or cry. She opened both her hands: an orange knife lay in each hand.

"What?" Jesse quizzeled, "H-How?"

Gemma spoke creakily. "When I was ten years of age, shortly after World War I, Papa returned from a special trip he took to England. He was to meet someone he had not seen in years and years. He had purchased these two orange-bone, Toledo-steel knives. One for his friend, and one for him. The larger knife has a cat, the smaller has the butterfly. Like Jesse's."

Jesse interrupted, "What happened?"

Gemma paused. "Papa never met his friend. I do not know what happened. But Papa had bouts of ... quiet ... sadness ... after that." She brightened, "He gave the butterfly knife to me. And, oh, I carried my little knife everywhere. I used it for any and every occasion. Unfortunately, I snapped off the smaller blade. I was quite distressed. But Papa told me that, now I had a wonderful little screwdriver! Just as you said, Jesse."

Conor sat with something shivering up his spine. He suddenly knew beyond all certainties that Jesse's knife, at one time, belonged to Gemma.

Jesse, too, was fiddling with this puzzle. "Gemma, my knife. I ... you ..."

Suddenly, Gemma's face moved through a panoply of emotions. She looked amazed, doubtful, sorrowful. She sat very still, and another huge tear trembled on her lashes. It seemed to just sit there. Finally, it fell, dripping down her cheek. She pulled both knives to her heart.

Her mouth grimmeled. She spoke. Quietly. Determinedly. "Yes. Jesse's knife was, once upon a time, my own little knife."

"Wha-a-a-t?" Jesse nearly shouted. "How can your knife be my knife?"

Gemma took in a deep breath. And laughed! "I thought I should never again see this little butterfly knife. You have all spoken of your Dearie's connections, the weavings of our lives. I have something to tell. Of such weavings."

She looked to the sky, "Oh-h-h!" Her words stuttered in her throat, "Do you know where I lived? When I was an actress in New York City?"

Their heads wagged back at her, and Jesse replied, "Nooo."

"I lived in a five-story apartment house. Betwixt 5th and 6th Avenues. Near the Princess Theater."

"Oh no, you didn't!" Amanda's hands flew to her face, as Gemma's eyes peered into her memories.

"My apartment house had an oak tree in the courtyard, and a

Laundry next door. The owners were Mac and Bridget McCarthy. Mac was the spellbinding storyteller I once knew."

Collective gasps gulped the wind. The sail jounced up and down with their jolting thoughts.

"What?"

"Truly?"

"You …?" Jesse puffed. "You lived in OUR apartments in New York City?"

Gemma nodded with an enigmatic smile. "Yes, I did. And no, I did not."

"Wha-a-at …?" Jesse puzzled.

Conor questioned, "Why so contradictory?"

"Contrary, indeed!" Amanda spouted, still incredulous.

Gemma closed her eyes, and Jesse's irrepressible brain worked on another tiny puzzle: "*Contradictory … contrary …*" he murmeled, "they're kangaroo words."

But no one paid him any mind. Gemma opened her eyes … and her lips parted.

"It was the last of October, 1929. Daniel and I … on our beautiful wedding day. Dearest Papa and Uncle Trevor were with us." Gemma beamed, "Daniel and I," she repeated. "Always." But a shadow instantly filled Gemma's eyes. "How could we know? The very next day …? The Stock Market, the world—*my world*—would come crashing down?" She looked down at the knives, her lips trembling.

"That night, my little butterfly knife disappeared with all the other treasures of my life. That night I lost everything. My darling Papa. My steadfast Uncle Trevor. My beloved Daniel." She whistered her Shakespeare, "*I encounter darkness as a bride, and hug it in mine arms.*"

Conor and Amanda and Jesse each felt their hearts tremble as Gemma's eyes seemed to whirl with the memory. "I thought I had gone mad."

Jesse wanted to hug this madness out of her. But he sat quietly, wondering … marveling. *Another secret.* His hand felt the long, smooth wooden tiller. Like the long, smooth wooden railing, back in Mac's apartment house. They felt connected.

Jesse held the tiller, feeling the water pulling on it … pulling him into something … something new. Gemma gently put her hand on his, and they held the tiller, together, pointing the way like a compass in a new land.

"Ohhh …" she looked at Jesse and spoke the words to his song: "*The greatest thing … you'll ever learn … is just to love and be loved in return.*" She touched his cheek. She touched her heart. "I have loved. I have lost. But I have loved." Her face was shining. Her eyes were gleaming. "I remember."

Jesse felt her Light, unfurling, shining out all over. He wanted to know her story. Her secret. He could feel it, becoming more a part of him. "Gemma?" Jesse boggled. "What did you mean when you said, *You did, and you did not, live in our apartments?*"

She looked at him. She looked at Conor and Amanda. She looked at the glittering water that lay ahead. The wind touched the sail, and the catboat rose up, rolling on a cresting wave.

Spellbound, Jesse felt the tiller tug and felt a tug at his heart, "Gemma? Will you tell?" He gazed at Gemma, and she spoke softly. One word. One complicated, overflowing, simple word. "Yes."

Here is the stardust that dreamers know.
  Wonder ... glittering. Secrets ... awakening.
  It's your magic. Your Light.
  Becoming.

GLOSSARY OF IMAGINATOR PEOPLE

Algonquin Indians – A large subfamily of Native American people who inhabited eastern North America from Canada to Virginia. Examples of Algonquin words: opossum, skunk, chipmunk, moose, raccoon, husky, woodchuck, hickory *(chinquapin/chinkapin),* pow-wow, quahog (type of large clam), wampum.

Barrie, James – (1860-1937) Scottish novelist and playwright, best known as the creator of *Peter Pan,* inspired by the Llewlyn Davies boys (1902) originally about a baby in magical adventures in Kensington Gardens, London; (1904) it was a "fairy play" about an ageless boy and young girl, Wendy, who have adventures in *Neverland.*

Berlin, Irving – (1888-1989) Russian born, American immigrant; popular songwriter of hits like "Alexander's Ragtime Band," and "White Christmas." Personal notes: Berlin wed Dorothy Goetz in 1912, but she died months after their honeymoon (typhoid fever). In 1925, he fell in love with heiress Ellin Mackay. Her father was against the courtship and sent her to Europe, during which time Berlin wrote beautiful tunes of yearning: "What'll I Do" and "Always." Upon her return to the United States, the couple eloped. Married until Mackay's death in 1988, they had four children.

Big Joe Turner – (1911-1985) American singer, famous for recording "Shake, Rattle and Roll" (1954), written by Jesse Stone (a.k.a. Charles F. Calhoun, his songwriting name); the song was later recorded by Bill Haley & the Comets and Elvis Presley.

Cetus – Rock (and Lighthouse - destroyed in '38 Hurricane); a group of stars—a constellation—sometimes called "the whale" or "sea monster"; In *The Secrets of Windy Hill*, Jesse is tricked into thinking Cetus rock is a submarine emerging from the sea.

Christopher Robin – a character created by A. A. Milne (1882-1956) based on his son, Christopher Robin Milne. Christopher appears with the animal characters in Milne's *Winnie-the-Pooh* stories and poems (1924-1928).

Christie, Agatha – (1890-1976) English mystery writer and playwright; created famous characters Miss Marple and Hercule Poirot, as well as the famous play *The Mousetrap*.

Cole, Nat King – (1919-1965) American singer, jazz pianist, songwriter, and actor, Nat King Cole recorded over 100 hit songs like "The Christmas Song," "Mona Lisa," "Too Young," and "Nature Boy," which in *Becoming Jesse* and *The Secrets of Windy Hill* is referred to as "Jesse's Song."

Dahl, Roald – (1916-1990) British author of fiction and children's literature; Squadron Leader, Fighter Pilot, Intelligence Officer in the Royal British Air Force during WWII.

Dvořák, Antonín – (1841-1904) world-famous Czech composer, often inspired by folk music of Bohemia; a best known and beloved piece is *The New World Symphony* (9th Symphony), written while he lived in New York City. He is also remembered for his opera, *Rusalka*, which was based on *The Little Mermaid* by Hans Christian Andersen; later became the basis for Disney's *The Little Mermaid*.

Elgar, Edward – (1857-1934) English composer known for his *Pomp & Circumstance* and *Enigma Variations*—14 variations on the same four-note, musical theme, of which *The Nimrod* is the most famous and inspiring.

Freemason – a member of an international order established for mutual help and fellowship, which holds elaborate secret ceremonies. The original Freemasons were traveling, skilled stonemasons of the 14th century; modern Freemasonry is usually traced to the formation of the Grand Lodge in London in 1717.

Gibson, Charles Dana – (1867 -1944) American illustrator who created the iconic, beautiful, independent Gibson Girls (inspired by his wife and her sisters); also editor/owner of *LIFE* magazine.

Gulliver, Lemuel – fictional protagonist and narrator of *Gulliver's Travels*, a novel by Jonathan Swift (1726).

Kipling, Rudyard – (1865-1936) English journalist, short-story writer, poet, and novelist; born in British India, which inspired much of his work, such as *The Man Who Would Be King* and *The Jungle Book*.

Knights Templar – (1119-1312) originally founded with a vow of poverty, the Catholic military order became vastly popular, wealthy, and powerful; headquartered in the Temple Mount in Jerusalem, Templar knights wore white mantles with red crosses, and were the most skilled warriors of the Crusades in the Middle Ages. When the Holy Land of Jerusalem was lost, support for the Knights Templar faded. Pope Clement V disbanded the order in 1312, yet the legends of their secrets and mysteries persist even today, especially in reference to the Freemasons.

Martin, Dean – (1917-1995) American singer and actor; born Dino Paul Crocetti. He became known for his comedy and singing act with Jerry Lewis in 1946. His song, "That's Amore," became a popular hit in 1953. He joined with Frank Sinatra (1915-1998) and Sammy Davis, Jr. (1925-1990) in a number of movies and had his own television show, "The Dean Martin Show" (1965-1974).

Marx, Groucho – (1890-1970) American comedian, actor, writer, radio personality, vaudeville performer, and stage, film, and television star.

A master of quick wit, he was one of America's greatest comedians.

Monet, Claude – (1840-1926) French painter and founder of Impressionism (paintings with obvious brush strokes, filled with light); *Seacoast at Trouville* is in the Boston Museum of Fine Arts in Massachusetts.

Montessori, Maria – (1870-1952) Italian educator, advocated child-centered learning; today her schools are found all over the globe.

Newton, Isaac – (1643-1727) highly influential English mathematician, physicist, astronomer, alchemist, and author; built the first practical telescope, theorized white light in a prism of color, and calculated the first idea of the speed of sound—but he is best known for his formulations on the Law of Motion and Universal Gravitation.

Potter, Beatrix – (1866-1943) English writer, illustrator, natural scientist, and conservationist. She is best known for her children's books featuring animals, such as *The Tale of Peter Rabbit, The Tale of Tom Kitten,* and *Squirrel Nutkin.*

Pythagorean Diet – practiced by the ancient Greek philosopher, Pythagoras. Its name was changed to the Vegetarian Society in 1854 at Ramshead, England.

Rachmaninoff, Sergei – (1873-1943) famous Russian romantic composer and pianist, resident of the United States beginning in 1917; composed "Rhapsody on a Theme from Paganini."

Richards, William Trost – (1833-1905) Philadelphia-born, famous American landscape artist, highly acclaimed for this marine watercolor paintings.

Rogers, Roy – (1911-1998) American singer, actor, and television host, most notable as the star of more than 100 Western films, such as *King of the Cowboys*. His TV Western-themed comedy-variety show featured the theme song "Happy Trails to You."

Rogers, Will – (1879-1935) born a citizen of the Cherokee Nation (Oklahoma), he was a popular actor (silent films from 1918-1929 and talkies post-1929), vaudevillian star, cowboy, nationally syndicated columnist, humorist, and radio personality. His folksy, inoffensive style poked fun at controversial politicians, gangsters, and government.

Scylla & Charybdis – ancient Greek tale of Homer's "Odysseus": He was trapped between the "horrifying, devouring of six-headed, Scylla—or swallowed and drowned by the terrifying whirlpool of Charybdis!"

Sargent, John Singer – (1856-1925) An American artist who lived most of his life in Europe, John Singer Sargent is considered the leading portrait artist of his time. He created 900 oil paintings, mostly portraits, and 2,000 watercolors of his world travels.

Shakespeare, William – (1564-1616) English playwright, poet, and actor, widely regarded as the greatest writer in the English language and the world's greatest dramatist. His use of language helped shape modern English, and he invented or recorded almost 2,000 new words, such as *lonely, alligator, eyeball, gossip,* and *hurry.*

Theremin, Leon – (1896-1993) Russian and Soviet inventor of the Theremin, an early electronic musical instrument; he also worked on TV research. His listening device, called "The Thing," was hidden for seven years in the Great Seal of the United States Ambassador's Moscow office and enabled Soviet agents to eavesdrop on secret conversations; discovered in 1952, it was presented to the United States as a token of friendship.

Wordsworth, William – (1770-1850) English Romantic poet who penned *Ode on Intimations of Immortality from Recollections of Early Childhood*, which includes "trailing clouds of glory do we come ... and heaven lies about us in our infancy."

GLOSSARY OF IMAGINATOR WORDS

* ~ an actual word, though sometimes archaic or literary

*Aurora Borealis – N. a natural electrical phenomenon characterized by the appearance of streamers of reddish or greenish light in the northern sky; also called the Mirrie Dancers in Scotland: *Jesse saw the Aurora Borealis of colored lights streaming through the sky—just like the Mirrie Dancers!*

Baby Grand – N. grandchild – music of our souls: *Dearie has two children and only one Baby Grand.*

*Ballygomingo – interjection. An expression of surprise – also, 'bally' is a common prefix to town names in Ireland: *Ballygomingo! You scared the b'jeekers out of me!*

*Banshee – N. Irish legend of a female spirit whose wailing warns of an impending death in a house: *She sends 'em packin,' screamin' like Banshees, down Windmill Road.*

*birl – v. (Scottish) to whirl: *The Mirrie Dancers birl across the night sky, dancing in the Aurora Borealis.*

blabber-gab – v. jabber – blather: *Greta blabber-gabbed on and on, making no sense at all.*

B'jeekers! – interjection. exclamation of surprise or fear: *B'jeekers, Jesse! You scared me!*

bliss-t – 1) adj. (bliss-ed) joyful – elated – feeling blessedness: *Jesse had a bliss-t expression and laughed with joy.* 2) n. that which is the most excellent or desirable: *Mac wished Jesse all the bliss-t on his journey to Elizabethtown.*

blisterquick – adj. speedy – quick – swift: *Blisterquick, Jesse ran after the goat.*

Blue ribbon, you! – interjection. An expression meaning "good for you" – praise: *How clever! Blue ribbon, you!*

*****brî** – n. inner energies: *Jesse could feel their inner energies, their brî, bouncing between them.*

brillish – adj. 1) bright: *The day was brillish with sunshine.* 2) clever, brilliant: *He rallied with a brillish idea.*

*****brogan** – n. a coarse leather shoe: *Conor cut up Jesse's brogans to make summer sandals.*

Bunky-dinks – interjection. An exclamation meaning "Oh no!": *Bunky-dinks! We'll never find our way!*

*****chinquapin** – n. (chink-a-pin) in the Algonquin Indian language, an edible nut—like a hickory nut: *Jesse whittled a clothespin into the shape of a little hickory nut, and he called it chinquapin.*

chorkle – v. chuckle quietly: *Charlie chorkled over Peter's lovey-doveys with Bethesda Philhips.*

*****collywobbles** – n. a weird feeling in your stomach (Latin – from *Cholera morbus*, referring to the disease): *Jesse's stomach retaliated with a groaning case of collywobbles.*

confuzzled – 1) adj. confused, baffled: *I'm confuzzled, I thought you wanted just the facts.* 2) v. to confusedly ask a question: *Jesse* *confuzzled,* "Why did we live in New York City if you like this place so much?"

daisy-daster – n. a mishap or low-key disaster: *Jesse's calamity with the animals was a complete daisy-daster.*

*Diddly-ahten-dah! – interjection. An expression in Irish song tradition: *Diddly-ahten-dah! How clever!*

Diggity-boo! – interjection. A catchall exclamation, usually positive in nature: *Diggity-boo! Let's go have fun!*

dreadly – adj. terrible – disagreeable: *August was dreadly hot and steamy; He was in a dreadly mood.*

*Erector Set – N. originated in 1913, a metal toy construction set, including metal beams with holes for nuts and bolts, hinges and clamps, to create different structures: *The Elizabethtown Bridge looked like an Erector Set.*

*FairLight – N. enchanting glory-Lights in a human being: *Jane was a true FairLight in the glow of her being.*

feisty-dregs – n. determinedly touchy – miserable: *Miserable, Greta took her feisty-dregs out on Jesse.*

*folderal – n. trivial or nonsensical fuss: *Jesse couldn't make sense of the girl's folderal.*

gahslahzerous – adj. a glamorous attitude: *You're all dressed up! You look gahslahzerous!*

*Gargoyle > gargoyle – v. to mix up words (*actual dictionary word: a carved face or creature on a building, whose throat and mouth act as a spout to carry water off the roof): *Oh, it's not* 'in-GUESS-ti-vate,'—it's in-VES-ti-gate! I gargoyle my words sometimes ... like water spouting out of a gargoyle.

gasper – v. gulp – exclaim – choke: *Mac gaspered in utter surprise.*

giggle-snickens – n. fun laughter: *The children burst into giggle-snickens at Mr. Bonheur's joke.*

glintaling – adj. gleaming – glittering: *The glintaling light looked like diamonds on the water.*

glinty – adj. expressive flashes of emotion and light, usually through the eyes, and usually of suspicious origin: *She stared with her glinty, glaring Fox eyes.*

*****gloss** – v. elucidate – explain: *Conor glossed on, describing Jesse.*

gossywims –adj. whimsical – inventive – dreamy: *The heron's gossywim feathers swept over the water.*

Great Illuminations – N. expression for Heaven, Nirvana, Paradise (many words, same Light): *Dearie died last Christmas and is now in the Great Illuminations, which some call Heaven.*

grimmel – 1) n. closed mouth, playful grin, sometimes of surprise or disbelief: *Her lips corkscrewed into a grimmel of satisfaction.* 2) v. to purse the lips, expressing doubt or playfulness: *Amanda grimmeled, "She looks like she could start an argument in an empty room!"*

*****grotty** – adj. unpleasant: *What are all these terrible, grotty, ridiculous surprises?*

guffiggled – n. silly laughter: *The children guffiggled at Queen the goat's royal highness.*

gusher – v. flow with a quiet shushing noise: *A silence gushered into the room.*

*****Haunts alive!** – interjection. An expression of surprise – a "haunt" is a ghost: *Haunts alive! How'd you do that?*

*****Heavens to Betsy!** – interjection. chiefly Southern, a catchall used to express exasperation, surprise, shock, elation: *"Oh! Heavens to Betsy!" Amanda jumped up, "What on earth?"*

Imaginator – N. An out-of-the-box thinker: *A true Imaginator, he created everything in his magical shoppe.*

jigger – v. to react to a fun little surprise; to quickly and delightedly move others to action: *Peter jiggered a laugh, corralling the children up the plank.*

Jigger Jollies! – interjection. expression of delighted surprise, often inciting one to action: *Jigger-Jollies! I have my own family! I'm going to write everything to Billy and Mac!*

Jiggery! – interjection. expression of surprise: *Jiggery! The sun'll set in the east afore things are quiet again!*

jim-jams – n. chills – frights – thrills: *Conor felt the jim-jams shivering up his spine.*

*****jot-and-tittle** – n. old-time expression: every little thing; (jot = iota = the letter 'i' in the Greek alphabet; tittle = old typing symbol = the tiny dot atop the letter 'i'): *He counted every jot-and-tittle on the list.*

*****judder** – v. shake or vibrate rapidly: *The rain juddered across the barn rooftop.*

kafluffle – v. act in a quick, disheveled manner: *Jesse kafluffled into his clothes and ran out the door.*

*kangaroo word – n. a word that contains all the letters of one of its synonyms, called a "joey" word;

example: *'Masculine' contains the letters of 'male.'*

*Kitsune – N. Japanese mythological fox; magical, shape-shifting; as it learns its magic, it grows up to nine tails; there are two Kitsune: good 'zenko' and bad 'yako.'

Light – N. the energy of the Universe; everyone is born with their Light; inner Light, heart-Light, Soul, Spirit, Chi, Qi, Tao; *Jesse was taught to know his Light and shine it out all over.*

love-adore – 1) v. cherish: *Dearie love-adores her Jesse.* 2) n. darling – dear-one: *Jesse is a little love-adore.*

memory-fizz – n. remembrance – reverie: *She gazed into the clouds in a far off memory-fizz.*

merri-cheers – 1) v. to overtly share happiness and joy: *Jesse merri-cheered Greta with his funny expressions.* 2) n. happy, joyful acclaim: *He raised his glass in a toast of merri-cheers.*

mincey-toe – v. tiptoe quietly or secretly: *He mincey-toed silently down the hall.*

moogle – v. speak hesitantly – confused or depressed: *His eyes closed as he quietly moogled an answer.*

murmel – v. murmur, sometimes confusedly: *His voice murmeled quieter and quieter.*

*netsuke – n. a small carved Japanese ornament, especially of ivory or wood, often worn as part of Japanese traditional dress: *Jesse's favorite netsuke was the little wooden bird in its nest.*

peeps – v. pass water – take a leak – use the toilet: *"Oh, I have got to go to the bathroom. I gotta go peeps!"*

*Peg-Puff – N. expression, derogatory in nature: *She's a Peg-Puff—a young lady who acts like an old one.*

pilfer-looter – n. a thief: *"Pilfer-looter!" Jesse gaspered, wondering who was stealing from Gemma's house.*

*pshaw – interjection. an expression of scorn or impatience: *Conor pshawed at Murphy's arrogance.*

qualmed — v. to become nervously or awkwardly silent at the sudden realization of a touching or tender incident: *Everyone qualmed at Jesse heart-touching yearning to find his disappeared grandmother.*

*Quatschkopf – German word (kwach – kopf) – just plain silly: *Jesse dropped the drink into his lap and thought, 'Ohhh, I am a Quatschkopf!'*

quirkle – v. to show an array of emotions: *Her face quirkled in confusion.*

quiver-quaver – v. to shiver – tremble, especially in fear: *The dreadly sound made him quiver-quaver in fear.*

quizzel – v. 1) to ask curiously: *"What's your name?" Jesse quizzeled.* 2) to discover curious events, people, or objects: *Jesse's eyebrows knit together as he quizzeled Sergeant Hannity.*

Rule of Tongue – n. a rule that one must use only highest and best words (also, an expression reminding one of the rule); Let the words on your tongue taste delicious: *"Rule of Tongue! No name-calling!"*

rusheled – v. movement with a soft, muffled, swooshing sound; *Jesse felt Ellie-cat rusheling about his legs.*

scallylag – v. to dawdle – goof off – waste time: *Don't scallylag—we have too many chores!*

shiveral – 1) n. chills – frights – fun thrills: *Jesse's shoulders twitched in a little shiveral.* 2) v. to get goosebumps or shudder at a fearful thought: *Jesse shiveraled, thinking of Tim Braedon.*

slidder – v. to move in a snake-like manner: *He shimmied and sliddered out of his clothes.*

smirf – v. to grin playfully: *She smirfed at the playful cat's shenanigans.*

smuffle – v. to take one's breath in a close hug: *She hugged him so close, he muffled, "Gemma, I'm smuffling!"*

sniggle – n. small reverberating snort: *She snorted a little piggy sniggle.*

*****snollygoster** – n. a menacing person who says or does things for their own advancement: *Miss Peggy is a very slick con artist—a snollygoster—and she has been robbing you blind.*

snorkle – n. a short snorting snore: *With a little snorkle, Jesse drifted off to another dreamland.*

*****snuggery** – n. archaic term for a warm, cozy place: *Jesse fell asleep on the bed in his cozy snuggery.*

squintle – v. peer – look closely: *He squintled at her face, looking for a clue.*

tattle-lips – n. exaggerator – liar: *You are stretching the truth, you little tattle-lips!*

thrill-digging – adj. enthusiastic – reveling – exciting: *He leapt up with a thrill-digging whoop!*

*__titchy__ – adj. (British: informal word) something tiny: *One titchy little thing was bothering him.*

tinteling – adj. frosty – cold: *He shivered in the tinteling cold.*

trapture – v. to trap and capture: *There's no way out! We're traptured!*

*__Travellers__ – N. the Lucht Siül (Loook See-ul), the "walking people" of Ireland – Irish gypsies: *The Travellers moved north in the summer season.*

tribble-trap – adj. craziness – nuttiness – nonsense: *Don't talk tribble-trap!*

*__Triquetra__ – N. trinity knot pattern of three intertwining circles: *She traced the Triquetra pattern of intertwining circles on the metal mug.*

twirly-purr – v. winding oneself about, resonating contentedly: *Gypsy cat twirly-purred around Jesse's legs.*

whirly-wander – v. travel: *He whirly-wandered from one continent to another.*

whister – v. to speak hoarsely, or just above a whisper; *In the dark, Jesse quietly whistered to Conor.*

***widdershins** – n. a feeling of moving in the wrong direction, counter-clockwise or backward: *It felt like the train was moving backwards and Jesse was in a dizzy of widdershins.*

wisky-dooley – interjection/adj. expression of unexpected, sometimes wild, quickness: *Wisky-dooley! Jesse's bike flew down the hill!*

wispy-slips – n. sleep – the Land of Nod: *He fell sound asleep into his dreamland of deep wispy-slips.*

wonderlush – 1) n. a state of wonder: *In a wonderlush, Jesse marveled at the beautiful sight.* 2) adj. marvelous – full of marvels, miracles, and surprises: *Jesse lived a wonderlush life filled with his everyday magic.*

zippity-pip – adv. very fast: *He ran zippity-pip all the way up the steps.*

DISCUSSION QUESTIONS

1. Dearie is the narrator for this story, and her intimate relationship with Jesse is clear when he hears her voice inside him. She explains his predicaments and reminds him to always keep his Light on. What does this mean to Jesse? How does he use his Light to change his attitude? Does it change his situation? Give examples from NYC, along his journey, and at Windy Hill Farm.

2. When does Jesse perceive why he is truly leaving New York City? What does this mean to Jesse as he moves through his story?

3. Jesse has prepared for his quest to find his 'disappeared' grandmother, Lady Jessica, but things do not all work out according to plan. What are some of the mishaps he encounters along his journey and at Windy Hill Farm?

4. Regan Murphy tells quite a tale about the women of Windy Hill Farm: Avery, Susan, Jane and Jessica. He says they are all bad apples. Why? He calls Jessica the Black Widow. Is this an apt name for Jessica? How does Jesse's arrival change this narrative?

5. Why are Peter Murphy's words about the Depression important in understanding Jessica – as Connor learns when they meet face to face? How do events from the Depression later connect to the characters of Tim and Tina Braedon?

6. What does Jesse think of Miss Lily when he first meets her? When did you feel his – or your – attitude toward her changing?

7. Discuss how and why Jesse changes Jessica's name to Gemma. How does this impact her? Do you think she grows into her new name?

8. How do Greta and Matts help Jesse find his way on the farm? What is the arrangement between Gemma and Margarethe and her children? On the farm? At the market?

9. What are the secrets, mysteries, and riddles Jesse finds in the gadgets and the people and the history on Windy Hill Farm? Discuss how some of them impact Jesse's story and how some of them are resolved.

10. Jesse still loves his word-play. Give examples of his fun or intriguing Spoonerisms, Kangaroo Words, malapropisms ('gargoyling' his words), riddles and song.

11. Who are some of the characters Jesse suspects of stealing from Windy Hill Farm? Give examples of who they are and why Jesse suspects them.

12. How does Jesse find his Light after he discovers the truth about who Miss Lily really is, especially when he discovers the evidence against her? What is the magic that reminds him?

13. Music plays an important part in Jesse story. What are some of the songs or compositions that stand out? How do they help frame the mood and attitudes? How does Rachmaninov's personal story and music help Jesse?

14. With family or friends, how does Jesse behave like a "love-y – dove-y" cupid?

15. Does Dearie's stone or Mac-Elliot's silver dollar bring Jesse luck? Is there a treasure on Windy Hill Farm? What is The Greatest Thing? What mysteries do you think Gemma and Jesse will share next?

ALSO:

Visit www.PatsieMcCandless.com
for these resources for educators and readers:

TEACHER'S GUIDE
A guide to further discussing this book
with your students

LIGHT LESSONS
Inspirations culled from the
pages of *The Secrets of Windy Hill*

ACKNOWLEDGEMENTS

My husband, Tom, for his love, his *sherpa* support, and his endless patience and belief in me and my stories.

The inspirations of all our Baby Grands: our grandchildren – though they are not babies any more, they are still the music of our lives.

Our children: Scott, who offered his Light thoughts and prodded me with his expressive clarity, and Kate, who helped me with the German idioms and translations, and who listened and counseled through all of Jesse's iterations, reading it aloud to her boys, making me believe all over again.

My generous readers, who spent their precious time and energies perusing my first pages and offered their words of appraisal and support: Saverio Rebecchi, Janet Auinger, Paulette P. Smith, Adela Bateman, Gay Wasik-Zegel, Patricia Cook, Mary S. Wright, Kathy Dickenson, Patsy Snyder, Lauren Helmer, and K.R., a young reader and Jesse fan.

Plus, all those I taught over the years, who, as it turns out, were some of my best teachers.

Technical supporters:

- Lauren Helmer, my superb editor and proofreader, who fell in love with Jesse and made him and his story shine like the starlight he is.
- Maggie McLaughlin, editorial director/ IT specialist, Constellation Book Services, for her expert eye and her tender heart in bringing Jesse to the world.

- Christy Day of Constellation Book Services, the book designer who patiently and beautifully put all the cover and interior details in place.
- My publishing consultant, the inimitable, irreplaceable, ever-at-the-ready Martha Bullen of Bullen Publishing Services.

ABOUT THE AUTHOR

A speaker, artist, author, musician, educator, mother and grandmother, Patsie McCandless grew up on a rural island in Rhode Island, where she taught sailing and took a ferry to school. She earned her MFA at Rosemont College, PA, and returned to her island, where she taught primary school for thirty years, while becoming a musician and composer. Patsie is also an award-winning artist in cut paper (PaperSolo.com), exhibiting in Miniature Societies in Florida, South Carolina, Washington, D.C. and Pennsylvania. Her *PaperSolo* artwork series is in the permanent collection of the St. Petersburg Opera Company in Florida.

A special gift led her to a monastery on the Hudson River in upstate New York for a writing retreat with Madeleine L'Engle, and she has not stopped writing since. Her first novel, the family classic *Becoming Jesse: Celebrating the Everyday Magic of Childhood*, won the prestigious Mom's Choice Gold Medal Award, the Family Choice Award and is on the SCBWI Recommended Reading List. Patsie created the cover for *Becoming Jesse* in paper, which won the Book Cover Image Award from Zamiz Press.

This newest novel from Patsie, *The Secrets of Windy Hill (Becoming Jesse, Book II)*, is the thrill-digging sequel, for which she created the color cover and all of the illustrations.

She and her husband live near Philadelphia, PA and enjoy the everyday magic of their children and grandchildren.

To learn more about Patsie and her United Nations Presentation, TEDx talk, Light lessons Blog, as well as her writing and art, please visit PatsieMcCandless.com.

Made in the USA
Middletown, DE
25 August 2022

71396579R00210